FRUITS
OF THE
EARTH

Frederick Philip Grove

*

FRUITS OF THE EARTH

*

*

*

Introduction: M. G. Parks

General Editor: Malcolm Ross

New Canadian Library No. 49

MCCLELLAND AND STEWART LIMITED

The Canadian Publishers
McClelland and Stewart Limited
25 Hollinger Road, Toronto

0-7710-9149-4

PRINTED AND BOUND IN CANADA

CONTENTS

*

PART II / THE DISTRICT

W HEN *Fruits of the Earth* was first published in 1933, its author could look back upon nearly forty years in which it had gradually taken shape in his imagination. In 1894, when Grove was a young farm hand on the Canadian prairies hauling wheat over a thirty-mile trail through unsettled territory, a chance meeting set off a train of thought which led to the genesis of this novel. He encountered a man who had arrived that very afternoon from Ontario and, having promptly filed on a homestead claim and unloaded his horses and possessions from a freight car, had set to ploughing the land as the sun dropped to the western horizon. Grove later recalled that "outlined as he was against a tilted and spoked sunset in the western sky, he looked like a giant" embodying "the essence of the pioneering spirit which had settled the vast western plains." Thus was born Abe Spalding, the central figure of *Fruits of the Earth*. Later experiences served as stimuli to Grove's imagination as he filled in the unwritten pages of the novel: a trip across the sodden, rain-drenched prairie in 1912 led him to conceive the episode of Abe saving his bumper crop of wheat in Chapter X; his observation of farming conditions in the spring of 1913 was later transmuted into the account of the great flood that en gulfs Spalding District; the sight of a pupil being crushed under the wheels of his load of wheat suggested the death of Charlie Spalding. The most vital of all such "explosions," as Grove calls them, was set off when, in a drive through the country near Rapid City, Manitoba, Grove noticed a magnificent home-stead—a great house of red brick and two huge white barns set in a four-acre yard. When he stopped to investigate, he discovered that behind the imposing façade lay nothing but decay and ruinous neglect: two decrepit horses and one miser-able cow were the only animals in the enormous barns, and in the mansion a family of poor tenants crowded into one room which they heated by ripping up the many floors of quartered oak for fuel. That same night, profoundly moved by what he had seen and applying it to the life of Abe Spalding, Grove began to write the novel. He had glimpsed the eventual fate of Abe's great farm after its forceful owner had died and his ageing widow had retreated to the town.

Fruits of the Earth has a definite setting in time and place

Its structure is chronological, built upon succeeding episodes or periods in Abe's life which depict his changing fortune and the growth of the district. The action covers about twenty-one years, beginning in the summer of 1900 when Abe appears on the prairie to settle on his claim. The locale is the flat prairie some fifty miles south and slightly west of Winnipeg, a district bounded by the Pembina Hills and Morden on the west and the Red River on the east. Grove knew this part of Manitoba very well—so well, in fact, that he catches its prevailing tones and moods again and again in the novel.

While few readers would question the veracity of Grove's setting or his success in using but transcending the literal scene, many have found his imaginative vision much less perceptive in the artist's central investigation of the human heart. If his people lack psychological depth, the reason is at least partly that Grove was primarily concerned in this novel with social forces and their effects on individuals. *Fruits of the Earth*, he once told a correspondent, "was never intended to figure as a novel. I meant it to be taken as a piece of pioneer history." Indeed, its original title was *Chronicles of Spalding District*, and Grove was deeply annoyed by his publisher's insistence that it should appear under the more fanciful title by which we know it. His didactic purpose, his desire to base his fiction on his thesis of man encountering the resistance of nature and society, would naturally tend to make his characterization typical or symbolic rather than fully rounded.

The role he assumed was nothing less than that of spokesman for the Western pioneer: "I, the cosmopolitan, had fitted myself to be the spokesman of a race . . . consisting of those who, in no matter what climate, at no matter what time, feel the impulse of starting anew, from the ground up, to fashion a new world which might serve as the breeding-place of a civilization to come." As an interpretation of a sociological phenomenon, the novel is often impressive. Grove creates in Abe a type of the successful pioneer—not a typical pioneer, for Abe is clearly a man of epic proportions, but rather the kind of man best suited to combat and, in a significant measure, to control the forces of nature and human society which oppose his success. To be successful, Grove decided, a pioneer had to be "dominant" and "rigid"; he had to have "a single-minded preoccupation with the specifically-pioneering task." In such a man's success lies his ultimate defeat, for as Grove explains, the successful pioneer is a tragic type:

Its whole endeavour is bent upon reshaping and doing away with the very condition in its environment which gives it its economic and historic justification; and when it has been done away with, when the environment is tamed, the task is done; and the pioneer has used up, in doing it, the span of life allotted to him. He suddenly realizes that he has been working for a purpose which has defeated its end. He cannot, now, settle down to enjoy the fruit of his labour.

This is the tragedy of Abe's life that, having devoted the best part of his life to the "specifically-pioneering task" and its attendant materialistic goals, he finds himself in middle age a spiritual pauper and, in the eyes of the new generation, a social anachronism. Because he finally recognizes his failure and is painfully aware that his material success has cost him dearly, his life becomes tragic. Though Grove does not allow Abe's defeat to be untempered by the gift of insight that is the hero's boon in regenerative tragedy, we are apt to be most impressed by a sense of loss and futility that overshadows the growth of wisdom in Abe; at the end, though not included in the novel, stands Grove's vision of the farm after Abe's death, in the hands of strangers and falling into ruin.

Grove's depiction of Abe's wife Ruth also serves to dramatize his thesis about pioneer life. In a pioneer society, he remarks in his autobiography, woman is perforce a slave, a mere helper of man. Unfortunately for pioneer women, the qualities in their husbands which make them successful pioneers are "incompatible with that tender devotion which alone can turn the relation of the sexes into a thing of beauty"; they lack "the gift for idealization and sublimation." Such a man is Abe, and he marries (mainly through physical desire) a woman who is not herself a fighter. Ruth, in fact, is a woman "fitted for the life in towns or cities rather than for the life on the open prairies."

The two main characters of the novel, then, were conceived by Grove as types of the pioneer, as elements in the fictional demonstration of a sociological thesis. The action is also carefully chosen as a chronicling of prairie farm life during the first two decades of the century. When Abe first settles on his claim, the flat landscape is unbroken by human habitation. Gradually projections spring up as Abe's example of determination and success proves the district to be arable. In the years 1912 and 1913 Abe reaches the apogee of his achievement (he saves a huge wheat crop when the price is unusually high and uses his small fortune to build his mansion and enormous barns), and the district approaches the end of an era. The First World War engenders a host of economic and social changes, and in the post-war years Abe and other farmers of his persuasion find themselves isolated in a brash new world of urban values which invade even their own families.

As Grove's prairie farmers feel the backwash of the Jazz Age, a wider social dimension broadens the regionalism of the novel. On another level, *Fruits of the Earth* ceases to be regional at all, for its action takes on philosophic, universal implications. The controlling theme on this level is summed up elsewhere by Grove as "the age-old conflict between human desire and the stubborn resistance of nature." Men impose their wills on nature; the Abe Spaldings seek to dominate it by forcing wealth from the fertile soil and by erecting tall buildings and windbreaks to challenge the monotonous level to which nature would reduce all life. But the efforts of men are pitifully mutable. The great drainage ditches made to carry off the spring floods are in a few years "like the prehistoric remains of a system devised by some mightier race gone to its accounting," covered with prairie grass and choked up with willow-thickets which thrive on the soil brought down from the hills. Abe's proud house is only five years old when its owner notices that "already little sand grains embedded in the mortar were crumbling away, already the edges of the bricks were being rounded by a process of weathering." And Abe reflects that "The moment a work of man was finished, nature set to work to take it down again. . . . And so with everything, with his machines, his fields, his pool; they were all on the way of being levelled to the soil again." This great commonplace of literature serves Grove well, for he weaves its universal poignancy into the texture of his scene and makes an awareness of its truth the ground of Abe's awakening wisdom.

If the material things built by man are so ephemeral, so inexorably destroyed by nature, what greater folly can there be than devoting one's life to a philosophy of materialism? Abe's consideration of this corollary of mutability brings into the novel another of Grove's favourite themes, the folly and eventual tragedy of materialism. He devotes several pages of his autobiography to a criticism of material progress, arguing that "for everything we acquire, so-and-so-much life has to be paid" and deploring the North American philosophy which holds that "to have is more important than to be or to do; in fact, that to be is dependent on to have." In the novel Abe learns this lesson through bitter experience: his house he comes to see as "a mere ostentation"; his numerous labour-saving devices save labour, but they squander his time and shorten his temper. He finally arrives at his creator's Carlylean theory that "The use of machines might 'pay' in a money sense; it did not pay in terms of human life. The thing done is nothing; the doing everything."

Abe's tragedy is therefore partly the result of false values. But Grove is too astute an observer of human life to attribute tragedy entirely to a close chain of cause and effect; the mystery is not so easily penetrated. Fate and circumstances seem to conspire to mock Abe's dream. The children who were to inherit his empire never succeed him. Charlie, his favourite child, is accidentally killed just when Abe's fortunes are at their peak—though, ironically, if the sensitive and idealistic Charlie had lived he would have been a most unlikely successor; Jim, the remaining son, becomes an addict of the machine and leaves the farm to work as a mechanic in town; Marion marries a lawyer and settles down in Winnipeg; Frances, who disgraces Abe by becoming a devotee and a victim of the fast living that is corrupting the younger generation, will never assume Abe's burden. His family having failed him, Abe must fall back on his inner resources and find some satisfaction and some meaning in renewed public service to the district bearing his name. The novel ends in the twilight of Abe's hopes, for not only has he been defeated on every crucial matter—his economic success means nothing to him, his family has disappointed him—but even his resumed leadership of the district can be no more than a fleeting triumph; Abe is not the man to cope with the complex world replacing the old agrarian democracy. Yet Grove deliberately chose to avoid a tragic climax for the novel, eschewing a more dramatic and possibly more aesthetically satisfying ending for the sake of "truth" to conditions in the West. We may suppose that Abe will live out the rest of his days opposing his iron will to the new age, but there can be no hope of his ultimate success. Though Abe is unbroken when we leave him, beyond the end of the novel stands its real conclusion.

Fruits of the Earth is a realistic novel, most obviously in the sense that it consistently avoids the sentimentalizing and falsifying of experience which characterized the typical Western "romance" of Grove's time. It is also realistic in other ways. In his essay "Realism in Literature," Grove defines what realism means to him: it is never concerned merely with surfaces and appearances, as "naturalism" tends to be; it is never predominantly subjective but always strives to mirror "a more or less universal human reaction to what is not I"; it is never closed within the exceptional experiences of the narrow present but always seeks the eternal; it never centres upon the expression of what the artist wishes to see or seems to see, but is always bent upon what "becomes clearly visible to the eye or perceptible to the ear, the sense, the mind, the soul." Within his limits, Grove has tried, with considerable success, to conform to these requirements. If one considers that he was writing in the late nineteenth-century realistic tradition, that he conceived his novel as a "chronicle," and that he held a narrow and over-simplified view of romanticism, it is not surprising that he is sometimes unconvincing. It is particularly ironic that he, a declared anti-romantic, should unconsciously succumb to one aspect of the attitude that he detested. For the pastoral ideal is strong in Grove: urban life, so-called "civilization," corrupts the soul; its baleful influence contaminates the purer countryside, alienating children from parents, breaking down moral restraints, engendering the false values that stem from avarice, and sounding the call of the machine. The reader will find all of these ideas expressed in the action of this novel. They fit the character of Abe—who, as Grove rightly insists, is by no means a reflection of his creator—but they also happen to be the prejudices of Grove himself. The greatness of a realist, Grove tells us, lies in the degree to which he can approach the ideals of psychological and philosophical depth, objectivity, universality, and imaginative breadth. Judged in company with the great realists he names—Aeschylus, Sophocles, Shakespeare, Goethe, Tolstoy—Grove obviously belongs to the more humble assembly of honest but flawed artists who stand, to use his own metaphor, on the lower slopes. His penetration into the human personality is seldom deep, and the reason is undoubtedly, as has been observed by Edward McCourt and will be recognized by every reader of Grove's autobiography, that Grove's rather cold self-centredness severely limited his sympathetic understanding of other people, real or fictional. His realistic painting of external reality also falters badly at times, as it manifestly does in the dialogue of his characters—in the stilted formality of Abe's speech, in the appallingly inept language of the girl's letter that Dr. Vanbruik shows to Abe; generally Grove is unable to give his uneducated characters the colloquial English natural to them.

To end a brief survey of his novel in this negative fashion, however, would be grossly unfair. Grove's penchant for ideas and his tendency to create people to illustrate his theories may be insufficient compensation for his frequent failure to make his characters live. But the philosophic concepts in this novel —especially the themes of cosmic time and mutability, with their emotional overtones—give to it a dignity and stature too often absent from contemporary fiction. In Grove's "old-fashioned" novel we find much that is impervious to mere changes in fashion. What he conceives as the tragedy of the human condition is ultimately as true and as moving for us as it was for the Elizabethans.

Dalhousie University   M. G. PARKS
August, 1964

WHEN Joseph Conrad in 1917 reissued *Nostromo*, he accompanied it by an author's note the first two paragraphs of which so exactly fit the case of the present book that I cannot refrain from reprinting them here, substituting the present title for *Nostromo* and *Jane Atkinson* for *Typhoon*. *Jane Atkinson* is an unpublished novel which, at the time of its completion, I considered the last volume of what I have come to call my (still largely unpublished) Prairie Series.

"*Fruits of the Earth* is the most anxiously meditated of the longer novels which belong to the period following upon the completion [Conrad says 'publication'] of *Jane Atkinson*.

"I don't mean to say that I became then conscious of any impending change in my mentality and in my attitude towards the tasks of my writing life. And perhaps there was never any change, except in that mysterious, extraneous thing which has nothing to do with the theories of art; a phenomenon for which I cannot in any way be held responsible. What, however, did cause me some concern was that after finishing the last story of the Prairie Series it seemed somehow that there was nothing more in the world to write about.

"This so strangely negative but disturbing mood lasted some little time; and then, as with many of my longer stories, the first hint for *Fruits of the Earth* came to me in the shape" [here I leave Conrad's text] of certain hints dropped by a real-estate dealer with whom I was driving along over the prairie, regarding the history of a certain farm which we were passing.

This farm was such as to suggest a race of giants who had founded it; but on inquiry I found that it was held by tenants who tilled a bare ten per cent of its acreage. In a barn built for half a hundred horses they kept a team of two sorry nags; and they inhabited no more than two or three rooms of the outwardly palatial house.

I have since found many more farms like that in Manitoba; and in every case I have investigated their history. Slowly, the composite impression gained grew into a compelling urge; and the result was the present story.

F. P. G.

PART I

* *

ABE SPALDING

*

WHEN, in the summer of 1900, Abe Spalding arrived in the village of Morley, in the municipality of Somerville, Manitoba, he had been travelling in the caboose of a freight train containing a car with four horses and sundry implements and household goods which belonged to him. He came from the old Spalding homestead in Brant County, Ontario.

He had visited the open prairie a year before and, after careful investigation, filed a claim on the south-west quarter of section five in the township beginning four miles north of Morley. He had had good and valid reasons for choosing that particular location. The neighbourhood as such he had fixed on because his twin sister Mary, who a few years ago had married a doctor by name of Vanbruik, and who up to 1897 had lived in the county seat, was at present, for somewhat obscure reasons, domiciled in this very village of Morley, where her husband, having sold his practice, was conducting the business of a general merchant. The particular quarter section on which Abe Spalding had filed seemed, to the casual observer, to offer no advantage over any other that was available; but he had found that, while the water which covered the district in the spring of the year stood for months on other parts, this quarter, and the whole section to which it belonged, as well as the sections north and south of it, dried several weeks in advance of the rest of the prairie. Further, he had been informed that the province was on the point of drawing two gigantic ditches through the district, one of them being surveyed to pass exactly along the south line of section five. These ditches were not primarily designed to drain a seemingly irreclaimable swamp, but rather to relieve an older settlement farther west, around the town of Torquay; but, while they were not meant to drain the land which he had chosen, he had shrewdly seen that they could not help improving matters. With his mind's eye he looked upon the district from a point in time twenty years later; and he seemed to see a prosperous settlement there. The soil was excellent, and there was no fundamental farming problem except that of drainage. Lastly, he was not the first settler to make the venture; the two quarters composing the north half of the section had been taken up a decade ago. The men who owned them, it was true, had not been able to make a success; they had left after having wasted their substance and energy, but not before they had received their patents, which they held on the chance that the land might in time become worth a few dollars per acre. A third settler, a bachelor by name of Hall, was actually in residence on the quarter adjoining Abe's claim to the west.

Abe came from a small Ontario farm of eighty acres, half of which, on account of rock and sharp declivities in its formation, could not be tilled. He was possessed by "land hunger"; and he dreamt of a time when he would buy up the abandoned farms from which all buildings had been removed; and, who knows, perhaps even the quarter where Hall was squatting in his sod-hut. In his boldest moments he saw himself prosperous on so great a holding and even reaching out north; for the section there adjoining was No. 8, held, as part of the purchase price paid by the Dominion for the rights of sovereignty in the west, by that ancient institution, the Hudson's Bay Company. In any other place, where his land would have been surrounded by crown land, any one might have limited Abe's expansion by settling next to him; for no settler could acquire more than a hundred and sixty acres by "homesteading." Here, all things going well, Abe might hope one day to possess two square miles; for the Hudson's Bay Company held its lands only in order to sell them. Abe was a man of economic vision.

As the lumbering freight train banged and clattered to a stop near the little station, in what was euphemistically called "the yard"—distinguished by nothing but a spur of the track running past a loading platform to the three grain elevators along its southern edge—Abe alighted from the caboose and stood for a moment irresolutely by its side. The conductor had told him that the car containing his chattels was going to be shunted to the loading platform, where it would be ready in an hour or so. Abe was not anxious to go to his sister's house; but his impulsive and impatient temperament made him desirous, above all, to get over that interval of waiting without being too conscious of his wasting time.

He swung about and strode swiftly across to the station, where a few idlers were lounging. Emerging on the east-west road, he found himself at the west end of the village, which had nothing in its aspect that could be called urban. The buildings of Main Street were aligned on one side of this road into which three short by-streets debouched from the north; to the south, the growth of the settlement was arrested by the right-of-way, no buildings but the grain elevators having been erected beyond it. Like the whole landscape, Main Street was treeless; and only the side-streets were shaded by tall cotton-woods which seemed to lose themselves, to the north, in what resembled a natural bluff—a deceptive semblance, for all trees had been planted. Main Street, with its single row of buildings, hardly deserved the name of a street, just as the agglomeration of houses hardly deserved the name of a village; it formed a mere node in the road running, in a straight line, from Somer-ville in the east to Ivy in the west, a distance of twenty-two miles.

Just beyond the first side-street rose the one building which gave the street a measure of distinction : a store unusual for a small prairie town by reason of its dimensions as well as of the solidity of its red-brick structure; it might have stood in the streets of any small city. The whole of its long, two-storied façade consisted of large show-windows filled with a miscel-laneous and effectively arranged exhibit of what could be bought inside, the assortment including everything from farm implements and furniture to groceries and tobacco.

Behind the store, facing west, on the first side-street, stood the one residence which, like the store, had an air approaching dignity. That was where Abe's sister lived; and the store was the Vanbruik Department Store, owned by her husband and managed by a high-salaried young man, Mr. Diamond.

Abe was very fond of his sister Mary; he wished he had sent her a wire message announcing his arrival so that she might have met him. A frown settled on his large round face, under the peak of the grey tweed cap which he wore. If he hesitated about calling at the house, it was on account of his brother-in-law, the mysterious doctor who a few years ago had suddenly given up his large flourishing practice at Somerville to turn merchant. Coming as Abe did from a small Ontario farm, in-herited five years ago from his father who had died a sudden death, and now advantageously sold to an industrial concern, Abe had the prejudice of the man who made his living by what he called "work" against the merchant who made "money" by calculation. Besides, Dr. Vanbruik was in every-thing Abe's antipode, physically as well as temperamentally. The mere fact that the doctor was a professional man had seemed to place Abe at a disadvantage in what little intercourse they had had. The doctor was a graduate of Queen's; and King-ston stood, to Abe, for all that was provincial in the spirit of Ontario; it seemed strangely eastern; it represented all that Abe had abandoned in coming west. Abe had deliberately chosen the material world for the arena of his struggles; the doctor, though he had turned merchant, seemed to live in a world of the spirit. Mary had, with Abe's own early consent, received a high-school and college education as the equivalent of her equity in the farm, there being only two children. The cost of her education had been defrayed by placing a mortgage of five thousand dollars on the parental place. Mary, too, therefore, was in a sense Abe's superior, though Abe was fully aware of the difference between an informational education and native intelligence, in which latter he did not feel himself to be deficient. Yet he could not help begrudging his sister that refinement of manners and forms which is imparted by the association with cultured men and women; he begrudged it while secretly admiring and imitating it. This was all the more the case with his brother-in-law, who had a way of quietly listening to an argument and then settling it by a display of superior information.

Physically, Abe was extraordinarily tall, measuring six feet four; the doctor was almost correspondingly small, for he lacked an exact twelve inches of Abe's stature. Abe was built in proportion to his height, broad-shouldered and deep-chested; the doctor was slender and fine-limbed, and yet he stooped. Temperamentally, Abe was impulsive, bearing down obstacles by sheer impetuosity; the doctor was deliberate, hesitant even, weighing every aspect of a matter before aligning himself. Consequently, at the age of thirty, with his life a blank page before him, Abe was disinclined to seek the company of this man who, besides, was his senior by fifteen years, having lived his life.

The struggle between Abe's desire to let his sister help him over the next hour or so and his disinclination to meet his brother-in-law was plainly visible in his face, which, above any pair of shoulders but his, would have looked disproportionately large. And there was still another reason for his hesitancy. Before leaving Ontario Abe had married Ruth, against the, at least implied, advice of Mary and her husband. When, a year ago, he had mentioned his intention, neither had voiced any open disapproval; but, in the course of the few weeks which he had spent at Morley, they had somehow conveyed a lack of enthusiasm over it, now by a silence, now by a hesitant question. "Will she be able to adapt herself to rural conditions?" "Won't she suffer from the unavoidable isolation on a pioneer farm?" For Ruth was the daughter of small-town merchants; her father had a bake-shop at Brantford; her mother, a confectionery operated in conjunction. The worst of it was that Abe himself had his misgivings when he pondered the matter; to have his own unvoiced fears put forward by others, if ever so tentatively, disconcerted him. The conclusion could not be evaded that he had been in love with a face and a figure rather than a mind or soul.

Yet he strode impulsively forward at last, diagonally crossing the sleepy street of the ugly village and hoping that his brother-in-law would not be at home.

That hope was fulfilled. His sister met him in the door of the wide-spaced living-room in the white house which was surrounded by an extensive veranda. At sight of her brother, Mary exclaimed:

"Abe! . . Why in the world did you not let me know?"

Abe shrugged his shoulders; but he bent down and kissed her cheek.

"Charles isn't in," Mary said. "He went to the city on business."

Mary, too, was tall, even somewhat large and rather heavy.

"I'm in town only for an hour or so," Abe said as they were sitting down—Abe on the large, grey chesterfield, his sister in an arm-chair of the same colour and design. "I have my stuff in the train and I'm going out at once."

"Surely not," Mary said, scanning his face through her glasses. "Or do you intend to come back to-night?"

"I don't think so. I want to start work."

"Not to-day, Abe?"

"Not to-day, perhaps. I have a tent along. I want to do as much breaking as I can this summer; and to build. Ruth will be out in a week or two."

Mary gave him a quick look. "So you got married after all? Why did you not let us know?"

"It was all done so suddenly. I sold the place and didn't know where to go. We got married, and two days later I started west."

"Why did you not bring her? She could have stayed with me."

"I came by a freight train and had the horses to look after. I'll put up a shack at once."

Mary nodded and rose. "I'll get you a cup of tea, shall I?"

"I won't decline."

When Mary had left the room, Abe sat for a few minutes, looking straight ahead. Then he rose and walked about, stopping in the bay window which looked to the street, turning again and stepping over to a library table covered with books. Of these he picked up one or two, and, finding that they were poetry, dropped them again, resuming his walk.

"I had a late dinner," Mary said when she returned. "I won't partake, if you don't mind." She moved a small low table to her brother's side, placing the tray upon it, and went out again to fetch the tea.

When she brought it, Abe helped himself.

"Why not let Ruth come at once, Abe?" Mary asked shortly. "You know I'd be glad to have her."

"Oh, well——" Then bluntly, "I believe she'd rather not."

There was a pause.

"And the old farm is sold? I can hardly believe it."

Abe, knowing that he was unjust, took that remark to hold a vague reproach. "What could I do? Eighty acres! And mortgaged at that."

Seeing that the money raised by the mortgage had paid for her education, Mary might have been offended in turn. But she smoothed all occasion of offence away. "It was the logical thing to do. The same amount of work put in here is bound to bring better results. We have both gone west, after all. You will miss the trees, though."

"I shall plant trees here."

"I suppose. But no cedars."

"No," Abe said after a silence. "Nor hard maples."

This addition to what his sister had said restored the inner understanding between them; they spoke of their old home for a while.

Then Abe rose.

"You won't return for the night?" Mary asked once more.

"No. I shall have to keep an eye on the horses."

Half an hour later Abe was unloading his chattels at the platform, leading his horses out first and then manoeuvring his wagon into a position where he could pile it high with a minimum of lost motion. Having taken as much as he could, he hitched two horses in front—Belgians these—and tied a team of Percherons behind. Thence, driving along the trail between track and elevators, he went west till he was opposite the station building. There, leaving his teams, he crossed the right-of-way and spoke to the agent, to tell him he would return for the remainder of his goods next morning.

At last he climbed to the top of his load and started north for the six-mile trek over open prairie.

A few hundred yards from the Somerville Line, as the east-west road was called, he reached that flat and unrelieved country which, to the very horizon, seemed to be a primitive wilderness. North, east, and west, nothing showed that looked like a settlement, and the impression of an utter loneliness was perhaps even enhanced by the knowledge that somewhere it harboured at least one man by name of Hall, half-crazed with work and isolation, and destined to be Abe's neighbour. As for others, the two who, probably under an impulse to huddle close together in this immensity, had a decade ago filed on the two northern quarters of the same section, they were gone, and having "proved up" on their claims, had vanished again in the outer world.

Abe's brief call at his sister's had somewhat unsettled him. For a year he had mentally lived on that open, flat prairie, planning and adjusting himself. He needed room; he needed a country which would give scope to the powers he felt within him. Forbidding as it looked, this was that country. But Mary's casual remark about the cedars had reawakened in him the vision of the old farm as a place to live in: the house in its cluster of cedars, with the gnarled apple trees in the orchard behind; with the old furniture in the rooms—not very comfortable perhaps, but harmonious in the half-light admitted by the scanty windows half closed with vines: mellowed into unity by being lived in through generations. Here, everything was of necessity new and raw. Ruth in the midst of this? She knew nothing of what she was going into except that Abe was to create some sort of home for her: Ruth, whom a year or so ago he had met casually when buying oranges in a store. . . .

Well, he would conquer this wilderness; he would change it; he would set his own seal upon it! For the moment, one hundred and sixty acres were going to be his, capable of being tilled from line to line!

He would conquer! Yet, as he looked about, he was strangely impressed with this treeless prairie under the afternoon sun. This utterly undiversified country looked flat as a table-top. Differences in level, small as they might be, must exist. Why, otherwise, should there be bare soil here and there, with the smooth and cracked surface of a dried mudhole in clay? Whereas elsewhere the greyish-green, silky prairie grass grew knee-high. Why should the spring floods which he had not yet seen drain away to the east, into the river which carried them to the great lake? Why should it have been observed by those who had preceded him that certain sections of this wilderness dried sooner in spring than others? There must be undulations in the soil.

A year ago, Abe had scanned the district from a purely utilitarian point of view. Apart from the bush land in the far north, this had been almost the last district where free land was still available. Within it he had looked for depth of topsoil, for nearness to possible neighbours, for a convenient distance from a shipping-point.

Nothing but such considerations had had any influence with him a year ago. That the general conformation of a landscape might have to be considered, such an idea he would have laughed at. Yet this prairie seemed suddenly a peculiar country, mysteriously endowed with a power of testing temper and character. But that was exactly what he had wanted: a "clear proposition" as he had expressed it, meaning a piece of land capable of being tilled from line to line, without waste areas, without rocky stretches, without deeply-cut gullies which denied his horses a foothold. He wanted land, not landscape; all the landscape he cared for he would introduce himself.

Yet, half unbeknown to him, there was a dream: of a mansion such as he had seen in Ontario, in the remnants of a colonial estate—a mansion dominating an extensive holding of land, imposed upon that holding as a sort of seigneurial sign-manual. Dominating this prairie.

Had he undertaken more than he could do?

So far he had allowed his horses to idle along the faint trail. At this thought he straightened on top of the tent which covered his household goods. There, just ahead of him, came the turn; so far he had gone north, covering four miles in that direction. Now two miles west; and then look out for the stake which marked his corner.

He shook the lines over the backs of the horses and looked up. There did not seem to be even birds about! But this immense and utter loneliness merely aroused him to protest and contradiction: he would change this prairie, would impose himself upon it, would conquer its spirit!

At last he arrived on his claim and stopped just within his lines. Before he climbed to the ground, he scanned the quarter section immediately west. On close scrutiny the monotony of the flatness proved to be broken there by what, at this distance, looked like two blisters in the soil: sod-hut and sod-stable of his neighbour; built by cutting with a spade squares of the prairie turf, matted with ancient roots, and using them like enormous flat bricks. Not thus was he going to build his first abode!

He slipped to the ground and unhooked his horses, throwing the traces over their backs; then he hitched them all four abreast and, behind them, strode over to Hall's place.

Hall was at home: a short, fat man of forty. As he issued from the sod-shack, which had two small square windows and a plank door fitted into its shaggy wall, he betrayed no surprise.

"Well," he said, "you got here, eh?"

"Yes," Abe replied. "Can I water the horses?"

"Sure. Help yourself. Help yourself to anything you can find on the god-damn place."

"Have a crop in, I suppose?"

"They's seed in the ground; an' it's up. Quite a height, too."

"How much?"

"Thirty acres. But whether it's going to make a crop——" And the man shrugged his shoulders and flung an arm which came naked out of a sleeve ripped from the shoulder down.

"What's wrong with it?"

"Put in too doggone late. Water didn't go till nearly June." There the man stood, hardly raised, mentally and in his aspirations, above the level of that prairie from which he had come to wrest a living. "Truth to tell, if you want to know, if it were to do over again, I wouldn't do it. That's flat."

Abe nodded. "Well, I'll take the horses down to the pool."

"Help yourself. Anything you can use, just help yourself."

"I see you've a drag-shovel there."

"Take it. Take it. It ain't mine. But the fellow what owns it ain't hardly going to come back for it. He's done and gone."

Again Abe nodded. "Shall have to dig a pool myself." And he turned away with his horses to where, behind the stable, a dam of yellow subsoil circled the waterhole in which a supply of the precious liquid remained from the previous thaw-up and the summer rains.

Half an hour later, back in the south-east corner of his own claim, Abe tied the horses to the wheels of his wagon, took a steel measuring-line from a pocket, and marked off a hundred and twenty yards to west and north. That was to be the site of his farmstead. It was done half in protest against a rising discouragement; and, yielding completely to that need for a protest, he returned to his wagon, threw the tail-gate out, and pulled from under the load a huge hand-plough, which he lowered to the ground with a supreme effort. For a while he was busy fitting evener and trees to the implement. Then, looking up at the sun, which was approaching the western horizon, he hitched his horses in front.

"Get up there!" he shouted; and, throwing the plough over, so that the share slipped smoothly along the ground, he went north, to the point where, from his measurements, the line of his yard was to be. Reversing the plough, he slanted the point into the virgin prairie and began to step out behind his team, throwing his weight now to right, now to left, according as the plough threatened to be thrown out of the ground by such resistances as the soil afforded. Thus he drew a furrow around the site of the yard; and, having finished it, he returned once more to the point whence he had started and began the task of breaking his first field. He did shallow ploughing; for he knew that the prairie should be broken and back-set. As he stepped along, he did double work: he guided his plough and counted his steps; and when he had taken three hundred and eighty strides he turned, for on the trip west he had figured out that that line squared would give him thirty acres.

At the end of his back-furrow he stopped and hesitated. Should he let it go and put up his tent, so as to have shelter for the night? If he was to have a meal, he must get ready for cooking.

No. He reversed the plough for another furrow; and once he was committed to more than one round, he stayed with the work till it was too dark to see. He was here to conquer. Conquer he would! Before long he had opened ten furrows; the sun was down; and still he went on. A slight mist formed close to the ground, and he had the peculiar feeling as though he were ploughing over an appreciable fraction of the curvature of the globe; for whenever he turned at the north end of his furrow, he could no longer see his wagon, as though it were hidden behind the shoulder of the earth.

By the time he left off it was after ten and quite dark. He had gone sixteen rounds. He unhitched and unharnessed near the wagon, fed his horses a modicum of oats poured on the ground, staked them out, and supped on bread and raw bacon. Then he rolled up in a blanket under the wagon, with the tent for a groundsheet, and fell at once into a dreamless sleep.

II * THE IDYLL

A YEAR had gone by. Again Abe Spalding was in town, driving a team of rangy bronchos hitched to a topless buggy. He had taken a can of cream to the station, to be shipped to the city. Every motion of his betrayed hurry. Having dispatched the can, he drove to the Vanbruik store and, among the many other teams that were slanting back into the road, tied his horses to the rail of steel piping which ran along the sidewalk in front of the windows.

As he entered the swing-door, clad in a dark-coloured suit of combination overalls—jacket and trousers in one—and began to make his way through the crowd—for the store was flourishing and attracted custom by special Saturday sales, one of which was in progress—the manager of the establishment espied him from his vantage-point on the mezzanine landing of the flight of stairs leading to the upper story where furniture, rugs, and similar goods were displayed.

This manager, Mr. Diamond, was a smart young man of good build and appearance, well dressed, with a dash of metropolitan refinement, his blue-serge trousers being sharply creased, his linen spotless, his face freshly shaved to the quick. That he went about in shirt-sleeves seemed done, not to spare his coat or to make him comfortable, but to put himself on a level with the crowd. He was a shrewd business man, willing to give liberal discounts for the sake of a quick turnover; yet hard to deal with when a note given in payment was not redeemed in time or when a long-term credit was asked for. To such pleas the doctor was less inaccessible; he had been known to take over a debt owing to the store, accepting a personal note and allowing it to be forgotten. Mr. Diamond's motto was "Cash and Carry"; though with such as worried more over their debts than their bills receivable he urged the convenience of a charge-account. To travelling salesmen he said, "We discount our bills." He would not have been out of place in a large city store; but this rural establishment he might own one day.

As he caught sight of Abe, he came running down the stairs. That Abe was singled out for personal attention may have been due to the fact that he was the owner's brother-in-law; but it was sufficiently explained by the consideration that he had one of the largest and most reliable monthly accounts, which he settled with "cream cheques."

Mr. Diamond flashed a gold-filled smile. "Anything for you, Abe?"

"Yes," Abe replied and produced a slip of paper on which Ruth had written out a list of her needs. "Have these put into my buggy. The bronchos, right at the door." The better customers' horses were known to the clerks as well as the customers themselves.

"I'll have it attended to at once." And Mr. Diamond held up a finger to one of the white-frocked clerks.

"The doctor at the store?" Abe asked.

"I don't think so. He'll be at the house."

But the manager led the way to look about, for the store was too large to be swept by a glance. Abe's physical superiority reduced the other man to a mere satellite. He himself looked like a fact of nature.

They made the round without finding the doctor. Abe stood irresolute. In the course of the year he had learned not to resent his brother-in-law's ways any longer. But now he half blamed his sister for the fact that she and Ruth did not pull together.

"I am going to the post office," he said at last. "I won't be back. I am in a hurry." He always was.

"No need." Mr. Diamond nodded. "You'll find your things in the box."

Abe passed through a door and went briskly along the sidewalk fronting a second, much smaller store conducted by a tiny, square-bodied Jew. Crossing the second street, the far corner of which was occupied by a hardware store, he reached, a few hundred yards beyond, a white frame building in which the post office was housed.

Like every place accessible to the Saturday crowd, the public room was filled with people who stood about conversing, the weekly trip to town being made quite as much for the sake of the social intercourse it afforded as for the purpose of trading. All these men came from south of "the Line." It would have been easy for Abe to strike up acquaintances and to have himself admitted to the general conversation about the weather, the prospects of the crops, and provincial or municipal politics. But he merely nodded; and, under a general cessation of the buzzing talk, a few of those present silently and casually returned his nod. As if to expedite matters, they stepped aside and opened a lane for him to pass on to the wicket.

The reason for this reception was that Abe had not only made no advances but had even met such advances as were made to him with an attitude of reserve. He was considered proud; and he did look down on people satisfied with a success which secured a mere living. His goal was farther removed than theirs, and the very fact that he had so far realized few of his ambitions made him the more reticent; he was not going to allow himself to be judged by what he had done rather than by what he intended to do.

Having received from the aged postmaster that bundle of circulars which constituted his weekly mail, he left as briskly as he had entered.

He went to his sister's house, where Mary met him at the door.

"You'll stay for a while? I'll make a cup of tea?"

"I just want to see Charles for a moment."

"He's in the study." Mary looked queerly at her brother.

When she had so much wished to have him in the district, he kept aloof !

The study was a small room opposite the dining-room. In contrast to the rest of the house its floor was bare; the general impression it made was that of an untidy litter. Its walls were lined with unstained bookshelves made by a local carpenter; the furniture consisted of a table strewn with papers, a roll-top desk, and two Morris chairs in one of which the doctor was sitting, a book in his hand; the seat of the other was encumbered with pamphlets and letters.

As Abe entered, Dr. Vanbruik looked at him over his glasses, dropped the hand holding the book, bent forward to sweep the encumbrances of the other chair to the floor, and said unsmilingly : "Sit down, Abe."

If the doctor's whole physique was small, his face was diminutive. It looked contracted, as if its owner lived in a perpetual concentration of thought. His dark clothes, though old, still bore traces of having been well tailored; but the creases at shoulders, elbows, and knees were worn in beyond the possibility of being removed by pressing. He had his right foot drawn up on his left knee and, with his free hand, was nursing its ankle.

As Abe sat down, there was a moment's silence.

"Hall's ready to sell," Abe said at last. "He's entitled to prove up if he gets the buildings he needs."

The doctor nodded. "You know my views. The farmer who isn't satisfied to be a farmer makes a mistake. You want to be a landowner on a large scale. You'll find you can't get the help you will need. At least you won't be able to hold it."

Abe gave a short laugh. "Machines."

"Well, we might thresh it all out again. It would lead nowhere."

"What I want to know is this," Abe said. "I could put up the buildings for Hall; or I could buy them and haul them out. But it's illegal for him to pledge the place before he has his patent. You have known him in a business way. Is he going to do what he promises when I can't force him?"

"No. You want his farm. If he owes you money when he proves up, he will sell to the man who offers cash, if he can find him."

"I offer him eight hundred dollars."

"Don't pay a cent till he turns his title over."

"He must have that house, worth three hundred dollars. And meanwhile he must live."

"Get more work out of him."

28

"That's your advice, is it?"

"If you must have more land, that's the way to go about it. As for Hall, I wouldn't trust him across the road."

Abe rose. "That's what I wanted to know. I must be going."

As he passed through the living-room, Mary stopped her brother. "You won't stay? Not for half an hour?"

"I can't. Work's waiting."

"It's Saturday. Other farmers have time."

"They!"

"How's the baby?"

"All right as far as I know."

"Ruth?"

"The same."

Mary stood and looked at him. Abe laughed, patted her back, bent down to kiss her, and turned to the door.

As he backed out of the row of vehicles in front of the store he looked at his watch. He had acquired the trick of timing himself on his drives. When the trail was dry, he tried to beat his own record, cutting off seconds from the time required.

He was sitting bolt upright and held his lines tight; the wheels bounded over the road. It took him twenty-four minutes to cover the four miles to the turn west. Having made the turn, he used the whip, just flicking the horses' rumps.

As he approached his claim he looked about. What he had achieved in a year might justify pride. There was a two-roomed shack, built like a shed. East of it lay a pile of poplar boles, hauled from the river, a distance of twenty-five miles, in winter; there was a year's fuel left, well-seasoned now. Along the west edge of the yard stood a frame stable large enough to house six horses and four cows, but too small right now. The yard was fenced with woven wire; and a strip thirty-two feet wide, inside the fence, was ploughed and kept black, to be planted with four rows of trees next spring. South of the stable loomed two large haystacks, cut of the wild prairie grass west of Hall's. North of the barn there was a huge water pool, forty by a hundred feet, fifteen feet deep. The whole south line, too, was fenced; with barbed wire only, it was true; but the posts were of imported cedar; and along the other lines posts and coils of wire were laid out, the posts all pointed, ready to be driven into the ground with a wooden maul after the next soaking rain. North of the yard lay the field, forty acres of good wheat. The remaining hundred-odd acres were all broken; black as velvet they stretched away as far as one could see.

That being so, Abe needed more land; with more land he would need help; a good thing that so far he had a thriftless neighbour willing to work for wages rather than to attend to his own claim.

Abe had lived through one spring flood. For three weeks in April Ruth had never left the square plot about the shack where he had piled the earth dug from the pool, thus securing the house from being invaded by water and doing away with the eyesore of the raw clay at the same time; he himself had had to don rubber hip-boots to cross his yard. But the flood had run out in time for seeding. One trouble was that the water had spread the seeds of foul weeds all over his land. Where the prairie remained unbroken, the grass had held its own, apart from small patches where skunk-tail had gained a foothold. But on the breaking where his crop was seeded, a damnable mixture of charlock, thistle, and tumbling mustard had sprung up with the wheat. These pests the water had brought from the older settlements to the west, in the famous Torquay district, south-east of Grand Pré Plains where, so they said, farming was already becoming a problem.

One other change Abe noted as he drove into his yard. South-west, seven miles away as the crow flies, a new grain elevator was being constructed, at a flag station called Bays, after the oldest settler south of the Somerville Line. That building, with glistening planks still unpainted, was a reminder that the country was being settled; land was going to rise in value; it was time to secure one's share of the prairie; no longer did a half section seem such a bountiful slice of the universe to build a mansion on.

As he drove to the house, Abe looked again at his watch. He had made the trip in thirty-three minutes and thirty-five seconds, cutting twenty-five seconds off his last record.

Ruth, in a long, dark print dress, was standing in the door, a smile on her pretty face and a child a few months old in her arms. She was not exactly small; but she was getting plump; and the plumper she grew the less tall she seemed.

Abe answered her smile by a nod, alighted, and at once carried the box with her groceries and the empty cream can into the house. Then, from old habit, he glanced at the sun; and without a word, he took the baby, helped the young woman to a seat in the buggy, and, returning the child to her keeping, reached for the lines to drive to the stable.

In front of the open slide-doors he unhitched, allowing the horses to go to the huge trough of corrugated iron which reached through the yard-fence into the field beyond. Between trough and pool stood the pump, which he worked vigorously for five minutes. When the bronchos had drunk their fill, he entered the stable and stuffed their mangers with hay; having tied them, he slipped the harness off their backs. Next, he filled the mangers and feed-boxes of the remaining stalls and finally went to the door where he stood for several minutes, one hand raised to its frame, shouting at the top of his voice, "Come on —come on—come on!"

This was the signal for the work-horses and the cows to return to the stable; and since they were always fed a measure of oats and a handful of shorts, a scarcely visible cluster of animals began at once to move from the open prairie towards the farmstead. As soon as Abe saw that they were on their way, he ceased calling, turned back into the stable and turned the drivers out into the yard. There being no room for all his stock in the barn, he had to feed in relays. Then he went to the gate and waited for the rest of the horses to come. Even his waiting he seemed to do briskly, calling again for the horses when they lingered to snatch another bite of good grass. At last they started their nightly comedy of a struggle between their love of freedom and their love of oats. Invariably the desire of the belly conquered; and, leaving the more deliberate cows behind, they entered the yard in a galloping rush, tossing their heads and raising their tails. The cows followed at a walk, breaking into a short run only as they passed the master who impatiently closed the gate behind them.

All this while Ruth had been sitting in the buggy and looking on. A somewhat empty smile never left her lips. Was this routine of the farm still new enough to her to retain its charm? Or was she so intensely in love with her vigorous and swift-moving husband that she was unwilling to lose a minute of his company?

Abe was occasionally conscious of a twinge of impatience with her—or was it with himself? He would have liked to say something; what was there to say? He had tried to speak of his plans; the topic, endlessly repeated, had exhausted itself. Sometimes she looked as though she were waiting; for what? He was doing his best.

The milking next, for evening was coming fast. Meanwhile, in the house, supper was waiting; and Abe was conscious of being hungry.

Ruth descended from the buggy and stood in the door, looking on. A year ago she had tried her hand at the traditional woman's task, with poor success. Laughing at herself, she had given it up; and Abe preferred to do all outside work himself.

Together they went to the house, Abe carrying the brimming pails. At the table, nothing was being said, either, beyond such brief words as were called for by the task in hand. Abe was thinking of his coming negotiations with Hall; Ruth—of what?

Supper over, Abe separated the cream while Ruth cleared the table and washed the dishes. It was seven o'clock; but the sun was still high. Abe carried the skimmed milk to the pigpen beyond the pool.

When he returned, he stopped in the centre of the yard. "Coming out?" he called to Ruth who was still in the shack.

She came to the door. "Might as well."

Might as well! Yet every bit of the work was Abe's.

They went to the field where the wheat stood knee-high, being in the shot-blade; and for two hours they went about pulling weeds; bright-yellow charlock and paler tumbling mustard. As always, Abe worked like a whirlwind; Ruth languidly, she being pregnant. Abe kept slapping neck and hands, for mosquitoes were bad. Ruth laughed, immune.

Suddenly Abe straightened and listened. "By jingo!" he exclaimed.

"What is it?" Ruth asked; for she, too, had caught a faint pulsation in the air.

"The ditchers," Abe said. "Come on!" And, turning, he ran for the yard, leaving Ruth behind.

The sun was almost setting; and as they passed through the gate where Abe had waited, they saw, straight west, little puffs of steam and smoke rising into the clear evening air.

"It *is* the ditching machine," Abe said. "They'll get past here after all this summer. I'll hitch up to-morrow; we'll have a look at them."

He took Ruth's arm and, bending down to kiss her, led her back to the field where they rogued for another hour till it was too dark to distinguish weeds from grain. The weeds Abe piled in the margin, at right angles to a rope which he had brought and by the help of which he swung the huge bundle on his back. Thus, through the dusk, they returned to the yard where Abe kindled a fire with chips from the wood pile, smothering the flames with the green weeds till they disengaged a dense, acrid smoke which dispelled the increasingly troublesome mosquitoes. Ruth brought two chairs from the shack; and they sat down in the smudge, Abe in the thickest of it, Ruth near the margin.

They had been sitting there for half an hour, Abe yawning with that abandon which comes from overwhelming drowsiness, when, from the trail beyond the fence, a voice sounded across: "Seen the ditchers?"

Abe and Ruth gave a start. "Yes," Abe said. "Heard and seen them."

"Both?"

"What do you mean?"

"They're working on both lines," said Hall's voice. "They're nearer on the south line."

"Come," Abe said to Ruth; and again he took her arm.

"Do you mean to say they work at night?" Abe asked at the gate.

Hall laughed and spat. "They had better. They've contracted to finish the work before freeze-up."

The bright glare of a headlight was visible against the dark sky from which the pallor of the sunset had vanished; and farther south a second similar light pointed eastward, less brightly, for these three humans were not in the line of its focus.

"That there machine," Hall said, pointing ineffectively with a chewed-off pipe-stem, "is two miles south. It's the bigger one; they work three steam-shovels there; that's why they've overtaken this here devil. They've shipped in two carloads of forriners, Ukarainians, dogdast them. I was thinking of asking fer a job my own self. But the white man don't stand a chancet in this country any longer."

"That reminds me," Abe said. "I'm going to build a granary. You can get a job right here."

"All right, bo'. What about that there house you were talking of?"

"I'll get you the house. Trouble is, I'll have to owe you the money it costs. You have to sign under oath that the house is yours."

Hall chuckled. "So long as I gets my money when I pull out."

"You don't need to pull out till you've got it."

"That's so. It's all right then. I'm danged if I stays on this prairie a day longer than I've got to."

Three, four miles to the west, lights shifted, crossing the pointed finger of the headlight. The night seemed to intensify into a more palpable blackness; and the pulse of the engine ceased. Startlingly, two or three of the movable lights were reversed, pointing converging beams backward, against the face of the machine that was straddling the ditch it excavated. Magically, it seemed drawn nearer.

"Something wrong," Hall said, spitting. "Lighting up for repairs."

They stood and stared but could not, of course, see what was going on. The second outfit was visibly forging ahead. Whenever Abe looked away for a second, he noticed the progress made in the interval.

"That there outfit," Hall said, "lifts three yards of dirt at a bite; the ditch is forty feet wide and thirty deep; but that there monster digs it at the rate of two rods an hour. Twenty rods in a ten-hour day; that's two miles a month. They're speeding her up now to five miles a month, what with night work and more help. They've got to finish her, or they lose their deposit."

"That so? How do you know?" Abe felt Ruth pressing against him.

Hall, however, did not take the slightest notice of her. Again he spat. "I've been down. Foreman told me."

"Well," Abe said, turning away, "I was thinking of hitching up and driving down myself to-morrow, it being Sunday."

"No work on Sundays," Hall said. "Stop at midnight. Wait till Monday."

Abe was fingering the gate. "No time on weekdays."

"You're in a blasted hurry. Learn better by-m-by. When do I start on that there granary of yours?"

"Report on Monday. We'll haul the lumber . . . Good night."

And once more husband and wife sat in silence within the smudge till the excitement of the trip to the road had worn off and drowsiness reconquered body and mind.

III * FIRST NEIGHBOURS

AGAIN a year had gone by; and Abe, with the help of a huge steam-tractor rented from Anderson, the round-faced young hardware dealer in town, and operated by Bigelow, the powerful, club-footed blacksmith, had hauled out for Hall a three-roomed farm-house which he had bought from Wilson, postmaster at Morley. The price, three hundred dollars, had been figured, as Dr. Vanbruik had advised, against the wages which Abe owed Hall for work done during the year.

It was in that spring of 1902 that Nicoll first came out to

look the district over. He was renting a farm along the southern edge of Grand Pré Plains.

"Renting!" he said to Abe. "You don't know what that means. No chance to do as I think best. My landlord wants me to summer-fallow eighty acres. 'Very well,' I say, 'give me a lease so that I can count on some return from my labour. Unless I know that I can crop that fallow next year, I won't earn wages for my work.' 'I can hardly do that,' he says. 'I may want to sell; or another tenant may offer a better rent.' 'Then,' I say, 'I'll crop what I till or go where I can do so.' 'You've got your living,' he says; 'what more do you want?' I always leave my land better than I found it; but it's no use. I have to have land of my own. I have my own horses and implements, such as they are. And I've a little money besides. I've *got* to have land of my own.'

"The land's here," Abe said, irritated by the man's hesitation, yet liking him. "It has its drawbacks, like any land. It's subject to floods coming down from the hills. They bring weeds. But *I'm* farming. Seems to me I'm getting ahead; though, of course, it's hard to say where you stand in this game. So far I've been tying my money down, what little I had. But this year I'll have a crop of a hundred and fifty acres; and it's doing well. I came when there wasn't even a ditch. We are getting the better of the water. I'm buying more land and proving up on the homestead. Seems to me I'm on the safe side."

"It looks that way," Nicoll said.

But he did not, that year, file on the quarter section which he had picked and decided upon.

In the summer of 1903 he returned. During the previous fall Abe had built a huge barn and added a room to the shack, financing his operations by using his last capital and borrowing at the Somerville bank—a process which he found surprisingly easy. True enough, it was a short-term loan of only fifteen hundred dollars; but, after threshing, he had paid off only eight hundred, covering the balance by a renewal note. In the spring he had planted a four-rowed wind-break of black poplar, with spruces interspersed along the north and west lines of the yard. There were other changes which Nicoll inspected and duly admired. The whole of what was now Abe's half section was fenced; and the land was divided by a cross-fenced pasture of twenty acres, extending from the rear of his huge, red, curb-roofed barn for twenty rods west and for half a mile north. In the house which he had bought for Hall lived Bill Crane who had been a notorious idler in town but who, having married, seemed to have changed his ways, for young Mrs.

Crane could often be heard shrilly driving her man to work in the morning. Hall, having received eight hundred dollars, had turned over to Abe his newly acquired title and left for parts unknown. Abe had a hundred acres of this new land under crop; and sixty acres were freshly broken when Nicoll appeared. The total number of horses on the place was eleven now, not counting three colts born in the new barn. Ten cows were being milked; and there were steers and heifers besides, and pigs and fowl.

Nicoll, medium-sized, middle-aged, bearded, deliberate, went about and looked at it all. "You say you came here with a few wagon-loads of truck and slept on the ground for the first two weeks?"

"That's what I said." They were standing in the open door of the magnificent barn. Opposite, in front of the house—for with the new room and the gable roof it was hardly a shack any longer—two youngsters played about; and a cradle stood in the shade north of the building. This cradle held a little girl called Mary, after her aunt, though, to avoid confusion, her parents had resolved to change the name to Marion, which was the first name of Ruth's mother.

Nicoll smiled up at Abe, sighing. It would have been hard to define his expression. Ordinarily he seemed to look into himself rather than at the things surrounding him. Now he seemed ready to be impressed. At times his look verged on adoration and yet seemed on the point of turning on itself and, in a smile half veiled by the reddish beard streaked with grey, of becoming tinged with a gentle irony. Abe was by far the younger man of the two; but the way in which Nicoll looked at him might have suggested that he gave him credit for superior wisdom and experience while at the same time half mocking at it.

In spite of the fact that Abe could not understand the man's hesitation he was attracted. To him the world was a thing to be conquered, waiting to take the impress of his mind and will. Nicoll seemed rather to look for a niche to slip into, unnoticed and unobserved.

"You," Nicoll said at last, "were of course in a different position when you arrived. "You had capital."

"I had five thousand dollars."

Nicoll seemed to shrink within himself. "As I said," he muttered, with his curious smile. "Dukes and lords . . ." He had said nothing of the kind; but perhaps he had thought it.

"But look what I've got!" Abe said impulsively. "This barn cost me three thousand dollars. My stock is worth two any day. And all that"—indicating, by a sweep of his arm, the

36

fields with their crops—"is clear profit, not to mention the rest of my equipment. I had nothing but a hand plough when I came. Before I'm through, I'll be farming whole sections of land, ploughing with tractors, an acre every two minutes."

"No doubt," Nicoll said. "Dukes and lords. How about the margin?"

"The profit? Before I'm through, I'll build a house over there fit to stand in any city."

Nicoll repeated, "No doubt!" not hesitatingly this time, but decisively. "Not a doubt on earth! . . . But I didn't mean it that way. Do you find time to live? Besides, I've half a score of kids."

"I've three," Abe said with a laugh. "There hasn't been time for more. What we want. A population. What do I want more than anything else? I'll tell you. Neighbours."

Nicoll laughed; and, with an intonation almost of archness which sat strangely on a man of his age, he added, "To buy out?"

Abe frowned but took no offence. "Tell you. I'll buy out every no-account fellow who settles next to me. Rather than let his claim revert to weeds which would be a menace to me. But if a man shows he can make a success, I'll help him all I can. Why, man," he burst out vigorously, "I'll tell you why I need neighbours. Because I need roads; because I need cross-ditches and other improvements. And as the kids grow up, I'll need a school. That's why I need neighbours. There's been a Yankee snooping around. I don't like him. A runt of a fellow, with an eye and a nose like a terrier dog. I've encouraged him. Why? Because he might know the business end of a rake from the handle. And Germans have been looking the district over, from the reserve down south. Even a Ukrainian came last fall; had been working on the ditching machine. I'd like to have men of my own colour about. But rather than stay alone, let niggers and Chinamen come."

"Good farmers," Nicoll said pensively, "those Germans and Ukrainians. And Chinamen, too. . . . I believe I'm going to do it. I'm not quite ready. But that corner suits me to the ground if it can be farmed."

"I've been steering others away from the place."

"I believe I will," Nicoll said, and went to to his buggy as though to start at once for the land-titles office.

But in the spring of 1904 there was no sign yet of any Nicoll in the district.

Abe had suddenly seen himself forced to buy a third quarter of land, unless, indeed, he had been willing to let it go to someone else. It was the north-west quarter; and, together with other parcels in other districts, it had been put up for public sale. Abe had been taken by surprise; and though the price was low, he had had to borrow at the bank. Not that it mattered; but his increased acreage demanded an ever-rising investment in implements; and Ruth was plainly getting impatient about the house. What could he do? He could not afford to let the land go to any one else. If, for a few more years, they had to put up with a house less roomy and less well built than their hired man's, it could not be helped. He had bidden the land in, paying seven hundred and fifty dollars for it.

Yet he was worried and restless. He was in debt. He worked frantically; he even pulled weeds again by hand, a thing he had not done for a year or two; and he did it alone now; for Ruth no longer kept him company. The crop did not promise so well that year; the flood had been slow in running out; and after that there was a drought; in patches the wheat was turning yellow before it had headed out. It was, of course, impossible to rogue three hundred acres of grain; he did what he could. Yet there were odd little twinges of a lack of confidence. With his thirst for conquest he lived dangerously, always assuming new debts before the old ones were paid off; he was discounting the future; he was selling himself into slavery. Such curious, harrying thoughts could be shaken off only by desperate spurts of work. Never was the day's task finished before eleven at night; he never sat about with Ruth any longer. The hired man had his more or less defined hours; Abe had not. Conscience-stricken over his neglect of Ruth, he tried to compensate for it by an occasional ostentation of solicitude. There were four children now: two boys and two girls, the name of the youngest being Frances. He urged Ruth to get help for the house. Ruth asked scornfully, "Where should I put a girl? In the hay-loft?" Yes, yes, the house was too small.

All this was worrying Abe when, one evening, Nicoll drove into the margin of the field where Abe was roguing. Sitting in his old, wobbly buggy, he asked whether he could spend the night in the barn.

"Sure," Abe said. "Had your supper?"

"Had a bite in town. Well, I am coming at last."

"To stay?"

"Not yet. We'll move next spring. But I've filed on the place."

"A wonder nobody got ahead of you."

"That risk I had to take. But I'm coming; provided I can

38

count on getting occasional work on your place for a year or two."

Abe laughed. "You're a godsend. Want to start to-night?"

"Not this summer. I've only a few weeks to spare before harvest. I need that for building. But if you say I can make enough to pay my store bill next summer, I'll go to town to-morrow and buy the lumber I need. I must have the house. There's been another kid during the year."

"Same here. A girl. Number four." Nicoll's coming would solve Abe's most pressing problem: that of help for the summer-fallowing while he and Bill did the breaking on the new quarter. An extensive fallow had become imperative unless he was willing to look on while his acres were being fouled with weeds. "I've bought a new quarter," he added.

By way of answer, Nicoll looked at Abe with his queer, half-ironic smile. "I'm honestly tired," he said.

"I haven't the time to feel tired," Abe replied.

Thus the spring of 1905 saw Abe's desire for a neighbour fulfilled. North of the bridge across the ditch a house had been built, with a commodious, roofed-over porch. Behind it, a small stable with a granary as a lean-to on one side, and a hen-house on the other. A strip of ploughing, for the wind-break, surrounded the two acre-yard. West of it, twenty acres of new breaking extended to the north.

Blessings, like disasters, have a habit of coming in pairs. Two miles east of what was henceforth to be known as Nicoll's Corner, a log-shack went up, south of the ditch. For a long while neither Abe nor Nicoll knew who was building in this furtive way. Whoever it was did his hauling and fitting at night, after dark. For hours there was a continual going and coming about the place by lantern light. Nicoll at last rode over on horseback. He reported to Abe that the walls of a house twenty by eighteen feet were going up there. Not a soul had been visible about the place.

The next time Abe was at Somerville he dropped in at the land-titles office and inquired. The man had given his name as Shilloe; he was a Ukrainian who had little English. When filing his claim he had produced naturalization papers. He lived at a town called The Coulee, eight miles south-west of Somerville, where he was employed as a section man by the Great Prairie Railroad.

Abe felt encouraged. For five years he had been alone; now he was going to have two neighbours at once. They would help to bring in other settlers. He had also noticed that the ditch along the Somerville Line was being deepened and widened; it had been taken over by the provincial government. But when he mentioned at Morley that this was evidently being done to attract settlers, he was laughed at. It was done, he was told, to attract votes to a certain party.

As for Nicoll, he and Abe became more than neighbours that summer; they became friends. Considering their almost antipodal outlook on life, this was a remarkable fact. . . .

Abe was breaking the newly acquired quarter section; and, belatedly, he was fallowing the south-west quarter. This ploughing Nicoll did while Bill Crane helped Abe with his breaking. Sometimes it happened that Abe and Nicoll met at the line dividing the two quarters where Abe had taken down his fence and replaced it by a shallow ditch.

Often, when they met, Nicoll jumped across to join Abe while the horses rested; and they talked; sometimes, as is often the case with farmers, on curious and recondite subjects.

Thus Wilson, the postmaster at Morley, having suddenly died, leaving his daughter Susie in charge, Nicoll said with seeming irrelevancy and in that light tone with which we touch on things that disquiet us, "Strange thing, death, isn't it?"

"I don't know," Abe replied. He had a definite aim in life: to be the most successful farmer of a district yet to be created; he was a materialist and felt uncomfortable when facing fundamentals.

"I wish we could know!"

Abe turned and picked up the lines of his team. "Best not to inquire, I guess," he said, and clicked his tongue.

When they met again, Nicoll pursued the topic. "I read an article recently," he said. "The doctor gave it to me." He meant Dr. Vanbruik, not Dr. Schreiber, the practising physician at Morley. "It said a life after death was impossible unless we had existed from all eternity."

Abe's eyes swept over the landscape beyond his fences. He did not often allow it to do so. Rarely, during the first years of his life on the prairie, had he given the landscape any thought. It had offered a "clear proposition," unimpeded by bluffs of trees or irregularities in the conformation of the ground; the trees he wanted he had planted where he wanted them. But when Nicoll spoke as he had done, Abe felt something uncanny in that landscape. Nicoll's words impressed him as though they were the utterance of that very landscape itself; as though Nicoll were the true son of the prairie, and he, Abe, a mere interloper. Incomprehensibly he was drawn to this man even while resenting the fact that his, Abe's, brother-in-law should loan him things to read. Abe read nothing but farm papers; and in them only what might enable him to farm more land more efficiently than any one else.

Again he picked up his lines. But, still standing in his place, he shrugged his shoulders. "What of it? Suppose we come from nothing and go to nothing? While I'm here, what difference does it make?"

Nicoll gave him a troubled glance.

"Get up, there!" Abe shouted, shaking the lines over the horses' backs; and as they bent into their collars, he caught up with the plough by running a few steps before he lifted himself to its seat.

Here and there, in the long strip of pasture, cows were grazing in groups; others were lying down and chewing the cud. To the east, two miles away as the crow flies, a slight indentation of the sky-line marked the spot where Nicoll's farmstead lay. Shilloe's buildings were quite invisible. Abe's own barn was so far the only landmark to be seen from Morley.

Conquest of that landscape depended on ways and means of speeding up the work Abe owned three quarter sections now. No doubt the man who held the remaining quarter of the section would turn up one day prepared to sell. Abe would have a square mile then; how could he farm it? Hired men? Bill Crane needed too much supervising right now; when he milked, he did not milk dry; when he fed, he seemed to grudge the hay and yet wasted more than he saved. Why in the world, he had recently asked, did Abe not turn the horses out at night? Even the horses liked it better. "They can't pick up enough green feed to keep in trim for the work and sleep besides," Abe had answered. What was the solution? There was only one: power-farming as it was called: machinery would do the work of many horses and many men. But Abe liked the response of living flesh and bone to the spoken word and hated the un-intelligent repetition of ununderstood activities which machines demanded. Yet sooner or later he must come to that; he would have to run the farm like a factory; that was the modern trend. . . .

At noon, when the men went to the yard for dinner, two little boys, four and three years old, crossed from the house to the open door of the barn, plying their little legs as fast as they could and holding each other by their hands. Three teams, sixteen horses in all—for Bill and Nicoll worked with six horses each, while Abe drove his "crack" team, four full-blooded Percherons—crowded around the water trough north of the barn. Abe left them and entered behind the children.

The two little boys were in the first stall opposite the door, south of the driveway, a stall never used except to drop hay into from above. Abe began to take oats to the various stalls.

But as boys will do, Charlie and Jim ran to the door every now and then, to scamper back to the protection of the stall, crowing.

They were on such a run when the first horses entered: a cunning mare with colt at foot. "Watch out!" Abe shouted.

The children jumped into safety; and the mare ran successively into several stalls to stick her nose into the feed-boxes. This was a trick of hers to steal a mouthful of oats here or there while the other horses filed in; but every time Abe gave a lusty shout; and, tossing her head and slipping on the planking, she backed out again. The children laughed at her antics.

Abe was still carrying oats into the various stalls, greeted wherever he went by impatient whinnyings and the thuds of shifting feet, when Bill and Nicoll entered and distributed the hay. The feeding done, Bill climbed by the ladder into the loft to throw down enough hay for the evening's feeding. This was a special delight for the boys, who allowed themselves to be buried as each forkful came down.

"Bill!" Abe called when there was enough hay.

"Yah?"

"Look into the bin and see how much oats is left."

The answer came shortly: "Not much. A bushel or so."

"We better fill up to-night before we quit," Nicoll said.

That was it! If all helpers were like Nicoll, it would not be bad. Bill would never have suggested working overtime to fill up a feed bin that was running low. The feed was there, in the granary. . . .

Abe picked up Jim, the smaller one of the boys, and put him on his shoulder; Charlie reached for his hand. And, with a nod to the other men, he strode off to the house, frowning.

He always frowned when he went to the house while Nicoll was there. He resented it that Ruth had suggested Nicoll might take his dinner at Bill's. At first Abe had flatly refused to agree to such an arrangement; but Ruth had made their meals so uncomfortable that he had broached the matter to Nicoll who had at once consented. "I quite understand. It's all right."

What was the matter with Ruth? Much was the matter.

Immediately after dinner Abe rose from table and returned to the yard where Nicoll joined him. Nicoll never got tired of admiring that barn of Abe's; but he did so with his peculiar smile which seemed on the point of turning from admiration into irony.

"I've often wondered," he said, making futile attempts at

using a straw by way of a toothpick, "whether this sort of thing pays."

"What sort of thing?"

"Buying more and more land. Working with hired help."

"Does it pay to farm? Seems to me that is the question."

"I don't think it is. While you do your own work, farming is bound to pay. It has paid since the world began. You make better wages for your labour than anywhere else and remain your own master."

"I'm hanged," Abe said, "if I'll work for a dollar a day. That's all I pay you. There must be some profit over."

"You pay more than the wages. You need two ploughs instead of one; or three or four. You feed two or three teams instead of one. You pay more in taxes. And—— Oh, well, it's all right when you hire a neighbour with time to spare. But when it comes to what you call a hired man! He won't work so hard; he won't work so well. There's more wear and tear on your implements, and on your horses. Right now, I believe, the greater your acreage, the less your yield per acre."

This argument told; for already, within five years, Abe had to contend against a decreasing yield. Yet he defended himself. "The soil gets poorer. You'll be up against the same thing."

"Perhaps." Nicoll shrugged his shoulders and pushed out his lips. "I don't say. But the moment I gave up moving from place to place, my yield increased. . . . And it gets harder to find help."

"Machines," Abe said, struck by the coincidence of Nicoll's arguments with those of his brother-in-law.

"That's so," Nicoll said pensively. They were squatting in the narrow strip of shade along the east wall of the barn. "When you hitch an engine to your plough, you know it won't slack. But the thing's got to be built. You get your hired man one degree removed. He's going to get the better of you. And then . . . I've been watching these threshing outfits. Do a lot of work. But . . . just for the fun of it, I threshed a strawstack over last year, in winter time, with the fanning mill."

"And what did you find? I've often wondered."

"I fanned a hundred and three bushels of wheat out of that stack."

"That a fact? I'll be hanged!"

And with that Abe rose, more disquieted than ever. . . .

In the fall of the year Shilloe moved out to his claim; but not before section crews were dismissed for the winter. He proved to be a pleasant, round-faced, clean-shaven man of thirty-odd, good-looking in his way, though unmistakably

Slavic. As for his wife, neither Abe nor Nicoll ever saw her; and whenever either of them passed the place, a flock of children scampered for house or stable to hide.

IV * HUSBAND AND WIFE

ABE had been married for nearly six years; and in rapid succession four children had arrived. Then, there was a cessation of births.

Just what had happened between Abe and Ruth? Neither of them knew; they had simply drifted. There had been a time when both had forseen the coming estrangement and dreaded its approach. Both had tried to forestall it. Abe had asked Ruth to accompany him on necessary drives : calls here and there, rounds of inspection when planning operations for the following season. Ruth had again sought his company in the long summer evenings. Gradually such attempts had been abandoned till, in occasional retrospection, both were often struck by the fact that a day, a week, a month had gone by without their having spoken more than such few words as were demanded by the routine of life.

Physical attraction had died in satiety, renewing itself in ever-lengthening intervals; on Abe's part because he immersed himself more and more in his work : he came home exhausted and overtired; on Ruth's part because, unperceived, a revolt flamed in her against she hardly knew what : the rural life, the isolation, the deadly routine of daily tasks. She had become used to exhausting her emotional powers on the children. These children had been born as the natural fruit of marriage, not anticipated with any great fervour of expectancy; yet they had come to absorb her life; for Abe, engrossed in other things, had left them to her. When, occasionally, she had told him of their progress in growth or development, he had listened absently, had treated her enthusiasm with an ironic coolness which made her close up in her shell. In his presence she had ceased to let herself go in her intercourse with them. When she was playing with them, and he entered, a mask fell over her face. Gradually, she ceased to play with them.

A peculiar development was the consequence. The children, always thrown with her, began to take her for granted; Abe was the extraordinary, romantic element in their lives; mostly he was away, driving or working in the fields; he did not encourage their familiarity; he tolerated them as an adjunct to his life; but he was also the dispenser of such rare glories as a ride on horseback, in buggy or wagon. When they begged for such favours and he briefly declined to comply with their wishes, they accepted his verdict as that of a higher power; but they soon learned that their mother's "no" need not be accepted.

Both Ruth and Abe were aware of these things. Ruth resented them; Abe, noticing that she did, took them with a humorous good nature which had often an ironical point. Suppose the children were noisy and Ruth tried vainly to quiet them. Abe waited till she had worked herself into a state of nervous excitement, the worse for his observant eye; then suddenly he would "settle them" by a word of command. His instant success had an effect as though he had said, "I'll show you how to deal with them." Ruth felt that it was easy for him to retain his power over them, but that he made no attempt of exerting it in her name or to her advantage. Although he corroborated her own demands, he did it in such a way as to damage her authority rather than to confirm it.

On the rare occasions when Abe gave these things a definite thought, he realized his own lack of consideration; but somehow he seemed unable to remedy it. His regret was always retrospective; he could not foresee it. His material struggle absorbed him to the point where he had no energy left to ponder nice questions of conduct and to lay down rules to govern his intercourse with wife and children. When, in a flash of insight, this became clear to him, he postponed the difficulty. The "kids" were still small; he would take them in hand later; let him build up that farm first, an empire ever growing in his plans.

There was another point of friction between him and Ruth: the house. Ruth did not forgive him the fact that the hired man of whom she disapproved had a better place to live in than herself. When Abe said that this was provisional, that one day he would build her a house which was to be the envy of everybody, she could not summon any enthusiasm; she wanted comfort, not splendour; convenience, not luxury. That was the reason, too, why she adopted an attitude hostile to the Nicolls; she envied them their house: but the Nicolls were mere peasants; she could not rid herself of the conceit of the city-born.

She was city-born! In this she was handicapped.

Abe had never expected Ruth to do any farm work, not even to carry water or fuel into the house. Winter or summer, he rose at four in the morning and started the fires. He milked the cows and fed the horses before he called her. But that call in the morning! In the first year of their marriage Abe had entered the bedroom and sat down on the edge of her bed, awakening her with a caress. Now he knocked at her door.

She was aware that he had begun to look critically at her. She had caught herself wishing that she could make herself invisible; She was getting stout. Not that Abe said a word about it; but she knew he disliked stout women. Abe was heavy himself; he weighed two hundred and fifty pounds; but, being so tall, he did not look it. Ruth had been slender at the time of their marriage; as she began to put on weight, she had become shapeless as she called it. She suffered from it herself but resented Abe's disapproval. Perhaps he never meant to convey such a disapproval. It was true that the bed which they had so far shared was becoming uncomfortable; but when Abe, in the fourth year, jestingly referred to the fact, his very jest offended her, the more so since, ostentatiously, he spoke only of his own increase in girth. "By golly!" he said. "Work agrees with me. It's about time we bought another bedstead so I can turn around without bumping you." A week later he brought that new bedstead home; and henceforth they slept apart. Ruth cried.

Nor was she unaware of her own shortcomings; she was getting less and less careful with regard to the common amenities of life. At first, she had omitted the white table-cloth only when Abe was absent from a meal. Why go to unnecessary trouble? It was hard enough to keep a house tidy which, with four children in it, was much too small. There was a kitchen cabinet; she had a good dinner-set; but, when pieces were broken, she replaced them with heavy white crockery, saving her better dishes for social occasions which never came. When Abe saw these substitutes for the first time, he lifted a cup in his hand and weighed it; but he never said a word. Next, to save steps, she took to washing the dishes in the dining and living room, leaving them on the table for the next meal. Then she left the white table-cloth out altogether, preferring oilcloth. The room took on a dingy appearance.

In her dress, too, she became careless. Her house-frocks were ready-made, "out-size" garments bought from a catalogue. Feeling "driven", she ceased changing her aprons at meal-time.

Abe noticed all this. The more lordly his own domain grew to be, the less in keeping was his house. For weeks he never said a word, till his distaste reached an explosive pressure. He knew that it was dangerous to let a grievance rest till it has become impossible to discuss it in a pleasant way. But time and energy were lacking; he closed his eyes while he could. When calling on his sister at Morley, he scanned everything and compared the way in which Mary, with the help of a servant, ran her house. Mary rarely mentioned her husband; the doctor rarely mentioned his wife; but when they did so, they spoke of each other with a great considerateness; not exactly tenderly, but with an unvarying mutual respect which showed that they were at one on every question of importance. The great secret in the doctor's life, the reason why he had given up his flourishing practice, lay between them as something jealously guarded from others' eyes. Abe, presuming on his twinship, had one day half asked Mary about it; she had at once withdrawn. Abe wondered whether Ruth would be as reticent, as loyal as Mary. He himself never even hinted to Mary of his criticism of Ruth.

Every now and then he tried to get Ruth to call on his sister. Mary had been at the farm; the doctor kept pony and buggy for her. But between the two women yawned an abyss. Neither could utter a word which found the other's approval. Abe had hoped that Ruth would enter into neighbourly relations with Mrs. Nicoll, a huge, talkative, and pathetic woman who made him laugh. But Ruth was consciously isolating herself, making that a point of pride which had been a grievance. Abe mentioned it to her as a duty that she must call on the new-comer. "That woman and I have nothing in common," she said. And this led to a "scene" between husband and wife.

"Listen here," Abe said. "You blame me for your isolation——"

"Who says I do?"

"Nobody needs to tell me. I feel it. You make me feel it."

"How, if you please?"

Abe stood helpless, uncomfortably aware that Charlie's eyes were on him from a corner of the dusky room. He paced up and down on the far side of the dining-table, Ruth standing in the door of the kitchen. Things pent up in his breast cried to be let out. He knew that this was the moment to shut them away in the depth of his heart; but he was consumed by the desire to revel in his misfortune. He also knew that, if he went over to Ruth and kissed her or patted her cheek, making her feel that she was something to him, he might easily win her co-operation in the endeavour to remove what was keeping them apart. He could not do so. "Oh!" he exclaimed, shrugging his powerful shoulders and raising his hands, "by a thousand little things, insignificant in themselves, that I can't lay my hand on. You know."

"Perhaps I do," she said, a white line around her lips. "But how about you? Don't you show me every hour, every minute we spend together that you disapprove of me, of all I am?"

Abe veered to face her, stung to the quick. What if she was right? He must conciliate her, or an abyss would open and swallow them. "Listen here," he said, shaken, and his voice betrayed him.

She sank into a chair by the door, covering her face with an apron. "Listen here," he repeated, steadied. "I have my work. It takes every ounce of my strength; it takes every thought I am capable of."

She looked up, her eyes dry and red. "What is it all for?"

He looked puzzled. "What is what all for?"

"That work. I don't know. To me it seems senseless, useless, a mere waste. Work, work, work! What for?"

He was thunderstruck. She disapproved of him, of all he was. But his voice was even. "Don't you know?"

"I don't. I had my misgivings. Farming! There are farms all over the country, down east. But I never dreamt of anything like this. It's like being in prison, cast off by the world. Don't hold Mary up to me. She despises me and thinks you a sort of half-god or hero. She looks at this shack and wonders how I can exist in it. She is right. I wonder myself. What can I do about it? This isn't a country fit to live in."

"Exactly," Abe said with rising anger. "I am making it into a country fit to live in. That is my task. The task of a pioneer. Can't you see that I need time, time, time? In six years I've built a farm which produces wealth. Give me another six years, and I'll double it. Then I'll build you a house such as you've never dreamt of calling your own."

"I know, I know. . . ."

"If you know, what's the fuss about? You said you didn't know what the work was for. That's it. To build up a place any man can be proud of, a place to leave to my children for them to be proud of."

Ruth looked up. "Where do I come in?"

"Aren't you going to profit by my labours?"

"Profit! You probably pride yourself on being a good provider. You are. I've all I want except what I need: a purpose in life."

"Don't you have the children?"

She burst into tears.

Abe drew a chair to the table and sat down by her side. Thence he caught sight of the boy. "Where is Jim?" he asked.

"I don't know, daddy."

48

"Go. Run along. Find Jim and play with him."

Obediently the child slipped from his chair and left the room, passing through the door into the dusk.

"Listen here," Abe said for the third time. "I am willing to do anything in my power. Do you want to read? Buy books or magazines? Whatever you wish. Why don't you spend money on clothes, on pretty things such as girls and young women want?"

"What for? For whom should I doll myself up? I am ugly. What's the use? I am getting stout."

"I'll tell you," Abe went on. "Next time I go to Somerville, I'll open an account for you at the new bank. I'll deposit a couple of hundred. I'll give you that much or more every year. To do with as you please. What you need, for yourself or the children, I'll pay for. This is to be yours. I don't want you to feel that you have to give an account of what it's spent on. I won't ask. I promise you that. Use it in any way you please. I know it's hard, living that way, all by yourself. It will get better. The children will be company soon. That right?"

Ruth did not answer; but she was drying her tears with her apron.

Abe went to the door. "Charlie, Jim!" he called. "Bed-time."

And the children, who were only to well aware that something was or had been wrong, came in at once, casting furtive glances at their parents. They went straight to the bedroom.

Abe returned to the barn where Bill Crane was milking.

For a while things remained normal between man and wife. No more than normal; they kept swinging about the neutral point, with only one change, namely that both made an endeavour to smooth matters over by a mutual show of tolerance and consideration.

But the essential difficulty was not removed. Abe was uncomfortably aware of the fact that, at the decisive moment, he had evaded the issue. But he had his hands full. The weed problem was becoming acute. As soon as the plough had done its work, the cultivator had to be started, followed by the drag; or the weeds would choke the wheat next year.

Then came the harvest. It was a good year, but the work was not easy. The rains had been ample; the straw was heavy; and a new weed had made its appearance: wild buckwheat, commonly called bind-weed. Its long, tough vines wound themselves about wheels and sickles of the binder till the horses could no longer pull the machine. Ordinarily, two men are kept busy stooking the sheaves which one binder cuts. This year, what with the delays met by the machine, that proportion was reversed: one good man could have kept up with two binders. But since Abe had fallowed a quarter section, he could not afford to buy new implements. He fretted when, a dozen times a day, he saw Bill and Nicoll going idle while he stood between horses and sickles and furiously cut and slashed at the choking weeds. At last, in order to keep two men busy where there was work only for one, he made them haul the sheaves from the west of the field to the east, to clear the stubble for ploughing. Even so, he knew he would be crowded for time.

Summer and fall went by. Night after night Abe came home after dark—hot, dusty, exhausted. There was no time, no energy left to devote to his household; and the fact that he knew he was neglecting a thing of fundamental importance made him cross and monosyllabic. He began to have glimpses of the truth that his dream of economic success involved another dream: that of a family life on the great estate which he was building up. At the early age of thirty-six he had moments of an almost poignant realization of "the futility of it all."

When he threshed—rather late, for no thresherman cared to come into this district till the work in more settled areas was done—he was disappointed; in spite of heavy sheaves the crop averaged only nineteen bushels to the acre, with an acreage of only a quarter section. His income from this source was below two thousand five hundred dollars.

Yet he deposited two hundred dollars in Ruth's bank; and eight hundred he set aside for building. By the time he had paid his debt to the implement dealer and his taxes, reducing his indebtedness at the bank by half, he had nothing left. He told Ruth of his deposit to her credit and the sum set aside for enlarging the house; but he withheld the fact that he had been unable to balance his accounts. He expected her to express satisfaction at the growth of her account—or was it growing? But she received the announcement with a mere nod and, on the doubtful point, volunteered no information.

Winter came. It had been Abe's intention to use coal for fuel; but, being determined not to touch that eight hundred dollars, he made up his mind to haul wood once more. To do so, he had to go a distance of forty miles, for timber of a size sufficient to make the trip worth while could no longer be found at any point nearer than that. He had to stay out overnight. He left Bill at home to look after feeding and milking; for he did not trust him with any but routine work.

Altogether, this was the most anxious winter he had spent on the farm. He resented it that he, a man farming three quarter sections, should have to make these long, tiring drives to save a hundred and fifty dollars. He never spent money unreasonably; yet he had to effect petty economies. He *must* have more land! He *must* get to a point where he farmed on a scale which would double his net income from a decreasing margin of profit. Nicoll's way was not his. He could not be satisfied with the fact that, if he killed a pig and a calf in the fall, there was meat in the house. To him, farming was an industry, not an occupation.

Spring came. He was planning to add two rooms to the house. Yet, since it was a makeshift—for never would he be satisfied with a patchwork house—he was unwilling to go to the expense involved. Still, Ruth must be considered.

One day, just before it was time to overhaul the implements needed for the spring work, he stopped in town and called on his sister. The doctor was at the store, to which a fully equipped dispensary and drug department had just been added, an extension of the business urgently needed since the necessity of getting prescriptions filled still diverted a good deal of trade to Somerville.

As Abe entered, Mary mentioned the fact of her husband's absence.

"That's all right. It was you I wanted to see."

"Sit down, Abe."

"How does it look to you, Mary? Am I making progress?"

Mary laughed. "You are the talk of the neighbourhood. Never was there a farmer like you, they say."

Abe felt comforted and encouraged. "Sometimes I am getting despondent. I am everlastingly short of money."

"Is not that very natural? You are always buying land and equipment."

"Not always. . . . I suppose it is foolish to worry."

"Look at what you have done. You have three quarter sections, clear, paid for. And such a barn."

"I have the money to add two bedrooms to the house. It does seem necessary, does it not?"

"Well——"

"There isn't room for Ruth to turn around in."

"Does she complain?"

"No, no. . . I believe she resents the fact that Bill's wife has a better place to live in than she. It's only temporary, of course. The fact is, I hate to spend money on a makeshift which I'll tear down in a year or two. I need an additional seeder and binder and God knows what."

Mary pondered. "I've always feared it. She doesn't co-operate."

"I don't say that," Abe forestalled her hurriedly.

"I know. I see what I see. Suppose I make another attempt?" She looked at Abe out of friendly eyes, from behind heavy-rimmed glasses.

Abe mused dejectedly. Then he rose. "Perhaps——"

"I'll go to-morrow."

"Day after. I'll have to go to Somerville. I've got to have that additional seeder before the work starts." ...

On the last of March—there was still snow on the ground—Mary, in fur coat and close-fitting hat, alighted in the yard where Bill was sawing wood. He came to take horse and cutter. The three older children were playing about the granary. Frances, no doubt, was asleep.

When Ruth opened to the knock, her lips tightened. She stepped back, inviting her sister-in-law by a gesture to enter; her very movement declined the other woman's kiss.

"Bill tells me Abe went away," Mary said.

"I believe he did. He isn't in."

With a glance Mary had swept the interior of the room. Plates were inverted on the oilcloth of the table; cups in their saucers. It *was* a small room for the family of four children. Ruth seemed enormous in girth. Mary removed her glasses to wipe them. It was hard to begin. She had planned to admire things to find the way to Ruth's heart. But there was nothing to admire. She resolved upon perfect frankness.

"Ruth, I know it is hard. The fact is, Abe is living through a crisis."

Ruth stiffened. "He has told you, has he?"

"You may think I have no right to interfere."

"I do. Why does he not speak for himself? Why send you?"

"It isn't as simple as all that. He doesn't send me. He came to speak of his difficulties."

"He went to discuss his wife with his sister."

"Not at all. He never mentioned you. I'm afraid you don't quite undersand Abe. He has a dream which is all-in-all to him. He is in financial troubles. As I said, he is living through a crisis."

"He has been living through one crisis after another."

"It's the pioneer's lot. The pioneer used to live through periods of actual starvation. To-day, with settled districts all around, distress takes the form of financial stringency. It was bound to come. Perhaps you don't give him full credit for what he has achieved."

"Who says I don't? But why buy more and more machinery and land?"

"It's the way of the west."

"But that isn't the point."

"What is, Ruth?"

"I can't discuss it."

Mary shrugged her shoulders. "Frances asleep?" she asked at last.

Ruth rose and opened the door to the bedroom. That room, no larger than the dining-room, held four beds and a wardrobe. On one of the beds the little girl was lying, her head surrounded by yellow curls, damp with sleep. She was two years old.

Mary entered, bent down, and kissed the child without waking her. Strongly moved, she turned back to the dining-room. She had no children of her own, much as she longed for them; and her emotion made her forget that Ruth had shown her the child only in order to let her see the crowded condition of the house.

"I am more than sorry, Ruth," she said as the door was closed.

Ruth went with her into the yard, wrapping her apron about her bare arms. She called the other children; she could afford to be generous; her victory over her sister-in-law was but too apparent.

"This is your Aunt Mary," she said as in formal introduction.

The boys held out their hands; but Marion hid behind the skirts of her mother.

Mary bent down, a pained look in her eyes. "I am not only your aunt, I am your godmother too."

But the child remained shy, and escaped. Bill came with horse and cutter.

"I am more than sorry, Ruth," Mary repeated, holding out her hand, which Ruth touched with her finger-tips, a triumphant smile on her lips. . . .

Just as Mary who had been crying, turned the corner into Main Street on her way home, she caught sight of Abe coming from the east and stopped to wait for him.

Abe, in the cutter drawn by his bronchos, sat erect and stern. As he saw her, he drew up his eyebrows in a questioning way.

Mary shook her head. "I am afraid, Abe, Ruth is right."

Abe nodded. "So long then." And he proceeded on his way. It did not matter! Was Mary against him too?

Arrived at home, he went straight to the house. What he

had to say had only been made harder by that ill-judged mission of Mary's.

The children were sitting at table, having their supper. That discomposed him; he must wait. He entered the bedroom and changed into overalls. Then he went to the barn to keep himself busy.

When he returned, Ruth was waiting for him. He spoke at once.

"Look here, Ruth. I want you to help me. I can't build this spring."

"Was that the news your sister was to break to me?"

"It was not. She didn't know. Listen here. I've got to have more land. That fellow Fairley who owns the north-east quarter saw me in town. I didn't know he lived there. He wants to sell and had a buyer offering a thousand dollars. I couldn't afford to let the land go into other hands. It's vital for me to have it. I offered eleven hundred. That's what he was waiting for. I had to use the eight hundred set aside for the new rooms. You will consider that a breach of faith. I *am* breaking faith with you. But I'll add at least one room to this shack in the fall; that's the best I can do. I am not my own master."

Ruth laughed. "Do you notice it at last?"

"Notice what?"

"That you are not your own master?"

Abe stared. This extension of his meaning might be just or unjust as you looked upon it. "Can't be helped. I've got to have the land."

Again Ruth laughed.

"Ruth," Abe said stormily, "don't you see how I'm fixed? It took all I could do last fall to make both ends meet. I had to use cream cheques to pay off part of my loan at the bank. Once I get that quarter broken, things will ease up. My hand was forced. It would be a waste of money anyway to enlarge this shack beyond what's absolutely necessary. In a year or two I'll build a real house. Surely I should be able to ask my wife to put up with things for a while."

"If you asked her. But you send your sister instead. Besides," she added, rising and trembling with the audacity of what she was going to say, "you could ask me if in other things you treated me as your wife. With strangers one keeps one's word."

"With strangers?"

"What else am I? I am living alongside of you. What do I know of your dream as Mary calls it? What do you know of me?"

Abe raised his hands and moved to leave the room. "For goodness' sake!" he said. "Don't let's have another scene! If you can't understand, you can't understand. I am doing my best."

When, that night, Abe had finished such chores as, in the division of labour, fell to his share, he found the dining-room empty, which had never happened before. Ruth had gone to bed.

V * THE SCHOOL

SHILLOE proved an exceedingly shy but accommodating neighbour who, once propitiated, would have gone to any length to help Nicoll or Abe. He had a large family, but nobody ever saw anything of the children except their backs, when they were running away. His wife seemed to have the gift of making herself invisible.

In the fall of that year Abe went out of his way to secure an old French-Canadian thresherman with his crew, his name being Victor Lafontaine. He lived at St. Cecile, a village along the international highway to the city, sixteen miles north of Somerville. To get there, Abe went east over trackless prairie. Twice the man was out; but, being determined, Abe made a third trip. Shilloe was always in the field when he passed, laboriously breaking land with a hand-plough drawn by two pinto ponies much too light for the work. Abe had the queer feeling that eyes were peering at him from behind corners or through the curtains veiling the diminutive windows of the clay-plastered house.

But on the last of his trips he saw, on the prairie north of Shilloe's claim, a man who, in outline, resembled his one-time neighbour, Hall. An old plough horse, a dirty blanket on his back, was grazing near the ditch. At sight of Abe the stranger made for the trail; and Abe stopped his horses. It was a bright, crisp morning of the early fall.

The man who approached, medium-sized, pot-bellied, spindle-legged, with a dirt-grey moustache dividing his face, was clad in a multitude of successive ragged coats which increased the bulk of his upper body and made him look even more disproportioned than he was.

"You Spalding?" he asked when within speaking distance.

"Spalding's my name."

"I've filed on this yere homestead. Filed on it yesterday.

Name's Hartley. You don't happen to have some second-hand lumber to sell?"

"No I haven't."

"Nor a horse or two?"

"I have some colts."

"No good," Hartley said. "What I want is nags, gentle and aged. And I want them cheap and on time."

"No," Abe said. "I have nothing in that line."

"What's the name of the feller there at the corner?"

"Nicoll."

"How 'bout him?"

"I don't think so. He keeps only four horses."

"Hm. . . ."

"Well," Abe said, none too favourably impressed with the stranger, "if there is nothing else I can give you information on——"

The man eyed him in a curious way. Then, "Don't think so. However, seeing as I'm going to move in here, I guess I'll meet you again."

Abe nodded and moved on.

During the next few weeks he often saw a one-horse team drawing a little spring wagon along the road from Morley. On top of a load of old boards and joists, among boxes and packing crates, perched that grotesque figure of a man who had spoken to him.

On these drives Abe found that there was, nearer the highway, between his trail and the Somerville Line, at least one other settlement, and a rather compact and considerable one. He could count a dozen farmsteads, while from the Somerville Line only two or three could be seen. He began to be interested in municipal affairs; and the councillor representing Ward Six —the ward in which Abe lived—a man called Davis, had his domicile in that district which went by the name of Britannia.

On one occasion Abe turned farther north. A cluster of grain elevators came into view in line with Morley. That was the town of Arkwright, twelve miles west of St. Cecile where a railway branched off from the main line, running via Arkwright and other towns to Torquay, to describe a loop there and to return via Ferney, Morley, and Somerville; from Morley one could go to the city by starting either east or west. Why was there no settlement south of the Arkwright Line? Some three miles north of Nicoll's Corner the slope of the land began to change, towards a tributary of the river which bounded the prairie in the east. Large stretches of country, there, consisted of an impenetrable swamp which could be crossed in winter only. Thus, by the mere chance of his having gone east for a thresherman instead of south, Abe's horizon was suddenly widened.

He was beginning to worry about the slowness with which settlers moved into the district, for his children were approaching school age. Already he had been amazed to hear of the frequent changes of teachers at Morley. These teachers were invariably young girls; and he doubted their ability to handle a school. That was why, when one day he was taking his dinner at the hotel at St. Cecile, he was much interested to find that a bearded old man who sat down at his table proved to be a teacher who, for many years, had been a schoolmaster in various districts near Arkwright. His name was Blaine. Abe was so much interested that he gave the man his exact location and asked him to call.

"I see you ride a bicycle," he said when the other man rose. For his trousers were held by steel clamps around his ankles.

"I do," said Mr. Blaine. "But you can't cross from Arkwright except in winter, when the bicycle is useless."

"Well," Abe added and rose to shake hands, "the snow may hold off."

Mr. Blaine was small and slender, with a head disproportionately large for his body, and a sandy beard streaked with grey disproportionately large for his head. When he turned, one was oddly reminded of a lion turning in a cage. He wore a dark suit of heavy cloth, his trousers hanging about his legs like curtains.

Abe heard more of him. He was seventy years old and had come from Ontario; he had been a high-school teacher and had married a pupil of his. For her he had built a small house at Arkwright where he had been teaching at the time; but his married life had been short, his young wife dying in childbirth and taking her baby with her into the grave. He had returned to rural life and now had the distinction of being the teacher with the longest record in the Canadian west.

One day Abe met the local school inspector at his sister's house where he had had dinner; for Morley boasted only a fifth-rate boarding house. Abe heard high praise of Blaine's work, his only trouble being that, with increasing age, he found it difficult to secure a school. Westerners hold experience and expertness in small esteem; they prefer the young girl who will dance and gad about. "Too bad," the inspector said. "There isn't a better man to be found for rural work."

Abe made up his mind there and then that Mr. Blaine was to be the teacher of his children.

But so far there was no school. The district must have at least five settlers before he could move in the matter.

As winter came, Hartley built a two-roomed shack on his claim, of old, half-rotten lumber, some of it mere box-lumber, half an inch thick. He put no foundation under it, but propped the corners up on railway ties placed at an angle. There the structure perched precariously through the winter, the wonder being that the February winds did not blow it over. In the spring of 1907 he covered the outside with tar paper tacked to the walls with a network of lath. He had brought a stove and put a flue-pipe through the roof.

Soon after, Nicoll came to Abe's one day, about seed-oats. Abe and Bill were at work, filling the loft of the barn with hay against the spring work. Nicoll at once climbed up, reached for a fork, and helped for an hour or so.

"Say, Abe," he said after a while, "I'm going to have a new neighbour."

Abe, who stood on top of the load, looked up. "Who's that?"

"Fine, upstanding sort of man. Name's Stanley. He's got only one arm; the other was caught by the belt of a threshing machine and torn clean out. They took him twenty miles to the hospital. A wonder he lived. A big fellow, your build, though not so tall.'

"Great news," Abe said. "Where is he going to locate?"

"A mile north of my line. East of the trail."

"Any children?"

"Six. One boy, five girls. The boy's thirteen."

"Nicoll," Abe said in sudden elation, "we'll get that school!"

"We surely shall."

Again the blessing did not come singly. East of the new Stanley homestead, where building operations began at once, another Ukrainian settled down, a small, determined man with a reddish-brown moustache on his Slavic face, his name Nawosad. More, two miles south of Nicoll's Corner somebody was building a sod-hut. This proved to be a young Mennonite by name of Hilmer, a quiet, well-built, almost handsome lad, so far unmarried. His clothes were black, down to his shirt. He fenced a small corral for the two oxen with which he started to break land. He lived in complete isolation, though, when spoken to, he answered with a ready courtesy which sat quaintly on his broken English.

At once Nicoll's Corner became the social centre of the settlement. Nicoll had drawn a shallow ditch along the south line of his yard, bridged, in front of his gate, by a culvert.

North of the fence, a wind-break was beginning to grow. There, of an evening or a Sunday afternoon, the settlers would assemble, sitting on the culvert, their feet dangling in the ditch; and all affairs that concerned the district were discussed, besides many questions concerning God and the universe. Only two men appeared rarely: Abe Spalding and Jack Hilmer.

And there, in the summer of 1908, the school district was formed.

By that time it was know that Abe planned to buy the section north of his holdings; rumour had it that he was getting wealthy. He had had a bumper crop last year and was building concrete pig-pens. That Hudson's Bay section, then, must form the north-west corner of the district; which placed the south line at the "first" ditch, half-way between Nicoll's Corner and the Somerville Line. Hilmer's claim would be just within the district. According to law they could include twenty square miles. That brought the east line to a point just beyond Hartley's and Shilloe's claims. It looked as though all these settlers had picked their location with that very thing in view.

What, next, was to be the name of the district? Various more or less far-fetched proposals came from Hartley, who never missed a meeting; but whenever he mentioned some new impossibility; it was greeted by a silence which condemned it.

One evening, late in June, Stanley rose and addressed the others in a brief, formal speech. All except Abe were present: Shilloe and Nawosad were sitting nearest the road, both resting elbows on their knees and looking at the ground. Hartley, a willow-switch which he used as a whip in his hand, sat in the centre of the group. Stanley had had the place next to him; and, nearest the gate, Nicoll was squatting on his heels. Hilmer was standing behind them all, ready to eclipse himself.

It was a warm night, with no stars visible; and a fine haze had overspread the sky: the only sort of night which is ever warm on the prairie, where radiation is swift. A slight breeze wafted the scent of fresh-mown hay from the west: as usual, Abe had been the first to start haying. No doubt that was why he was absent; he was always busy.

"Gentlemen," Stanley said, "why is the town of Morley called by that name? Where does the name Arkwright come from? I could easily multiply instances. It is a time-honoured custom on these prairies to attach the name of the first permanent settler to town, station, or district."

"Hear, hear!" Nicoll said without moving. "Just what I had in mind. There's only one name fitting for this school we are going to build. If there's a man among you who hasn't had help or advice from that first permanent settler, he hasn't asked for it, that is all."

"Well, now," Hartley began, "I don't see that we should be so doggone obsequious as to bow down before wealth——"

"Gentlemen," Stanley exclaimed, raising his one arm to impose silence, "are you ready for the question? It has been moved by myself and seconded by Mr. Nicoll that the district be called Spalding School District. I can't see much in the dark; so I'll ask those in favour to stand."

All but Hartley and Hilmer rose; the latter was standing already.

"Contrary?"

Hilmer squatted down; and Hartley did not rise.

"Carried."

Nicoll, who helped Abe next day in haying, brought him the news.

Abe listened in silence; but he experienced a thrill. That moment his aspirations underwent an extension which embraced the whole district. He suddenly felt it to be inevitable that, in the long run, he should enter municipal politics and look after the district which bore his name. There was the matter of roads; with increasing traffic the trail to town had become almost impassable; with deep ruts cut into it in spring, it held water till late in summer and remained a mire for months on end; and was it not intolerable that during the flood the district should be cut off from the rest of the world?

Since that spring when he had been confronted with what he considered the necessity of buying the fourth quarter of his section, Abe had recovered his economic balance. He might have built a house this year. But, having added the fourth room to the old building, he had postponed more ambitious changes till he would be in a position to "do things right." Ruth's opposition had put him on his mettle; to justify what he had done so far, he must carry out his plans, which were ever extending in scope. He would have to acquire the Hudson's Bay section; nor would it do to wait too long; land values were rising. For that purchase he would have to prepare in other ways: he must have at least one tractor of the most powerful type, to speed up the work in the spring and the fall; perhaps he would have to build another shack for a second man. In spite, then, of his undoubted prosperity, he was as much preoccupied with things to be done as ever; his life lay in the future; for the sake of that future he slaved from dawn till dark. What he had achieved was little compared with what remained to be done.

All the more did he feel flattered by the recognition which

was coming from the later settlers. As matters proceeded and took definite shape, he even felt a twinge of jealousy at the thought that the moving spirit in these things was Nicoll, not he.

Yet that was natural. Abe had already suggested that Nicoll be the secretary-treasurer of the district. It was generally taken for granted that the school was to stand on the corner opposite Nicoll's place, south of the ditch. Nicoll would be the one most available if teacher or inspector wished to communicate with the school board.

Two weeks later the organization meeting took place. If the school was to be opened in the fall, there was need for hurry.

This meeting had been called by the school inspector for two o'clock in the afternoon. Every settler attended. From the moment when Abe appeared on the porch of Nicoll's house, where a table and a few chairs had been placed, he had the curious feeling that nothing really needed to be discussed: it had all been agreed upon beforehand. A loan of two thousand dollars was to be taken up, secured by debentures; three trustees were to be elected; and Stanley proposed that they be the first three settlers of the district. Even when Shilloe, in confusion, declined for his part and suggested Hartley, it seemed as though this had been prearranged.

The election over, the inspector proposed that the new board hold its first meeting at once, in his presence, to elect chairman and secretary. Shilloe, Nawosad, Hilmer, and Stanley retired to the culvert; the board meeting was adjourned five minutes later. Abe had been elected chairman for the year, Nicoll secretary-treasurer. The inspector took his departure in a great hurry; all this was mere routine to him; and Abe and others felt defrauded of that formality and ceremony in the proceedings which they had felt entitled to expect.

Somewhat grimly, as the inspector drove through the gate in his buggy, Abe said. "Well, that's that."

A moment later, Stanley was shaking him by the hand, congratulating him on his election. "Nobody," he said, "expected anything else. We know you'll do the right thing by the district."

In the background, on the porch of the house, Mrs. Nicoll appeared, huge, smiling, overflowing her clothes, and surrounded by half a dozen of her younger children. Her head seemed lost in upper shadows; and her smile poured a blessing on the finished proceedings. Abe nodded to her; Stanley lifted his wide straw hat; Hartley stared; and the other three shifted uneasily on their feet.

Henceforth all school business proceeded automatically. Plans arrived, and one of them was recommended by the inspector. The board met and endorsed the inspector's choice. Abe never spoke; he sat in his chair, feeling oddly that they were tools through which others worked their will. The matter of the debenture issue was attended to by the provincial government; and they were told that they might proceed with construction, arranging for credit at one of the Somerville banks. Law and usage prescribed all proceedings. Tenders were asked for. A single bid was necessarily accepted. Twice Abe and Nicoll had to go to Somerville to sign papers at the municipal office. Matters took their course.

At home, Abe broke the news one night at the supper table. "Well," he said, assuming an air of importance which he did not feel, "we're going to have a school at last. No loafing next winter."

"Good," exclaimed Charlie, nearly eight years old; though he spoke as if sitting in the council of grown-ups, he fidgeted with excitement.

"Where's the school going to be?" Jim asked pertly.

"All settled," Abe replied with that assumption of irony with which he invariably treated the children. "Opposite Nicoll's Corner."

Ruth stared, not so much because she objected to the site as because she resented Abe's way of communicating accomplished facts. "That is over two miles to go. How about the winter when the snow is deep?"

Abe did not answer at once. He resented the sharp tone in which the objection was raised. "It's the centre of the district," he said at last. "Somebody has to be on the outskirts. Most of us are. Hartley and Shilloe are as far away. Stanley and Nawosad a mile and a half. Hilmer nearly two."

"Hilmer has no family."

"That can be remedied by and by. I can best afford to be far away. The Hartley and Shilloe kids will have to walk, I suppose."

"And we, daddy?" This from Marion who, in a coltish way, was growing into a particularly pretty little girl.

"I'll get you a pony and buggy for fall and spring; and a box-cutter for winter. When it storms, you'll go in the bobsleigh."

"Hurrah!" Jim crowed.

"Have you a teacher yet?" Charlie asked pensively.

"No. But I've one in mind. . . ."

During the rest of the summer three carpenters worked on

the school site; and occasionally Hartley put in what he called a day's work. This arrangement was made on Abe's suggestion; Hartley had hinted that Nicoll was "making a fortune out of the thing"; for the carpenters boarded at his place.

Meanwhile the summer's work was proceeded with; and late in August harvest began. Nicoll and his oldest boy Tom worked for Abe; and so did Shilloe, Nawosad, and Hilmer; for Abe had two binders going at last.

On one occasion, when Abe was resting his horses, Nicoll, having finished his round, came over to chat for a moment.

"Some crop!" he said admiringly.

"Too many weeds," Abe replied.

But Nicoll laughed. "If you go on like that, you'll be knighted one day. Sir Abe of Spalding Hall."

"Some Hall!" And Abe waved his arm toward the patchwork house.

"That'll come."

With an emphasis which seemed uncalled for, Abe replied, "You bet it'll come. You bet your life!" And he reached for the lines. When he returned to the spot, he called Nicoll.

"About that school," he said. "It's time to engage a teacher. This is a meeting of the board. There's a quorum present."

"A meeting must be duly called," Nicoll objected.

"Nonsense. Unless you and I run that school, they're going to make a mess of it."

Nicoll scratched his greying head. "Thinking of any one, Abe?"

"Yes. I've got him picked."

"Him? Is it a man?"

"It is. Old man Blaine, from up north, Arkwright way."

Nicoll stroked his beard. "Tell you frankly, Abe, we'll have trouble over that. I'd rather have a girl myself for the little tots."

"Blaine's all right. Ask the inspector. An old bachelor's as good as a girl. And he'll keep the boys in order."

"I don't know," Nicoll said doubtfully.

But Abe cut him short by reaching for his lines. He was a power in his district. Yet——

Even in his own house he met opposition. Once more Charlie asked one evening at supper, "Have you a teacher yet, daddy?"

"You bet." At this time Abe often used slang phrases.

"Who is it, daddy?"

"Old man by the name of Blaine."

"A man?" Ruth exclaimed, stiffening.

"Mighty good man at that."

"If it's to be a man, I won't send Frances."

"Suit yourself. I want the boys kept in order. No slip of a girl for me!" He was so angry that he rose and left the house.

Yet, when he saw Nicoll again, he condescended to argue. "You know as well as I do that we can't keep a girl in the district. Talk it over with my brother-in-law. Most of the time children spend in school they are readjusting themselves. Every new teacher brings new methods."

Nicoll hesitated. "We'll have to have a meeting over it, Abe."

"Have that meeting if you must. But not till we're agreed."

"I guess you know best, Abe."

"I do. I've thought this over from every angle. You ride the binder to-morrow. I'll get Hartley to stook. I'll go and see Blaine."

It was the first time that Abe left his work for the sake of public business; it showed Nicoll how important the matter seemed to him.

Two weeks later a special meeting was held. It took less than five minutes, but it gave Abe a foretaste of what public business might be. As before, the scene was Nicoll's porch; the next meeting would be held in the school which was nearing completion.

"The matter before the board is the engagement of a teacher."

"Move we advertise," said Hartley.

"Well," Nicoll drawled uncomfortably, "there is an application supported by a recommendation from the inspector."

For a minute or so there was silence. They made a strange group under the lamp. Nicoll was stout, Abe stouter, Hartley fat. Hartley, quite at his ease, glanced from Abe to Nicoll, from Nicoll to Abe.

"Move we advertise," he repeated doggedly.

"Let's deal with the application first," Abe said at last. "Just read it, Nicoll."

Nicoll did so.

"We'll dispense with the formal motion," Abe went on. "Those in favour signify in the usual way."

Nicoll raised his hand.

"Contrary?"

Hartley raised his.

"I've the casting vote," Abe said. "I'm for accepting."

Again Hartley, ragged and cynical, glanced from one to the other.

"That's settled, then. Motion to adjourn?"

A minute later Abe and Nicoll rose. Hartley kept his seat.

Abe knew what this man was going to say to Stanley and the rest; but he felt he was doing what was best for the district, as time would show. He was content to force his better judgment on them if need be.

What Hartley said was this: "By golly! If that wasn't cut and dried! I'll be hanged if it wasn't!"

VI ✳ THE GREAT FLOOD

WITH the last year of the decade a series of three wet seasons began, bringing momentous developments.

Hilmer had built a frame shack of three rooms, a long, shed-like building facing the road. His mother, a woman of sixty or so, had joined him, bringing two children of ten and eleven respectively and a man much younger than herself to whom she had recently been married. This man, Grappentin by name, did not settle down on the place but appeared and disappeared periodically. Mrs. Grappentin owned another farm, in trust for the two children of her second marriage, south of the Somerville Line. This farm her third husband was supposed to work; but it was said that he allowed it "to go to the devil"; that, when the spirit moved him, he went and fetched horse or cow or a piece of equipment to sell and to spend the proceeds on drink or intercourse with loose women. Mrs. Grappentin became a frequent visitor to most farms in the district. Vigorously she strode over the prairie, a grotesque sight, for she was lean and ugly and resembled the idea which children have of a witch in the woods. She would sit about and gossip in broken English till she was given a trifling something—a piece of meat, a small bag of grain, or a handful of eggs; when, with fantastic praises of the givers, she would promptly take her leave. All of which she did, under protest of her son, as a means of paying for "her keep." There was only one place where she never called, and that was Abe's.

Abe, early in 1910, surprised the district by acquiring the whole of the Hudson's Bay section north of his place, for which he was variously reported to have paid from four to eight thousand dollars "spot cash." As a matter of fact, he paid three thousand six hundred—four hundred dollars more than the price quoted to him when he had made the first inquiry regarding the land. With values rising, he could not wait.

Spring opened with heavy rains. Just as the first great thaw had begun to honeycomb the deep snow which covered the prairie, a blinding snowstorm turned into a washing downpour —a thing unusual for the latitude. As a rule, the thaw proceeded by stages, interrupted by sharp frosts which stayed the waters; and the land would be bare of snow before the flood came from the hills. This year the rain condensed a process which ordinarily took a month into the short space of a week. The winter's snow melted within a few days; and the rain added to the flood. The sky remained clouded; and no check retarded the thaw.

Nor did the water seem to move for a day or two except in the ditches, whose presence was indicated by dirty-white foam-lines streaking the otherwise mud-coloured expanse. Underneath, the ground remained frozen. Nobody could leave his house except in hip-boots of rubber.

The first twenty-four hours Abe remained at home. Although the foundation of the barn was raised well above the ground, the flood stood two inches deep on its floor. One of the granaries still held grain. Throughout the first day Abe worked with Bill at the task of raising it, going from corner to corner, jacking the building up by a few inches, and forcing pieces of planking under it. The cellar of the house brimmed with water.

The second day, he walked over to Nicoll's, in hip-boots; and there he found a crowd assembled in the yard: Stanley, Nawosad, Shilloe, and Hartley. He heard of much damage done.

The bridge had been carried away; Hartley's shack had been swept from the railway ties and tilted up: wife and children were climbing about on a slanting floor; Shilloe had had to abandon his place; Blaine, who had converted what was meant to be a teacher's office in the school into a small bedroom, was a prisoner there, without food, for he had been boarding at Nicoll's.

"Where did you go?" Abe asked of Shilloe.

"To Mr. Stanley's. I am staying in his granary."

Stanley and Nicoll had no damage to report except that their cellars were flooded and the floors of their stables covered with water.

Abe assumed command. "We must get Blaine out."

"By golly!" Hartley exclaimed. "This isn't a country fit to live in, what with no roads——"

"We'll get the roads," Abe said briefly, and, turning to Shilloe, "Take one of Nicoll's horses and go to my place. Tell

66

Bill to hitch up the Percherons and bring them along, with a wagon. Tie Nicoll's horse behind. You take the Clyde team. Put some eveners into the wagon, and all the chains and ropes you can find."

"All right." And the Ukrainian went to the stable, splashing.

"What are you going to do, Abe?" Nicoll asked.

"Get the culvert back into place. We can't leave Blaine there."

Shilloe and Hartley had turned their horses out to shift for themselves, for there were haystacks scattered through the meadows.

Abe sent Nawosad and Stanley to get a team and a wagon with which to rescue the Hartleys. Nicoll harnessed his horses.

An hour went by; then, splashing the water over their heads, plunging and all but beyond control—for the slippery ground made it hard for them to keep their feet—Abe's eight horses came from the west, with Bill standing in the wagon-box, dripping and drenched at every step with ice-cold water though he was hooded in canvas.

Abe, in hip-boots, short slicker coat, and wide-brimmed southwester, was the only one who had adequate protection against rain and spray. He took over the wagon and dismissed Bill. "Tell my wife," he said, "I may not be home before night."

Nicoll hooked his four horses together and, paying out their lines, climbed into the rear of the wagon. Shilloe rode one of the four Clydes.

"If it gets any worse——" Nicoll said dubiously.

"It won't," Abe replied. "But we've got to be able to get out. When we get this culvert into place, we must see about Hilmer's. Come on, Hartley. We need every hand we can get."

When all was ready, he swung his lines over the sleek backs of his Percherons; and they started with a rush, throwing the water house-high, for it covered their knees. As they left the wind-break behind, they saw Nawosad and Bill Stanley, a lad of fifteen now, coming from the north. Stanley himself had remained at home, for the boy had two arms. Without stopping, Abe waved to them to fall into line. This was an emergency in which his captaincy went unchallenged. None of those who saw him that day disputed his leadership for years to follow. He did not complain; he accepted things as they were and did what had to be done.

There had been trouble about the school. But nobody denied any longer that Blaine's work was more than satisfactory. Yet, had it not been for Abe, he would never have been called into the district; and Abe upheld him when a feeling, characteristic of the west, asserted itself that it was time for a change. After the work of this spring, opposition ceased; and this was going to be of importance shortly.

Davis, councillor and road-boss for the ward, had visited the district a year ago. He had promised to get these settlers a road to town; but last fall it had become known that he had used his influence to have his own outlet to the Somerville Line raised by a foot and surfaced with gravel. Abe was the only man who could be opposed to him with any chance of success; but when, during the winter, matters had been discussed at Nicoll's Corner, Hartley and one or two others had been afraid of entrusting Abe with power : he might use it too autocratically. Meanwhile Davis was offering inducements right and left to secure his own re-election. After this spring, there was only one feeling from which even Hartley dared not openly dissent. Abe might refuse to consult them; but he was the man to do the right thing.

Arrived at the point where the culvert had lodged slant-wise across the ditch, with the swirling current tugging at it, Abe stopped the horses, of which there were eighteen in all. To the south, Shilloe's buildings seemed to float on a lake; to the north, Hartley's shanty stood tilted up. Abe sent Nawosad with Stanley's two horses to take the family out on Hartley's hayrack. "Take them to my place. To the empty granary. Let them take their own bedding. Tell Bill to look after them in the line of food." He glanced at Hartley, as much as to say he had better join his family for the moment; but Hartley did not stir from the floor of the wagon-box.

Abe, Bill Stanley, Shilloe, and Nicoll descended into the water which stood here nearly two feet deep.

Together they fastened a chain to a corner of the culvert, securing it to projecting timbers. To this chain they fastened two four-horse eveners, close to the corner; then, leading the chain forward, they fastened one evener to its end; and another, a matter of ten feet behind it, in such a way as to make Nicoll's team straddle the chain. Abe and Shilloe gathered the lines of the last two teams, and Nicoll and Bill Stanley took charge of those in front.

At a signal from Abe, following the brisk question, "Ready there?" all the horses bent forward; and the culvert slipped to the northern bank of the ditch. A few timbers crashed with splintering sounds.

Abe shouted a signal to stop and to breathe the horses. Then they swung on to the trail to the west. The broken braces underneath stayed behind; and the sledding of the structure, buoyed up by the water, grew easier at once. Again Abe called a halt.

"You'd better unhook, Nicoll. We'll manage with three teams. Go back for the wagon. We'll need the chains."

And forward again, the horses plunging wherever they met with soft footing. When the water was thrown aloft in sheets, Shilloe and Bill Stanley laughed. Abe's broad face never moved under the projecting southwester; he took the brunt of it all; unlike the others, he stayed behind his horses, watching them closely, for Beaut, the leader, was with colt.

At last they had covered the mile and a half and came to the crossing. But the biggest piece of work remained to be done: the culvert, forty feet long, had to be manoeuvred across the swirling ditch; they waited for Nicoll. Nawosad passed them, with the Hartleys on the rack. Hartley himself had, after all, chosen to join them and was reclining on a miscellaneous assortment of bedding.

Abe frowned when he saw him. Was he going to be content to let others rescue him and his without lending a hand?

There followed three hours of titanic struggle. With poles and timbers they pushed the culvert into the wild current, often themselves in danger of slipping into deep water. The near corner was anchored, by a long chain, to Nicoll's corner post, with enough slack to let the structure swing to the edge of the ditch. Another chain was fastened to the far corner which would be the forward one on the other bank. That chain lay coiled on the floating floor. Three times they almost succeeded in lodging the culvert against the far bank; one of them ran to pick up the coiled chain and to take the leap; but whenever the strength of a man was withdrawn, the culvert, caught broadside on by the current, swung back and frustrated all that had been done.

Meanwhile, at the school which faced them with its northern row of windows, there was a spectator. Old man Blaine, as people called him, stood on the cement stoop of the trim, white building, his trousers clasped at the bottom as if he expected to use the bicycle for his escape. He looked on out of haggard eyes, a soft felt hat on his grey hair, his sandy, grey-streaked beard reaching to his waist. He seemed to stoop under the weight of his head, unconscious of the cold drizzle which interposed a veil between him and the men, so that he looked like a creature of mist.

Nobody, so far, had thought of stopping for a meal when Nicoll proposed to fetch Tom, his oldest boy, to help. They must have another hand. But Abe shook his head and pointed to the south where a black spot was approaching out of the rain-dimmed distance, cleaving the surface of the huge lake. Hilmer had seen them from his place.

They rested, waiting.

When Hilmer arrived, Abe shouted directions. And once more they manoeuvred the culvert into the stream till its far point touched the submerged bank on the other side. Hilmer showed that he could at least carry out instructions. With a jump he landed on the raft, picked up the chain, and was back on the flooded prairie before the culvert had swung out again too far to take the leap. Heedless of the fact that he was getting drenched to his shoulders, he ran till the chain was taut and gave it two or three quick turns around the corner post of the school yard. But still the culvert lay at an angle. So Abe slackened the chain on the north side, allowing the culvert to drift till it bridged the ditch at right angles. Hilmer joined the other men.

The next problem was how to get a team across. But, Hilmer reporting that his culvert was still in place, though in need of being anchored, Abe changed his mind. "We'll go down by and by," he said. "Let's have something to eat. You go home," he added to Bill Stanley. "We won't need you again. Take your team and get into dry clothes."

"How about Blaine?" Nicoll asked.

"I'll carry him over. Can you feed us all?"

Half an hour later, Abe, carrying the teacher on his back, entered Nicoll's yard where the horses were munching hay and oats from the box of a wagon, up to their hocks in water.

At the house, dinner was ready. Two tall, slender girls and the enormous woman waited on the famished crew; three big boys and a host of smaller girls sat about in the dim room, devouring every word that was spoken. To them this was a red-letter day: the men were heroes and giants fighting the elements. Outside, the rain was thickening again.

It was past five o'clock when Abe, leaving his Clydes at Nicoll's Corner, himself straddling the Percheron gelding, tackled the task of taking horses and wagon across a culvert which moved under foot. Two or three times he made the attempt; but when their feet touched the floating edge of the timbers, the horses reared and backed away. At last Nicoll, Shilloe, and Hilmer bestrode one each of the other horses; and though they still scattered water all about them, their riders forced them on.

At Hilmer's Corner they anchored the bridge; it was dark

by that time; but for fear that the worst might happen and they be cut off from the world, they did not give in till all was safe. It was midnight before Abe got home; and the rain was falling with that steady swish with which it falls on a sea becalmed.

VII ✳ ELECTION

THE district needed a new man on the council. Davis, huge, bottle-shaped, the typical politician, could not be trusted. He abused his position for the sake of his "pickings."

The trail to town became a thing to be dreaded.

So far, the traveller had been able to avoid the worst spots by circling over the prairie. But the road-allowance was being fenced. Blaine had filed on the school quarter and was enclosing it. He had no intention of farming; but Abe had promised to haul his cottage over from Arkwright if he secured the land to place it on. It looked as if Blaine were permanently established in the district; Abe's ascendancy in matters of local policy seemed assured.

The three quarter sections remaining between Nicoll's and Hilmer's Corners had been filed on by three brothers, young fellows who intended to farm in partnership. In imitation of a commercial firm they called themselves Topp Brothers Limited. They, too, started operations by fencing their long strip of land.

This made the problem of the road vital. Often one of the settlers got stuck on his way to town, especially after a rain, when the water stood yard-deep in the ruts.

Davis promised whatever was asked for. "I'll do my best, fellows. I'll see that you get what you need." But he had disappointed them once too often. Besides, while it was known that the council had already discussed the situation in plenary session, Davis tried to create the impression that everything depended on him. At least he allowed it to be inferred when they were assembled in groups; by appointment he met the settlers at Nicoll's Corner and made a speech. But he overshot his mark. At a time when everybody was busy seeding, he kept dropping in on individual farmers. Who was looking after his place? He could not afford to hire help; how, then, could he neglect his fields unless his position—to which no salary was attached apart from mileage fees—yielded "pickings" enough to carry him through the year? He used his very need for money as a plea; and to such a plea most of the settlers were accessible enough; they all knew that need for money. Poor devil! The trouble was he could not be trusted.

The ward comprised, in addition to Spalding District, Davis's own settlement and the village of Morley. Who was to take Davis's place?

Abe's prestige had grown enormously. He owned the biggest holding, not only in the ward but in the municipality. He paid the highest taxes. His progress was watched even at Somerville. He was buying a tractor. Hilmer, Nawosad, and Shilloe were fencing his new section. Abe, Bill Crane, and Nicoll had all they could do to get his seed into the ground: he seeded eight hundred acres.

Nicoll was sent to sound him as to his willingness to "run" for a seat on the council. Having long played with the idea, Abe did not decline; but he refused to canvass the ward. "Elect me if you want to," he said. "I'll act. But I won't go around and beg for votes. If you think I can do something for you, it's up to you. I won't stir a finger." He pleaded the urgency of his work; but it was known to be pride which prompted his refusal to do the usual thing. This gave a few men from Britannia District the material to work against him. "Give Spalding power," they said, "and he'll rule you with an iron rod."

Among those, on the other hand, who were most active in the interest of Abe's election was Blaine. As soon as the roads were dry, he straddled his bicycle every Saturday to go to town. His huge head with the long beard floated over the handle bar, trembling on a slender, corded neck; he did not go fast; but he pedalled along as though automatically.

Thus he passed the cottage which the Topp brothers were building in the centre of their long holding—a neat little thing twenty feet square, perched on a high foundation, with a porch in front. And next Hilmer's shack where old Mrs. Grappentin followed his progress from a window or through the open door. "There he goes," she would say in German, "to win votes for the duke and lord!" This name had stuck.

He would spend all day in town, talking to the farmers from the east half of the ward; he knew everybody who was not a new-comer to the prairie: years ago, he had taught in Britannia District.

One day, when Abe and Bill were disking the new breaking, such as there was of it, the rattling noise of a motor car running with exhausts wide open caught Abe's ear. He was facing north and nearing the line of the Hudson's Bay section; and soon he saw a curious vehicle lumbering over the prairie from the north-east: it was that once familiar sight of an ancient Ford car of the first vintage, covered in all sorts of places with tarnished brass. It jolted and tilted and tossed along, with an ever-increasing bellowing noise at which the horses pricked their ears; for, level as the prairie looked, it was by no means as smooth as it appeared to the eye. Everything about this car shook and rattled; the cloth of the top dangled behind in strips like a bunch of streamers; the fenders were suspended with binder-twine.

The car came to a stop in front of Abe's horses which were prancing with fright. The driver alighted, vaulting briskly over the door without opening it; and he came at once to where Abe was sitting perched on his harrow. Small and clad in grey overalls, the man looked more like a schoolboy than an adult of forty years. His face was freckled; his eyes grey-blue; his hair reddish. Abe recognized the Yankee who had been "snooping about" in the district before Nicoll's time.

"Hello, Spalding," he greeted Abe informally and in a business-like way. "Running for councillor, I hear. Remember me? Wheeldon, in case you've forgotten. From Destouches, Iowa. I've filed on the north-west quarter of eleven." He pointed over his shoulder towards Stanley's place. "I'm thinking of moving out next spring. Provided you and I can come to terms." This on a rising note.

"Come to terms?"—distantly; these two had disliked each other at sight.

"I want road work for two men and two teams for three months, at current rates. I'm willing to pay the usual rake-off."

"I am not a councillor yet," Abe said, stiffening.

Wheeldon laughed. "That's all right. Subject to your being elected. I've fixed the other fellow. He's O.K."

Abe saw a lane of new vision opening up. "What's your offer?" he asked, sitting motionless.

"The usual thing. Ten per cent."

"The other fellow took it?"

"Like a shot."

"How much down?"

Again Wheeldon laughed. "Thought you'd be all right. Trouble is I can't afford a payment down. I'll endorse the first cheque over to you. It's between gentlemen."

"You've got the horses?"

"I have."

"What about buildings?"

"I've got the wherewithal to build this fall."

"Why the road work, then?"

"A year's living. Second year I'll have a crop."

"What are you doing at present? Farming?"

"I'm a tinsmith Work's falling off. What with mass production in the factories."

Abe sat silent. Then he spoke. "As for the deal you propose, I don't do that sort of thing. But we want the settlers. If you move in, we'll look after you. There'll be six or eight miles of road to be built next summer. If I'm road-boss, I'll use local labour if I can get it. Some of us don't want the job though we'll keep a team on the road if it's needed. You can figure out what your share will be."

Wheeldon looked pensively at Abe. "The straight game, eh? That's one way, of course. Something new. It's as good as a promise?"

"It's as good as a contract," Abe said slowly.

"Fine. I'm in a hurry. Shake."

And he returned to his car, abstracting a jack from the litter in the back seat. Having raised one of the rear wheels, he put the car in gear, cranked, and, as the engine started with a roar, adjusted the levers under the steering wheel. Having replaced the gears in neutral, he pushed the car off the jack and, a moment later, turned to the east.

Abe sat and looked. Instinctively he had wiped his hand on his trousers. Was that the way it was done? His contempt for the man had an undercurrent of pity for one who had to have recourse to such means of making a living. "A nice story to tell on the platform!" he muttered.

A week later Abe went to town to get some repairs done at the blacksmith shop. While Bigelow hobbled about between forge and vice, rotund, swarthy, and preoccupied, Abe sat on the frame of a plough.

Placing Abe's broken guide-rod on the anvil, the blacksmith spoke between hammer-blows. "Fellow from south of the border. Name's Wheeldon, I think. Davis says—got promise of road work from you. That right?"

"Quite right."

"Looks bad, Abe."

"Looks bad if local work's to be done by local labour?"

"That all?"

"That's all."

"No promise in return?"

Abe hesitated and frowned. "Tell you. I'm not campaigning. But did Davis give you to understand that Wheeldon made me a promise?"

"He allowed that conclusion to be drawn."

"Then he allowed himself to lie. Wheeldon offered me ten per cent. Same as he offered Davis. Davis took it. I didn't."

Bigelow remained silent till Abe had paid for the work. Then he added, "You'll have my vote."

"Not that I'm asking for it, you know. . . ."

Before going home, Abe did some shopping at the Vanbruik store. As usual, Mr. Diamond came to meet him.

"Well," he said, "the campaign is becoming interesting, with one of the candidates missing all meetings!"

"Meetings being held?"

"Quite a few. Informal most of them. But Davis is always there."

"He'll have things all his way, I suppose?"

"That's the funny part of it. The more meetings he holds, the less votes he has left. If he did all he promises, he'd beggar the county."

When harvest began, Abe forgot about the election. Every settler worked on his place. He bought a third binder; and, long expected, the great tractor arrived at last. When it was driven over from Somerville, people came to their doors and stared. Henry Topp, oldest of the three brothers, acted as engineer. One of the difficulties had been to find a man who could operate such machinery; Henry Topp had moved in; and like other difficulties confronting Abe, this one had vanished. Two binders were hitched behind the huge engine which used kerosene for fuel. With Henry, who was small, his two brothers came to stook: David, second in age, medium-sized, quiet, efficient; and Slim, the youngest, barely nineteen years old but already six feet in height, boisterous, raw-boned, a youth who thought nothing of walking to town to meet a girl when the day's work was finished.

Meanwhile a house went up on the north-west quarter of eleven, north of Stanley's homestead, with two carpenters at work.

Thus, by the time harvest was finished, there were twelve resident ratepayers in the district, including Blaine. The ward comprised one hundred and five votes, so that Spalding District furnished, after all, only a small fraction of the electorate.

The decisive battle for which the ward had prepared itself during the summer was fought when all fall work was finished, on the third Tuesday of the month of December.

Two weeks before, Abe's nomination had been duly recorded at the municipal office at Somerville, Nicoll acting as proposer and Bigelow as seconder. Davis being renominated, a poll was necessary. Anderson's implement shed, north of his hardware store, was the polling place, with Dr. Vanbruik acting as deputy returning officer and Mr. Diamond as polling clerk. The shed was heated by a number of coal-oil stoves and lighted—for windows were small and scanty—by a gasoline lamp suspended above the table on which stood the ballot box.

Davis was present as was his right; in addition, two farmers of his district acted as his authorized agents. Abe had not even come to town, but Nicoll was there to represent him. "One witness to the proceedings," Abe had said. In a corner of the shed a space was curtained off where the electors were to mark their ballots.

The forenoon went by quietly, forty-two electors from the east half of the ward presenting themselves. All of them winked at or spoke to Davis and his agents. Occasionally Davis or one of his agents followed an elector into the store which served as a waiting-room. Such electors climbed into their buggies or wagons and left the village, going east; and an hour or so later they returned with a passenger. There was a crowd, it is true; but all remained quiet. Young Anderson improved the occasion by turning over a large stock of mechanical toys.

Several people presented themselves who were not resident in the ward though they owned land there. These voted "on certificate"; that is, they had procured a certificate stating that they had the right to vote at this time and place. Their appearance gave the proceedings an air of importance unusual in municipal elections.

When, at noon, Davis left the polling station to have his dinner, Nicoll followed him. In the store, Davis became elatedly vocal. "Boys," he said, "it's a walkover. Forty-two votes and none for the enemy!"

The crowd cheered.

They left the store. The whole north side of the street was lined with wagons, buggies, democrats.

From the west, along the sidewalk, come Aganeta, Mary Vanbruik's maid, carrying a tray with the doctor's luncheon. She was a big girl, high-bosomed, high-coloured. On her feet she wore a pair of man's goloshes. As she approached the crowd, she shouted, "Careful there!"

A young fellow veered about, jumped aside with exaggerated gallantry, and, as she faced him, laughing, pinched her cheek. She, unable to defend herself, stamped a foot, holding her tray aloft. Emboldened by the laughter of the crowd, the young fellow sidled in and tried to plant a kiss on the nape of her neck. She turned unexpectedly and, raising one of her heavy-booted feet, kicked him squarely in the pit of the stomach. He slipped and fell. This time the crowd cheered the girl.

That moment Nicoll stepped forward and relieved her of the tray.

The girl, enraged, abandoned it and threw herself on her assailant before he could rise. Under her weight he fell back; and, taking his head in both her hands, she knocked it repeatedly on the sidewalk. Then she ran to the door of the store where Nicoll had preceded her. Dazed, the young fellow picked himself up, laughing sheepishly.

Davis returned immediately after dinner. Aganeta had just gathered the doctor's dishes and left the room with a furious look, muttering something about the "Davis crowd."

Davis, on the ground that an elector was present, at once objected to the latter's voting. The elector was Nicoll.

But Dr. Vanbruik overruled the protest. "Mr. Spalding's agent can hardly be presumed to be influenced by such a remark."

Davis took note of the incident in a statement signed by his agents.

Not before three o'clock did the voting become brisk again. The new wave of electors was led by Shilloe. Davis "challenged" his vote. "I require the elector to be sworn."

Dr. Vanbruik picked up a printed form and read the oath required from an elector whose right to vote is doubted or challenged. This formality took ten minutes.

Hartley came next and went unchallenged. Then followed half a dozen residents of Morley; and Davis challenged every one. It was nearly four when they had voted. A huge crowd was dammed back in the store.

Nicoll was worried. If Davis went on challenging votes, not half of Abe's supporters would get a chance at the poll before the closing hour. He turned to the doctor. "May I ask the opposing candidate a question?"

"I don't see what could prevent you."

Nicoll turned to Davis. "Do you intend to challenge all voters opposed to you?"

Davis laughed. "I'll challenge as many as I see fit to challenge."

The doctor, though ignoring Nicoll's silent appeal, yet spoke to the man guarding the door. "Call Mr. Anderson, please."

When young Anderson looked in, the doctor asked him to get hold of Mr. Watt, the provincial constable.

"He's right at the door."

"Ask him in, will you? Ready for the next voter."

The elector entered and was challenged. The constable, handsomely filling his uniform, followed.

By this time there was tension inside and outside the room. The store was packed with those waiting. Even children had squeezed in when school had closed. Davis's tactics were transparent: he had had his henchmen vote in the morning, "rolling up" forty per cent of the total for himself. Now he was holding up his opponents. Such a proceeding did not fall under the heading of "corrupt practices" as defined by law. But even if it had done so, Abe would never have condescended to an appeal to the courts; and Davis knew it.

"Don't let the next man enter," Dr. Vanbruik said. Then he raised his voice. "Mr. Watt, I, deputy returning officer of this polling place of the hamlet of Morley, charge you to swear in a sufficient number of deputies to handle the crowd. You will next, by telephone, get into touch with the clerk of the municipality and give him a message as coming from me. Please take the message in writing. It is this: "The vote polled at this station is so far fifty-one; there are fifty-four more votes to be cast. Since one of the candidates pursues the policy of challenging indiscriminately, I can at best handle six votes an hour. We need at once a number of deputy returning officers to handle the vote within the time required by law, with full equipment."

The officer saluted and, admitting the next man, left the room.

Davis changed his tactics at once. Leaving one of his agents behind, he gave the other a signal and pushed his way through the now hostile crowd in the store. In the street, he crossed the driveway and the dry ditch to the fence of the right-of-way. There, nobody being near to overhear, he jotted a few names on a piece of paper. "Here," he said to Searle, the agent. "I'll go back and send Armstrong out. Between you get hold of every one on this list. You'll find the needful in my buggy at the livery stable. I rely on you that these fellows don't vote."

"All right, boss."

"Look sharp now."

In the polling room the voting proceeded smoothly.

At a quarter to five a car arrived in front of the store, stopping in the middle of the street. A small, stout man with a pointed grey beard alighted. This was Mr. Silcox, municipal secretary, respected by every one. The crowd, now quiet enough, opened a lane to let him pass.

The doctor looked up when Mr. Silcox entered. "The trouble seems to be over, Silcox."

Silcox nodded but remained at the door. Behind him, Searle looked in, raising three fingers to Davis. Ninety-nine votes had been polled. Davis felt sure of forty-five. It was a matter of five votes to him.

But no more electors appeared. A drowsy silence settled on the room, accentuated by the sizzling of the gasoline lamp. In street and store, people stood about in whispering groups. The result? That would be announced next day at Somerville, at the hour of noon. . . .

Davis and Nicoll went to hear the announcement. Nicoll brought the news to Morley where Abe met him at the post office. One of the ninety-nine votes had been rejected, having a cross against each of the names. The remainder were divided evenly between the two candidates. Mr. Silcox who had the casting vote had declared Abraham David Spalding elected.

Late in the afternoon, Abe entered the Vanbruik store in company with his brother-in-law. At sight of them a number of farmers who had come to town to hear the news broke into cheers.

The doctor, with dry humour, turned to a young man and asked, "Whom are you cheering for?"

A blank look came into the face of the rustic. "I don't know."

"Well . . . who's elected?"

"I don't know. Davis, I guess."

The doctor laughed in his mirthless way, saying to Abe, "That's the sort of people you are going to represent."

VIII ✳ THE DISTRICT

WITH his election to the council Abe became the undisputed leader of his district. Yet it did not make him popular among those who were temperamentally opposed to him.

In the spring of 1911, as soon as seeding was finished, the long-expected road work began, with Abe as road-boss. It was late in the year; for, while in 1910 the flood had arrived with unheard-of suddenness, subsiding as quickly, it came this year in successive steps of unusual slowness, taking three weeks to run out. Again there were rains; but they did not start till the bulk of the winter's snow was gone. Yet well into the month of May these rains kept turning into snow. It was June before people had time for anything but farm work; and the road work was repeatedly interrupted by the necessity of using such dry spells as there were for haying.

Abe found the additional drain on his time which his duties as a councillor involved almost more of a burden than he could bear; for he was consciously working up to a grand climax in his farming operations. In 1910 he had had six hundred acres under wheat; his crop had been of more than twelve thousand bushels; yet his margin of profit had been small. He found that the greater the acreage, the higher the cost of tillage per acre. It would be the same this year; but he still felt convinced that only by increasing his acreage could he reach a point where his total return would once more show a disproportionate profit. In the course of years of planning he had evolved a scheme whereby, once his land was broken —as it would be this summer—he would fallow a certain part of his land every year for a given number of years; and periodically there would be one year in every twelve when no fallow was needed. On such a year he counted for the realization of his bolder dreams; and it would come for the first time in 1912. Whenever he thought of it, he was visited by fears. Not all years yielded equally well; it depended on the sort of season it happened to be. To work for eleven years in hopes of getting the proper return for his labour in the twelfth was plainly in the nature of gambling. If that twelfth year was a year of subnormal yield, it would prove disastrous. In order to put in a wheat crop of twelve hundred acres, he would either have to have a considerable reserve of capital or to strain his credit to the breaking point. Yet he had been lucky so far; he must count on his luck to continue. Only once had he been really straitened: when he had suddenly seen himself forced to buy land before he was ready. Such a contingency could not repeat itself: he had all the land he could get. Besides, he had lived through even that crisis and come out on top. But there was so much more at stake now. He strained every muscle; he effected every possible economy in order to be prepared for that great year when his whole acreage would be under crop.

So, when the crews began to work on the road, starting at the north end, two miles from Nicoll's Corner, he found it impossible to be here and there, supervising, and to attend to his own farm as well; supervision was needed everywhere. His bronchos were never turned out on pasture; they stood ready at all times, harnessed and bridled. The road work had to be pressed forward at an unusual rate. It was hard to get enough teams. Abe fairly begged Nicoll and Stanley to put four horses each on shovels. Hilmer, Shilloe, Nawosad, and the younger Topp boys were "holding scrapers"; they guided the handles of the drag-shovels as the teamsters drove them up from the newly-opened ditch. Hartley, with a two-horse team, did the ploughing, loosening the soil for the scrapers. None of these had the four horses necessary to operate a drag. Remained Wheeldon with two teams, and Nicoll and Bill Stanley with one each. Five men without horses could have looked after twice as many teams.

The spring of 1910 had given conclusive proof that the road was needed. If there had been a grade, the flood would not have cut them off. Abe, of course, needed the road more than any one else. He did more hauling than the rest of them together. So, when he appeared in his buggy and found the crews resting, he looked more like a taskmaster to them than the benefactor who had won them that road and the chance of making money at the expense of the county. They resented it that Abe had taken Henry Topp away by offering him five dollars a day to operate his tractor.

Hartley and Wheeldon did not hesitate voicing such sentiments when Abe was not present. "He's got an easy job talking! Sitting in his buggy collecting mileage."

But Nicoll who acted as foreman spoke up. "That's where you're wrong. Abe won't collect a cent for mileage. He wants the road."

"Right, mister," Hartley said. "He wants the road; and we are to build it for him."

"As to that, he pays half the tax-bill of the whole district."

Wheeldon and Hartley gave more trouble than the rest together. Wheeldon wanted the money even more urgently than Hartley; he was ambitious; Hartley was satisfied not to go hungry from day to day. But even Wheeldon threatened to quit unless more frequent rests were called than Nicoll thought necessary. Hartley did leave once. But when Abe engaged an outsider to replace him, he abandoned that policy.

Yet these two trouble-makers found allies and abettors in the two younger Topp brothers, especially Slim who, in the afternoon when the heat grew oppressive, groaned and swore as though completely exhausted. But when Nicoll told him to take an hour off, with corresponding loss of pay, he laughed, danced a jig, and shouted, "Hi! Look here, you fellows!" And, catching his drag by handle and clevis, he lifted it stalking in huge strides after the fidgety team, and threw it down again when he reached the bottom of the ditch.

The net result was that the district defined itself into three groups, one of which was formed by Abe alone. There was, first, the Nicoll-Stanley group, consisting of these two who saw Abe more or less as he was: autocratic, intolerant of opposition, but absolutely fair and concerned with nothing but the welfare of the district. Hilmer and the Ukrainians belonged to this group; they regarded him as superior in knowledge as well as in power and wealth. The group opposed to them was led by Wheeldon. Behind him trailed Hartley and the three Topp brothers, more perhaps, at least in the case of David and Slim, from a desire for mischief than from any reasoned opposition to Abe.

This grouping showed itself most distinctly when, on Sunday afternoon, or when a rain had stopped the work, both groups met at Nicoll's Corner. There, great discussions were held these days. The culvert took the place of a sort of community hall. Sometimes even old man Blaine came over on his bicycle which he laid down in the grass by the roadside. When he appeared, there would be a sudden silence; and he knew they had been talking of him. As elsewhere in rural districts of the west, the teacher was the most common topic of discussion. The school is the one institution over which the district has immediate and absolute control; and every ratepayer thinks himself entitled to a share in the running of it which is in inverse proportion to his qualifications. Nobody denied any longer that the children were making progress; the inspector's reports were brilliant. Yet when Blaine had filed on the school quarter, murmurs had been renewed. Did he presume himself so secure of his tenure? Was he counting on remaining for the rest of his days? Did he think, because Spalding supported him, nobody could dislodge him? In winter Abe had hauled his cottage from Arkwright, a diminutive building with three tiny rooms and a corner porch. Even Nicoll had thought this step incautious; but Abe had allayed his fears. "We are just as independent as ever. Blaine's getting up in years. He wants a roof over his head, that's all. When we don't want him any longer, he'll retire." Wheeldon was all the more allusive these days since Abe had taken occasion to point out that, not being a British subject, he had no say in matters of the school.

With rare exceptions Abe kept away from these meetings;

he had no time; he was not "a mixer." When he happened to pass while a meeting was in progress, however, a feeling almost of envy came over him: *he* was everlastingly living in the future; that future might never come; *he* could not stop to look about; *he* must plan and calculate. Life was slipping by, unlived.

He, too, was aware when, that summer, he passed the spot for the first time, that a silence fell at his approach. Like Blaine he divined that they had been talking of him. At the culvert he drew his horses in; but the animation had dropped out of the conversation which turned to the weather and the crops.

Democracy had been the topic.

"Democracy!" Hartley had sneered. "If this district isn't run by one single man, I'd like to see one that is."

Nicoll had answered: "Democracy means putting the right man in the right place. That's what we've got our vote for; not to interfere with every detail. Look at the school. It's the best school for many miles around. I'll be the first to oppose Abe when he can't show me that he's right. But to put him down *because* he's right is silly, not democratic."

"Yeah!" Wheeldon had exclaimed. "But I'd like to see him drive a team on the road."

"There's another point," Nicoll had replied. "We've been wanting that road for years. We put Abe on the council, and we get it. We don't get the frills which Davis promised: concrete bridges and a culvert for every farm. Ask any one on the council. For the first time there's system in the road-building of the municipality. Trunk roads are built; nobody gets a little private drive-way for himself. I don't blame Abe for not working on the road. I can hardly afford it myself. And I've only eighty acres under crop and four horses to provide with hay."

On another occasion, rain having stopped work in the early afternoon, Abe used the unexpected leisure to go to town. As he passed the culvert, the conversation did not stop. Old man Blaine was present though the mud had prevented him from using his bicycle. The conversation had taken a quasi-scientific turn.

"Say," Henry Topp exclaimed, "how can a man walk faster than a train?"

His brothers laughed. Nawosad and Shilloe bent their heads to listen. Only Hilmer was absent.

Stanley, sitting at the far end of the culvert, portly yet alert, his single elbow resting on his knee, said quietly, "He can't."

"I've seen it. By gosh and by gum, I've seen it! Perhaps I should say jump, not walk."

"No," Nicoll said. "Nonsense!"

The whole group, comprising ten men, exclusive of Abe, was in that relaxed, lazy state of mind and body which, in the country, is induced by the fact that an event beyond man's control has decreed a holiday. Not even the Sunday brings such utter relaxation of tensions; for the Sunday is, after all, part of an established routine. The relaxation is all the greater when this rain happens to come on a Saturday.

"Well," Henry went on, "they were shunting a freight train in the yard at Morley. The train was moving quite fast. And there was a fellow walking on top of a box-car, in the same direction in which the train was moving; and when he came to the end of the car, he went right on and jumped to the one in front."

Nicholl, reclining on a plank at the edge of the ditch, raised himself to a position of attention. "You're joshing."

"By golly, no. I saw it with my own eyes."

Stanley laughed. "What next? He jumped from one car to another. That's nothing. Four or five feet. But the car was moving, you say. How do you explain that?"

Blaine, sitting nearest the road, was whittling a weedstalk with his pocket knife. "I've seen that myself," he said. "I could do it. You could do it. Nothing mysterious about it."

"Well, explain," Henry challenged. "Now show your science."

"Science"—this with the emphasis of authority—"never explains."

"What's the use of science if it doesn't explain?" Nicoll asked. "I thought that's what science was for."

"Science gathers facts and puts them in order. Then they become law."

"Now you're talking!" said Henry. "Laws have to be obeyed. If you've got a law, you've got an explanation. If any one asks me why I pay taxes, I say because it's the law that I should if I can. Out with your law!"

The reference to taxes brought a laugh.

"It isn't so simple," Blaine said. "I've forgotten most of my science. But it's something like this. The motion of the car puts something into the man that carries him over; and they call it inertia."

There was a silence as if at an anti-climax. Nobody cared to contradict; but nobody was quite convinced.

Abe stirred, picking up his lines. "Too much rain," he said.

"We could do with a dry spell," Stanley agreed.

"Well, I must go," and Abe shook his lines. The thin wheels of his buggy were picking up wide rims of mud.

The silence continued till he was out of earshot. Then, "Going to town!" said Hartley with a sneer.

Nicoll looked at him, a question in his eye.

"That's the place for politicians."

"Well," Stanley said, "Spalding's hardly a politician."

"At any rate," Nicoll added, "he's straight as a die."

"And he'll go far," Blaine said slowly, his head bent over his knees. "Most progressive man in the district."

"Doing well," Stanley nodded. "Considering he's been on his place no more than twelve years."

"No trick!" This from Hartley. "With money to start with."

Besides these men who were in constant though half-formal contact with Abe, there were the women. To him they remained vague; but he was to them a huge figure of somewhat uncertain outlines, resembling the hero of a saga. What most of them saw in their immediate surroundings was squalor, poverty, and desperate struggle; what they heard of him grew into the conception of wealth and magic success, especially since he allotted work and paid out public money. When Hartley quitted work, his wife looked to Abe for the reason. To him she looked for his reinstatement. At Abe's place every one could earn wages in seeding or harvest; and most of them did; their own harvests were barely sufficient to cover payments on live stock and implements. He piped, and they danced; and even though some of them swore at him before they went to his dance-floor, Abe remained a hero and a saga-figure, loved by few, hated by some, but willy-nilly admired by all.

Nobody, not even Nicoll, had an idea of the tension in which Abe was getting ready for the great and decisive year. Nobody knew how he worried. He worried about everything, about the weather, the flood, and about help; for it was clear that he could not hold Bill Crane. He had found another man, Harry Stobarn; but he disliked him and did not trust him with his stock. Bill was getting restless and talked of taking up land himself; he did not know when he had a good thing, for Abe had raised his wages by five dollars a month, in spite of the fact that he gave less and less value for his money. Abe felt as though he were staking his whole existence on a single throw next year: twelve hundred acres under wheat! The cost of putting that crop in the ground! If the season proved inauspicious? . . .

These thoughts never left him. The present season was wet:

rain followed rain; the straw was too long; and when the ears should have been setting and filling out, even the blades remained green.

Never did these thoughts leave him; and they were passing through his mind as, on that Saturday afternoon, he drove south on his way to town. Slowly he drove, for the road was heavy; and the mud picked up by the wheels measured a foot across. It was still cloudy; and on all sides the prairie looked as though lifted up to the sky.

From everywhere eyes were focused on him as he drove along. Nobody ever went to or came from town but everybody in the district knew it. The prairie is too open for any move to remain hidden. When a caller came to a settler, all of them knew and talked of it at once; when a settler went to call somewhere else, remarks were made in every house.

Thus, as Abe approached Hilmer's Corner, there was a discussion going on about him in the Mennonite's shack.

This shack, the roof of which slanted from front to rear, was divided into three rooms. At the north end was a bedroom where the Grappentins lodged at night. Next came a large, hall-like space which served as the general living-room and Hilmer's workshop combined; for Hilmer plied the trade of a harness-maker; and south of it followed his own bedroom, a mere cubicle six feet in width. When Mrs. Grappentin's husband was at home, the children were at night bedded down on the floor of the shop; when he was absent, they slept in his bed.

On the Saturday in question, the whole family was assembled in the central room. The children were playing in a corner; at one of the two small windows piercing the front wall sat old Mrs. Grappentin, looking out; her head resembled a bird of prey perched on her shoulders, her hooked nose corresponding to its beak. Near her, on a canted chair, lounged a middle-aged man of ferocious aspect, with prominent teeth slanting forward in his mouth, below a straggling red moustache; his blotchy, purplish complexion betrayed him to be addicted to the copious use of liquor. This was the third husband of Hilmer's mother—a man who had married the older woman under the promise that he would work the farm left to her by her second husband; but it proved that he had done so chiefly in order to extract, through her, from her industrious eldest son the wherewithal to support his idle, drunken, dissipated life. While he had money, he was never at home.

Young Hilmer himself, in black sateen shirt and black cotton trousers, a small black cap on his head, for he was sensitive to draughts, was working in the centre of the room, in front of the open door, where on two planks supported on trusses a set of harness in need of repairs was spread out. His chief characteristic was introspectiveness.

Among the grown-ups a desultory conversation went on in German.

The mother at the window was the first to see Abe coming from the north; and from that moment on an unbroken stream of abuse flowed from her lips. "Da kommt der grosse Herr!" she exclaimed. "There comes the great lord! Silent and haughty as ever, looking over the land as if he owned the world. Pride comes before the fall! What's made him so great? What has he done? He settled down here when this was a wilderness, with money in his pocket, that is all. He made it hard for his neighbours, so he could buy their land cheap. And then he waited till we came and made it worth money. He's been lording it ever since, running school and ward and county—die Grafschaft—as if he had not only the money but the knowledge and the power and the right all to himself. When any one else wants something, he puts his foot down and says he mustn't. . . ."

"Sein Sie doch still, Frau Mutter!—Be quiet, Mrs. Mother!" said her son, walking about with awl and waxed thread. Yet, in spite of his ostentatious preoccupation with the work in hand, he too, bending forward, peered through the door at the proud figure of Abe behind his bronchos. "Everybody lives in his own way. He lives in his. I've never heard it said except by his enemies that he has acquired land and position by anything but hard work and ability, Mrs. Mother."

Grappentin, the stepfather, spat contemptuously on the scoured floor which was covered with a thin layer of white sand from the river. "Hard work! Nobody gets rich by hard work. He's played his tricks, I'll warrant, the son-of-a-gun!— Der Hundekel!"

"Now, now, Herr Stiefvater!" Hilmer muttered. "I don't like to hear such things said in my house. I am glad Mr. Spalding has made a success. It shows what I may be able to do, with hard work and industry."

"Look at him, look at him!" the woman screeched. "There he goes around by the field! As if the road were not good enough! Perhaps he has done something there by which he's got all his money!"

"Hush, hush, Mrs. Mother!" exclaimed Hilmer as though oppressed by the vicious imagination of the old woman. "I know better. And so do you. The mud is deep at the spot. A regular hole."

"I can't stand the sight of the great and rich. It wasn't to see them that we came to this country."

"Right, Mrs. Mother. We came to get great and rich ourselves."

Grappentin burst into a guffaw; but Hilmer worked quietly on. Grappentin rose, bent his arms over his head, and stretched with a yawn.

"Look at that!" the old woman cried; for, beyond the trail, Abe's horses were taking the sharp, slippery incline to the culvert in wild bounds, nearly upsetting the buggy. Mrs. Grappentin broke into a shrill senile laugh. "I wish he had broken his neck!—Ich wollt er haett sich den Hals gebrochen!"

"For shame, Mrs. Mother!" Hilmer reproved without looking up.

Grappentin stood before the young man in a spreading sprawling attitude, hands on hips. "Would you mind," he said with an ironic imitation of Hilmer's sobriety, "would you mind, Mr. Stepson, telling me why the great lord is always alone and does not mix with the rest of us as other Christian people do?"

Hilmer fixed a mild but steady eye on the other man, holding it there for a moment, before he answered. "Because," he said at last, "he thinks greater thoughts and aims higher than all the rest of us do."

IX ✳ THE CHILD

IT was in connection with his work on the council that Abe succeeded in solving the problem of finding a successor for Bill Crane.

Ward One of the municipality, in its south-east corner, was represented by a man called Rogers with whom Abe found himself voting most of the time. One needed only to look at this man to see that he was of a different type from the rest of the councillors. The council was divided into two groups, three of its members being typical politicians, as was Mr. Eastham, the reeve; these four were ostensibly also farmers; but they occupied their farms chiefly for the purpose of qualifying for their political positions; their income came from "pickings."

They were opposed by Rogers, Abe, and a Mennonite from the so-called Reserve by name of Bickert.

But Rogers was different from all others. He owned and

operated a farm; but he worked it along English lines. He was what is commonly called a "remittance man," i.e. being a younger son of a landed family, he drew an independent income from an estate in England. He preserved a distinctly English accent and used words which, though comprehensible to the others, yet marked him off as belonging to a different level of education. From the beginning he felt drawn to Abe, and admittedly because Abe was Mary Vanbruik's brother. While the doctor had practised at Somerville, Mr. Rogers had been a frequent caller at his house; and Mary had spent weekends at the Rogers place. Though of medium height, Rogers looked tall and slender; his handsome, tanned face with the appressed ears was divided by a short, brown moustache. He was always well dressed; yet he never looked as though dressed for the occasion; he felt too much at home in his clothes.

Now and then, some matter being put to the vote, he would raise a smiling glance to Abe's eyes; and Abe invariably understood its meaning. Invariably, in such cases, they voted together, supported by Bickert; and the reeve gave his casting vote to the other side.

After meetings, Rogers and Abe often spent a few minutes in conversation; and one day, towards the end of the summer, the subject of the brief exchange of words was the problem of help.

"I," Rogers said, "always advertise for Ukrainian families new to the country. I keep an Englishman or two besides. For the routine work I prefer the foreigners; they are willing and reliable."

"How much do you pay?"

"I give them house and garden; they help themselves to all the milk they want. In addition I pay the man three hundred dollars; and the woman at the rate of a dollar a day when her help is required."

"Do they stay?"

"Till they take up land. Three, four years. One man has been with me for twelve years now. He gets four hundred."

"How much do you farm?"

"Three quarters, nearly. The river cuts away a corner of my land."

"I'll try that," said Abe.

The consequence was that, just before harvest, Bill Crane left Abe. A Ukrainian by name of Horanski moved into the house west of the yard. Abe fenced a three-acre lot for him; for he had a family of five children. Abe wanted to give him a chance of making additional money by raising potatoes and garden truck. Horanski was a squarely-built man of middle age who knew no English but proved adaptable and indefatigable in his work. Nor did his wife, a broad, comfortable woman, shrink from such tasks as she could do. Abe was ready for the coming year.

The yield of the crop in the fall of 1911 turned out better than Abe had expected. He threshed late, Victor Lafontaine furnishing machine and crew as he had done for a number of years. Consequently, fall-ploughing remained incomplete. Yet, when the first frost came, more than a thousand acres were ready for the seeder. In a reasonably early spring, the tractor would take care of the rest. The whole district was aware of the extraordinary preparations which Abe was making; and the whole district adjusted itself. Since work a-plenty could be had for the asking, people held back on their own land while wages flowed.

Abe now planned building a new barn, partly in order to separate cows from horses, partly because his ever-increasing store of machinery would find room in its eastern half, for the open shed admitted the snow in winter. As for the house, he might have built that fall; but he wanted to be sure that he could, next summer, carry on without using his credit at the bank, so that the whole crop would be available for what he might care to do. Once he had built, Ruth was never again to complain about lack of space!

When spring opened up, without extraordinary developments, there was the usual rush of work. The tractor, driven by Henry Topp, drew a ten-share plough; behind it, drawn by horses, trailed two disks; and endless units of drags were followed in turn by the seeders of which there were six, two belonging to Nicoll and Stanley. The weather was singularly propitious; but the more propitious it seemed, the more Abe worried.

He had heard it say by old-timers from south of the Line that wet years run in threes, as do dry years, with one normal year completing a seven-year cycle. A few of the weather-wise even went so far as to say that, the first year, it was the spring which was wet; the second year, it was the summer; the third year, it would be the fall; and the year 1911 had borne them out. Neither a wet spring nor a wet summer did Abe any harm. In 1910 and 1911 he had had a surplus of hay, so that he had been able to give a whole stack of such as were short of roughage. Even Wheeldon had taken advantage of the offer. As for the grains, the straw had been heavy; and it had "lodged"—had been laid down by the heavy rains—so that it had been hard to cut; but the yield had been above the average of nineteen bushels per acre. Most settlers had complained that half their crops had been "drowned". If it had not been for the detested road work, there would have been outright distress.

Abe worried; too much was at stake. If the prediction of the old-timers came true, the wet weather would come in the fall—the only time when it could ruin him. Before long it was clear to Ruth and Mary that Abe was living through a new crisis. But this time he did not drown his worries in work; more often he was seen stalking along the margins of his enormous fields, inspecting his crops. The work he left more and more to the broad, obsequious Ukrainian and his wife, there being no fallow to plough. Mrs. Horanski was glad to earn an extra five or ten dollars a month by doing the milking; and Abe thought it good policy to give her all the work she wanted.

When Abe stalked about his fields, he did not pull weeds as in the past; what could be done with an acreage of two square miles? And his idle walks led to a new development in his life.

One night when the children were playing about the house, the weather being just right for the crops, neither too hot nor too cool, and the soil just right, neither too wet nor too dry, Abe's oldest boy, now a child of eleven, spied his father north of the yard and, obeying an impulse, left Jim and the girls and joined that man who was almost a stranger to him. He took his hand and walked along as though he respected his worries and were getting God knew what enjoyment out of it.

Encouraged by his father's toleration of his presence, Charlie sought him out again next Sunday morning when Abe had inspected the empty stalls of the barn; the horses had long since been fed, the cows milked, and both turned out into the pasture which ran north for two whole miles, comprising now eighty acres.

Thence Abe meant to go to the west field, to circle it—a walk of five miles—and to see the young wheat in that part of his holdings. There had been no rain for a week; and though the plants did not yet suffer from lack of moisture, a little rain would not be unwelcome, to keep conditions as nearly ideal as they had been so far.

The morning was bright and clear. It seemed almost too bright and clear; not a cloudlet showed: a rare thing for a Manitoba summer day which is normal only when flat-bottomed, round-topped clouds sail whitely through the blue.

As Abe turned to the gate, Charlie took his hand and hopped along by his side. They passed through the gap in the wind-break, now twenty feet high, and out on to the road. Towns were dotting the distant skyline, raised by the mirage. Silver-white vapour mirrors were overlying the land. Every blade of grass sparkled with dew.

They passed the wind-break and the pasture; Horanski's house, north of them, made almost the impression of an independent farm. Here, Abe meant to turn into the fields; but there was a tug at his arm.

"Daddy," said a sing-song voice, "I know a vesper sparrow's nest on the road past the field. Won't you come along to see it?"

"Can't you go alone?" Abe had stopped.

"Sure. But I'd like to show you, daddy."

Abe felt vaguely flattered. "What's a vesper sparrow?"

"Don't you know?"

"Did you before you went to school?"

"Didn't they teach you about birds when you were a boy?"

"They taught us to read and write and figure."

"We learn lots of things besides."

"Well, you haven't answered my question, sonny." Abe never called Charlie "sonny" except when he was teasing him. On such occasions, the word had become habitual since years ago when Abe had happened to use it Charlie had tearfully protested, "I *am* no sonny."

"A small bird as big as a sparrow, with white stripes in his tail."

"Haven't all sparrows white stripes in their tails?"

"Only juncos and vesper sparrows."

"That so? And where do they build their nests?"

"On the ground."

Even at this point the conversation had become an adventure to Abe—an excursion into the mysterious realms of childhood. "Well," he asked, "where is that nest of yours?"

The boy led the way west, south of the farm. They had left Horanski's place a few hundred yards behind when the child exclaimed, "Oh, look, daddy! There on the fence. That's a vesper sparrow."

"Is that the one from your nest, do you think?"

The boy considered. "No. It's too far."

"How far is it?"

"Quite a piece. More than half a mile."

They went on. Both were in their Sunday clothes, though Abe wore no coat. The sky was undergoing one of those sudden and subtle changes which follow a cloudless sunrise; it lost its polished appearance and became dull. A breeze sprang up from the north-west.

"I'll tell you," said Abe. "Maybe we had better go another day. It looks like a shower. What do you say?"

"Oh no, daddy! Come on."

The sky became whitish. But they went on along the trail which lost itself in the prairie. Now and then there was a tug on Abe's arm; for the child picked up clods of earth and shied them across the ditch to their left into the meadow beyond. For every step Abe took, the boy took two or three, jumping ahead and doubling back. Abe mused. He was making this child happy; and that made him happy in turn: with a happiness unknown to him at less magic times: this hour was fraught with something which redeemed the workaday week. Why had he never enjoyed it before? With a pang he realized that he was missing much in life.

He felt poignantly that he loved the child; that he approved of his very existence; that he must tie him to his heart by a bond. The boy was himself re-arisen; finer, slenderer, more delicate, more exquisitely tempered. It affected him like a miracle bursting on earthly eyes.

As they approached the south-west corner of Abe's holdings, Charlie abandoned his other pursuits and stayed by his side. "Ssh!" he said and, with the exaggeration of childhood, began to walk on tiptoe, sideways, restraining his father as if they were stalking game. "There!" he whispered tensely as, a rod ahead, a bird flew up with a startled chirp.

When they reached the nest, built of dry blades of grass and cunningly concealed in a hummock, a few inches above the surrounding level, the boy went into ecstasies of delight. "Oh, daddy, come quick, come quick! They're hatched. Look at the little ones! They're all mouth! Oh, come, daddy! What's that yellow stuff around their beaks?"

Abe came and bent over the boy who was on his knees.

They stood and looked, the mother bird anxiously fluttering near and perching plaintively on the wire of the fence.

Suddenly Abe felt a heavy drop of rain and straightened. From the north-west a low-fringed cloud came sweeping along, aquiver with lightning. Half a mile ahead of them the long, silky grass was wildly waving in the wind which had not reached them yet. Abe felt worried. As for himself, he might spoil a suit of clothes; but the child was apt to take vicious colds. In the corner of the wild land ahead stood the remnant of a haystack.

"Run," he said, leading the way in huge strides to the stack.

The child followed, putting forth all the powers in his thin body to keep up with his father. It took only a few minutes; but they had barely reached the shelter when the squall struck. The fact that they were in a pocket of calm gave them a delicious feeling of being saved and of an isolation which they shared. As the rain swept over, it blotted with veil after veil all things to the east. Abe scooped a hollow in the wall produced by the hay-knife. There they squatted as in a cave.

A brief rattling shower passed east, shot with hail and followed by a lull. Then, with a sharp flash of lightning and a simultaneous bellow of thunder, a steady downpour began, slanted by the wind. Abe winced at the flash; but the child remained unconscious. of the storm. He was dancing about from foot to foot in front of his father. "Oh, daddy, it makes me *so happy* to see those little birds!" And, after a while, "I wonder, will they get wet?"

"I don't think so," said Abe. "The mother is sitting on the nest."

"Mr. Blaine says we must never disturb a bird when it rains."

A second flash was followed by a long, rolling peal of thunder which ended with a sharp, detached explosion. The boy laughed at the peculiar rhythm. "That sounds like a crocodile lifting his tail," he said.

Abe joined in his laugh.

The boy snuggled against his father's knee. "Like this," and he ran his hand along Abe's thigh, using two fingers as legs; then, laying hand and forearm down and bending his fingers up, backward, "Like that," he said.

"Do you know what a crocodile is?"

"Of course!" And, turning, he looked out from under the shaggy roof of the cave. Drops were falling from the edge of the opening. "That's like a curtain of beads." He was never at rest, twitching with vitality.

Abe felt as though he had been lonely for years. He drew the boy between his knees. "Do you like to go to school?"

"Yes." But it was said without enthusiasm.

"Much?"

"Ye-es." This time there was distinct hesitation.

"Why?"

"That's where Mr. Blaine is."

"You like him, do you?"

Charlie turned, playing with his father's watch-chain. "Don't you?"

Abe laughed. "I don't matter. Do all the children like him?"

"Some do; some don't. Some say he's too strict."

"That's what a teacher is supposed to be."

"The Hartley kids have been to school elsewhere. They say it's nicer to have a lady teacher."

"You think so too?"

"No."

"Well, you'll keep Mr. Blaine."

They remained where they were till the storm was over. Pools of water dotted the prairie. They could not get home dry-shod. But the clouds were dispersing, and the sun shone through their rents. When they reached the first cross-ditch, a black, turbulent current was running into the master ditch south of the trail.

They came to the nest. "I wonder," said Charlie, "whether they are all right? Oh, daddy!" he cried as the mother bird flew up. "They're quite dry. There's water all around; but the nest is dry."

"The mother bird knows where to build. She knows about rain."

When they entered the yard, Abe felt a poignant regret that the hour was over. . . .

A week later, a Presbyterian minister held divine service at the school. Although Abe was indifferent, he took his family. During the following night Abe was in the deepest of his sleep when he felt a pull at the covers of his bed. "Yes," he said, starting up into a sitting posture. And a moment later he became aware of Charlie standing by his side, barefooted, shivering in his night-gown. "Daddy," he whispered, "I had such a terrible dream. May I come into your bed?" Abe threw his blankets back; and the child dived in.

On Saturday, Abe said to Ruth at dinner, "Let Charlie put on his good suit. I'm taking him along to town."

Ruth did not reply. She had grown still stouter. The features of her face had hardened, heavy, unlovely; her waist-line had disappeared. She had abandoned the last attempt at making herself attractive.

On the way to town, Abe was in no hurry. Haying was in full swing; but a competent man was in charge; never had he put as much confidence in any one as in Horanski. The season still remained ideal.

Abe was thinking of that night when the child had come to his bed. He had not closed his eyes again. Why had the boy not gone to his mother? Was it the new relationship between father and son?

"What were you dreaming about," he asked when they were well on their way, "that night when you came to my bed?"

"Devils," said Charlie succinctly.

"What?"

"Devils."

"What are they?"

The boy fidgeted, various expressions chasing each other over his delicate features. "Oh, I can't tell. Terrible things."

Abe looked at the child. What was going on in that little head with its fine, fair hair? Love him as he might, he could only feel what the boy permitted him to feel.

But Charlie became confidential. "Daddy, can God do anything He wants to do?"

"I suppose so."

The child pondered. "I've been praying for something; ever since we went to church the other day. But I haven't got it."

Abe felt overwhelmed with the difficulty of the situation. He must not even smile at the child. "We know nothing about God," he said hesitatingly. "I don't. But there are people who think they know all about him. They tell us that sometimes, when we ask for a thing, we don't get it because it wouldn't be good for us to have it."

"Oh!" The boy pondered again; and, with sudden irrelevancy, "Daddy, how do children come into the world?"

Abe was thunderstruck. Of all questions this was the one he was least prepared to answer. He realized at once that his relationship to the boy had reached a crucial point. He could not refuse to answer; he could not evade; he could not deceive; for the child would detect any reluctance, any evasion, any untruth. The boy had had contact with others; the school had interposed itself between parent and child. On his reply would depend which way, in years to come, this boy would turn for truth, to his father or to his classmates. Abe must make a bid for the child's absolute and utter confidence. It seemed a daring thing to do, contradicting all conventions. Like a tremendous weight, the responsibility of parenthood settled down on Abe. So far he had given more thought to municipal problems than to the welfare of his children. No other course, therefore, remained open but to trust his instinct.

"I don't know," he said slowly, "how much you can understand of this. You saw Beaut, the mare, in the spring, didn't you?"

"Before she had the colt, you mean?"

"Yes. And you've seen a change since the colt arrived?"

"She isn't so big."

"Exactly. That colt, you see, had grown inside her body."

The boy laughed; and the laugh sounded almost silly; but Abe divined that it sprang from excitement.

"In the same way a child grows within the mother."

Again the boy laughed his excitedly silly laugh. "Then only mothers can have children?"

"Only mothers."

For the third time came that laugh. Then a thoughtful pause; and next an almost pouting question. "But, daddy, how does it get in? And how does it get out?"

"That I'll tell you when you are older. Listen, Charlie."

"Yes?"

"Other boys will tell you things. They don't know. You didn't know. How could you? Few parents tell their children."

"I have asked mother."

"Have you? Now let's make an agreement. I promise you to tell you the truth as far as you can understand it. I may tell you to wait. I may tell you I don't know myself. But I won't tell you an untruth. In return I ask you one single thing. Don't ask other boys for information which they can't give. Come to me. Will you do that?"

"Yes," Charlie said; and once more he laughed, but in a different key. Then, boastfully, "Sure! I'll always come to you, daddy. You tell me the truth. *Now I know.* Shall I tell you what I've been praying for?" He was standing and playing with the lapel of Abe's coat.

"Well?"

"But you mustn't laugh! I've been asking God for a baby."

Abe did laugh; and the boy laughed with him. Both laughed at the silly child which Charlie had been. . . .

One day Abe stopped at the school as he passed it. Although these were holidays, Abe found Blaine in the building where he spent most of his time reading. As Abe entered, the old man looked up from his desk, his steel-rimmed glasses on the tip of his nose.

Abe nodded and squeezed his bulk into one of the larger seats. This was an up-to-date classroom, spacious and airy; and the windows, all on the north side, looked out on the prairie east of Nicoll's.

"Blaine," Abe said, "I've never asked you how the kids are getting on. I didn't want you to think that as the chairman of the board I asked for special consideration. But I'm beginning to realize that I know nothing about them."

"I've wondered," Blaine said. "The only one inclined to give trouble is Jim. He doesn't like school. The girls are up to grade."

"And Charlie?"

"Well, Charlie!" the old man said slowly, looking queerly at Abe. "I don't know whether you realize——"

"What do you mean?" Abe asked huskily.

"It's hard to put into words. . . ."

Something passed between the two men, like an electric current.

Abe rose, a lump in his throat. "I know," he said; and awkwardly he stood for a moment before he nodded and turned away.

Henceforth there was a secret understanding between them.

X ✳ THE CROP

THROUGHOUT that summer of 1912 Abe never ceased worrying about his crop. Things going well, he was apt to feel that some disaster was preparing itself. Never did the grain suffer from excessive moisture or lack of it. Never a blade turned yellow before the second week in August; and then a golden spell brought the very weather for ripening wheat. The straw was of good height but did not lodge. The stand was remarkably thick and even; and not on Abe's place only but throughout the district and even south of the Somerville Line and in the river valley to the east. Unless some major disaster intervened, a late hailstorm or a prairie fire, unheard-of wealth would be garnered that fall throughout the southern part of the province. Even though, with such a crop, the price of wheat was bound to fall, there would be plenty. Abe estimated his yield at forty bushels per acre. The grade could hardly be less than Number One Northern, coveted by every grower of wheat. Unless some major disaster interfered, this crop would place him at the goal of his ambitions. But could it be that no disaster was to come? He felt as though a sacrifice were needed to propitiate the fates. He caught himself casting about for something he might do to hurt himself, so as to lessen the provocation and challenge his prospect of wealth must be to whatever power had taken the place of the gods.

He had read of such crops; he had heard tales told. South of the Big Marsh, a man had bought a farm on credit for ten thousand dollars, with only his equipment and his industry on the asset side of his balance sheet; his first crop was said to have paid for the farm. Such cases were used by the great transportation companies to advertise the west. They were on everybody's lips. But Abe knew that against them stood hundreds of cases of failure, of bare livings made by the hardest work. Was his going to be the one case in a thousand?

Yet, no matter how he looked at things, even allowing the price of wheat to fall to an exceptionally low level, *unless some major disaster interfered*, he was bound to see his material wishes fulfilled. Twelve hundred acres under wheat! Forty bushels per acre. At, say, sixty cents a bushel—surely, that was the lowest possible price? Thirty thousand dollars were growing in his fields—a fortune sufficient for his needs.

This was the harvest for which he had worked through all these years since he had first bought additional land. Slowly, as his holdings increased, the plan had dawned on him to arrange the rotation forced on him by the problem of weeds in such a way as to make it possible once in a decade to put his whole area under crop, staking a decade's work on a throw of the dice: a venture so costly as to make failure seem a catastrophe.

Everywhere the young were elated at the prospect; everywhere the aged, the old-timers, in the Mennonite Reserve, for instance, shook their heads. Wet years had always come in a three-year succession. This year spring had been normal; summer, a marvel of favouring conditions: no human intelligence, endowed with the power of determining seasonal events, could have planned things in a more auspicious way. But there was still time for rains to come; and if they came now, they would come at the one and only time at which they could endanger all Abe's work. He might not be able to cut his wheat; being cut, the grain might sprout in the stook and be ruined. The fall was his vulnerable point, his only one.

Already, in certain districts, people spoke of a year in the early nineties when, in the settlements to the west, it had been impossible to thresh in the fall. The crops had stood in the fields through the winter, to be threshed in spring. Farmers had considered themselves lucky to save a fraction of their wealth. Could nothing be done to save all? In August Abe did what he had never done before. He went great distances into the districts to the west: to Ivy, eleven miles from Morley; and thence south-west, to Wheatland and Ferney, standing about in stores and listening to the gossip of farmers. Wherever he went, reports were the same: unless something went wrong at the last moment, it would be a bumper crop. One danger was pointed out: before this, an early killing frost had overtaken the west. When Abe reached home, he went into his fields and rubbed a sample of his wheat from ears here and there till he arrived at the conclusion that his crop was safe; frost might lower the grade; it could not ruin the whole.

Others who shook their heads in anticipation of what must go wrong were fatalists in spite of misgivings. What must come would come; no use trying to fight; no use worrying. Too bad if anything happened; but if it did, it could not be helped.

But Abe rebelled at that thought. He was changing. His ambitions had been material ones; but there were other things in life, dimly seen as in a mist. A happiness based on things not material was blindly emerging. Abe was a slave to the soil; till he had satisfied that soil which he himself had endowed with the power of enslaving him, he must postpone all other things; only when he had done what he must do, would he have time and energy for anything else. This crop he must have.

And cutting started. Abe began with two binders drawn by horses: the problem of help was acute. Harvest was general. Abe asked Nicoll for his boy Tom, seventeen years old. Nicoll was obstinate.

"I'll hurry things along," he said. "I'll let the girls stook. Loan me a binder and a team, and I'll let Tom drive my own outfit; I'll drive yours. That way I'll get through in half the time. When I finish I'll come with three boys. But I can't afford to let my sixty acres wait. With an additional binder it's a question of two, three days."

Abe went to see Henry Topp and received the same answer. It was late at night when he got home; he harnessed five horses to one of his binders and drove it over to Nicoll's Corner. It was after midnight.

People had heard him for miles around; sounds carry far over the prairie. Next morning Stanley came to Abe's asking for a repair part for his binder. He spoke in a peculiar vein. "You know, Spalding, I can drive a team; but I can't stook with one arm. When such an affliction comes, you learn patience. When I look at you, I see myself as I used to be. I thought I could force things. I've learned to trust in the Lord. That's what's wrong with us all; we have lost our faith. You are going to have that crop or to lose it; and if you're to lose it, nothing that *you* can do will save it for you."

Abe looked at the man who had spoken with an insistence unusual between people who are not intimate. "That may be," he said. "But it may also be that God helps them that help themselves."

He could not afford to sit back and look on. A few days later, the weather remaining incredibly golden, Abe's harvest got into its stride. He paid his stookers three dollars a day: wages unheard of except in threshing, and they drew every hand. Even Stanley sent Bill; and Harry Stobarn came from a distance of ten miles—a man who was to play a part in Abe's destinies two years later.

On Sunday Abe went to Somerville to fetch a fifth binder: what was the cost of a binder when such a crop was at stake? Three acres of wheat would pay for the machine. Abe was still financing on last year's crop; not a cent did he owe at the bank

Twice, during the first day, there was trouble with the two oldest binders. Abe sent to town; the assistant to one of the grain buyers was a binder expert; henceforth this man, drawing five dollars a day, remained in the field, driving the bronchos hitched to a buggy, available wherever a binder stopped. A supply of repair parts lay in the box.

At noon, the whole crew was fed at Horanski's where the woman seemed glad of this overflow of harvest joy lapping about her door. At five, a lunch was served to the men, with beer or coffee to drink as they preferred. The binder expert brought baskets full of sandwiches and jugs full of coffee and beer to the field. Abe's driving power told; for two weeks, work in the fields became an orgy.

Then, just before the end, a slight rain fell like a warning. It was after dinner; by night they would have finished. The rain ceased almost as soon as it had begun; but work had to be suspended. Abe was in a panic. When, three days later, on 3rd September, the last sheaf was stooked, some of the binders and the tractor were at the northern line of the Hudson's Bay section; the stooks stood so close together that it was impossible to take the machines across the field. In a buoyancy of exultation, Abe took a pair of pliers from the tool-box of the nearest binder and went to the fence to pull the staples holding the wires to the posts. The whole caravan crossed over to the wild land in the west and circled the farm in the dusk.

Two days later a heavy rain fell. But dry weather followed immediately and continued for several days. Yet signs began to multiply that more rain was to follow. Abe lived in a frenzy of worry. If all went well, there were forty thousand dollars' worth of wheat in the stooks. Abe, full of forebodings, began to wish for an early frost.

On 11th September Abe was up at four in the morning, feeding the horses himself from sheer nervousness; for more than a year now he had left such chores entirely to Horanski who seemed famished for work; but Abe felt as though, by keeping himself even uselessly busy, he was doing his share to avert a disaster; nobody would be able to say that he had been sitting idly by while his crops were being ruined.

Always he had thought fastest and to the best effect when at work. He could never grasp all the bearings of a problem sitting down; at work, difficulties seemed to solve themselves as by magic.

Thus, having done the chores at the barn, all but the milking, he climbed into the loft, taking a lantern, to throw down hay for the day; and, happening to look into the grain bin, he saw that there was little oats left near the chute. He climbed in and, with a half-bushel scoop, shovelled the grain over from the talus-slopes of the margin.

Suddenly he straightened under the impact of a thought.

Yes, *he would stack his crop*!

Nobody throughout the length and breadth of the river valley had to his knowledge ever stacked his grain. In thirteen years he had not seen conditions which might make it necessary or desirable to do so. It would cost hundreds of dollars; he would have to pay threshing wages. Yet, since threshermen would not come into the district till the work in more densely settled parts was done, his crop would be safe.

He dropped his scoop, climbed out of the bin and down the ladder.

That moment Horanski entered the barn.

"Quick," Abe said. "I've done the feeding. Take Pride. Make the round south of the ditch. Four dollars a day. Let the Topp brothers and Hilmer bring a hayrack each. Start at six. Hurry up now."

Horanski was jumping. "Ya, ya. But what?"

"Never mind Hurry. We stack."

Abe had four ordinary wagons; only two of them were still fitted with hayracks; in threshing, boxes were needed. By almost superhuman exertion he managed to tilt the boxes of the other two to the ground and to replace them by flat racks lying near the shed. Having done so, he did not go to the house to light the fire in the kitchen but took Bay, Pride's sister, from her stall, threw a blanket over her back, and in a minute was galloping east to see Nicoll.

Nicoll, harvest being done and threshing far afield, came down in his night-wear when he heard Abe's frantic hammering. When Abe told him what he wanted, he was amazed. "Surely not. Nobody ever stacks here."

"Never mind what others do. Four dollars a day for man or boy. Six for a man with rack and team."

With that he was away. Similar scenes were enacted at Shilloe's, Hartley's, Nawosad's, Stanley's. Back to the farm in the grey of dawn.

Even now he did not go to the house for breakfast. He harnessed eight horses and hitched them to the racks in the yard. Daylight came, and with it the first helpers arrived.

Abe started them at once to gather sheaves, north of the yard. He drew a load of hay to the margin of the field and spread it on the ground. By half-past six the whole crew had arrived; eleven hayracks were gathering sheaves; Abe and Nicoll were stacking.

At seven, Charlie appeared beyond the fence. "Daddy, daddy!"

It was several minutes before Abe heard. "What is it?"

"Aren't you coming in for breakfast?"

"No. Bring me a cup of coffee and a slice of bread."

The day was white and hazy, a distant, rayless sun lighting the world. At noon, they changed horses rather than give those they had been using time to digest. At night they went on till it was dark. Only then did it strike Abe that this was the night of the council meeting at Somerville. He had never yet missed a meeting. "Can't be helped," he muttered, "I've got to save that crop."

Two stacks had been finished, thirty feet in diameter, twenty high: giant stacks thatched with hay. The third one, just begun, Abe covered with a tarpaulin, working by lantern light.

But it did not rain next day. Hilmer reported that he had seen threshing south of the Line. Surely all was going to be well; there was no need for this extra expense? He meant kindly, wishing to save Abe money even though part of it flowed into his own pocket.

Abe knew that not a man in his crew approved of what he was doing. They were glad to take his cash but thought him crazy to spend it.

At ten o'clock Wheeldon appeared in his rattling car. "What the hell——" he began.

Abe stared. They called Henry Topp the "runt"; this man was a pigmy.

"Who's ever heard of such a thing?" Wheeldon asked. "In a semi-arid country as this claims to be."

"Never mind," Slim Topp shouted. "Come on. Lend a hand."

"Be hanged if I do. What sort of wages are you fellows licking up?"

"I pay threshing wages," Abe said.

"I'm going south," Wheeldon boasted. "I'll bring a fellow back to thresh me at once."

"Nothing like trying."

Wheeldon returned in the afternoon.

"What luck?" Horanski asked from where he was pitching sheaves to the fifth great stack that was rising into the air.

"Every doggone fellow laughs at the idea of coming up here."

Abe heard what he said. "If you want a job——"

"By golly, I believe I do."

"To-morrow morning at six. Bring a rack."

The third day dawned grey and threatening. By eight o'clock Abe moved the scene of operations to a point west of the pasture. With the menace of a clouded sky overhead, the men worked feverishly, Horanski setting a frantic pace. In routine work nobody would have exerted himself; but this was so quixotic that work seemed sport or play.

That night, with a high wind from the east, slight drizzles began to sweep over the prairie like painters' brushes, continuing for more than a day. Then a dry sunny spell; but it did not turn warm. As soon as the stooks dried in the fields, everybody went south, east, west, to induce a thresherman to come, using Abe's huge crop for a bait. Threshing fees were running high; there were reports of heavier rains in the south. Nicoll reported several engines to be stuck on the roads. Victor Lafontaine tried to get through; in vain.

Once more Abe sent word around. Four and a half dollars a day! Already a few doubted the wisdom of working for wages. Yet, when the Topp brothers and even Wheeldon came —the latter saying, "By gosh, four and a half is too good to miss!"—Nicoll and the others threw their misgivings to the wind.

And things looked brighter again. Soon frost would come. In freezing weather the crops would be safe. But Abe stacked.

The scene of operations had shifted to the Hudson's Bay section when one afternoon a large, new car appeared on the trail west of the field. A tall man in city clothes alighted. He climbed the fence and came to the stack where Abe and Nicoll were working.

"Well, well, well!" said Mr. Rogers, for it was he; "you must be anticipating foul weather, Mr. Spalding."

"I am playing safe," Abe replied and slipped to the ground.

"What are you afraid of?"

"Nothing, nothing at all."

"Threshing is beginning to be general again."

"Some machines are stuck right now."

"They were in too much of a hurry after the rain. I can understand a man stacking if he farms in a small way. But you——"

There was a pause. Then Abe asked, "Any business you came for?"

"Why, yes. Let's step aside. You know Mr. Eastham's term as reeve expires in December. There is a certain deal pending. Some of us have been waiting for just what is going on. We want an honest man for the place. In fact, we want you."

"For reeve?"

"For reeve. Will you accept nomination?"

"I don't know." Municipal honours were far from Abe's mind just now.

"It won't take more of your time than you are already giving to the public business. You are the only man from a north ward who can swing the south wards as well."

"I wouldn't canvass."

"One of the assets which we are counting on. The position you take on that point is known. It will win us more votes than anything else. One joint meeting, adroitly managed. You say a few words——"

"I am not a speaker."

"Again, all the better."

"I'll think it over." Abe's eyes were on the horizon.

"I'd like to take your answer back."

"All right," Abe decided. "I'll run."

"Good!" And, picking up a sheaf, "There's weight in that. Well, so long. I see why you were absent from the last meeting.' . . .

On 25th September Abe finished stacking his crop. Next day it began to rain; and, with low welts of cloud driven over the prairie by dismal winds, ever shifting, it went on raining, with few let-ups, till 20th October. The ditches ran full; water began to stand in the fields.

This fall of 1912, when farmers throughout the south of the province could not thresh, is still being used to date certain events. "You remember." people will say, "that was the year before—or the year after—the fall when we could not thresh." The stooks stood in water. Everywhere people prayed for frost. Ordinarily an early freeze-up is undesirable; even if the crops escape, it interferes with ploughing; which means that work will be late next spring. But that year it rained and rained; and when the rains began, it turned warm again.

Abe might have exulted. Instead, he felt like a man who

has, without knowing it, crossed a lake covered with thin ice. The fact that he had been very near to losing the greatest crop he had ever raised drove home to him how much uncertainty there is even in the most fundamental industry of man. If he had not stacked!

Day after day, clad in a glistening slicker, he went into his drenched fields and, with the rain descending fitfully about him, reached into his stacks, extending a long arm, and made sure that no moisture was penetrating the sheaves. He had an old book on farming, printed in England, and re-read the chapters that treated of stacking. A good deal was said of the sweating of grain which improves its quality. He watched that process, rubbing a handful of grain from the ears, to look at the kernels and to compare them with the pictures in the book.

With nothing to do in field or yard, he took once more to going to town. The village was always crowded now; for everybody was, as to leisure, in the same position as Abe; what was the use of sitting at home and worrying? In town, they had at least company. Abe heard people describing what was happening to their crops: the grain sprouting in the stooks, the roots weaving the sheaves into a solid, cohering mass.

Of his own wheat Abe took handfuls to the elevators. Number One Northern. "Have you threshed?" the buyers asked. "I have stacked." And the buyers whistled through their teeth. Abe's crop became famous.

Threshermen sought him out. The general disaster hit them as hard as any one else. "Say, Abe," one would say; "Say, Spalding," others; a few went as far as, "Say, Mr. Spalding —have you made arrangements for threshing yet?" "No." And the men would underbid each other, coming down from sixteen cents a bushel which had been the peak to fifteen, twelve, ten cents. Abe listened; but suddenly, without giving an answer, he walked away. "Getting queer," some said. "His good luck's affecting his mind." A man who had spoken to him before drew him aside. "Abe, there's no chance of moving my outfit till after the freeze-up. But you've stacked. Good crop, they say. I wouldn't want this known. But I'll thresh you for six and a half." And when Abe made a motion to leave him, he detained him by a finger on his arm. "Abe, listen. I'll knock another quarter of a cent off." But Abe turned away, the thresherman staring after him. On forty thousand bushels a quarter of a cent meant a saving of a hundred dollars.

Mr. Diamond surpassed himself in smiles. "Some weather, Abe. But you can laugh. You were wise. How about a new fur coat for the winter?"

"We'll see."

"Want to buy this store, Abe?"—with a broad laugh.

Abe was restless; it seemed incredible that he should have escaped.

On 21st October, a grey, chilly day, but without rain at last, Abe saw Nicoll at his stable as he drove past. Anxious for company, he turned into the yard, cutting a deep, sharp rut into the ground which looked like the bottom of a freshly drained pool.

Nicoll came dejectedly and stood between the wheels of the buggy.

"How's your wheat?"

"Bad. Think the rain's over?"

"Hard to tell. I hope so."

"Not that it matters."

"Is it as bad as that?"

"It's as bad as can be."

"I'm sorry. Thought I'd ask. So long."

"So long, Abe."

From the culvert bridging the ditch Abe looked down on the slow, yellow flood which ran even with the banks. He had done it! Next year he would build. But never again would he allow himself to be caught without a threshing outfit of his own!

In town he met Eastham, the reeve.

"Hello, Spalding," the latter said. "Running against me?"

"I?" For in his preoccupation he had not thought of it again.

"So they say," the squarely built man with the big, red moustache said ironically and grimly.

"Come to think of it, they did ask me."

"When you ran for the council, you got in by the skin of your teeth."

"That's a fact," Abe said. "You know I don't do any campaigning. You'll have it all your own way. I won't stir a finger."

"Well-l-l" Mr. Eastham said and raised a hand to the edge of his expensive hat of soft grey felt. . . .

In the district, people were more excited over the fact that Abe had saved his crop than that they were losing theirs.

"What I'd like to know," said Henry Topp, "is how he could tell."

"He's a wise one," Hartley replied. "If he hadn't stacked, we'd have threshed, I bet."

"Nonsense!" Stanley exclaimed. "You'd have worked on a threshing crew while threshing lasted. But no outfit would have come in here. We're out of the way. He had the luck."

"He has the luck every time!" Henry said.

But it was left to Mrs. Grappentin to find the true solution of the problem: Abe was in league with the devil, or he would never have thought of stacking. And Hartley and Henry laughed enough to split their sides.

On 25th October it rained again; but the rain turned into snow, and it froze up. The crops, half ruined by sprouting, froze to the ground: the fields looked like skating rinks. Not one of the farmers threshed that fall; and when they did, next spring, the yield was low; the grade was "no grade"; the grain was sold for feed.

XI * SUCCESS

INCIDENTALLY, Abe was, that winter, elected reeve of the municipality, "by acclamation"; for his candidacy hotly contested for a while, remained unopposed at the last moment.

Rumours were afloat about a deal engineered by Mr. Eastham and his henchmen. At the meeting which Abe had missed, they had done a clever stroke. It had been moved that the council resolve itself into "committee of the whole." The difference between an ordinary meeting and a meeting in committee consisted in the fact that the deliberations of the council were public, whereas, in committee, the members could be pledged to secrecy. Rogers and Bickert had connived at this move.

The matter which was up for discussion was the application of a foreign railway for permission to extend its yards so as to permit their being linked with certain territories on which the railway wished to erect repair shops. The scheme was in the interests of the town of Somerville; and the town council had given a favourable decision; but a piece of road needed belonged to the municipality; and the site of the future shops was in private hands. The railway submitted two alternative plans. Both involved concessions from the municipality as well as the town; but which of two private holdings was to be acquired, depended on the previous decision of the municipality with regard to its roads. The council made its decision in committee. A few days later Rogers, who had seen through the scheme, found undeniable evidence of the fact that the farm which the railway would have to acquire had changed hands just before that meeting of the council in committee. Ostensibly, the buyer was a man unknown in the district; but Rogers suspected him to be a dummy. Shortly after, rumour insisted that an unheard-of price had been paid by the railway for the land. Rogers went on with his campaign for Spalding as though he knew nothing. But on the morning of nomination day he sprang a mine by dropping a casual hint of certain disclosures to be made shortly. The very vagueness of his threat, pronounced with the utmost urbanity, made the information on which it rested seem vastly more definite than it was; and he was careful not to make a positive statement which might betray how little he knew. Eastham was in town and showed a bold front; but at twelve o'clock, when nominations closed, a thrill went through the town : Mr. Eastham had declined renomination. Rogers boldly treated this as an admission of guilt and made his assertions specific. When, in the afternoon, friends of the reeve went to his house to plead with him about the necessity of a blunt denial, they were told that Eastham had gone to the city. Before the day was over, Rogers's guess that he had crossed the border was confirmed by a telegram addressed to Mrs. Eastham.

It was a week before Abe heard of his election, for he was threshing. When he did, it did not mean much to him : he was planning beyond his boldest dreams.

The threshing was done by Victor Lafontaine who brought his old steam engine and the huge separator over the snow from St. Cecile. No bundle wagons were needed. The separator was drawn between two stacks, and Nicoll and Horanski pitched sheaves while a dozen teams hauled the grain away. There were three granaries in Abe's yard, each holding seven thousand bushels. These were attended to by three teams; nine hauled directly to town. Even at that it was necessary at times to thresh on the ground. Huge sheets of tarpaulin were spread on the snow; the grain was shovelled into a pile and covered with other tarpaulins weighted down with whatever could be found in a country devoid of stones. If the indicator at the grain spout of the separator was correct, over seventeen thousand bushels of wheat were left in the fields. Twenty-one thousand bushels were waiting in the granaries; more than fourteen thousand had been sold outright, with the price of wheat rising sharply. Besides, there were barley and oats, vastly more than needed for feed and seed : these were stored in the loft of the barn.

Even Ruth gasped when she heard the figures from the children. She could not defend herself against a feeling of admiration for the man who had saved such a crop.

One night at last, coming home late and sitting down wearily at the table to have his belated supper, Abe said grimly, "That's that!"

"Finished?" Ruth asked.

"Finished," he replied.

He had recently bought a gasoline lamp which hung suspended above the table, shedding a cruel light on everything in the room. Abe felt this evening to mark an epoch in his life. He was awed by his own achievement. In the whole world there seemed nothing left for him to do.

He looked at Ruth who was waiting on him. For years they had lived side by side, speaking of nothing but the trivial matters of the day. They hardly knew whether they were in agreement on the fundamental questions of life. Were there such questions?

Abe had been dimly aware of changes going on about him. The years were piling up. He had given it no thought; it could not be helped. Slow work, the work of the farm! Every step took a year. But the last step had been taken. He could afford to look back.

Yes, there, in the door of the kitchen, stood Ruth. That was how she looked; not a sight to make a man's glance linger. Between her heavy bust and her wide, massive hips, the last trace of a waistline had vanished. In the short, wide face, the wrinkles furrowing cheeks and forehead showed a thickness of skin such as to preclude any delicacy in the mouldings which increasing years were bound to bring. Her expression betrayed a sense of disappointment with life.

Abe was aware of a wave of distaste flooding through him. This feeling he tried to hold down by sheer force. He averted his glance. He was afraid that anything he might say would widen the estrangement between them rather than bridge it; about her dress, for instance, with its heavy, cast-iron folds; or about the incomprehensibly unattractive, grey-brown cloth of which it was made; or about the way in which she tied her hair into a knot on top of her head.

And this room! Dingy and dismal. The inexorable light showed up its threadbare, worn-out fittings.

He pushed his cup back and, without looking up, said, "Well, all this is going to be changed at last!" It was meant as a consolation; as conveying a sense of his own shortcomings; he was sorry that he had left Ruth in such surroundings for so long. He had been an unconscionable time in fulfilling his promise. After all, she had had to live in the place; to him, it had been just a lair to go to at night.

Ruth sat down at the table. The silence was full of unexpected meanings. "Abe," she said, looking first down then straight at him. "I don't know——" And tears ran down her cheeks.

Uncomfortably he leaned back in his chair.

"This crop," Ruth went on; "it means a fortune. Why build?"

Abe gasped. "Why build? What else?"

"We have enough to live on. Move to town."

"Do you mean retire?"

"Perhaps."

"Do you know that I am not yet fifty?"

"Well——" Ruth moved a dish with nervous fingers. "I feel sixty."

Abe stared at her. She looked it, too. His fault? Partly. But he could not help himself. For years he had been careful not to touch on matters which might provoke a scene; he had done so for his own sake : in order not to be disturbed in his work and his plannings. All his energy had been claimed by the farm, summer and winter. In winter he had cleaned his seed three, four times; all his wheat had been hauled to town between fall and spring. No doubt, to be thus left alone had been hard for the woman.

"Abe," Ruth began once more, trying to be considerate. "You work and work and work. What for?"

Abe felt he had reached the limit of his endurance. Yet he kept his temper under control. "What does any one work for? We work because we must, I suppose. We are all going to die one day if that's what you mean. But before we die, we want to find some satisfaction. You ask me to give up when that satisfaction is within reach."

Ruth hesitated. The sacrifice she demanded was beyond the man's power to give. It was beyond her power to yield. Yet he was human; so was she. Was there no common ground between them? She made a last attempt. "Look what this life has made of me. When I am to talk to any one but the children, I am nervous. Rather than go to town and show myself, I stay at home, day in day out, year in and year out."

Abe had risen. He felt shaken. He pitied the woman. Yet, was it his fault? A vague gesture preceded speech. "Isn't that just where you are wrong? You should force yourself. Here's a whole district, but nobody comes to see us. Why not? Because you don't go to see anybody. They think you consider yourself better than they are. They say we're stuck-up. I've got to mix with the men whether I want to or not. But are they wrong? I have wider ambitions and bolder aims than they. If you and

Mary don't pull together, there are other women. Make friends. For God's sake try!"

"This life has taken the desire away."

"This life! Do you realize that it's the freest, most independent life on earth? Your part in it is your own making. I—" And he shook his head in utter disgust—"I can't live in town. Years ago you bore me a grudge because you had to live in this patched-up shack. I want to raze it and give you a real house. If I've left you to live here, I've done so in order not to put up another makeshift. It would have been waste of money. Sooner or later I was going to be in a position to do things right. I am in that position now."

Ruth rose as if to break off. "Build if you must."

But now he would not accept that verdict. "You act as if it were my fault that things are as they are. You act as if I were to blame because you've got stout. You make your whole life a silent reproach to me. I can only say there are other stout women. They can't help it. But they try at least to remain a little attractive. I've never grudged you money; not when I was hardest up. Every year I've given you a few hundred dollars. I've promised not to ask you how you spend it. But I will ask. Have you spent it? Have you spent any of it?

"No."

"Why not? That's what money is for. To be spent."

"What should I spend money on myself for? Living as I do."

"There you go. Turning around in a circle like a dog chasing his tail. For my sake.—For the sake of the children."

"Perhaps the children will thank me one day that there are a few pennies left when they're needed."

Abe threw up his hands. "Let me look after that. I'll double what I've been giving you. I'll treble it. I'll write you a cheque for a thousand dollars to-night. But spend it! Spend at least part of it."

"I will," she challenged, "if you build."

Abe stood as if struck speechless. "If I build! I'll build. Of that you may be sure. I'd rather build with your co-operation than otherwise. But build I shall. What else should I do? Go to town? Open up a butchershop? Lick my fingers for other people's dirty cash?" And, slamming the door behind him, he went to pace the frozen, snow-covered ground.

Shortly after the new year Abe left the farm to go to the city. Horanski was in charge; a crew had been hired to haul the grain. In thirteen years this was the first time that he had gone away. He had offered to take Ruth and the children. Ruth had declined.

When he returned towards the end of the month, he gave orders that every sleigh going to town with wheat was to bring home a load of red brick which was piled along the railway track. He put Horanski to work cleaning the seed. He himself was rarely at home. Many people asked for a job, from town and from south of the Line. He investigated their circumstances and gave work or denied it according to the urgency of the case. People learned to depend on him.

He spent long hours at Somerville, in conference with Duncan and Ferris, implement dealers. A contractor from the city came to measure the ground between the old house and the wind-break in front where the brick was being piled. Other supplies were brought out: rolls upon rolls of ornamental fence-wire; hardwood for floors, to be stored in the granaries as they were being emptied; windows and doors; cement for foundations and sills; parts of some complicated machinery to be assembled on the farm; coils upon coils of insulated copper wire; building paper; bundles of lath and green-stained shingles; shiplap and scantling; no end of things; the district buzzed with their list.

Abe was secretive; he had plans and papers; ground plans and elevations; he showed them to no one.

"Well, Abe," Nicoll said, "I suppose you'll do this thing as you do everything, on the large scale, won't you?"

"Large enough for my family, if that's what you mean."

"Spalding Hall?"

Abe made neither answer nor motion.

"What's all that machinery?"

"Motor and dynamo."

"Electric light for the house?"

"Light and power."

Nicoll nodded. "I see. I see.' . . .

"You would think," said Mrs. Grappentin, "he's building a village."

"He gives bread to the district," Hilmer replied. "Wenn die Koenige baun, haben die Kaerrner zu tun.—When kings build, the teamsters find work, Mrs. Mother." . . .

Every load that went to Abe's place was watched and discussed; and not only in the district, in town as well. Day after day load after load went out, throughout February and March.

Mr. Diamond was enthusiastic. "That's the way, Abe. I've always believed in you. Show them how to farm." . . .

The brick had been hauled; and still there was wheat. To the amazement of his men Abe gave orders to bring lumber now. He did not explain; but carload after carload of lumber was shunted on to the siding at Morley—huge timbers such as are used for frame and flooring of barns. These he piled at the north end of the yard, in front of the granaries.

The thaws came, and the flood appeared. It ran out, and everywhere farmers began to thresh. Abe fretted; he could not get help. He had to be satisfied with a small acreage of wheat. By the time Henry Topp came to operate the tractor it was too late to seed anything but barley.

Then, in the beginning of June, a string of bunk wagons came from town, drawn by Abe's horses: little houses on wheels, one of them fitted as a cook-house. Other things followed: an excavating machine with a steam engine; a concrete mixer; many things. All were put just inside the wind-break: a regular village with all sorts of shops.

Abe had to be everywhere: in the field where the spring work was still going on: in the yard where the exact location of the great house depended on his say-so. It was more than he could do. Often the foreman directing the work came out to the field; or he waited for Abe late at night to discuss this or that. The crew, forty-odd men, consisted almost entirely of "foreigners"—men willing to work, pleasant, obliging; but rough and wild-looking not a few of them were.

And the children had to be kept within bounds; there was danger among the machines where chains dangled and derricks swung while horses struggled with their loads of wet earth to be dumped on the trail past Horanski's. Would that trail be mud, mud for ever after?

Yet when Abe, years hence, looked back on this summer of 1913, it seemed as if never in his life had he been happier than at that time. When the foreman asked a question, on Abe's answer depended something akin to creation: for decades or centuries that spot of his yard would present itself to the world as he willed it.

Then, excavations being finished on the sites of both house and barn, the scene cleared itself up; and concrete was poured into moulds. This was the most important part of the work: there must be no water in cellar, engine room, and manure pit. Pitch was enclosed between two layers of concrete to make the foundations waterproof.

Whenever Abe went to look at anything, the children came running; for holidays began and they were at home. Without him, they were not allowed to cross a certain line where he had stretched a rope. Jim was rapidly outgrowing Charlie; the latter putting all growth into mental and nervous development; Jim, into muscle and sinew. The girls, Marion and Frances, offered a similar contrast; Marion was tall, yet otherwise she resembled Charlie; Frances was short but resembled Jim in disposition. Both girls were exceptionally pretty in their individual ways.

On the building site, Charlie, now twelve years old, showed by his questions that he was trying to visualize the building as a whole; and Abe showed him the elevations. Jim, less than a year his junior, was curious to see how the concrete mixer worked, how mortar was made, how it hardened between the bricks. The girls looked on.

New excavations began; trenches were dug across the yard, from the house and both barns; just east of the pool they united. In these, pipes were sunk below the frost-line, for the water supply. Before the floors were laid, all sorts of machines were set up in the basement: pumps, to be operated by electricity, a washing machine with a rotary drier; the furnace was installed, and sheet iron coal-bins fitted in.

"How could you think of all that, daddy?" Jim asked.

Abe felt flattered; but he destroyed the child's belief in his omniscience. "I've employed an architect to write the specifications. He's responsible for it all."

"Does he get paid for that?"

"Of course. I paid him six hundred dollars for the plans."

Jim whistled.

Ruth betrayed no interest. Yet, with the warmer weather, she changed for the first time in years to light-coloured clothing. Not all of her new things were to Abe's taste; nor did they all fit well; but she had made an attempt, and he gave her credit for it. He went further. One day he returned from Somerville with a parasol of pearl-grey silk; she stared as she thanked him; the thought of the money it had cost appalled her; yet he had thought of her while in town. He promptly bought her a fur coat, of grey Siberian squirrel.

Haying began. The work in the field became frantic.

Meanwhile the walls of the house went up. The crew that had been pouring concrete moved to the barn. Electricians wired house and farm buildings: horse-barn, granaries, pigpens, and the large hen-house the front wall of which was replaced by canvas. Two poles were erected in the yard; and power wires slung overhead. Four huge incandescent bulbs were suspended there: even the yard was to be lighted.

"Spalding," said Hartley, "is wiring his hen-house."

"What?" Wheeldon asked. "Chickens going to lay by electricity?"

"Exactly," Nicoll replied. "If you want to get eggs in winter, you've got to give the hens as much light as in summer."

"I'd put a lantern behind the roost," Wheeldon said.

And the crowd at Nicoll's corner laughed an Homeric laugh —only Nicoll looked worried.

It became known that Abe had spent a week at the Agricultural College near the city, a new institution in course of construction.

"College farming!" said Wheeldon.

And Hartley added, "If I'd enough money to build a pig-pen like what I hear they've got there. I'd live in it myself."

"I believe you," Nicoll parried.

Yet Abe was anxious. Once more he had started a vast machinery going which he had controlled at the outset but which had begun to control him instead. The cost of the building had been fixed at fifteen thousand dollars; but point after point came up for reconsideration. This or that, the foreman said, could be done at the original figure; but . . . And Abe invariably decided for the better way which involved increased expense. Whenever that was done, the foreman made him sign an order authorizing the alteration in the plan. What would the total be when all was finished? Abe knew only that the total was growing, growing.

The roof was raised. More machinery arrived in town. This was for the new barn: hay-slings, elevators to raise the grain into bins; grain crushers; pumps for the milking room; cooling vats for the cream; a huge cream separator to be driven by electricity. The district marvelled.

But more than anything else was one piece of machinery discussed, with long, flexible tubes that ended in rubber cups. Many a guess was made as to its purpose before any one dared to ask Abe. Nicoll ventured the question at last and was himself dumbfounded at the answer.

"That's a milking machine."

The district roared with laughter.

At last, when Abe was cutting his crop, the dynamo was set up in a roofed-over pit behind the house. Four huge cement blocks were cast for it to rest on; four more to carry the gasoline engine that was to drive it; these were set to a depth of six feet below the floor of the pit in which holes had been left when it was laid. Nowhere did the concrete of the floor which was continuous with that of the basement touch the cement of these blocks; the interstices between them and the floor were filled with pitch. This was done to prevent any vibration from reaching the house. All this interested Jim more than anything else; he obtained permission to stay with the electricians.

Ruth was impatient for the work to be finished. The tall new structure took away the light from the old house. In fact, when the wiring system was to be tried out, even she was quite excited.

To the last, the electricians worked in the old barn where the wiring had given most trouble. All lights were to have a mysterious triple control: from a master switchboard in the dining-room of the house; from a smaller switchboard in each of the buildings; and from each individual light the turning on of which started the engine.

At last the day for the trial had come. It was half-past ten at night when the chief electrician announced that he was ready. There were two small lights on the gate-posts fronting the road, with individual switches under hoods of japanned tin. The system was to be tested by turning one of these guide-lights on—their bulbs were frosted, so as not to blind the nocturnal traveller seeking entrance.

The children had been allowed to remain awake for the occasion. Who could have slept? The men working in the field had scouted the idea of going home. They were assembled west of the low roof of the pit; that roof was provided with a skylight which was open.

There they stood, breathless with excitement. The engineer blew a whistle as a signal that he was going to switch the gate-lights on; and as he did so, the underground cavern burst forth in a blaze of light. They heard nothing—which was disappointing; and, blinded, they saw nothing either.

Then Jim exclaimed, "Look, look, she's running!"

"Is she?"—from a dozen mouths, incredulously.

But Jim pointed to the dynamo. "See the sparks? At the brushes."

"By golly!" someone said.

The wheels ran so true that their roatation was imperceptible. Jim skipped to the far side of the pit where the exhaust pierced the low wall. "Here you can hear it!" And everybody followed him with a rush.

Across the pitch-dark yard the electrician came to the house and went up the rear steps to what was going to be the kitchen. "I'll turn the whole system on," he said, vanishing into the building.

Everybody ran to the gate in the ornamental fence dividing house-yard from farm-yard. A second later every window in house, barns, granaries, pig-pens, and hen-house blazed forth as in the streets of a city; even the lights overhead came on, flooding the yard as with daylight. Mysteriously, all about, the leaves of the wind-break rustled in the reflection of the glow.

"Hip, hip . . ." cried a voice.

And all present broke into a cheer, the children most unreservedly.

"Well," said Ruth, herself half aglow, "and now to bed."

But they ran to hide behind the grown-ups, giving vent to their protest by a long-drawn-out "O-oh no-oh!"

Ruth smiled and yielded when Abe said, "Let them sleep to-morrow. I'll give them a holiday." For school had started again.

The test was not finished. The electrician made the round with Abe, to turn on every light separately and to show him how the switches controlled the machinery in house and barns. This electrician, whose time was valuable, intended to leave on the morrow, delagating what was left to be done to subordinates.

One by one the men working in the field drifted away; it was past midnight; even the children grew sleepy, and Ruth took them to the old house. There was nothing spectacular any longer.

And the days went by; once more the crews changed; and only the cook remained through it all, a round-faced, pleasant little Chinaman. The new barn was painted; and when the new red did not harmonize with the darkened tint of the old barn, the latter was repainted, too. In the house, plastering was done; woodwork was stained; floors waxed.

Every night all lights were turned on, much to the surprise, no doubt, of horses, cows, pigs, and chickens; and the children verified the fact that the hens did not go to their roosts but went on scratching in the litter of straw on the floor.

One evening Abe found a pretext to go to town after dark; and when the children exclaimed, "Oh, daddy! You just want to see the place from the road!" he grew almost angry because they had so accurately guessed his design. But when he gave orders that the lights were not to be turned off, and they crowed over him, he could not help laughing himself, thereby admitting that they had been right.

He went in the buggy; and he never looked back till he had reached town. From the Somerville Line he peered through the night at the pool of light on the horizon. It did not loom high but seemed rather to form a dent in the sky-line. That was the proudest moment of his life; and he raised an arm as though reaching for the stars.

This lighting system had not formed part of the original plan; but dreams have a way of realizing their potential growth. The best thing a man can say of himself is that he has grown with the growth of his dreams.

Work in the house was not finished before the freeze-up. The year had been dry; the crop was fair but no more; and Abe's acreage had been small. He knew that he had exceeded all his estimates. If he wanted to furnish the house that winter, he would have to borrow. "If he wanted?" Not a piece of old furniture was going into that house, no matter what the cost. By and by he would draw the old, patched-up place into the field beyond Horanski's, for a second hired man.

"Never again!" he had said last year when he stacked his crop; and the purchase of a grain separator had formed part and parcel of his plans; but as fall had come, he had made arrangements with Victor Lafontaine of St. Cecile. There was no money left for machinery.

It froze up early, with no snow covering the ground; and Abe could not haul his wheat to town. So, in November, he went to Somerville to make provision at the bank for credit and then took the train to the city in order to buy the furniture for the house. When he returned, he had spent an additional three thousand dollars.

They moved in in December. The old shack stood deserted behind the mansion, a bit of an eyesore for Abe whenever he looked at his place from anywhere but the road.

Again he urged Ruth to get help for the house, but she declined. "Well," Abe said, "I've given you every labour-saving device known: electric washer and drier, dish-washing machine, vacuum-cleaner, septic tanks, bathroom, hardwood floors, and so on. You'll have to make out, then, as best you can."

XII * THE BRIDGE

ONCE more a year had gone by. On Abe's place, hens laid eggs in winter; cows were milked by a machine. In the west half of the new barn water was supplied to the animals by turning a single tap which caused twenty drinking pails to fill. Manure was rinsed away by a powerful jet of water and, in well-arranged drains, run into a concrete pit where it was rotted by fermentation and, therefore, never froze. The other half of the barn, accessible from stable or yard, held tractor and implements, milk-room and workshops.

Even in the old barn things were changed. Feed grain was elevated directly from the tanks into huge hopper bins whence the mixture was fed into a crusher and thence to the feed chutes. Water was pumped by a force-pump into an overhead tank.

At the house, there was a bathroom with a large tub and taps of hot and cold water. Every bedroom—there were six, one for each member of the household—had a white-tiled wash-basin set into the wall, it, too, with running water, hot and cold. Nobody needed to clean or light lamps; a switch was turned instead. The engine was fed with liquid fuel from an outside tank. A huge furnace for which Abe bought anthracite by the carload needed to be looked after only twice a day.

Labour-saving devices galore; and they did save labour; but did they save time? There was less hard work; there were more errands to run; there was more fixing to do: annoying little jobs which, though he did not admit it, made Abe very impatient. Occasionally he had to send for a mechanic. There was less labour; but there was more ill temper.

The milking took less time; but when Horanski, who still proved skilful and adaptable, had finished with the cows, his wife had to clean and scald no end of tubes and bowls.

Perhaps Abe had, in 1913, not given quite as much thought and energy to the field work as he might have done. Perhaps the fertility of the soil was beginning to show the effects of many croppings. The yield, that fall, had been disappointing: less than fifteen bushels per acre; the fallow had not been extensive enough; there had been little fall-ploughing. In 1914, spring was late; Abe owed money; more than he had ever owed before. His credit was unquestioned; he could borrow when he pleased; but it was imperative that he seed a large acreage, larger than could be properly prepared. In desperation he did what he had never done yet; he seeded stubble, merely disking four hundred acres cropped the year before.

1913 had been dry. According to the weather-lore of the old-timers two more dry years were due. But 1914 denied their doctrine; there was plenty of rain. Abe was favoured by his usual luck. Had there been a drought as in 1913, his stubble seeding would have been a total loss; it had been a total loss for the Topp brothers and others when, after the disaster of 1912, they had threshed in spring and neglected their land.

For the first time, the district seemed actually retarded in its progress by the opportunity which Abe offered the settlers of making good wages. Nicoll and Stanley, it was true, forged slowly ahead; even Wheeldon did well. But Nawosad, Hilmer, Shilloe, and the Topps were always working for Abe instead of attending to their own farms. How Hartley held out was a mystery. He peddled groceries and patent medicines; but who could make a living by such means?

In the fall of the year, war had come in Europe. As for the district, another quarter section, west of Hartley's, had been filed on by a young man by the name of McCrae; but he promptly enlisted. An example thus being set, further enlistments followed. First Dave Topp went, then Bill Stanley, glad, people said, to get away from home where it was now praying and Bible-reading from morning till night; and finally Tom Nicoll and Slim Topp left together. Henry Topp, too, volunteered; but, being below the minimum height, he was rejected. All which meant that Abe was suddenly deprived of half his help.

Nobody thought as yet that the war was going to have far-reaching consequences for the settlement; but it upset many plans.

Every Saturday that summer, Abe had taken Charlie along when he went to town or when he worked in the field. There, he had as usual ridden a sulky plough drawn by his great Percheron team in which by that time Jim and Beaut had been replaced by two colts of the mare.

Having the boy between his knees, Abe allowed him to hold the lines and to turn at the end of a furrow; it was time to initiate him into the work of the farm. He would soon finish his eighth grade at school.

When, after the outbreak of the war, Abe saw himself deprived of his local supply of labour, he began to dream of the time when his boys would be able to assist in the field. In the fall, having somehow managed to do his harvesting with what help was still available in the district, he went finally far afield, before threshing started, to find additional hands. He took Bill Crane back who was glad to come, for his family had multiplied; and a man he had occasionally employed before, Harry Stobarn, from east of Morley. These two "bached it" in the old, patched-up house. But still he was short of help; the more so since his crop was widely scattered over his land.

When at last the fields east of the pasture had been cleaned up, the lay-out of the remaining areas was as follows. The threshing machine occupied the centre of the north-west quarter of the Hudson's Bay section, a mile and a quarter from the east-west road to Nicoll's Corner. There, the work had been proceeding for a day or two. Two trails led south, worn into the soil of stubble and fallow by many haulings. One of them angled south-west and crossed the line of the farm near its corner; thence it followed the fence, on the wild land, till it reached the east-west road. This trail was used by the teams going directly to town, of which there were six. The second trail angled to the south-east, to a gate in the fence enclosing the pasture; leading out again on the far side and, through the east field, into the yard north of the house. This second trail was used by the teams hauling to the granaries.

Even though Abe sent part of his wheat to town, more than half of it had to be stored on his place. The four-horse teams working here were hitched to huge grain tanks; and often it was necessary to fasten a wagon behind, triple-boxed, such as the teamsters used who went to town.

It was the last day of September, about ten o'clock. Abe's tank stood under the spout. Horanski had taken the last but one load; Nicoll, the last; and both had been double loads. Relief was expected; the first teams that had gone to town must soon be back, anxiously waited for; it was no easy task for even four horses to draw a tank holding a hundred bushels and a wagon-load of sixty over a distance of a mile and a half; nor for the men to empty them at the granary and to get back to the field before the engine blew its warning whistle.

Yet, while a tank was being filled, there was time to rest; and Abe had always enjoyed these intervals of leisure. The engine was humming its harvest song, fed with straw by a swarthy young Frenchman; and two more of Victor Lafontaine's sons were pitching sheaves from their bundle wagons to the feeding platform of the vibrating and shaking separator. The air was filled with chaff and dust which gave a bronzed colour to the sunlight as it filtered to the ground. All the men were grey with that dust; the chaff stuck in their hair and eyebrows.

The engine was placed at right angles to what wind there was, to lessen the danger of sparks being blown into the ever-growing strawstack. The breeze being from the north, Abe could not see the trails. Throughout the field, bundle wagons were scattered among the stooks.

Victor, small, mouse-eyed, sixty years old, kept crawling and climbing about, under and over his antediluvian engine, oil-can in hand. Abe was fond of the man who, year after year, substituted sons of his own for one or two of his hired helpers.

At the feeding platform, two empty wagons were being replaced by fresh ones. Abe was leaning against a front wheel of his tank; but, seeing that the wheat had reached the height of the spout, he lifted himself on the hub of the wheel and shovelled the grain to the rear.

At that moment he became aware of a slight commotion. The drivers on their loads ceased work and looked to the south; and so did Victor Lafontaine who stood poised on the boiler of the engine.

Suddenly Victor exclaimed, "Oh, oh, oh!" disapprovingly.

Abe dropped to the ground and circled the engine.

Harry Stobarn was returning from town with an empty wagon. Apparently something had gone wrong in the harness; for he had jumped to·the ground and run to the head of the horses where he was cruelly tearing at their bridles. The horses reared, trying to back away. He jumped aside and aimed a vicious kick at the flank of one of the Clydes. The horse, beside himself, plunged and, carrying his mate away, was off at a gallop. Stobarn, shouting and waving his arms, started in pursuit. All this at a distance of half a mile.

Abe and such of the Frenchmen as were near ran to head the horses off. Abe was the first to reach them. As soon as he laid hold of their bridles, they stopped, breathing heavily.

Harry came running, the picture of spitting fury. "The doggone——" he shouted, on the point of having another go at the horses.

But Abe stepped in. "Get off my place!" he said sharply.

"What?" shouted Harry. "Gimme my wages, you bully; then I'll go."

"Get off my place," Abe repeated. Insult made him quiet. "You'll find the cheque in your mail to-morrow. I don't carry cash about in the field." He turned back to the horses, stroking their noses.

Harry looked from one to the other; but the young Frenchmen took their cue from Victor who gave no encouragement. Pushing his hat back from a beady brow, Stobarn said, "Don't ask me to work for you again."

"Small chance."

Harry turned away, performing antics to cover his retreat.

The French lads ran; and Abe took the horses to the engine and left them; they were willing enough to stand.

Meanwhile the separator had run idle; but the work was resumed as though nothing had happened. Horanski was returning from the yard with his empty tank. When Abe's load was full, he swung the spout over to Harry's empty wagon.

Horanski drove into place behind. Abe fastened the triple box which Stobarn would have taken to his tank and drove away. He had seemed quiet enough; but only now did he master his anger. Too bad! They had just been able to keep pace with the machine; now they would have to thresh on the ground—an undesirable proceeding in open weather. Part of the grain was sure to spoil.

As he neared the first gate of the pasture, Nicoll came from the yard. Leaving their gates open, they passed each other in silence.

When Abe had unloaded by shovelling the grain back into the hopper whence the elevator raised it to the trap in the roof of the granary, he entered the east half of the new barn to fetch a tarpaulin to take to the field. Movable granaries of corrugated iron, that was what he needed. Well, another year. . . . But when he had left the yard and was crossing the pasture, a new thought struck him. Charlie had driven horses; most settlers allowed even smaller and younger boys to take loads to town. At the worst, it was a matter of two loads for the day. It was Saturday; the boy was at home. If he gave him the old team, the greys which Hilmer was driving, surely the boy could manage?

Horanski was coming to meet him; another load was going out to the west; that must be Henry or Shilloe; a third team was coming empty from town. Abe stopped. "Go to the house," he said to the Ukrainian. "Tell Charlie I want him. Let him have lunch and come along with you."

"All right," Horanski replied and drove on.

At the engine, Nicoll was filling his second load. Abe did not drive into place behind him; town teams had the precedence. Nicoll went on, and Himmler took his place. Abe told him to change horses, giving him the team which Stobarn had driven. "You go straight back," he said, handing him fifty cents. "Get a bite in town and feed at the livery stable." Hilmer's team he led to a rack full of fresh hay, brought out for the bundle teams. A dozen boxes were standing on the ground; he poured a measure of oats into two of them.

Hilmer pulling out, Abe filled Stobarn's wagon before he drove his own tank into place. But he had hardly done so when Bill Crane arrived; and so he let him take Stobarn's wagon, giving him the same directions which he had given Hilmer. Crane's wagon he manoeuvred alongside his tank and filled it over the top of the latter. Horanski was approaching on the trail from the yard; and while Abe was waiting for him, he dispatched the first empty bundle wagon to the Ukrainian's house where Mrs. Horanski, aided by one of the Nicoll girls, had prepared dinner for the crew. The noon intermission was at hand.

Horanski came; another team from town was in sight. Abe made room under the spout by driving ahead.

"Here, Charlie," he said, for the boy had climbed to the ground. "I want you to take a load to town. Can you do it?"

"Sure, daddy."

"All right. There it is. Climb up." And he helped him. "Had your dinner? To elevator one; the first from the crossing. Listen here. While you have the load, you walk the horses. When you drive up the incline, hold your lines tight. On the platform, let the man do the work. On the way home, you can trot half the way."

The boy nodded and clicked his tongue.

Victor Lafontaine had been watching father and son. As Abe turned back to his load, the Frenchman caught his eye and smiled. "Nice kid," he said.

Abe looked at his watch. "Fill Horanski's tank. Then dinner." And he, too, drove on, separated from Charlie only by a narrow strip; for half a mile the trails hardly diverged. Abe met the hayrack bringing the dinner for the crew. Mrs. Horanski stood, precariously balanced, among baskets of food and boilers of coffee. As she passed him, she nodded with a smile at Charlie who laughed proudly back at her.

Then, just as father and son reached the point where their trails divided sharply, the whistle of the engine blew, giving the signal to stop work. The shrill sound made Charlie jump; and smilingly he looked back at his father, waving his hand; then he disappeared from sight.

Two hours went by. Abe had had his lunch at home and was back in the field filling his tank.

Wheat, wheat, wheat ran from the spout.

Then, just as in the morning, Victor and his lads stared south.

Abe looked up at the old man's face which he saw in three-quarter profile. He was conscious only of the sunlight playing in the snow-white bristles of the stubble of his beard. Incomprehensibly, a wave of fear invaded him, aroused by the puzzled expression on the man's face.

Again, as in the morning, Abe dropped to the ground and circled the engine.

On the trail from the yard a dust cloud was trailing along. It took Abe a second or so to make out, at the apex of the fan-shaped cloud, a man on horseback tearing along at a terrific speed. He was riding a draught-horse, which fact was betrayed by the lumbering though furious gallop. He had just crossed the pasture.

"He leapt the gate," Victor said from behind Abe's back.

Abe did not answer. Who could it be? Whence did he come? A dull and ever-increasing disquietude took hold of him.

Suddenly he recognized the rider. It was Bill Crane. He should have been back by this time. The horse he was riding was clearly doing its utmost; yet Bill was wildly lashing it with a long line.

Everybody in the whole field was aware of the rider's approach; all work had slowed down.

Then, at a distance of a quarter of a mile, the horse stumbled in full career and fell, throwing the rider who rolled over two or three times, to leap up and to fall again, fighting for breath and reeling.

Abe veered on Lafontaine. "For God's sake, shut that engine off!"

Victor jumped; the hum subsided into silence.

Bill had stopped, struggling for his voice. "Charlie!" he yelled. "Charlie's got hurt."

Abe's knees gave under him. "Where? How?" he shouted.

"Hilmer's bridge. Load went over him!" Bill was still staggering forward; apparently he had been hurt by his fall.

"Hurt?" Abe asked as if groping for a clue.

"Load went right over him."

For a moment it looked as if Abe were going to ask more questions. Then he turned and ran for the lead team of his grain tank. Feverishly he unhooked one of the horses, a Percheron colt, and, gathering the long line into loops, vaulted on his back. Lashing the heavy horse into a gallop, he shot past the engine out on the trail. Everywhere the bundle drivers were unhooking their horses. Abe's mind was singularly lucid. He noticed a number of things which, in the light of the tragedy with which he seemed to be threatened only so far, as though it might still be averted by speed, were mere trifles. Thus Bill lay motionless on the ground; the horse, a Clyde, was breathing but foundered. "That horse," Abe said to himself, "will never get up again." From the south-west, two teams were returning. . . . Precious time would be lost in the yard; for the colt he was riding could not stand the pace. With his eyes, Abe searched for the gate of the pasture; the trail was winding; he wanted to strike a straight line.

Nicoll and Horanski were in the pasture. What in the world were they doing? Then he understood. Bill had shouted to them in passing; they were catching Old Sire for him. Old Sire was an ancient racehorse, a hard and fast rider, recently acquired for a debt which Blake had owed him, an old loafer at Morley who attended all municipal race-meets.

Now they had him; and Nicoll was running for the gate to open it. Abe neither veered nor stopped. The moment he passed through the gate, he vaulted off the colt and ran on with the gathered momentum. In half a dozen bounds he reached Old Sire, the bony iron-grey, and was on his back. Horanski, with a swing of his arm, threw the halter-shank aloft; and, the horse already gripping the ground, the line hit Abe across his face like a whip. In less than a minute the horse doubled his speed. Never before had Abe asked a horse to give him the very last of his strength; but Old Sire caught the infection as though memories of the race-track had returned to him. The far gate of the pasture was open; but Abe held the horse at right angles to the fence which he took at a leap.

Straight on, over barley stubble, till they reached Abe's east line. Again Old Sire took the fence; and they were on the prairie. In five minutes they made Nicoll's Corner. Then south over the culvert.

Everything seemed quiet and peaceful. The sun seemed to stand still over the plain, his heatless rays bronzed even here. Chaff and dust from many threshing fields had spread over all this world.

Ahead, at Hilmer's Corner, there was a congestion. North of the bridge stood a wagon or two; between the road and Hilmer's yard half a dozen horses were grazing. From the yard, an old woman stared dully at the man who came tearing along. Beyond, one wagon on the bridge; three, four farther on. To the west, a car in the ditch.

A moment later, Abe saw it all. Pole and neck-yoke of the wagon on the bridge were trailing; the horses had been unhitched. Beyond, Bill's empty wagon barred the road. The load north of the bridge was Nawosad's; and as Abe vaulted to the ground, the Ukrainian stepped aside. Abe ran past him.

On the culvert, a group of men were crouching or kneeling to the right of the wagon. The first was Anderson; on the far side was Hilmer, looking strangely stern. Between them, Dr. Vanbruik, on his knees, bending over the motionless body of Abe's child which lay between the wheels, for it had not been moved. Below the bare ribs of the chest was a horrible depression, discoloured; even the doctor averted his eyes as he applied the stethoscope.

Abe felt, saw, heard nothing. Yet he asked a question.

Without looking up, Dr. Vanbruik shrugged a shoulder.

Mechanically Abe repeated his question. "Dead, you say?" The doctor gave him a brief, direct look and bent down again.

Abe, feeling the ground giving way beneath him, walked blindly on to the end of the culvert, staggered through the ditch, took a few steps over the open prairie, and fell forward on his face. . . .

An hour later, Charlie's body was taken home in Bill's wagon. The lads from the field who had arrived followed on horseback. The load which the boy was to have taken to town was pushed to the side of the road. At a word from the doctor, Anderson had returned to town to fetch Mrs. Vanbruik. At Nicoll's Corner his car caught up with the procession and passed it in silence.

In the yard, they were met by Ruth, Mary Vanbruik, and the three children. The girls were crying; Jim stood pale and silent, awed by the fact that never again would he tease Charlie, nor Charlie him.

Ruth did not cry; but her face was tragically set and hollow when Anderson carried the body past her, up the steps, through the hall, and into the great living-room of the house where he placed it on the chesterfield. Nobody was in a condition to say anything. Nobody even asked how the thing had happened till many days later.

In the field, Nicoll took charge. Abe sat about as though his mind were affected. Dr. Vanbruik went to Somerville to attend to the formalities. Old Mrs. Crane was sent for to lay the body out.

Mary Vanbruik stayed with Ruth. All neighbours who had not already been working for Abe came to help, even Wheeldon; and it was from the threshing field that the doctor finally pieced the story together.

Charlie and Bill had been approaching Hilmer's culvert at the same time, Charlie from the north, Bill from the south, with Bill a trifle nearer to it than Charlie. But the culvert could be crossed by only one wagon at a time; and the boy, seeing that Bill, with his empty wagon had the advantage over him, had, half in jest, urged his horses into a brisker pace, swinging the loose ends of their lines over their backs. Bill, wishing to let the boy win the race, had held his horses in. But at both ends of the culvert the many haulings had worn away the earth; so that a vehicle going at any speed was bound to hit the timbers of the bridge with a jolt; and the horses, knowing that, with the boy urging them on, had taken the incline at a bound. When the jolt came, the child had been thrown up into the air; and, the wagon below him being retarded, he had lost his seat and fallen between horses and wagon. Bill, from the far end of the culvert, had been yelling frantically, "Whoa, whoa, there!" And the horses, knowing his voice and seeing him blocking the road, had stopped; but not till the front wheels had passed over Charlie's body, just below the ribs.

Death, Dr. Vanbruik said when he had been called by Hilmer, had been instantaneous ⋏

*

PART II

* *

THE DISTRICT

*

THE years went by.

Abe had been stunned; but it did not show in his work. It was true that he pursued it in a grim and cheerless way, unaffected by the things stirring every one else to his depths : the events of the war.

For a while he had been inclined to do as Ruth had wished him to do : to give everything up and to go away; it was Ruth who had kept him from following the impulse. Then he had voiced an intention of withdrawing at least from his public duties; that step, Dr. Vanbruik had dissuaded him from taking. At last, as if driven by a force which lashed him on, he had resumed his work at a pace which appalled his neighbours. He had bought a threshing machine and added more labour to the load he was carrying already; but he had soon found that the thresherman's trade and the farmer's business were incompatible. While he threshed others' crops, his own fall-ploughing remained undone; in spring, the work was gone through in a rush; nothing was done as it should have been done. In the third year of the war, he showed a return of his old shrewdness by selling his outfit at peak price and realizing a profit.

Incidentally he had begun to read. One of the things which make up the fundamental web of life—that background of life which no so-called progress can change—had bidden him halt on his way; and as he realized that, his old preoccupations had suddenly seemed futile. When all a man's gifts have been bent on the realization of material and realizable ends, the time is bound to come, unless he fails, when he will turn his spiritual powers against himself and scoff at his own achievements.

If, at one time, he had thought that machines were going to bring the millennium, he came to see now that the machine itself is nothing; what is needed is the mechanical mentality; and that he did not have. The use of machines might "pay" in a money sense; it did not pay in terms of human life. The thing done is nothing; the doing everything. He began to formulate such things to himself; he tried to find how he felt about things and to put that feeling into words.

He also listened more patiently to others, trying to get their point of view. He became intimate with his brother-in-law. Often he went to town to talk to him though he never stayed long. Perhaps it was partly because Mary and Ruth had found a way of getting along with each other.

Every time a new contingent went overseas from the municipality, Abe saw them off, not with a speech as might have been expected from the reeve; but a look here, a pressure of the hand there were worth more than a speech. Throughout the municipality there were people now who, when Abe was attacked—as he often was, for he carried things with a high hand—rallied to his defence and silenced his opponents.

Between Ruth and Abe a new relationship had sprung up. It arose from the mutual recognition of the right of every human being to live his own life. Ruth encouraged Abe in the very things which she had once opposed, proposing innovations and improvements in house and farm; and Abe recognized this yielding of her spirit to his or to what she still thought was his. Abe gave her a free hand with regard to the children. Marion, the older girl, was, in 1917, sent to the high school at Somerville where she boarded out, of course; Jim and Frances were still attending the district school; but already it was understood that Jim was to join Marion if at last he passed his entrance to high school examinations. He was a year older than Marion but behind her in school.

As for the children, Abe felt lost. At first, after Charlie's death, he had borne them an outright grudge because they lived when the boy was dead. In 1915, he had one day come upon the three as they were playing on the lawn east of the house. He had given no more than a glance; but it had produced an utter silence. As Abe passed on, Jim and Frances had resumed their game; but Marion, twelve years old, had withdrawn behind the old house to cry. A distant bond had established itself between him and this older girl: she resembled Charlie. "When his ambitions were realized . . ." Abe had thought in the past. They were realized; but there was still much to think about, though it was of a different kind these days.

The farm? It had lost its right to exist. Yet Abe enlisted Jim's help in spring and fall. Since Hilmer, Shilloe, and Nawosad had in a modest way become prosperous; since Hartley had turned agent, selling brooms and brushes now; since Bill Crane and others, lured by a soldier's pay and a separation allowance, had enlisted, while conscription had claimed the younger men, outside help could simply not be had any longer. Immigration had ceased; and that was the reason why the old house had never been moved. Now even Horanski had filed a "cancellation claim" on the school quarter where Blaine had squatted down years ago.

Blaine and Horanski had come to a mutually profitable arrangement, for Blaine was willing to pay for the lot on which his cottage stood. The current year, 1918, was the last which Horanski was to spend on Abe's farm. Yet Abe gave the problem little thought. The children, he felt, would drift away; for whom should he go on working on that large scale on which he had worked in the past? He would retrench.

He had other things to think of. Often, strangers wondered when they saw him; occasionally Ruth shook her head.

He would stand at a corner of his huge house and look closely at brick and mortar. It was five years since the house had been built. Five years only! Yet already little sand grains embedded in the mortar were crumbling away; already the edges of the bricks were being rounded by a process of weathering. When he bent and looked closely at the ground, near the wall, he saw a thin layer of red dust mixed with those sand grains. The weathering process would go on and on; and what would come of it? Dr. Vanbruik told him of the clay mounds covering the sites of ancient Babylonian cities, loaning him a book or two on excavations. The moment a work of man was finished, nature set to work to take it down again. A queer thought, that. And so with everything, with his machines, his fields, his pool; they were all on the way of being levelled to the soil again. What would happen when the supply of iron ores was exhausted? For that supply had its limits. This great mechanical age was bound to come to an end; and the resources of the planet would be scattered all over its surface.

Abe looked about and seemed to see for the first time. There were his wind-breaks, tall, rustling trees, full-grown: poplars interspersed with spruces, maturing. They would age and decay and die; already some showed black knots of disease; others, their bark having burst, grew huge buttresses resembling proud flesh. They would die and decay; unless they reseeded themselves as they seemed to do; then they would spread and conquer his fields and the prairie, converting it into a forest-clad plain. Yet, if that prairie were capable of bearing a forest, would not the forest have invaded it long ago?

Even the prairie was engaged in a process which would do away with it. Abe looked at the ditches running full of a muddy flood; and his mind lost itself in the mysteries of cosmic change.

Sometimes, on his way from Somerville, when he came from a meeting of the council, or from having taken Marion back to school—his mind seemed to hover over ,the landscape as in flight.

There was the Somerville Line which passed through the village of Morley, hesitating on its way, forming something like the node in the stem of a plant, to run on again, to the west. Man's work!

North of that line—in the past it had been the same south of it—stretched the flat prairie, unique in America. The exceedingly slight slope with which it drained north-east to the river was hardly perceptible; it amounted to less than a foot in a mile. To the casual glance, it seemed flat as a table-top. No native irregularity, whether of soil accumulation or plant growth, broke its monotony. Whatever relieved the sky-line was man's work. The only native growth was the long, slender prairie grass which, in a summer breeze, gave the surface of the soil the appearance of a sheet of watered silk.

Once the buffalo had roamed here, supplying the eye with contours to rest on; they had been replaced by these scattered homes of man. A phenomenon characteristic of this prairie, though not restricted to it, lent it some interest: the frequency of mirages. Often a distant strip of land was lifted above the horizon like a low-flung cloud; a town or a group of farmsteads, ordinarily hidden behind the intervening shoulder of the world, stood up clearly against the whitish sky which only overhead shaded off into a pale blue. The strip of featureless air between the mirage and the solid earth below was of that silvery, polished whiteness which we see otherwise only in the distant mirror of a smooth sheet of water.

On this prairie, near things often seemed to be distant—a haystack no more than a quarter of a mile away loomed gigantic as though separated from the eye by two or three miles. Far things, especially such as in themselves loomed high —the huge storage granaries along the railways, for instance—seemed near. In certain states of the atmosphere, the layered air worked like a lens: roofs five, six miles away showed details of construction as though magnified by the glass.

Far in the west, a low swinging line indicated the series of hills which, geologists tell us, once formed the shore of the lake whose bottom has become the prairie. Occasionally, though rarely—mostly prior to one of the major storms of the summer season—these hills, too, seemed lifted and drawn nearer, but without the silvery strip below which was characteristic of the mirages on the unbroken prairie.

In the particular section where Abe's life as chronicled here unfolded itself, a traveller might, at the time, have gone in an east-west direction for a hundred miles without finding the slightest change in the essentials of the landscape. Two railway lines had been built, both branching from the international trunk line which ran roughly north-south, parallel to the highway. Both turned west in almost straight lines, twenty-five miles apart, till, at the foot of the western hills, they joined in a loop. Both were strung with towns at intervals of ten or twelve miles. From a distance, all looked alike, their salient features consisting in the tall, spire-like elevators which dominate western landscapes everywhere; below them clustered a few stores, a few dozen dwellings, and such groups or lines of trees as the aesthetic sense of their inhabitants had impelled them to plant.

But had such a traveller chosen to go from north to south, he would have been arrested at regular intervals by those enormous ditches, all running parallel to each other and sloping, at the rate of four feet in a mile, towards the river which bounds this steppe of the prairie in the east. To those who lived here, these ditches were of importance not only because they were the only means which enabled them to grow their crops by carrying away the water which once flooded the prairie for months at a stretch; but also because they determined the distances which the settler had to travel when going from one point to another not in exactly the same latitude. They could be crossed only where bridges were provided, which was once in four miles. People might be neighbours, their yards separated by nothing but a ditch; yet they might have to travel four miles to get from one farm to the other.

Even at the time these man-made diggings impressed the beholder who came from a distance, with perceptions undulled by familiarity—and it was less than twenty years since they had been dug—like the prehistoric remains of a system devised by some mightier race gone to its accountings; so completely had the prairie grass obliterated the traces of the tools used in their excavation.

Altogether it is even to-day a landscape which in spite of the ever encroaching settlements of man, seems best to be appreciated by a low, soaring flight, as by that of the marsh-hawk so commonly seen in the open season. Wild life is little abundant. Gophers—even they are rare—field mice, an occasional rabbit, meadow-larks, blackbirds—especially the red-wing—and ground sparrows, in addition to hawks and burrowing owls, pretty well exhaust the native share of the vertebrate orders. Insects are represented by a few butterflies and enormous numbers of beetles and crickets—subterranean kinds—

with clouds upon clouds of mosquitoes in spring and early summer. Birds that are recent immigrants congregate about towns and farms surrounded by wind-breaks.

Owing to the peculiar difficulties of drainage with which the farmer has to contend, man remains distinctly an interloper; the floods, though tamed, have not been done away with by the ditches; and in places these ditches have furnished the soil for willow-thickets which are choking them up. True, where the water once used to stand for months, it now stood only for weeks, at least in those elusive seasons which farmers call normal; but these weeks came toward the end of April and often the beginning of May when seeding was in full swing elsewhere; and the land, being the lowest, except in the far north, of the prairie provinces, seems to attract early frosts which hinders the due maturing of the grains when seeding was delayed by the flood in spring.

Such as live here, brought by those accidents of choice which commonly determine location in a new country: the nearness to the western metropolis, the possibility of breaking large tracts without the previous labour of clearing away stumps or stones, the vicinity of friends or relations, or lastly a predilection for this peculiar, melancholy landscape, bred into the blood by some atavism of sentimental tendency, are developing what is so far exceedingly rare on this cosmopolitan continent, namely, a distinct local character and mentality.

If they have lived here for some time, a decade or longer, and have stayed on in the face of all the inevitable and unforeseen discouragements and difficulties, so that the landscape has had time to enforce in them a reaction to its own character, they seem slow, deliberate, earthbound. In their features lingers something wistful; in their speech, something hesitating, groping, almost deprecatory and apologetic; in their silences, something almost eloquent.

It is a landscape in which, to him who surrenders himself, the sense of one's life as a whole seems always present, birth and death being mere scansions in the flow of a somewhat debilitated stream of vitality. It is not surprising, then, that, physical facts notwithstanding, the difference in the mood produced by day or night, or by summer or winter, seems less pronounced than elsewhere. True, the average day is hot in summer; and the night is cold. But the discomfort caused by the heat does not seem essentially different from the discomfort caused by the cold; the effect of both partakes of the effect of a lid placed over slow ebullition. Perhaps the time best fitted to bring out the characteristic impression of the landscape is neither noon nor midnight but the first grey dawn of day, especially a dull day; or the first dim dusk of night, that dusk in which horizons become blurred and the height of human buildings seems diminished. And similarly the time of year most in harmony with the scene is neither summer nor winter; but rather the first few days of spring while the snow still lies in dirty patches and, from the heights in the west, the floods send down their first invading trickles which follow the imperceptible hollows of the ground; or the first drear approach of November days, with indurating winds and desolate flurries of snow in the air.

The prevailing silence—for, apart from man's dwellings, not even the wind finds anything to play its tunes on—is accentuated rather than disturbed by the sibilant hum, in early summer, of the myriads of mosquitoes that haunt the air, bred in stagnant pools, and the shrill notes, in the early autumn, of the swarm of black crickets that literally cover the soil. That silence, like the flat landscape itself, has something haunted about it, something almost furtive. . . .

Abe, now that he was becoming conscious of this landscape at last, and of its significance, could at first hardly understand that he, of all men, should have chosen this district to settle in, though it suited him well enough now. But even that became clear. He had looked down at his feet; had seen nothing but the furrow; had considered the prairie only as a page to write the story of his life upon. His vision had been bounded by the lines of his farm; his farm had been floated on that prairie as the shipwright floats a vessel on the sea, looking not so much at the waves which are to batter it as at the fittings which secure the comfort of those within. But such a vessel may be engulfed by such a sea.

When, these days, he approached his place, the place built to dominate the prairie, he succumbed to the illusion that he who had built it was essentially different from him who had to live in it. More and more the wind-break surrounding his yard seemed to be a rampart which, without knowing it, he had erected to keep out a hostile world. Occasionally the great house seemed nothing less than a mausoleum to enshrine the memory of a child.

Abe felt defeated; at least in so far as he was what he had been; perhaps that defeat would slowly become apparent to the outside world. But the world defeats only him who has already been defeated in his heart. And was it a defeat? He was changing his aim; that aim was now to live on, not in a material sense, through his economic achievement, but in what he did for district and municipality. No rural school of the west had ever been guided like his; no municipality had weathered the war like that of Somerville. As far as his economic ambitions went, he had reached his goal. He might go on making money; what for? Material aspirations meant nothing. He had the house; and he found no pleasure in it. For fifteen years he had dreamed of what he would do when he had it; now it seemed useless.

Economically, the war had been hard on him. The price of wheat had been fixed for the farmer; for nobody else had the price of anything been fixed; by legislation, the farmer had been the prey of all preying interests. Everybody else in the district felt the same way; nobody was surprised at the fact that Abe had arrested progress. He was biding his time. For outwardly he had changed little. He had replaced his ageing bronchos by another driving team, still more magnificent. When he drove to town, he sat as straight in buggy or sleigh as ever. He spoke as little; whatever he had to say was always concerned with business; and it was always said to the point.

Abe was well-to-do. Did he not show it by the way in which his children were dressed? Was not Marion, at Somerville, paying thirty dollars a month for her board? Abe might be a little heavier and older. He was as headstrong as ever. Was he not running school and district?

How was it, then, that he was more and more discussed? That it was necessary for his friends to contradict such assertions as that he was "land poor," that he had sunk his wealth in the soil which, sooner or later, he would find himself unable to till? That the time was coming when he would have to withdraw from the offices which he held? That others would shortly take hold?

XIV   THE CHANGING DISTRICT

THE fact was there was unrest in the district; and that unrest was greatly increased by the coming of another settler. The story of John Elliot's coming was that of the rise in the price of flax.

Throughout the years of the war, flax had shown erratic tendencies; now its price was soaring towards a peak. John Elliot had repeatedly appeared in the district to look things over. He was a short, stout, round-shouldered man of thirty, with a round, full face, tanned brick-red from his eyebrows down; above that line, his bulging forehead was white, protected by a wide-brimmed sombrero. He had been farming in the short-grass country of Saskatchewan, a wheat district pure and simple. He seemed to have money and an equipment superior to that of any one but Abe; and he was what Abe was not, a "mixer". Though he was ugly—his mouth was large, and his nether lip shovel-shaped and pendent—he made friends at once. He was always laughing and joking, displaying gold-filled teeth. Even while travelling, he wore a white-and-blue checked shirt and a pair of cotton trousers; and somehow he conveyed the impression that he was too well off to need the appearance of prosperity.

He wanted land; and flax land at that. Nearly the whole district was flax land; and plenty of it was available. The trouble was that a man could homestead only a hundred and sixty acres. "Do you think I'd be satisfied with a measly quarter? I want a half at the least. Any of you fellows willing to sell? Good night, boys. Nothing doing. Not for me. What's that? Hudson's Bay land? Where?"

The south half and the north-west quarter of section twenty-six, opposite Hilmer's Corner, were vacant; and these three quarters, like Abe's north section, were part of that twentieth of land which was left to the Company when they surrendered their sovereignty.

"Ye-es," John Elliott said. That might suit him.

But land values had gone up since the war. Abe had bought his section for three thousand six hundred dollars. Now the price was four thousand dollars a quarter section. Time to pay in? Pay ten per cent down; the balance within thirty years.

One day somebody picked up the news at Somerville that a deal had been struck. Rumour, always willing to believe what flatters the interests of the many, had it that Elliot had paid spot cash for the land; but a private loan company registered a mortgage on the land which amounted to three thousand dollars more than the purchase price.

Still, it was staggering. Twenty years ago the site of a farm had not been worth taking; right now a quarter section could be had for the asking. And just because one quarter section was not enough for this man, he bought three quarters for twelve thousand dollars. As always in a boom so called, a temporary, disproportionate, and unjustified rise in price was taken for permanent; a condition that was bound to produce the corresponding slump.

"By gosh!" Wheeldon said at Nicoll's Corner. "What's the bright idea?"

"High finance," Henry Topp replied.

"The idea is flax," said Stanley.

Henry's brother Dave, invalided home during the previous winter, nodded in that peculiar way which he had brought back from overseas and which made people say that "he was not all there" any longer.

Nicoll, too, rarely smiled these days; his eldest boy Tom had been killed in action. "I suppose the man knows what he's doing."

And Stanley shrugged his armless shoulder. "If the war lasts——"

At which more than one head nodded; and everybody resolved that next year he, too, was going to "take a shot at flax."

"Look here," Wheeldon said into the silence. "The fellow's got children. We should have him on the school board."

The silence of the others remained unbroken. Everybody knew what Wheeldon was driving at. As soon as the war was over, consolidation was going to be an issue throughout the ward. More and more children in Spalding District had reached or were about to reach high-school age. As elsewhere in the Canadian west it was an ever-present problem what to do with or for adolescent children. There was land a-plenty; but it takes money to start a boy. Hiring out on the farm did not pay, though Horanski was drawing fifty dollars a month and had land for garden and potato patch, milk, and fuel besides. In the city and in construction camps a man could earn three or four dollars a day. Shilloe's and Nawosad's eldest boys had gone. Bill Stanley and the third Nicoll boy, Stan, made no secret of it that, if they returned from the wars, they had no intention of going back to the farm. And it was worse for the girls; for opportunities to get married were lacking: with half the youth of the country dead in Flanders or disabled at home, it seemed imperative that parents should train their daughters to make a living of their own. If a high-school education were within reach, girls could be nurses or teachers. Teachers' salaries were rising; and it was easy to become a teacher. A hundred dollars a month was being paid!

Years ago Abe had put in a good word for the plan of consolidating half a dozen rural districts into one educational centre at Morley; but incomprehensibly he had turned against the scheme, without volunteering reasons for his change of front. It took Nicoll's stubborn loyalty not to abandon an allegiance thus sorely tried.

Ever since Spalding District had been formed Abe had sat in the chair; and Nicoll had been secretary-treasurer. The third position on the board had been successively filled by Hartley, Stanley, and Wheeldon. As soon as Wheeldon was naturalized he had tried to have himself elected; but there had been a feeling that it was best not to embarrass Abe. At last, however, Abe himself had said, "Put him in office. Let him air his complaints at the meetings of the board. If he can convince one of us, he will have his way." Since his election, business had been conducted in a more formal manner. Thus, in the spring of 1917, Nicoll had been in need of a small sum of money due to him for having taken the census of the district; and Abe had simply signed the cheque. Wheeldon had kicked up a row. Such accounts must be passed at a regular meeting of the board. "Not," he said to Nicoll, "that I grudge you the cheque. You'd have got it anyway. But it isn't business; and it isn't legal." He was right; but in the rush of seeding it was inconvenient to hold a meeting. Most ratepayers considered the matter a trifle not worth the ado that was being made about it. Yet Wheeldon was beginning to have a following: Hartley, Henry Topp, and others.

The issue of consolidation was going to become acute as soon as peace came. If, therefore, Wheeldon suggested that John Elliot should be on the board, it could have only one meaning: that he should take Spalding's place. The district was growing; McCrae would move in when he returned from overseas; Horanski would have the vote when he left Abe. Others were looking for land; and as new settlers moved in, Spalding's prestige would wax or wane according to the attitude of the older settlers with regard to him. Already Wheeldon considered himself as one of the founders of the community. A priority of five or ten years in the date of settlement became negligible in the consideration of seniority.

"While I'm single," said Henry Topp, "I don't give a tinker's damn."

"That's where you're wrong." Wheeldon replied. "That's not what I call citizenship!" That word was just becoming the slogan of the hour.

"Oh well," Henry drawled, "I'll act the fool and make you laugh." And the way in which he danced his shoulders and moved his fingers, as though playing an accordion, did fetch a laugh from the meeting.

Other things troubled the district. Since Bill Stanley had

gone to the wars, against his father's wish, yes, defying his orders, the latter had become filled with missionary zeal. The world as it was was going to come to an end; and the kingdom of God on earth was going to be established. He and others of his creed, he said, had long prophesied the coming of that war which was shaking the foundations of the present world. By strange interpretations of certain passages in Holy Writ he was pointing out that the course of events in Europe had been predicted hundreds of years before the birth of Christ. Though nobody could follow his exegesis or believe in his prophecies, he succeeded in stirring the district into metaphysical shivers. Especially David Topp, who, since the war, had become quiet and introspective, gave himself over to silent and melancholy musings. "We must better our lives! We must live more closely in accordance with what our Lord preached when He walked on earth!" Such things he said in a tense and laboured voice and with unalterable conviction. His preachments, as people called them, made the more impression since they came from a brother of the man who remained an absolute scoffer. David spoke of his intention of leaving Henry to his perdition and breaking up the partnership of the brothers.

Shilloe, Nawosad, Horanski attended meetings at Morley where a preacher from the city conducted services in Anderson's shop; for the two churches in town were closed to what many called a freak religion.

Hartley and Wheeldon did not take sides in the endless discussions. But Hilmer made long trips on Sundays to attend such services as were held in his own church in the so-called Reserve.

While most of the settlers listened when Stanley talked, awed though unconvinced, Henry Topp contradicted. "That's all nonsense! Talk of the soul. There ain't no such thing. Ask any doctor. They've searched men's bodies. They haven't even found the seat of the soul."

"Exactly! If they had, the soul might be physical; but it isn't."

Perhaps Nicoll was most profoundly disquieted; he had always been given to metaphysical speculation. Yet he adhered to conclusions arrived at long ago. "I don't know what the soul is. But as it arises with the growth of the body, it must disappear with death. If it were to continue for ever, it could not have had a beginning either."

"Like everywhere else," Stanley argued, "it was created. And like everything else it will remain unless God uncreates it. All those who refuse to listen God will destroy. But those who find truth will be called into the kingdom. Millions now living will never die." . . .

Horanski still lived on Abe's place; but he broke a small field on his own quarter, seeding it to barley. Jim stayed at home for three weeks to help Abe; and Ruth raised no objection. Throughout the district new land was broken; and Abe did not even look for additional help. He, Horanski, and Jim did what they could; and the rest remained undone. He enlarged his pasture, seeding down a wide strip of his fields. Every one experimented with flax; but Abe did not.

After seeding John Elliot reappeared. He was not going to move out that summer after all; he had been unable to sell his place in Saskatchewan. This fact lost him part of his prestige. Still, he walked and talked as if he meant business, and as if, once ready, he would do unheard-of things. As for the price he had paid for his land, that was nothing; one crop—what *he*'d call a crop—would pay it off.

When Wheeldon heard that he was in town, he hunted him up "Too bad," he said, "you aren't coming at once. There's an election ahead. For the school board. You'd be our man."

"You bet." John Elliott pushed his sombrero back on the huge, sandy-haired dome of his almost bald skull, inserted his thumbs in the loops of his braces, and, splitting his face by a broad, exaggerated smile, "I'm the natural chairman."

"What about consolidation?"

"Ye-es. I've heard. I'm in favour. Who's not?"

"That's the point," Wheeldon said. "There'll be opposition. This district's been run for many years by one single man."

"Spalding?" John Elliot stretched himself in an endeavour to look down on Wheeldon who, however, was but slightly shorter than he.

"That's the man."

"Well-l-l," Elliot drawled, in that way which made people doubt whether he meant what he said, "we'll have to take him down a notch, I suppose. You don't mean to say consolidation's an issue now?"

"Not while the war lasts."

"Don't worry. That war'll last another year or two. If it doesn't, you'll see me here in a hurry. I'll build a shack this fall."

"Will you be able to sell out west?"

"Like a shot!" Elliot said, raising a finger and slanting his head. "When the war stops, there'll be a rush to the land."

And, soon after, carpenters began to erect a barn on Elliot's land.

Every step was watched by Mrs. Grappentin, who was alone with her son, the two children having gone to live with cousins of theirs; of her husband, the last thing reported—told by herself—was that he had fetched a team of oxen from her farm; these he had promptly sold at Somerville for what they would bring. Mrs. Grappentin had been compelled to insert a notice in the town paper that she would not be responsible for debts contracted by the man. She herself continued to visit in the district, retailing gossip in broken English.

"Yes," she said, "a good thing, this. That man Elliot moving in. A fine man he. A man of understanding and wealth. And not proud. Such a barn he is building! Three-inch lumber throughout! Bigger than the barns on the other place. As big as the two together."

Which, however, nobody with eyes in his head could credit. It was apparent that it would not be larger than half of one of Abe's barns.

The fact was that Abe had begun to weigh like a substantial shadow on the district. Did not Stanley have as nice a house as one could wish to have? A rectangular structure with a bay window in the south wall and a porch at the corner, pleasantly painted white, with roof, doors, and windows brown. He, too, had planted trees; and he had a good barn, a granary and a hen-house. But his hens did not lay by electricity.

A granary Wheeldon did not have so far; nor had he planted trees; and his house was only oiled, not painted. But he was a good farmer. With some people he would have carried more weight had he not been jealous. "He hates Spalding," Stanley observed to Nicoll. "Not because Spalding is rich; but because he is tall and broad. When Spalding is around, Wheeldon feels like a pup. I'm not a small man myself; and if we didn't have Spalding, I believe Wheeldon would make *me* a present of his dislike." Nicoll laughed. With him, it was a matter of personal pride that everybody's achievement was measured by Abe's.

So, when at the end of the summer another prospective settler looked the district over and found his way to Nicoll, asking where he might pick up second-hand lumber to build stable and shack, he referred him to Abe. For Abe still had the old house, crowding against the new one and detracting, in a rear view, from its impressiveness.

This new man became the butt of all jokes in the district. His name was Schweigel; and he was a Jew, well known in the settlements south of the Line where he had been a pedlar for a decade. He was fat, round-faced, with the hands of a plump woman. When he spoke, he held these hands clasped in front of his face, waving them forward and backward to give emphasis to his shrill, piping voice. He was always imploring whomever he happened to talk to, either to give information or to sell at a less exacting price whatever he had to spare. In this, he was extraordinarily successful, for people almost gave him what he wanted, taking out part of their price in laughing at him. He came with a horse lame on three legs and kicking with the fourth at each step while drawing the skeleton of a spring wagon on top of which, in a long coat of raw hide, perched the Jew. A Jew farmer was in himself a novelty; but Moses Schweigel supplied inexhaustible mirth.

For some reason Henry Topp, in speaking of him for the first time, called him Itzig; and in spite of the passionate protests of the man the name stuck. Over and over he would spell and pronounce his real name; Henry provoked him to do so. "What is that confounded doggone, Yiddish name of yours, Itzig?" And Schweigel spelt it, lisping the sibilant. Henry could hardly suppress his laughter, for the Jew pronounced every letter with the fervency of prayer. "And how do you pronounce that gibberish?"—"Shou-i-gel!"—"Well," Henry said, "that's too twisted for my outlandish tongue, Itzig." Whenever Schweigel heard that name, he lifted his hands as though stung by a needle.

He had filed on the south-west quarter of twenty-seven, west of Hilmer's, much to Mrs Grappentin's disgust; and with only two horses, both crippled, he managed to break a patch of ten acres. Out of half of Abe's old house he put together a small hut in which he lived with a beautiful young woman and two little children "pretty as angels"; his stable fitted the two crippled horses like a glove, people said. As for feed, he was not ashamed to beg it: an armful here, a few trusses there, carrying them home on his back in a ragged sheet of canvas; and soon he had a little stack. Whenever, on these trips, he passed Hilmer's Corner, Mrs. Grappentin, standing in door or gate, shouted abuse at the bent figure under its load. "Look at the yellow one! Taking home what he did not work for!" Yet, as for work, nobody slaved as indefatigably as he; and scarcely had the weather, in the fall, become the least bit inclement, when he was out again with his little wagon, clad in his long, loose horse-hide coat, with the mangy hair outside, and drove amazing distances to buy eggs and fowls to ship to the city, making a handsome profit on each transaction.

Horanski, too, built a shack before threshing time, using the remainder of the lumber from Abe's old house. That shack, of two rooms, stood in the extreme south-west corner of his land. Several of his children being still of school age, he was favourably placed.

Finally, just before the armistice, young McCrae turned up; and before the freeze-up he had his place fenced. A neat, shed-like shack was built which, however, he did not occupy during the winter.

With all these new settlers coming in, it was doubtful how things would stand should it come to a "show-down" between Spalding and Wheeldon. That such a decision was at hand, nobody doubted any longer.

XV * ABE'S HOUSEHOLD

IT would have been hard to tell whether the meta-physical disquietudes that rippled through the dis-trict found an echo in Abe. He had never taken part in the discussions. He had kept himself to himself. Instinctively he despised the intellectual powers of most of the "crowd." But he brooded; and in his broodings he sought help from his brother-in-law and old man Blaine. Their conversations were all of a type.

Sometimes he went through the great house, speaking to no one, his face clouded. Ruth respected that privacy which his mood seemed to demand. Absently he looked at this or that; at the furniture—chesterfield, arm-chairs, and rug—of the living-room which reached across the whole front of the build-ing, only the hall being taken out; or at the dining-room in the centre of the house; at the "den" where his little desk stood, with three or four shelves full of books and a library table strewn with papers; even at pantry and kitchen behind. Then he turned and entered the hall where there were hooks for hats and coats and a gun-rack with two guns which had never been used since Charlie had first started to go to school—for even in the fall when a steer and two pigs had to be killed for winter meat Abe had always left the farm for the day, hiring the butcher at Morley to do the work. And ultimately he went up-stairs to look into room after room, winding up at the east room which was locked.

For a while he hesitated at the door; but at last he unlocked it, entered, and looked about in the half light, blinds and cur-tains being drawn; at the bed, still made up; at the chest of drawers which still held a boy's clothing; at the open cupboard by the window where a few books stood, a few toys lay about, and a few curiosities were arranged in a sort of display: stones found on the prairie, plants dried and pressed, half decayed now, bird feathers, and a football which Abe always touched as if to make sure that it had long since become soft.

Having finished his round, he went to the barn and hitched his drivers to buggy or sleigh to go to town. There he stood about in the store and finally, having inquired whether the doctor was in, which he rarely was, he went to his sister's house.

Mary received him at the door and asked a few questions about his health which was always good, about Ruth and the children, and, seeing he was in his monosyllabic mood, she said briefly, "Charles is in the den."

Abe entered the den; and the doctor went through the ever-repeated ceremony of clearing a chair for him. "Sit down," he said.

They sat in silence, the doctor sucking the stem of his pipe. "I can't understand it," Abe said with darkening brow.

The doctor did not answer at once. When he did, his tone was didactic; he had said the same thing so often. "We can't know, Abe. But where knowledge is denied, faith comes in."

"Faith in what?"

"In whatever we have made the canon of our lives."

Another silence. Then, "What is yours?"

"I have discarded so-called beliefs. But there are obligations left, the more exacting since they are not imposed from without. Courage and fortitude; the search after truth——"

"If you can't know, what is truth?"

The doctor's small face seemed to contract. "That which we feel to be in harmony with the best and deepest within us."

Abe brooded. Then, in a whisper, "Where's the kid?"

The doctor nursed the ankle of a foot with the palm of a hand. But before he could answer, Abe had resumed, "I can see him move. I can hear his voice. I can feel his arm about my neck. Where is he?" A silence again. "*He!*" Abe cried. "The rest of the body...."

An hour or so later, he entered Spalding School. Perhaps it was five o'clock in the afternoon, and the schoolmaster was engaged in the task of putting away maps, books, and papers used during the day.

Abe sat down in one of the larger seats; and for minutes, while the old man went on with his work, not a word was spoken. Blaine, too, had learned to recognize and respect Abe's moods. He knew how surcharged this giant was with perplexities. At last Blaine sat down, skinny, ridged hands clasped about a thin knee, huge head bent forward, trembling on its pedicel, with the long, curly, snow-white beard touching his thighs. On his short, fleshy nose reposed steel-rimmed glasses; and the ruddy cushions of flesh which formed his cheeks seemed singularly clear-skinned and transparent. He stared through the windows.

Abe stirred. "How old are you, Blaine?"

"Seventy-seven, Abe. Getting up in years."

"Your time's coming. Ever think of it?"

"Yes. . . . Yes. . . ."

"Believe in an after life?"

"I don't know. I have my doubts."

Abe looked at him. "A man must make up his mind one way or the other."

Blaine's beard trembled. Then, slowly, "If sixty years ago my father had heard any one say that he doubted, he would have thought him insane or wicked. I believe in God; but it isn't the God my father believed in. He's changed."

"How?"

The old man stared at his questioner. "It's all for the best, they say. That doesn't go down with me."

The dreaded question came. "Where's the kid?"

The old man flung his hand in a helpless gesture. . . .

Abe often thought of Nicoll who had lost a boy in the war, taking his loss with great fortitude. Was he right? He had been right in many things. Nicoll was the only man who understood him, Abe. All the others, friend and foe, thought of him as unchanged; and they imposed their conception of him on all who were moving in.

But not, of course, on Ruth.

As in the case of many marriages, the lines of Abe's and Ruth's lives had neither merged nor diverged; they had run parallel. Both were mellowed by age and sorrow. Just how deeply Ruth grieved, Abe did not know; it was not his way to talk about it. Only his silence showed how deeply he had been moved; and he reaped what he sowed, namely silence.

Outwardly, and that was all Abe could judge by, Ruth had made an understanding between them very difficult. In this house with its polished floors, its oaken stairway, its wide, high windows, its shiny metal appliances which saved labour and demanded it, she did all the work herself and did it faithfully and well. So there was no time left to dress in; from morning till night she went about in the same house-dresses of dark print to which she had reverted. The two girls, especially

Marion, were never behind the latest fashions; every few months they had new dresses; no expense was spared to make them attractive; and they were attractive. What little vanity Ruth might once have had she had transferred to her children. What did it matter how she looked herself? No wonder that, on the rare occasions when she went to town, or when the Vanbruiks came to the farm, Ruth, "dressed up," looked even more awkward, more "countrified" than on weekdays at home; she had no taste; and her daughters were not quite old enough to guide her.

When she scanned herself in a mirror—as a rule she used it only as an indispensable means of putting hairpins and clothes in the approximately right places—she felt amazed at the change she had undergone in the last twenty years. Her massive jaw sprang forward from a triple chin; the skin of her neck was heavily corrugated. The line from her shoulder-blades sloped forward to the top of her head. On her back, the flesh bulged as much as on her bosom. In walking, she balanced her weight on one foot before she lifted the other.

It was tragic that this mockery of the human form should yet be the seat of poignant emotions. Abe did not doubt the fact; though tears, when he surprised her weeping, seemed facile to him. He withdrew: as though sorrow were a privilege reserved for himself.

But often they sat together of an evening now: Ruth sewing, Abe reading large-tomed books. They sat in the dining-room; both had sat too long on straight-backed chairs to feel at ease in an arm-chair. Perhaps the children were doing their home-work; or they were in bed.

Both Frances and Jim were backward in school; they did not apply themselves; they were preparing for a life of things among which scholarship held no place. In the spring of 1918, Jim had tried for the third time to pass his entrance examinations; he had failed again.

One evening Abe spoke of that. "He should help me on the farm. He's no good at school."

"He can help you throughout the summer," Ruth said. "In winter I want him to attend." She dropped her sewing, looking up at Abe.

"What's the use if he can't pass that examination?"

"He can go on to high school," Ruth said primly. "I have written to the Department of Education. Since he lost time through work in the field, they permit him to proceed."

Abe mused. "If he hasn't the brains——"

"All the more does he need the schooling. People with brains get through life somehow; the rest need instruction."

"A novel theory," Abe said listlessly.

"I want Jim to go to Somerville next fall," Ruth went on briskly. "If there is any trouble about the expense, I have the money."

"If it's got to be, I'll finance it, of course.' . . .

Frances was still a grade behind Jim; but Blaine had said she would be ready for high school within a year. She was only a little over fourteen, a very pretty girl, plump as Ruth had been, but with Abe's fine, light hair. She was prettiest when she was hot; her hair assumed a natural curliness, and her pallid complexion took on a rose tint.

When, at the beginning of summer, Marion came home for the holidays, Abe was greatly struck by the change in her. Her aunt had brought her out in the car; Abe had not seen her yet when he entered the dining-room for his supper; she looked like a strange young woman.

She was standing in the far corner, diagonally opposite the kitchen door through which Abe entered. She was holding her hands behind her back, a smile on her lips. Abe thought the pose arranged for effect; and the sight came indeed like a calculated surprise. It was the first time he saw her with her hair done up : beautiful hair, the dark brown of her mother's when young, with golden tints in reflected light. Her face showed that bony, thin-fleshed grace which had been Charlie's. Her body, tall and slender—the opposite of Frances's build—yet fully developed, held a note new to him in attitude and expression. She wore a maroon-coloured dress of light silk, very plainly cut, too plainly for a girl of not quite sixteen : too well adapted to display the forms of a young woman. According to the fashion it was open at the neck and reached just below the knee. The sleeves, wide, transparent, revealed long, slender arms. She came quickly forward, put an arm about Abe's shoulders, kissed him as he bent down, and stepped back. "Hello, daddy," she said with a laugh as of abated breath. "I hope you are well?"

"Sure," he said, sitting heavily down at the head of the table. "Why shouldn't I be well? What are all the lights on for?"

Marion, with a silvery laugh, switched them off.

"Well," Abe asked in the course of supper. "Do you think you passed in your examinations?"

"I think so, daddy." Which was said very readily, with a note of politeness foreign to ordinary intercourse in farmers' families.

Abe's eye was on Jim. Where in the world did these two get their complexions? Both were dark-skinned, with ruddy cheeks; but Marion had an almost Spanish *morbidezza* of the flesh and a velvet bloom on ivory and red. That thin-fleshed slenderness of facial contour, too, they had in common. But what was beautiful in Marion was coarsened in Jim to an angular boniness. Jim was the only one of the children who promised to vie in height with his father. At seventeen he stood six feet tall. But one feature of his head was repulsive: his large, prominent ears showed a peculiar deformity: their lobes pointed horizontally forward. . . .

The weeks went by. In the field, Jim was as good as a man. And, as fall came, Abe made arrangements for the boy to board at the same house with Marion, to attend high school at Somerville.

The crop was a failure. Drought was the trouble this time. In a drought Abe suffered more than his neighbours.

Twice before Abe had lived through a crisis: never through one like this. It would have relieved him to speak of his worries; but a habit of silence had established itself between man and wife. Every year Abe had given Ruth a cheque; and since the year of the great crop that cheque had been for a thousand dollars. In 1917, what with this cheque and the expense of sending Marion to Somerville, Abe had, for the first time, found himself unable to pay his taxes. The payment to Ruth was in the nature of a debt of honour on which he must not default; it had precedence over every other demand on his purse. He had waived all replacements on the farm; yet, throughout the year, he had not succeeded in straightening out his tax bill.

This fall, the wheat crop averaged eight bushels to the acre, on five hundred acres. The grade was low; his net income from the crop was less than three thousand six hundred dollars. The payment to Ruth and the cost of having two children in town consumed half his surplus. Horanski who was leaving had to be paid in full. When Abe balanced his accounts, he had less than a thousand dollars left to see him through till next fall. The taxes, amounting to more than a thousand dollars a year, would have to stand over again.

At bottom, there was nothing to worry about. Everywhere on earth the farmer suffers set-backs through failure of the crop. Abe had had two bad years in succession; it was unlikely that another would follow. A single fair crop—twenty bushels to the acre—would take care of his indebtedness. His credit at the bank was good; he had owed money before. The trouble was that in previous years he had been expanding; income had been bound to increase. He was retrenching now; he was re-organizing his operations on a smaller scale. Well, his land was broken; his difficulties were momentary only.

Abe being reeve of the municipality, the business of the corporation had, during the last few years, rested largely in his hands. Throughout the war he had enforced a policy of the strictest economy: all new road work had been postponed; nothing had been done except what could not be left over. Statistics showed that no other municipality in the province was in a better financial position. This policy would, of course, involve an enormous expense when the war was over. The ditches, for instance, would have to be looked after; for, though the province had established the drainage system, the various municipalities had been saddled with the cost of upkeep; and for years the council had been aware of the fact that a considerable amount of work would have to be done to preserve their efficiency; in various places the banks had caved in; in others, deposits of silt choked the flow of the water; east of Spalding District, willows had invaded the bottom, damming all current. For this work funds had been set aside, invested in war bonds. The fact that the taxes on two sections of land were unpaid could not possibly prevent the municipality from doing all that could be expected. Abe would see to that; in case of need he would go to the bank: at the worst, he would borrow from Ruth. . . .

But that fall the war did come to an end.

XVI * THE CAMPAIGN

WITH the armistice, the question of consolidation was an issue overnight, a long-prepared and hard-fought issue which was to unleash every dormant passion in the district and to divide its population into sharply differentiated camps. Abe forgot his personal worries and, for the first time, came out in a partisan fight.

How long-prepared the issue was Abe did not know till he stood in the battle. It became a test of the standing he had won in the community. At once, Wheeldon and he stood opposed as the leaders of two hostile factions.

John Elliot had moved in, after all; the moment hostilities had ceased in Europe, he had sold his place in Saskatchewan. For a few weeks the Elliots lived in a granary: John, his wife, a thin, cityfied woman who had once been a stenographer, and their three children, two girls and a boy. Meanwhile a small, square cottage was being run up by two carpenters: the Elliot glory was fading fast.

Another new settler, a Russo-German from White Russia, moved on to the south-west quarter of twenty-eight, a mile and a half west of Hilmer's Corner, a short, wiry man by name of Baker, sullen and silent, with whom nobody became acquainted to any extent. He brought the total of farmsteads in the district up to sixteen. Only one settler, the youngest Topp, was still overseas, apart from Bill Stanley who was not going to return. Thus, since women had received the vote, the number of electors was twenty-nine.

But the campaign reached far beyond Spalding District. Seven schools were involved; three north of the Somerville Line, including the hamlet of Morley; and four south of it. The armistice had hardly been signed before nobody spoke of anything but consolidation.

It went without saying that in town there was a solid majority for the scheme. The town had nothing to lose and everything to gain. Every prairie town is anxious to secure any building to be put up without regard to the cost. Stores and residences are makeshifts; false fronts and shoddy work prevail. A large public building gives town or village tone and stability. Besides, though Morley was already the distributing centre of the territory, the daily concourse of children from many districts would concentrate certain trades in town, such as the candy trade, not to be despised. The construction work would bring in carpenters, masons, and other craftsmen who would leave money behind; and finally there would be at least four, probably five or six teachers who, paid in part by the provincial government, would live or board in town, to say nothing of the traffic and repair work brought by the vans that they were to convey the children to and from school.

Every townsman, with the exception of Dr. Vanbruik, who stood aloof, became a booster for the scheme, in true American fashion: not a farmer came to town but found himself tackled by three or four enthusiastic canvassers trying to convince him of the superiority of a graded over an ungraded school. The inspector fanned the zeal of the townsmen; he was paid for that sort of work; it was considered a feather in his cap if he put the scheme through. The superiority of a graded over an ungraded school being granted, the chief argument was the acknowledged fact that the operation of a consolidated school involved no more expense for the individual district than the operation of their ungraded school had done. The excess in actual cost would be taken care of by provincial grants.

For a while Abe merely listened. He had never taken an active part in any campaign; this time he must : his whole nature revolted against the scheme. He saw the fallacies in the arguments advanced. He did not allow the fact that the cost of operation was bound to be in excess of former costs to be obscured by the fact that the distribution of that cost would be provincial instead of municipal. He saw that the district would lose control over what he considered its own affairs. He suspected that even such share of the cost as would remain incident upon each single farm would be greater than it had been in the separate districts. He knew from his own experience that children taken from the farm and transplanted into the environment of the town tended to grow away from the land and the control of their parents; ultimately they would look down on those parents and their ways, having themselves had the advantage of a surrounding which seemed more advanced. Above all, he felt in this innovation the approach of an order in which the control of the state over the individual would be strengthened through a conformity against which he rebelled. The scheme was in keeping with the spirit of the machine age : the imparting of information would be the paramount aim, not the building of character; spiritual values were going to be those of the intellect only. This he felt dimly; and since he could not have clearly explained it, it crystallized into an all the more powerful instinctive aversion.

When he discussed the matter with Dr. Vanbruik, the latter seemed unwilling to commit himself. He had no experience with the scheme.

What Abe needed was clear-cut arguments that would appeal to the practical sense of the settlers : he knew he could never make them understand objections which he realized but faintly himself.

Early in the new year, he left home for several days. To do so was becoming a difficult matter; Horanski had to be coaxed before he agreed to ride over morning and night to attend to Abe's chores.

Abe went to Ferney and thence north. Torquay had a consolidated school. There was another purely rural consolidation sixteen miles north. He gathered facts and figures a-plenty and heard of other schools which he should visit. He went on to Balfour and to Minor, in the bush country of Manitoba. In the district of Minor he found that the cost of educating the children was the highest *per capita* in the province. When, in the middle of January, he came home, he was armed indeed.

For weeks on end he spent most of his time in town, waylaying settlers of his district as they came in: Shilloe, Nawosad, Hilmer, Baker, the Topps, John Elliot, Stanley, and even Nicoll. He used only arguments which they could understand. Shilloe, Nawosad, and Hilmer were easily convinced. Baker listened but would not give any promise; Baker was careful and thrifty; he had built a log-house on his place and worked in town as a carpenter: had he been promised employment?

Next Abe spoke to the Topp brothers who nodded to all he said. Henry assured him almost too readily that he was opposed to the scheme. "I'm not going to pay a cent for all this tomfoolery. I'm a bachelor and intend to remain one, no matter what Wheeldon says."

Stanley and Nicoll were the two who, in the immediate present, had most to gain from the scheme; they had children, the majority girls, of high-school age. Abe modified his arguments. Granting that consolidation was desirable, was it wise to enter upon it now? "You may think hard times are over. I tell you hard times are only beginning. The war has to be paid for. Prices will rise not fall, except for the products of the farm. It would have been wiser to build during the war."

"Even so," Nicoll replied, "it was a matter of duty not to take people away from essential industries. How long should we wait?"

"Hard to tell. Four, five years"

Nicoll and Stanley laughed. "Till it's too late to do us any good.". . .

John Elliot listened, but while doing so he kept shifting his sombrero; he was standing sideways, hand on hip, looking up askance at Abe's face as at the stars. He exaggerated most of his motions.

"Tell you frankly," he said when Abe had finished, "I consider my own advantage only. I want my kids to attend high school and college. I've never gone to school much myself though I had the chance. I've come to see that I'm under a disadvantage."

"Let them consolidate without us. We can come in any time."

"Naw," Elliot replied. "Can't tell what we'll do later. If my vote counts for anything, I'm going to make sure that we're in it." . . .

Abe did not give up. Having exhausted his economic arguments, he began to hint at those underlying his opposition.

One day late in February Nicoll met Abe at the corner. "I'm sorry, Abe," he said, "but you're backing the wrong horse. Consolidation is bound to carry. You are going to lose prestige by your defeat."

"I don't care," Abe replied with such a power of emphasis as almost to shake Nicoll's convictions. "I am right; you are wrong. I can't explain my real objections; but that makes them no less valid. I've been right before. If we hadn't had Blaine, there wouldn't be a child ready for high school now; we'd have had change after change; the kids would have stuck in grade five."

"I know, Abe, I know. This is different."

"In what way? You think one thing; I think another. If this district goes in, every settler will be sorry one day. That's why I fight the thing."

Nicoll hesitated. "They attribute personal motives to you."

"What personal motives could there be?"

"They say you want the distinction of being the only one who can send his children to high school."

"Nicoll! If consolidation carries, my children will attend the local school. If I had my will, they'd be kept at home. But I leave that sort of thing to my wife.' . . .

Early in March Schweigel came to Abe's yard.

"Oh, Mis-ter Spalding," he exclaimed, clasping his hands in front of his face, "what a place!" And he looked at house, barns, and wind-breaks. "The abode of kings!" He alighted from his wagon, grotesque in his long horse-hide coat which flapped about him like a tent. His face, hairless except for a furry little beard below the chin, beamed like the moon. "This is farming indeed!" And his voice trailed off in a treble of admiration.

Abe stood towering at a distance. "Anything I can do for you?"

"Oh, mister, if you would! A little hay. Just a little. My poor horses have nothing to eat. I'll pay. I have brought my goods. A piece of print for your lady. Curtains for the house. Needles and thread. Whatever you wish. A pair of rubbers for yourself."

"Never mind," said Abe. "You needn't pay for a bit of feed."

"Mister!" the Jew exclaimed; and it was hard to say whether he implored Abe to accept a trifle or adored him for refusing to do so.

"Help yourself!" Abe said with a sweep of his arm towards the haystack in the yard; and he made as if to turn away.

"You are like a kind who commands," the Jew cried rapturously; "and the rabble runs. You shall have my vote."

Abe frowned. "As for your vote, you will do as you think best. I am not asking for support."

"You don't need to ask, mister. Your wishes are known."

"My wishes," Abe said sharply, "have nothing to do with it. When I argue, I do so to give facts which the people may not know."

"Who would dare to go against you, mister?"

"Help yourself," Abe repeated and strode away.

When the Jew left the yard, his lame little horse could hardly draw the load, though the man lent all the help he could by pushing from behind. . . .

During the next two weeks five of the seven districts concerned held their meetings to decide the question. Even into this matter of assigning the dates calculation entered. Next to Morley, Britannia District was most enthusiastically in favour of the measure; and therefore it was the first to hold its meeting; the vote was unanimous. Morley held back. The promoters of the scheme knew that any movement gathers momentum by its own progress. The final stage of the campaign must be opened by a favourable vote; but had it been the vote of Morley itself, the example might have worked the wrong way. Followed three districts south of the Line. In all three the measure was carried. Then came Morley; and Spalding was next. Five districts, therefore, were pledged; a sixth one was sure to follow : Bays. Spalding was the only really doubtful one; and that only on account of Abe's influence. Whenever probabilities were weighed, the result seemed uncertain. But Wheeldon was confident. "Wait and see !" he said.

The night of the meeting came.

From half-past seven on the ratepayers and their women began to assemble at the school where a gasoline lamp was suspended from a hook in the ceiling : that lamp had once lighted Abe's old house.

Shortly before eight came a mild surprise. McCrae appeared accompanied by a young lady who presumably was his wife. He was little known in the district, and people looked curiously at the pair. The lady was young, pretty, bashful; smilingly she looked about from under a lowered brow. McCrae had just moved out; as a returned man he had received clear title to his land, in addition to financial help for the purchase of equipment. They sat next to the Schweigels who had so far drawn the lion's share of attention. Mrs. Schweigel was more than pretty; she was a beauty; and she was surprisingly well dressed.

Apart from these two all the women were middle-aged or

elderly; in their apparel, fashion was strikingly disregarded. The Ukrainian women were sitting together, separated from their men who lined the wall opposite the windows. One of these women looked jaundiced, in contrast to Shilloe, her husband, who was handsome in his Slavic way.

Then the two Elliots entered; and Mrs. Elliot was scanned with curiosity; she was delicate and carried herself in a haughty way. Her presence put a stop to the last whisper of conversation. A dead silence fell, broken only by a cough here and there.

Nicoll was sitting gravely alongside the teacher's desk.

Then, following each other in rapid succession, the protagonists of the occasion arrived. First Wheeldon, small, erect, filled with the sense of his own importance, accompanied by his wife, still smaller, in spite of the enormously high hat by which she sought to correct this deficiency of nature. Then Abe, huge, towering, reaching up, as he passed along the aisle, into the shadows above the cone of light shed by the lamp. Ruth waddled to the first seat from the door.

Abe went straight to the front where he nodded to Nicoll and, bending down, asked him a question. As he straightened, his glance swept over the assembly. Not a ratepayer was missing. To his surprise he saw Nicoll's two eldest daughters. Had they the vote?

The meeting was opened by the usual formula; Abe asked Nicoll to read the minutes of the last public meeting. While this was done, he sat down, his face expressive of the utmost indifference. Yet, as his eye alighted on Wheeldon, his lips straightened. The point at issue was not so much consolidation as the question who should, in future, determine the policy of the district. The discussion to follow was mere pretence; the vote would go as Abe or his opponent was favoured.

Nicoll finished. Abe called for a motion to adopt or amend the minutes. Mover and seconder rose so promptly that Abe felt at once he was merely taking part in a prearranged play. Yet, the formalities having been gone through, he rose and stated the purpose of the meeting, known to all. "The question is open for discussion."

There was a minute's profound silence. A tension spread through the room, as though people knew what was to follow. All eyes were on Abe; through them the tension flowed into him.

Then the chief surprise was sprung. Wheeldon rose and, from a paper in his hand, read a motion to decide the question at issue by a poll. Elliot promptly rose and seconded the motion.

"Ladies and gentlemen," Abe said, "it has been moved and seconded that the question be decided by poll. We are assembled here to discuss that question. I have no objection to a poll, but——"

Wheeldon had risen and stood waiting. Abe looked at him without completing his sentence.

"Mr. Chairman," Wheeldon said pugnaciously, "there is a motion before the meeting. It is customary to put such a motion to the vote."

Abe frowned. Was the intention to muzzle him? "Ladies and gentlemen, you have heard the motion. All in favour—— Against——"

But the show of hands left a doubt. "The secretary will count hands."

Nicoll rose and went through the aisles. There were nine votes against the motion. "In favour——" Eleven in favour. Which meant that eleven had withheld their votes,

"Carried," Abe said. "There will be a poll. I repeat, it seems to me we came here to discuss the question at issue——"

Again Wheeldon was on his feet. "I move we adjourn."

Henry Topp seconded this motion; and it was carried.

Abe rose. "Just a moment." He bent down to Nicoll. As he straightened, nobody could have told that the course the meeting had taken affected him in the least. "The poll will, according to law, be held in this school, on April the second, one week from to-day, between the hours of nine in the morning and five in the afternoon. Mr. Nicoll will act as returning officer; Mr. Blaine as clerk. The meeting is adjourned." And, without stopping to speak to any one, he went out, backed his cutter away from the fence, behind the long rows of vehicles slanting into the ditch. There he sat, waiting for Ruth who was speaking to one or two of the women. Their roles had been exchanged.

XVII * THE POLL

DURING the week, Abe left his farm only twice, on Friday and Sunday, to fetch Marion and Jim from Somerville and to take them back. Apart from that, he prepared for the spring work.

Most people felt that the meeting had been used to settle the old score of envy. Spalding had gained by what appeared to be a defeat. To the new settlers, the old score meant nothing.

Abe was a picturesque figure personifying such success as was possible in the west.

Abe was ready to sink his personal wish in the general will. So far, democracy was a reality to him. Nor was he going to weaken what he felt to have been a moral victory; he would look on in silence. He was now convinced that his side would carry the day; Wheeldon had miscalculated. He had always claimed that Abe carried things with a high hand; if it was true, which Abe would not have admitted, Wheeldon had shown himself an apt pupil : what could have been more high-handed than the way in which he had imposed his will on the meeting? What drove Wheeldon to this revenge? That he had been unsuccessful in his attempt to bribe him; and that he was so small of stature !

If Abe did nothing, Wheeldon did a great deal. From his gate Abe saw the old car on the road to town, travelling at a furious rate, dangerous while there was snow on the ground; or it was standing in front of one of the farmsteads, outlined against the windy, white sky.

The poll opened on Tuesday at nine o'clock. Nicoll was at the desk, ballot-box and all the paraphernalia of a formal election before him. Beside him sat Blaine, his bearded head trembling over his papers. Not a person appeared before one in the afternoon; then, as is usual in rural elections, the whole vote was polled in an hour.

Wheeldon was the first to enter. He presented a certificate signed by the secretary of the municipality stating that he was entitled to be present in the polling room and to scrutinize such electors as might appear. A similar certificate, he said, had been mailed to Mr. Spalding.

Nicoll was puzzled. Every person entitled to vote was known to him. There could be no reason for challenging votes. His own honesty, he thought, was unquestioned. Such things were done in provincial or federal, perhaps even municipal elections where unknown people might appear. But in a school vote? However, it was perfectly legal; all rules applying to municipal elections also applied to a poll taken in a school district. If the machinery of the law was to be set in motion to no purpose, he, Nicoll, could not object.

To no purpose? A purpose there was. Nicoll felt vaguely disturbed.

Outside, there was a confused noise of voices. The electors were gathering in the school yard. It was a mild day; the road to town was soft though snow still remained in the ditches.

For another ten minutes nobody entered. Wheeldon was sitting in one of the school seats.

Then Stanley opened the door. Nicoll looked up and saw that at least a majority of the ratepapers and their wives were assembled. They were improving the occasion by turning it into a social affair. Perhaps only Abe was not yet present; him Nicoll would have seen on his way, through the window. He handed Stanley a ballot paper and pointed to the cloakroom in which he was to mark it.

Nicoll's musing proceeded. Abe had never fraternized; neither had he ever canvassed before. "Elect me or not; you know your interests." This time, however, Abe had condescended to argue.

Nicoll did not understand why Abe opposed the new order. There was that irrationality of all human decisions which arise from our nature and which, *ex post facto*, we prop and strengthen by arguments and reasons from which they do not spring. Even material interests count for little where something deeper is at stake. Abe was maintaining two children in town; yet he opposed a scheme designed to throw a not inconsiderable fraction of the expense on the public purse. Nicoll had known Abe too long to believe that he took his stand for selfish reasons. No matter what Wheeldon and others said, he had never decided a question involving others on the basis of private considerations.

As the voting proceeded, Nicoll looked from time to time at Wheeldon. Did Wheeldon act from purely interested motives? Not one of his children was of high-school age. But Wheeldon, though naturalized in Canada, remained at heart a citizen of the United States, and considering the ways of the country of his birth the best in the world, felt it incumbent upon him to keep alive the tradition or fiction that the Yankee is more progressive than any one else on earth. Change seemed progress to him. Wheeldon opposed Abe on principle. To outsiders, Abe looked like an imperturbable mass in repose; he had begun to move slowly and deliberately; when he spoke and acted, it seemed as though words and actions were based on things deeper than the impulses which caused others to speak or act. This gave him that appearance of an assumed superiority antagonizing those who themselves laid claim to a measure of superiority over others. Abe had a way of looking at Wheeldon as if he were lowering down on one whom it was scarcely worth his while to annihilate; though Nicoll knew that such was largely unintentional.

Wheeldon's presence in the polling room had a purpose;

and it was directed against Abe. Though Abe and Nicoll were, for the first time, irreconcilably aligned on opposite sides, Nicoll trembled at the thought that Abe might go down to defeat.

The voting proceeded briskly. Whenever one elector left the building another entered. All smiled or frowned at Wheeldon's presence.

Blaine, his glasses slipped down to the tip of his nose, his leonine head quivering over the poll book, searched for the name of the voter and, with a trembling hand, checked it off. During these intervals, such a drowsy silence fell over the room that it was almost possible to understand what was being said outside.

By two o'clock, four-fifths of the votes were polled. Nobody had left the school yard; everybody seemed to be waiting for a climax to come. Outside the yard, half a score of sleighs and cutters stood aligned; the horses, with blankets under the harness or robes thrown over it, stood motionless in the snow, their heads hanging low.

Nicoll sat, looking out through the windows. Across the corner lay his own yard, surrounded by a wind-break of poplars, bare of leaves. Black boughs and twigs traced an irregular lattice-work against the ever whitish sky. Here and there a branch was strung with swollen, bulbous knots. Fifteen years ago Abe had warned him against cottonwoods, the popular tree for planting on the prairie. "Quick to grow; but they don't last." He had been right, of course. Down to the nature of the wind-breaks, the district bore the imprint of Abe's mind.

Yet, Nicoll and Abe were aligned on opposite sides!

Suddenly the room was stirred by the touch of drama. Looking out through the windows, Nicoll felt his muscles tightening. Blaine raised his trembling head. Wheeldon twisted himself around in his seat.

At the corner, Abe was swinging up on the culvert, its timbers resounding under the hoofs of his horses. In his long, low cutter he was sitting by the side of his wife. He was driving briskly, touching his black hackneys with the whip as they slowed on the culvert which was bare of snow. He sat motionless, impressive, in an old raccoon coat and a wedge-shaped cap of muskrat. Both were bare of fur in places; but on Abe they looked like Royal attire. His smooth-shaven face, deeply lined, stern and inexorable, was like a red, weathered mask.

Ruth, in the squirrel coat which he had given her long ago and which had had to be widened from year to year, massive though she was, looked dwarfed by his side.

Somehow it was known in the district that Ruth would vote

against her husband; her appearance, as two dozen pairs of eyes scanned the pair, confirmed that rumour. There were those in the crowd who, in Abe's place, would have left their wives at home; and some accorded him a grudging respect because he could give the other side its due. Two or three, in their hearts, cried out, "Damn him!" For the mere fact that he had not joined the crowd an hour ago but came at his own time and pleasure, driving briskly up to cast his vote, and, no doubt, intending to leave as briskly, for he did not enter the row of vehicles but, having passed the school, turned in the margin of the road and stopped behind the sleighs, in the ditch—that mere fact marked him off from the rest of the settlers; *he* was no mixer; *he* followed a lonely path—worst of crimes in western Canada.

In the schoolroom, an enormous and incomprehensible tension took hold of Nicoll. From the moment Abe had come within sight, the stream of voters had ceased. The few who had not yet cast their votes waited to give Abe the precedence. Irrationally, Nicoll had a foreboding: something hovered over the building which was catastrophic.

Outside, Abe, heavily and slowly alighting, was seen to exchange a word with his wife, presumably offering to let her go first. But she shook her head, and he handed her the lines, turning away. The crowd looked on in silence, half sullen, half expectant; a few had a welcoming smile on their lips. As Abe entered through the gate by the flagpole, he nodded. A lane opened to the door. He went on without stopping.

In the room, the air of tension became enormously intensified by the fact that Wheeldon rose as the doorknob turned.

Abe went straight on through the central aisle, taking notice of Wheeldon's presence only by the slightest raising of one brow. He nodded to Nicoll and Blaine and reached for a ballot paper.

At this, Wheeldon took a step forward. "Mr. Returning Officer, I object to Mr. Spalding's voting."

Abe frowned. Nicoll and Blaine looked up, startled. Was this man out of his senses? Challenge Abe Spalding?

"Do you mean to say——"

"I challenge his right to vote. You know your duty. Tender the oath."

Nicoll shrugged his shoulders and turned to Blaine. "A Bible around?"

Blaine was so excited that, in trying to open a lower drawer of the desk, he went down on his knees. A moment later, Nicoll placed a worn copy of the Bible on the edge of the desk-top.

Abe stood motionless. Wheeldon had the right to challenge any voter. In tendering the oath, Nicoll was doing no more than his duty. Abe had only the vaguest idea of the wording of that oath. He knew he could be asked to swear that he was the man named in the voters' list. But not even Wheeldon could possibly doubt that.

Nicoll opened a copy of the Public Schools Act at the page where the various schedules were printed. He looked up, confused. "You know——"

"I know. Go ahead."

Nicoll read slowly, Abe speaking after him, word for word, with only the person changed from the second to the first. Blaine was filling in a blank form of Abe's signature.

"I swear I am the person named or purported to be named in the list of ratepayers shown to me.

"That I am a natural born subject of His Majesty and of the full age of twenty-one years.

"That I have not voted before at this election.

"That I have not directly or indirectly received any reward or gift; nor do I expect to receive any reward or gift for the vote which I tender at this election.

"That I have not received anything, nor has anything been promised to me, directly or indirectly, either to induce me to vote at this election, or for loss of time, travelling expenses, hire of team, or any other service connected with this election.

"And that I have not, directly or indirectly, paid or promised anything to any person to induce him either to vote or to refrain from voting at this election."

The atmosphere, during these proceedings, was that of an unbearable anxiety on one side of the desk; of scorn on the other; as though Abe, by the tone of his voice, were saying, "When is this farce to end?" Yet, when he repeated the last paragraph, a though flitted through his mind: "That's what he expected I could not swear to."

But there was one short paragraph left; and Nicoll read it.

The thunderbolt fell; Abe's voice ceasing repeating the words.

That paragraph, as read, bore the wording, "And that you are not indebted to the municipality in respect of taxes other than taxes for the current year. So help you God."

Abe's voice droned on, "And that I am not indebted to the municipality in respect of taxes——" And then it ceased.

A storm of impulses raced through Abe's mind. As if he were reaching out into the universe for a cosmic weapon to strike his opponent down. He would write a cheque for the amount, overdrawing his account at the bank; he would give an order on his brother-in-law; he would step into the road and ask Ruth for the loan of the money. . . .

The world was falling to pieces. Nobody in the district had ever been debarred from voting on such a score. Many a time, no doubt, many a one, if that was the law, had been technically in default. Every one, probably; he, Abe, never. This thing dishonoured. He had tried to cast a vote to which he was not entitled. He had held office in district and municipality and was not entitled to either. Things had gone on because nobody had happened to object. Nobody ever did object when the voter was a bona-fide settler. The letter of the law was disregarded to uphold its spirit; now the letter of the law was invoked to thwart its spirit. He, Abe Spalding, who had made this district—for how many settlers would have held out unless he had helped them : unless he had given them work; unless, on occasion, he had given them food or feed?—*he* was being deprived of his vote; and it was done according to the letter of the law! Then the law itself was evil!

He realized that none of his impulses would change the situation; that situation was without remedy. For the second time in his life he stood face to face with an unalterable fact. The first time the hand of God had advanced the fact; this time it was the hand of man!

Mentally, as he stood there, he shook himself free of all bonds of office. Never again would he meddle in public affairs!

Yet, if, five minutes ago, he had been a tree in the forest, he was now a tree at the root of which the axe had been laid!

All this time—it was less than a minute since Nicoll had ceased speaking—the others in the room had been staring at him, two of them as profoundly shaken as himself; the third one triumphant. In Abe's face, not a muscle had moved. But Nicoll realized what this meant to the district. In his breast cried a voice, "Go on, Abe; For God's sake, go on! What are you waiting for?" Blaine's head swayed and trembled.

Wheeldon's lips were twisted in a thin smile, not altogether of triumph. He realized that he had released in that imperturbable giant more than he had known to exist in his depth. He had not meant to bring him to the ground; he had meant merely to indent his armour.

Without a word, without a sound, without a flicker of eye, brow, or facial muscle, yet white-lipped, Abe veered, retraced his steps to the door, and went out, allowing the door to slam behind his back.

Outside, the crowd had been laughing; for since John Elliot's coming Henry Topp had found his match; the two had been "performing" for the crowd. At Abe's sight, a silence fell; the lane opened; and without glancing right or left, Abe passed on to his cutter.

There, Ruth rose and shook herself free of the rugs.

"Never mind," Abe said gently. "Sit down. We are going home."

"I haven't voted."

"You can't vote. Stay where you are. I have been disqualified."

Ruth sank back, her knees giving way beneath her.

Abe reached for the lines and clicked his tongue before he had entered the sleigh. The horses, stall-fed, jumped forward. He stepped in and hit the seat with a heavy thud.

One single laugh was heard behind—Henry Topp's. . . .

At midnight, Abe drove to town with two letters. One was addressed to Stanley Nicoll; the other to Mr. Silcox, secretary of the municipality of Somerville. They contained his resignations as a trustee of Spalding School District and as reeve of the municipality respectively. To the latter, Ruth's cheque for the amount of his arrears in taxes was attached; to the former, the stub of the cheque-book recording the payment.

Never again! Never again! But what?

XVIII * JIM

CONSOLIDATION was carried in Spalding District by a majority of one; in spite of the fact that Nicoll —who never mentioned it till many years later when even Abe could laugh over it—had voted against the measure, by way of protest against the method used to defeat Abe Spalding.

The manner in which Abe took his defeat was quite independent of the outcome of the poll. He might have contested the result; for Nicoll, who made it a point to inquire, found that no less than three others had voted without being entitled to do so, for the very reason for which Abe had been debarred. It also became known that Henry Topp had changed sides on the promise of his appointment as van-driver for the district; Wheeldon, had he been challenged, so Nicoll suspected, would have lost his vote because it was he who had made that promise to Henry. Nicoll told Abe; but Abe refused to make use of the information.

Nor would he reconsider his resignation as reeve. Rogers and others no sooner heard of it than they came to see him; he listened to what they had to say: never before had the council been in greater need of his level-headedness and honesty; never had his ward been in greater need of his championship; for that very spring, the heaviest snowfalls of the season coming in April, the ditches refused to function. When Abe had heard them, he said one single word, "No," and turned his back.

Nicoll thought it worth his while to take at least the sting out of Abe's defeat by speaking to him alone. He intercepted him on his way back from town. When Abe crossed the culvert, he stepped right into the road so as to force him to stop. Abe frowned as he drew in.

"Listen here, Abe," Nicoll said. "There'll be an election. We shall have one trustee on the consolidated board. Will you stand?"

"Haven't you realized yet that I was disqualified?"

"That was mere chance. You are in good standing again. Surely, Abe, you are not going to bear us all a grudge because Wheeldon——"

"Wheeldon was within his rights. There is nothing to be said."

"If you decline, he is going to be on that board himself. We want you. I could promise you an almost unanimous vote."

Abe clicked his tongue. "I have washed my hands of it."

"Abe," Nicoll pleaded, striding along by the side of the sleigh, one hand on the back of the seat, "if men like you refuse, politics is bound to be the dirty game it is. It isn't democratic——"

"Democratic!" Abe sneered with darkening brow. "I'll tell you what your precious democracy is. A system devised to keep the man who stands out from the common crowd down to the common level. That is all."

And, Nicoll falling back, he drove on more quickly.

Although it had been nearly dark, Abe had seen a hurt expression in Nicoll's face which haunted him without softening him. For the moment it made his mood all the more savage. "Why can't they leave me alone?"

At the house, it was different. In speaking to Ruth, Abe's tone was more than usually considerate. Yet he promptly arranged for the repayment of her loan to him; he sold half a dozen Percheron colts, a score of steers, and a few milch cows.

Abe having no help but Jim's, the measure was dictated by considerations other than financial.

He would have time now! Time for his family and for—what?

Meanwhile the lateness of the spring began to worry the district. Snow lay deep again; and it was the third week of April before the thaw recommenced. As is common in such years, the weather softened with a heavy rain shot with sleet. The flood which should have subsided by 1st May was just coming down by that date; and since the stages of successive thaws were omitted, it was unusually abundant, especially since the flow in the ditches was sluggish. Culverts and bridges were dislodged; and Abe witnessed, for the first time, a distinct current over his fields. In the barns, the beasts could not lie down. Only house, granaries, and hen-house remained dry. Abe reaped the benefit of double-walled foundations now; not a drop of water entered his cellar.

Often, while this second great flood lasted, he went in his big hip-boots to the gate of his yard to look on from a distance while the other settlers worked on the bridges with teams of sixteen horses, drawing them back into place and anchoring them. In previous years he would have organized the work; he had taught them in the past how to do it. Nobody would have dreamt of presenting the municipality with a bill for work done; and the council, on the other hand, would have been powerfully urged to prevent a recurrence of such an event.

Well, let them work out their own salvation now! Abe did not go near them. He took his spy-glass and watched them from the gap in his wind-break; and when things went wrong, the culvert floating off again after it had been dragged into place, but did not laugh; he merely grunted.

Seeding time came, and Abe fetched Jim. Together they ploughed.

Meanwhile curious, seismic movements shook the grain markets. Government control of the price of wheat had been continued; and all the speculative impulses let loose by the cessation of hostilities were directed towards the other grains, oats, barley, flax. Flax was selling around five dollars a bushel, three hundred per cent of the normal price. The very lateness of the spring favoured flax as a crop for the district. But seed rose to seven and eight dollars a bushel. Farmers had no money; the municipality had to help. Rogers was filling the vacancy left by Abe's resignation; and he headed a committee to deal with the situation, the outcome being that every farmer was to receive a small allotment of seed flax, according to the acreage under cultivation on his farm, the price to be a lien on the crop.

Abe would have been entitled to a considerable fraction of the seed set aside for his ward. But he declined. He did not wish to have further credit dealings with the municipality. But when Jim, who, having been in town for many months, seemed suddenly to have grown up, attacked his father's policy, Abe defended it on purely economic grounds. Flax was selling at an abnormal price, true; but last year no more than the normal acreage had been devoted to it. This year that acreage would be enormously increased. That was the way, he explained to Jim—a hit-or-miss way, wasteful and cruel—in which abnormal market conditions corrected themselves. The increased acreage brought a glut; the glut a disastrous drop in price. Even three dollars a bushel, with abnormal seed-prices, abnormal wages, and a yield of eight bushels to the acre, would mean a loss to the farmer. The price would fall even lower.

Sound reasoning—for normal times. But Abe was merely justifying his disinclination, not only to take seed on credit, but to go with the crowd. He had five hundred acres ready. He seeded wheat.

Jim was almost as tall as his father, though of course not of his massive and powerful build. Reports from Somerville High School had denounced him as mischievous. It is not uncommon to call that mischief in a boy which is the premature and inconvenient manifestation of propensities in which valuable gifts are foreshadowed. When Abe had taken Jim to task, half indulgently, the boy had admitted that he had tampered with such apparatus as was used in the teaching of science. He assured his father he had meant no harm; he had been curious to see how this apparatus worked. Abe, while not absolving him, had accepted his word. On another occasion Abe received a letter from the principal, complaining that Jim was disrespectful. Jim explained that, during a lesson in physics, he had expressed his disbelief in a fact asserted by the pedagogue. "It slipped out of me." Abe asked for details. The fact in question was that a bullet shot from a gun in an absolutely horizontal direction would touch absolutely level ground at precisely the same moment as a bullet merely dropped from the height of the muzzle of that gun. By his impulsive exclamation Jim had, according to Dr. Vanbruik, merely shown the true scientific spirit which refuses to accept facts of observation without verifying them. Abe refused to punish the boy and, in a note to the principal, told him of his decision. In this he was confirmed by Jim's protestation that physics was his favourite subject at school.

Jim was a born mechanic. When Abe saw him adjusting his disk-harrow and asked where he had learned that, Jim told him that he had spent most of his leisure time at Duncan and Ferris's implement shop.

"Do you mean to say working?"

Jim grinned and pulled out a roll of bills. "I made fifty dollars last month putting seeders together."

Abe nodded.

"Say, daddy," Jim asked, "can I do with this as I please?"

"It's your money."

Yet, personally, Jim was clumsy; his voice was hoarse.

One day, coming home at noon, they found Ruth "in a taking". It was washing day; something had gone wrong with the electric machine; she was using a rubbing board to get at least part of the work done. Jim promptly went into the basement. Within ten minutes he returned. "I've fixed that for you, mother; it was a short."

Abe knew what that meant; but he could not have effected the repair. Yet he disliked Jim's syncopation of speech. Since Charlie's death he had not used a slang word.

Jim worked on the farm for three weeks; Abe did not ask for more. By himself he seeded stubble to barley; he was not going to look for outside help; by the middle of June he started work on his fallows.

Throughout the spring Marion had not been home; it was her second year in high school, and there were Saturday lessons and reviews; when school closed, she and Jim went to Morley by train, and their aunt brought them out in her car.

Mary had not yet left when Abe came home in the dusk of the longest day of the year. Brother and sister met near the car in the outer yard.

"Abe," Mary said, "why don't you drop in as you used to do?"

"I've been busy. I have no help."

"But you've been in town. You've been at the store."

"I haven't been fit for company. You've brought the children?"

"Yes. I don't know where Jim is. Marion's at the house."

"Get in. I'll crank the car. Don't worry. We'll see."

The car swinging out, Abe looked gloomily after it. He went to the back of the house where the cellar of the old house, now covered with planks, was slowly caving in; Abe had never found time to fill the hole.

At that moment Jim issued from the new barn, depositing two pails at its door and bringing another to the house. "Hello, dad," he sang. "I've done your milking. That spotty one, isn't she a corker?"

"I leave the calf with her. If you milk her, she should be tied."

"Oh," said Jim, "but I milked with the machine."

Abe said nothing. Since Horanski had left, he had done the milking by hand. This boy of his had the spirit of the machine.

That night, Abe lay awake for many hours, puzzling over his relation to the children. While they were little, he had been preoccupied with the farm; while they were adolescent, he had been immersed in public business. Why should he think about these things now when it was painful to do so? Why indeed, except because he had withdrawn from that material world in which alone he had felt at home? They were preparing to depart and to enter that world which he had left. At the best could he hope to meet them at a cross-roads to catch a glimpse of them as they vanished along paths of their own.

At night, the next day, Jim dressed in his town clothes. "I'll walk to town, dad. I've got a deal on with Anderson."

"Take the pony," Abe said.

"No, thanks. I'll walk."

When, late at night, Jim came home, Abe was still sitting up; for though he had not objected to Jim's going to town, he yet felt that he could not go to bed before he returned. Jim entered the lighted yard with a great clatter and clanging; it sounded as though long iron rods were being dragged over cobblestone pavement. Abe rose from his chair in the dining-room where he and Ruth had been sitting.

In the yard, Jim received him with an embarrassed laugh; he was sitting on the floor of a single-seated Ford car which was stripped of everything inessential: running boards, fenders, top, cushions. So that was the deal he had had on with Anderson.

"What did you pay for that pile of junk?" Abe asked.

"Seventy-five. Fifty in cash; a note for the balance."

"Whose note?"

"Mine."

"You are a minor. Your note isn't worth the paper it's written on."

"Right. But Anderson's endorsement makes it good. My credit stands high."

Abe was silent. Then, contemptuously, "Looks like a plucked chicken." And, indeed, the machine looked high-legged and naked.

The name stuck while Jim kept the car. He placed it in the

old open implement shed between the granaries; henceforth, every rainy day, he tinkered there, tightening bolts, painting the body, disassembling and reassembling intricate parts till the whole car was transformed.

One day Abe, suspending the ploughing on the fallow, told Jim at noon to get the buggy ready. It was time to look at the hay.

"Come on, dad," said Jim. "Be a sport. Let's go in my racer."

The girls laughed, for Abe had never yet entered a car.

Abe did not answer; reluctantly he felt that he must indulge the boy: he half resented it that Jim should thus take the lead. When they went into the yard, the girls accompanied them; and Ruth stood at the window of the den to see them start.

Bumping about in the low body in which they reclined, they shot through the gate and turned west, with the exhaust of the engine emitting a deafening bellow. They went all over the western meadows. "All right," Abe said at last. "We'll go ahead a week from to-morrow."

They turned. "Say, dad," Jim asked, "there's a chance of selling this outfit for a hundred and twenty-five. I can get a real car for three hundred from Duncan and Ferris. They'll take my note for the balance. If you pay me fifty dollars a month and time and a half for overtime, I should be able to clear that off in three months."

"I might not have work for you on those terms."

"That'll be all right. I can get a job elsewhere. Lots of farmers asking me in town."

"That so?" Abe felt a pang in his heart. This boy also had the commercial spirit. He did not feel that he was debasing himself by working for the highest bidder: an effect of his stay in town. Did he not know that his father would rather give him any sum than let him go to work away from home?

The summer went by. Repeatedly Jim had criticized his father's methods; especially had he disapproved of Abe's refusal to "go into flax." "Look here," Abe said one day, "who's built the best farm in this district?"

"I know, dad. But this time you're wrong."

"We'll see."

Throughout the district excitement prevailed. Abe had only wheat, the price of which was fixed; he was in no hurry; *he* had no flax.

Everybody else had at least a few acres of his crop. Henry Topp had the largest acreage of all; it took the incentive of a gambling interest to make him work. The only thing which had prevented people from seeding more flax had been the cost of seed; now it looked as if the price of the market might run as high as that of seed in spring.

As usual, threshing started south of the Somerville Line; it had hardly begun when a new factor entered into the situation. Unheard-of wages were being offered to teamsters who had horses and tanks for hauling flax to town before the price broke; for, once the crop began to move, nobody expected that price to hold. Few threshermen, so far, would consider threshing wheat. Flax was the crop of the year. Yet, when a decline in the price level was followed by a prompt recovery, there was a retardation in the movement of the crop. A man with a hundred bushels to sell might make fifty dollars by waiting a day.

The consequence was that every farmer went to town from day to day and sat about at the elevator to listen to the announcement of the fluctuations in price which were made from hour to hour. At a given moment, when the price, having broken, stiffened again, there would be a frantic bidding for teams or a sudden rush of selling; for a few shrewd men came on top of a load which they parked to wait for a rise; when it came, they ran for their teams and drove up to the platform to sell before the next drop. Others, observing that every fall in price was made up for shortly by a rise beyond the previous level, took their loads home at night, to make an additional profit next day.

Into this excitement fell, like a bomb, the announcement that John Elliott who had only a small crop, for little was broken on his place, had been offered twenty thousand dollars for his land. Still more astounding, he declined, holding out for five thousand more. The would-be buyer, however, acquired two farms south of the Line instead. The district was drunk with the spirit of speculation.

Jim, who went often to town now, at night, brought the story home; and when farmers at last offered five, six, eight dollars, not for a day's work, but for hauling a load over a distance of four or five miles, he announced that he, too, was going to pick up easy money.

To his amazement Abe said briefly, "No. You won't."

Jim looked at his father. "Why not, dad?"

"Because I say so."

"But dad——" However, seeing his father's frown, he did not insist. "At any rate, I wish you'd give me the morning, dad. I'd like to see how things are going at the elevators."

"You can have the morning. But you won't haul."

"All right, dad."

Jim reached the first elevator south of the track at eight o'clock. A crowd was assembled. A number of farmers were leaving to fetch their flax; the price stood at the fabulous level of five dollars and sixty cents. The situation was the more exciting since the price was expected to break any moment; once broken, it would tumble till it reached its normal level of less than two dollars.

Jim backed his second-hand touring car into the row of vehicles south of the elevator and returned to the incline. He saw Elliott, Wheeldon, Horanski, Hartley, and Nicoll, with a crowd of strangers, and excitedly nodded to them all. On the dumping platform a score of men were standing about, among them Henry Topp. Of the two buyers, one was sitting in the engine room, next to the telephone; the other, loading a car on the track. All business except that of flax was suspended.

A farmer, who, the day before, had brought a load of wheat had met with a curious situation. His wheat had graded number two; but the buyer told him that he had only one bin with storage for wheat available; unfortunately it was partly filled with grain that had graded number five; if he would let his wheat go at that grade, he could sell; if not, he would have to take the load home again. The difference between the grades amounted to twenty-five cents or fifteen dollars the load. The farmer had tried the other elevators; and, curiously, the same situation had prevailed there. He needed money; he had come eighteen miles; his horses were tired and not of the strongest. He sold. At once a rumour sprang up that this was a put-up game to "do" the farmer; a few years later such things drove thousands into the pools.

Suddenly an announcement was made : "Five-seventy-five."

Henry Topp jumped like a clown in a circus. "They call me the runt!" he yelled "But I'm the guy who pays the fair price. Ten dollars a load."

A thick-set bearded Mennonite stolidly outbade him. "Ten and a half."

Suppose a man took seventy bushels in a load, this was fifteen cents a bushel for hauling. But nobody stirred. With flax close to six dollars a bushel, something spectacular was expected to happen. Should the price break, the scramble for teams would be even more frantic. When wages offered reached twelve dollars a load, with nobody taking the offer, Henry Topp had an inspiration. Jim, with most of the others, was sitting on the railing of the incline, his long legs drawn up angularly, his spine bent into an arc, his cap pushed back.

"Eat my shirt!" Henry yelled. "And my boots too, doggone you! I'll pay by the bushel. A quarter a bushel!" And to emphasize what he had said, he hurled his cap to the ground and trampled on it, turning his heels and grinding it into the cinders of the driveway.

His bid was followed by a silence; it sobered the crowd. They were figuring out what that amounted to by the load; just as previously everybody had figured out what a bid by the load amounted to by the bushel.

But the silence was only momentary. First Elliot, then two others outbade Henry Topp. A few teams aligned at the bottom of the incline; one, a four-horse team with a hundred-bushel tank, pulled up to the platform. People's thoughts were diverted: that man was going to take home five hundred and seventy-five dollars for his load. What did it matter what was paid for hauling? Bidding rose to thirty-five cents.

Bedlam broke loose. Nobody considered the distance. What did it matter? Nobody would get more than one load per team to town before the price broke. If it broke now, so much the worse for the farmer, that was all.

Wheeldon, however, waxed indignant. "Hi there!" he shouted. "Do you call that fair play? It's robbery! That's what I call it."

Elliot turned on him, a broad grin on his red, round face. "Forty cents," he said, bowing to Wheeldon as if handing a bouquet to a lady.

Everybody gasped. Twenty-four dollars for a small load! An hour's work with a team of horses!

"Dammit!" Henry Topp yelled at Elliot's back, "why don't you say fifty? Are you tight?" And with a war-whoop which made the horses nodding up the incline raise startled heads, he swung his arms, cheering, and shouted, "Half a dollar a bushel. Come on, you loafers!"

In the entrance to the platform, the buyer appeared. "Five-eighty."

This increased the commotion. Lightning-quick, deals were struck. Everybody offered half a dollar. Horanski and Nawosad, though they had flax to sell themselves, closed with Wheeldon; they had to fetch their wagons, for they had walked to town. Wheeldon would take them in his car. Hartley and Shilloe closed with Elliot; Hilmer and an outsider with Henry Topp. Nicoll had brought one of his three loads along. A man from south of the Line spoke to Jim; no settler from Spalding District would have offered Abe's son a job.

There was a rush for cars and teams. Elliot came over to

Jim. "Gimme a ride?" He had a wagon but handed it over to Shilloe.

When Jim started in the wake of Wheeldon, he carried seven people, two squatting on his running boards.

Nobody knew that a townsman had also been watching developments. Before noon Anderson had a string of new Ford cars coming in from Somerville, ready to take some of the easy money.

John Elliott sat with Jim in the front seat. "By jingo," he said. "I believe I'll buy a car to-night."

"Unless the price breaks," Jim added.

"Go on. That price will hold for years!"

As a matter of fact, Elliot did buy a Ford car that night; and so did Henry Topp and Wheeldon.

The road was in a poor state of repair; but Wheeldon ahead of Jim, drove with reckless expertness; and Jim, dropping his passengers at their respective destinations, followed closely in his wake.

When Wheeldon stopped to set Horanski down, it struck Jim that the Ukrainian, too, had flax; and yet he was going to haul for Wheeldon. "Horanski," he shouted after him, "haven't you flax of your own?"

The Ukrainian did not stop in his run. "Sure," he called back over his shoulder; "sell him to-morrow."

When Jim got home, he found his father in the east half of the new barn, putting his binders away for the winter.

"Dad!" he called in his hoarse, loud voice, from the door. "Flax is nearly six dollars. Fifty cents for hauling a bushel."

Abe straightened his back and looked at Jim without speaking.

"You were wrong this time!" Jim went on and plunged into a report of what he had witnessed.

Abe listened without betraying his thoughts. He was fifty years old; he felt older; but he did not mean to surrender the lead just yet. His own crop was by no means a failure; it had been seeded at small cost; it was wheat, which meant food for man. He could afford to despise easy money; he had declined to undertake what he abhorred, a speculation.

Jim went to town again next morning. Elliot had sold at five-ninety, Wheeldon at five-ninety-eight; and still the price rose. When Horanski brought his single load, he received six dollars and three cents a bushel.

But it snowed up on 9th October. Nobody in the district did any fall ploughing. All the work was left till spring.

Shortly, the new school was opened at Morley. It was a holiday for the neighbourhood; a deal of speech-making was to be done; and Ruth went with Jim and the girls in Jim's car. Abe stayed at home.

XIX * THE NEW SCHOOL

EVERY now and then, during the summer, Abe had seen something of the great building going up just east of the town.

It was an imposing structure comprising six classrooms, laboratories, teachers' offices, and an assembly hall; the whole built in the form of the letter H. A long, shed-like stable marked the east line of the five-acre yard, large enough to accommodate six summer and six winter vans with twelve horses. The summer vans resembled such stage coaches as had been in use twenty years ago; the winter vans, mounted on bob-sleighs, had box-like canvas tops with a flue-pipe projecting from the roofs. Inside there was a driver's seat; behind it, a stove screwed to the floor; and two benches running the length of the van.

The school was administered by a board consisting of one trustee from each district, Spalding District being represented by Wheeldon. The local school remained closed. Mr. Blaine retired.

As the time approached, Ruth spoke one evening of the advantage it would be for Marion if she continued at Somerville for her last year.

Abe mused in silence. "Very well," he said at last. "But if Jim and Frances are to go, they will go to Morley. Consolidation has been forced on me. I want to see how this thing works out."

"I am speaking only of Marion," Ruth replied.

Marion, accordingly, was taken back to Somerville. Abe was only too willing to make concessions.

On 1st November, the van service opened, with Henry Topp in charge of Spalding District. The route was prescribed by the board; and when his schedule was announced, Abe laughed. His was the first place at which the driver was to stop in the morning; thence he was to return to Nicoll's Corner; then to go north, to pick up Wheeldon's, Stanley's, Nawosad's children; back again to Nicoll's Corner; east to Hartley's and Shilloe's; a third time back to the corner, to admit Nicoll's children; then south. By the time the van reached the school, Abe's children had travelled fourteen miles; and the van held thirty-one children. Jim and Frances had to board the conveyance at a quarter-past seven, before daylight in winter. It was true that, correspondingly, they reached home at night so much earlier; for apart from Nicoll's children they were the first to be set down of those who lived north of the second ditch. Even so, however, they never came home before five. In 1920, the van was to start from the northernmost point; in 1921 from the point farthest east.

To this aspect of the matter Ruth had never given a thought; and she was dismayed. Often, during the winter, the children were late in getting to school; at night, it was often six and later when they got home.

Jim took things cheerfully. He was glad of the opportunity the new system afforded of meeting and associating with all the boys of his age. Few were in the same grade; for, since there had never been a high school within reach, not many had covered the work of the first year. But that did not matter. He frankly proclaimed that he liked the system.

It was different with Frances. In spite of her plumpness she was pale and of delicate health; she suffered from headaches. Often she felt excessively tired; and that made her ill-humoured. "Oh," she would say when Jim, his work finished, tried to entice her into a game of cards or checkers, "leave me alone. All I want is to go to bed." On Fridays, she heaved a great sigh. "Thank the Lord! Another week gone!"

She was nearly sixteen. Physically, she developed rapidly, though she remained small. Her face assumed a new and alluring prettiness, a plump and slightly anaemic charm, with fair curls hanging down in front of her ears. Abe watched and said nothing.

Every night after supper Ruth insisted on the two children doing their homework under her eyes. Two hours were reserved for the task. Jim sat down without a protest; but he often hid a cheap novel under his books. Frances groaned.

One Friday evening, however, shortly before Christmas, Frances, too, seemed willing enough. She and her brother occupied opposite seats at the dining table, under the frosted bowl of electric bulbs. Ruth sat at the far end in one of the straight-backed chairs, sewing. Opposite her sat Abe, turning the leaves of a great tome with illustrations of ancient buildings. Behind Ruth, in one of the deep, grey chairs from the living-room, Marion reclined, stitching a silky piece of lingerie—her usual occupation when at home.

For an hour a profound silence had reigned in that solemn room when Frances ceased writing and looked up with a laugh.

"Miss Garston gave us for a composition topic, 'Why I like Consolidation,' she said. "Anyone want to read what I've written?"

With a deep frown on his massive face, as though recalling himself from the infinity of space, Abe held out a hand. Frances handed the sheet of paper over with another laugh; she had hardly expected her father to ask for it. As he proceeded, she nervously chewed her pencil.

"Why I like Consolidation," Abe read: "The fact is, I don't like it at all. I have to get up at half-past five in the morning. Breakfast I have at a quarter past six. Before seven I leave the house, warmly wrapped, to walk to the corner of my father's farm. At seven I hand myself over to the jailer who takes me to school. He tries to bandy impertinent jokes with me. In the van it is hot, and I take my wraps off. For the first half-hour it is not too bad. I have at least ample room. Then we pick up a bunch of nine children from three families. Four of them smell of garlic; some of unwashed bodies and unclean clothes. After another three-quarters of an hour we pick up eleven children, nearly all of them objectionable on the score of smell. The air we breathe over and over begins to be so foul that it nauseates me. Whenever the van stops, I bend forward to get a whiff of the delicious cold draught. By this time I am sitting on my wraps; for we are crowded. I hate to do that, for I have nice clothes and like to take care of them. None of the other children will sit still.

"At twenty minutes past nine we reach school and are handed over to a new set of jailers. I am so stupefied with bad air and so tired with jolting that to study is the last thing on earth I want to do. But that is what we are sent for. I should like the work if I reached school fresh after a reasonable night's rest. As it is, I know that whatever I may still be able to do is not worth doing. All day long I watch the clock and resent that it is so slow. The only oasis in the desert of the day is the noon recess when I go down town.

"At four o'clock, which comes as a great relief at last, I must hand myself back to the jailer of the morning, for another drive of sixty or ninety minutes in evil-smelling captivity. When I get home, I have no life left and certainly no desire to write a good composition on 'Why I dislike Consolidation.'"

Abe sat and frowned, his eyes on infinity. As for the contents of this exercise, it confirmed his aversion to the whole system. He might have laughed at it. But over and beyond what he had read, he had received a shattering revelation of the character of the girl. That she was precocious he had known; children were precocious these days. But she was advanced in a way which he could not have defined.

It was Frances who broke the silence in which everybody looked at the father. "I don't think I'll hand that in," she said.

"Why not?" It had been half a minute before Abe spoke.

"They'd can me."

"'Can you?' Can't you speak decent English?"

"Expel me, then."

"Let them try!" Abe got heavily to his feet. "You make a clean copy and hand it in. If they object, you tell them I've read it and approved."

Frances looked at him with an uncertain light in her eyes.

"I want this sheet," Abe said. "Stay where you are. Write it over."

He turned to pace the room. In that writing the girl's soul lay bared; could he allow her to show it to others? There was passion in that exercise. Had Ruth not heard, he would have retracted.

Ruth pushed her glasses back on her bulging forehead. "Let me see that, Frances."

In a strange impulse Abe went through the swing-door into the white-tiled kitchen to reach for the sheepskin in the narrow closet by the side of the wash-basin. For an hour or longer he paced the yard; and not till the lights had flashed on upstairs did he re-enter the house.

Ruth was in the dining-room; she never went to bed before him now.

For a few minutes, Abe walking up and down, there was the silence usual between them. Then Ruth dropped her sewing.

"Abe," she said, looking up, "what can we do about Frances?"

He stopped and pondered, weighing her. Did she see the problem?

"Can't we make an arrangement for the children to drive themselves?"

No. She did not see the problem. Then, as if awaking, "You wanted consolidation, did you not?"

"I want the high school."

Abe stood silent. "You have a problem on your hands," he said at last, "in that girl of yours."

"She is yours as well as mine, Abe."

"Is she?"

This was a cruel thrust. In years gone by Ruth had consciously tried to raise the children so that they would be more hers than his. But Abe regretted what he had said; he knew only too well that he himself had failed his children in the past.

"You have a problem on your hands in the girl," he repeated; "and every parent in the district will have a similar problem."

"Just what do you mean by that, Abe?"

"Unless you feel it, I cannot explain," Abe replied.

On Christmas Day the Spaldings had dinner in town with the Vainbruiks. The weather was mild; for a week it had thawed every day; the eaves of all buildings were strung with icicles; and from the ground their drippings grew up in corresponding cones.

Dinner over, the two women withdrew upstairs; the girls went for a walk; Jim disappeared. The conversation of the men turned to the school.

"I can't say that I like what I see," the doctor said. "Here are two hundred children coming in from the country, fifty adolescents, a few young men and women: all released from patriarchal homes into comparative freedom. The common objection to all public schools—that, in a moral sense, they level down, not up—takes on the proportions of a menace. All become unified—standardized, they call it—in a common smartness. Not to know, say, do certain things stamps a boy as a 'sissy'. They smoke, they use objectionable language, and worse. Above all, they acquire the slang of the day—a stereotyped language capable of expressing only coarsened reactions. It is the same with the girls, of course. They are suddenly brought into contact with the conveniences of an advanced material civilization: post office, telephone, and so on. They conduct correspondences of which they keep their parents in ignorance. Over the telephone, they speak to distant friends. I have overheard such conversations. The sort of letters they write I had an opportunity to see when chance placed one in my hands. It was lost in the store. Since I know neither writer nor addressee, I am not violating any confidence in letting you see it. I kept it as a document."

He rose slowly—he was over sixty-five—went to his desk and abstracted a paper from one of its drawers. Abe opened it and read:

"My dear Vi,—Oh boy! I'm all tipsy and raring to go. Oh kid! Ma has relented. I'm going to attend a swell dance tomorrow night where the Tip Top Orchestra is playing. My togs are ready, compact filled, hair frizzed and all. Of course, Ma doesn't know; but Jack will be there with bells on. She thinks he's at Torquay yet. But this once I am going to have a fling. Dash it, though! I was mad at Jack the other day, a week ago. You know that nifty compact he gave me last Xmas? He smashed it; and I gave him Hail Columbia. He'll bring me a new one to-morrow night; that'll be jake with me. Didn't I feel punk, though!

"Last night I met Agnes Strong on the ice. For the love of Pete! How that Jane carries on! I'd be ashamed of myself, honest to cats, I should. You know Frank Smith, the new sheik? He's sweet on me, and, of course, I encourage him. Want some fun. But Agnes is cuckooed about him since he took her to a dance last week. It makes me puke to see her. Well, so long, kiddo. Must ring off. Think of me to-morrow night, all dolled up. Frank says I'm a spiff looker. Hug me tight. See you in the funnies!—Pansy Blossom."

"The worst of that sort of thing," the doctor said after a while, "is not the moral degeneracy which it may or may not imply. It is the coarsening of a whole generation." . . .

At night, Abe gave Ruth that letter to read; she was amazed; but, of course, "*her* girls would never condescend to a thing like that."

A few weeks later, having thought matters over, Abe went to town. It so happened that, in the store, Mr. Diamond mentioned casually that Mrs. Vanbruik was in. Abe, following up a half-matured thought, said at once, "I'd like to see her for a moment."

But someone else was speaking to her. While waiting, Abe asked to see his account. When the book-keeper, an elderly man of military bearing, brought him his ledger page, Abe, amazed at the total, turned to the manager. "What are these items here, dry goods, with three amounts of thirty, twenty-five, and forty-five dollars?"

"Let me see." Mr. Diamond, taking the paper, disappeared in the crowd. "Those," he said, returning, "were dresses for the young ladies, ordered through a traveller on approval. Miss Frances took them out, and Mrs. Spalding signed the bills."

Abe nodded as Mary approached, in fur coat, but without a hat on her still brown hair.

"Hello, Mary," Abe said grimly. "Ruth would like to put Frances out to board. The drives are too much for her. Would you take the girl?"

Mary hesitated. "Personally, yes. But I must consult Charlie."

"Of course," Abe said. "No hurry. It's quite a responsibility to assume. I want the girl under strict supervision."

"I see," Mary said. "Very well, Abe. I'll talk it over."

Thus, in February, Frances was taken to town to live with her aunt, coming home for the week-end only. Ruth did not know that Abe was trying, belatedly, to shoulder part of the responsibility for his children; she thought he had given in to her wishes and felt properly grateful.

When seeding time came and throughout the district people were getting ready for a record acreage of flax, Abe said, "I'll stick to wheat," and when he saw to what an enormous expense people went in order to put their crops into the ground —no ploughing had been done in the fall—he felt justified on that score alone. Unless the price remained around five dollars a bushel, where it still stood in spring, every bushel raised would mean a loss. But the gambling spirit had taken hold of the farmers; and had there been a prophet, they would not have listened to him. Harry Stobarn and Bill Crane were working for Elliot, at six dollars a day. Horanski, instead of hiring out himself, imported unskilled countrymen of his from the city; even Hilmer doubled his acreage by hiring a man. Wheeldon, Henry Topp, and others plunged to a ruinous extent. But all had credit at the bank. Abe Spalding, they said, had lost his grip.

His acreage, even of wheat, being unexpectedly small, he had seed left when he finished. Early in June he took it to town to sell.

He had just turned his horses beyond the elevator when he noticed that, near the crossing, the man who had preceded him had stopped and jumped to the ground. Abe knew him slightly; he was living three miles east of Morley, south of the track. As Abe approached, the man laid a mittened hand on the edge of his tank, lifting himself to the stepping board. "I want to talk to you," he said. "Drive to the side."

Abe did as bidden.

"You're Spalding from up north, aren't you? My name is Simpson. You've a girl going to that school over there? I know her. I have one myself. The two've been chums. I've seen them together.

"A week or so ago—it was the 1st June; I remember the date because I was hitching up to go to Somerville about a note at the bank; and the east-bound train was going by. My yard's right alongside the track. And there I saw your girl in the cab of the engine, sitting on the knees of the engineer. No. I know her well. Plump sort of a chit. Round cheeks and fair, curly hair. I know her. I've seen her often enough with my girl. The train was slowing down to go into that siding at Willett. . . .

Well, I thought you should know. She recognized me, by the way. Looked straight at me and stopped, laughing. The rest's up to you." And Simpson dropped back to the ground.

Abe stood, the lines slack in his hand. He could not think clearly; he had the almost physical sensation of a wish that he were dead. What do? Go to the school and annihilate it with all it contained? Go to his sister's to talk it over? Go home to hide?

He went to the school, entered, and knocked at the principal's door. A tall, gaunt young man appeared.

"My name's Spalding. I want a list of the days on which my daughter Frances has been absent from school."

"Just a moment." The principal returned into the classroom. When he rejoined Abe, he led the way to a small room in the central part of the building where he bade Abe sit down. He himself went to fetch the register of attendance. "For what month?" he asked.

"May and June."

The principal jotted down a few dates on a pad of paper. For June, there was only one, the third of the month.

"How about the first?" Abe asked.

"1st June? That was a Saturday."

Abe stared. Then Frances had been at home that day. He felt baffled. "Thanks," he said at last. "And now I want the girl."

"Very well, sir."

When Frances appeared, she looked apprehensive. Was it guilt betraying itself? Abe said nothing, however, and led the way.

At Mary's house, his sister met them. "What is wrong, Abe?" Abe motioned her and Frances to sit down. "Why," he asked the girl whose pallid face was flushed, "were you absent from school on 3rd June, last Monday?"

"I was ill."

Abe looked at his sister, and Mary nodded. "I don't remember the date. But I can look it up."

"Never mind. Any other day on which you missed school recently?"

"Not that I——" Mary began.

"Yes, auntie. The last Friday in May. Don't you remember? I had a terrible headache in the morning. I went home in the afternoon."

Mary looked as though in doubt. "What is the meaning of this, Abe?"

"On that day Frances left here as if she were going to school but did not turn up there."

There was the slightest pause before Frances said, "I never!"

"Be careful," Abe threatened, "I've witnesses to prove what I say."

"Abe," Mary repeated, "will you tell me what you are driving at?"

"That day she was in the cab of the engine on the east-bound train."

Frances rose in a paroxysm of sobbing.

"How could she have got back?" Mary asked.

"I don't know. I'll find out."

"Just a moment, Abe," Mary said. "The train leaves at nine-ten. It gets to Somerville at ten-twenty. There's no way of coming back till three-forty-five the next day."

"She was seen."

"What is the date?" Mary asked, reaching for a calendar.

Abe hesitated. "That is the one point on which I am not sure. 31st May or 3rd June."

"Where does the doubt come in?"

"I don't care to explain just yet."

Frances dabbed her eyes with a handkerchief. "Don't you remember, auntie? I went to school in the afternoon and then home."

"I don't remember, my dear."

"Friday?" Abe asked. "According to the register you were in school that day."

At last Frances said, "Mistakes will occur."

"They will." Abe rose to leave the house.

He went to the station. He had thought of freight trains.

"Can you look up the dates on which freight trains have gone west of late?"

"Can I?" Kellogg, the agent, said; and, taking a file from the shelf above the wicket, he turned its pages. "Not a one for two weeks. They've all been going east. Apart from the regulars, there was only a special. 31st May, going west in the morning and east at night. Field-day at Ferney. The east-bound mixed was run on the siding at Willett." Willett being a flag station half-way to Somerville.

"Thanks," Abe said and left.

He returned to the school which was being dismissed for the noon recess. He found the principal in the hall. "My daughter claims she missed school on Friday morning, 31st May," he said.

"Just a moment." The principal swung lankily on his heels.

Miss Carston, the high-school assistant, was coming down the stairway. "Miss Carston," he said, "this is Mr. Spalding. Could there be a mistake in your register? Mr. Spalding claims his daughter was absent on Friday morning, 31st May. Your register marks her present."

Miss Carston, a short, stout woman, frowned. "Mistakes will occur. But wait. 31st May? No. That morning we had a monthly test in French. Frances was present. I have her paper here."

"Thanks," Abe said and turned away.

He left town on the east road, going to Simpson's.

"Yes," Simpson said as, wiping his mouth with the back of his hand, he came from the shack. "You can see for yourself. This is where I was." And, placing a toothpick between his teeth, he led the way to the stable. "The train was slowing down to go into the siding. Another train was coming down the line as I left the yard."

"But that was 31st May."

"1st June. I had a note to renew before noon."

"You are sure about the date?"

"Absolutely."

"1st June was a Saturday. The girl was at home. Can I phone the bank for a confirmation?"

"If you want to."

Abe returned to town and waited till one o'clock for the bank to reopen. When he called the manager over the telephone, Simpson's renewal of his note was confirmed as of 1st June.

The evidence was hopelessly confused. . . .

At night, Abe gave a detailed account to Ruth, without disguising the fact that all seemed contradictory to a degree.

"Frances is truthful," Ruth said with conviction.

"But she says she was at home on Friday morning. The teacher says she was at school; and she can prove it."

Ruth spoke placidly. "We are human, Abe. Frances is a decent girl."

"I hope so. I can't make it out. I have tried to deal with the case. I have failed. I leave it to you."

A few days later Abe met his brother-in-law in the store.

"Bad business, Abe," said the doctor with more emphasis than he was in the habit of giving to his words.

"I know, but what could I do?"

"Hard to say. But a suspicion cast on a girl's character does not remain without effect. If she is innocent, it is a revelation to her."

Abe looked into an abyss.

That night, the matter came up once more between Ruth and Abe. Jim had gone to bed. Ruth was sewing at her end of the table. Abe was pacing the room, still baffled by his inability to see clear.

"Ruth," he said at last in a more moving tone than he had used for years, "you seem to feel sure of the girl. I hold you responsible."

Ruth looked up, resting her hands. "I am satisfied that Frances is truthful. I assume the responsibility. . . . Abe," she added after a while, responding to his tone, "I can't see what you worry about. Surely you don't believe the girl has been seduced?"

Abe drew a deep breath. For a moment it seemed in the profound silence which followed as though he were growing beyond the proportions of a mere man. When he spoke, his voice held a quality which sent little shivers over Ruth's spine. "I can't help myself. When Charlie died, he took something of me into his grave. I have been living like a shadow of myself these half-dozen years. . . . Seduced? The word is yours. But I want to say this, if a child of mine went wrong, in the sense in which the word is commonly used——" His look, as he swayed back against the frame of the door, had something erratic; and though he did not raise his voice, it assumed tone and pitch of an outbreak of primitive passion. "If that happened . . . I'd rather see that child dead before me in her coffin!"

And, having spoken, he seemed to shrink once more into his mere human form. Ruth sat, bent forward, staring into his face, white-lipped because she had had a revelation of his inner nature.

XX * MARION

SCHOOL had closed, and Marion had come home, changed again. Abe felt more deeply disturbed than ever.

On 14th July, a Sunday, he was in the meadow west of his land, sitting with Jim in the latter's car. He was looking at the grass; it being short, they would have to cut a very large area.

Square miles of land! What for? To live on; not to know why or what for. . . .

Jim's voice broke in on his musings. "If you want help, I

can get a man for you, dad." And he mentioned McCrae, the returned man who had settled west of Hartley's. Jim knew that Abe would not engage any one who had worked for him before. "You'd have to pay three dollars for a ten-hour day; and time and a half for overtime."

"All right," Abe said listlessly.

"You want him?"

"I suppose."

They turned to go back to the farm. Abe had of late fallen into the habit, whenever he was outside of his yard, of scanning the horizon. The weather was dry, the distance clear. Suddenly, the car crawling slowly over the prairie, Abe focused his eyes on a moving point in the south-east, just north of town. His eyes had learned to interpret the smallest trifles at great distances. It was not long before he knew that the moving point was a car.

"I wonder who that may be," he said half to himself.

"Who? Oh, I see," Jim said, following the direction of his father's glance; his chin was resting on the wheel. "That must be young Harrison. He's coming here, I bet."

Abe frowned. "Who's Harrison?"

"Don't you know?" Jim laughed. "I thought you did. Young lawyer at Somerville. Bright young chap. Lots of money. Well, sis would hardly tell you. I bet mother knows all about it, though."

"About what?"

"Well-l-l," Jim squirmed, "he's Marion's beau."

Abe's heart missed a beat. All about him a life was lived of which he knew nothing.

On the trail south of the farm Jim speeded up. In the yard, he alighted at once. "I'll tip sis off," he said.

But that precaution proved unnecessary; for Abe was still sitting in the car which had stopped in the middle of the yard, when, on the steps of the house, the three women appeared, festively clad: Ruth in a long skirt of black satin, with a *crêpe-de-chine* blouse and a white fichu; Marion in a gown of light, clinging cloth, mouse-grey, boldly trimmed with a flame-red border; Frances in her ordinary Sunday clothes, a watchful expression on her precociously saucy face. Jim was coming from behind the house, tall, jaunty, conceited in spite of his ugly ears; he, too, wore a new suit and a sailor hat. Slowly Abe left the seat of the car. He was in striped shirt-sleeves, though he wore a good pair of trousers and his vest, with a laundered collar and a blue silk tie; on Sundays he dressed when the chores were done. He did not cross the yard but looked at the family picture before him. He had dreamt of such scenes in the past; this might be fulfilment. . . .

A low, expensive, single-seated car, light blue, swung into the yard and smoothly came to a stop at the little gate of the house-yard.

A smallish young man in a blue-serge suit with very wide trousers—aggressively new and well-made, the coat excessively short—manoeuvred himself from behind the wheel and, taking off a light-grey hat of soft felt, uncovering abundant, glossy, rather long black hair parted in the centre, eagerly rounded the car to meet Marion with outstretched hand.

The girl, greeting him with a smile which seemed to surge forward in short little bursts of almost laughter, turned slowly, without releasing his hand, and introduced him to mother and sister.

To Abe it looked like a puppet-show. "So this," he thought, "is the way such things are managed these days."

Marion, at a loss, looked across to him; and he, feeling sorry for her, obeyed the appeal in her eye and relinquished the door of the car on which he had been leaning.

He and Mr. Harrison were introduced and shook hands.

Jim nodded familiarly in the background. "Hello, Bud! How are you?"

A general conversation ensued, guided by Marion and designed to bridge the awkwardness of the moment. Mr. Harrison was bringing news: the Saturday papers of the city had carried the results of the high-school examinations. Marion, Jim, and Frances had passed, though Jim with two "conditions"; it was more than he had expected.

Oh yes, the weather was marvellous; not a bit too warm. No, it had been no trouble to find the place; how could one mistake it?

Abe's glance rested on Frances; the expression in her face startled him: a luring, greedy, jealous smile with which she watched her older sister and the young man.

Marion, though taking part in the conversation with fluent readiness, seemed far away. But whenever her eye met that of the young man, a radiance rose into her smile which was invariably followed by the glow of a blush. Again little bursts of laughter broke from her lips, revealing strong ivory teeth. Unconscious of the fact that she betrayed her whole heart, she yielded, body and soul, to a power that swayed her as the wind sways a tree, its leaves flashing silvery undersides. From the very day when she had come home a month ago Abe had half divined it; it had been ever present with him, disturbing the flow of his moods.

A moment later Marion executed an adroit manoeuvre by separating the two men from the group. "Father," she said, "Mr. Harrison is dying to see the farm. Will you show him? We shall get dinner meanwhile."

Abe led the way; and as he did so, he saw from the corner of his eye a significant little by-play between the girl and her brother. With a broad, teasing smile Jim made a motion as if to join the men; but Marion, in sudden alarm, detained him by a touch on his arm. Jim laughed, scratched his head, and stood back.

As Abe and young Mr. Harrison crossed the yard to the old barn, the latter kept up a patter of talk. It might seem strange that, living in an agricultural country as he did, he had never been on a farm; yet such was the fact. Born and raised in the city, having no relatives in the west, his father, the judge, having come from Nova Scotia, he had seen the open country only from train or car. He had often felt it a handicap that he knew nothing of the work of his clients. . . .

"Well," Abe said as they reached the open door of the barn, "if you want to see stock, Sunday's a bad time. Horses and cows are out on pasture. They may be a mile or two north."

"Anything. It's all new to me." In the door he turned. "A world in itself," he said. "The trees shut it off." The wind-breaks with their lofty, rustling tops were at their best just then.

"It isn't as it used to be. We are more dependent on the town."

"I suppose so. There is less isolation. The car has changed that."

Abe did not answer.

Perhaps nothing on earth so reflects the Sunday spirit of rest as a large, high, and empty barn, with the light entering through the rows of dusty windows above the stalls. The very smell of hay and musty straw contributes to it. The air, pervaded with the slightest taint of ammonia and impelled by the currents which enter through the doors as if it were cooled by them, moves in a leisurely, lazy way. The world of work and worry seems far removed, veiled by a curtain of unreality. Time stands still. The paths which the sunspots trace over floor and walls are deprived of their significance as indicating the flow of the hours. The rectangles of brilliant light lie like palpable flakes, their edges curved and curled up by the chaff.

Abe felt disturbed by the presence of this stranger which

reminded him of the fact that life called for decisions binding on all time to come.

Nothing was said for a while as the two strolled along side by side, the one huge and powerful, but stiffened by work and advancing years; the other dwarfed by his side, but lithe and young.

"That is the cow barn," Abe said as they recrossed the yard.

Again they passed through the building, Abe handling a lever here or pressing a button there to illustrate the working of the equipment.

A small door led from the stable into the milk room; and thence into the east half where the implements were stored.

Between the new barn and the granaries lay the cool shade of the towering structure. West of the lane, just inside the wind-break, glistened the pond, a smooth sheet of water.

"Nothing much to see," Abe said; yet he unfastened the door of the last of the granaries through which a wave of intensely hot air, laden with the smell of sun-parched timbers, struck their faces. Inside, in the semi-darkness, they saw, suspended from the ridge of the roof, huge tins filled with binder-twine and other things which had to be protected from mice. Against the partitions dividing the bins from the aisle, garden tools leaned; bags were piled in lots of two dozen each.

"I have three granaries," Abe said, pointing by a swing of his arm. "We use a trap in the roof to fill them. For the rough grains I have bins in the lofts of the barns." And, after a short, frowning pause, he added, "Well-l-l," and led the way to the house. . . .

The sight of Marion in the presence of her lover haunted Abe for weeks. He tried to define the change in her; and whenever he did, he seemed to see a grey-white cloud just before the dawn and suddenly turned into a roseate marvel by the rays of the rising sun.

But there were other moods, induced by critical thought. This thing had come upon him with amazing swiftness. Why? Because nature plays human beings a scurvy trick in allowing a blind instinct to mature before thought and insight are sufficiently developed to act as a check. It was he, the father, who must counterbalance it.

Trifles changed in the day's routine. Abe still rose at half-past three; but instead of lighting the fire himself, he knocked at Jim's door and left it to him to do so. After a while Abe even proposed that Jim get breakfast for the two of them. Henceforth nobody stirred in the house till, all chores being done, the men had gone to the field.

McCrae was a small, wiry young fellow with a red, smiling face which impressed perhaps by reason of a striking ugliness rather than by reason of beauty, though the latter was not entirely missing. For two-thirds of its area, including nose, forehead, lips, and one cheek, its skin was glossy and of a silky texture, as if it had been scalded in his childhood. Nose and lips were slightly asymmetrical, giving him a look of evil boldness which might have been repulsive had it not been in such perfect harmony with the swaggering nonchalance of his bearing. As it was, his very deformity lent an additional attraction to him.

Jim and McCrae were on the most friendly terms; they never met in the meadow without a challenge of wits.

Abe worked harder than either. Whenever he stopped, the power of consecutive thought seemed to leave him. Yet, at every halt necessitated by the horses' need for a rest, he looked about over the prairie as if to verify that every landmark was still in its place. For miles around nothing stirred in the fields unnoticed by him. Wheeldon, Stanley, Nawosad, Nicoll, Shilloe, Horanski, Topp, Elliot, Hilmer, and Schweigel—all were ploughing; wherever they went in their fields, a dust cloud trailed after them; for the soil was excessively dry, cracked with dryness; too dry to plough. Only weeds thrived in such weather; and to keep them down, the ploughing had to be done. As usual Abe was the only one who was haying so far.

Marion? No doubt Ruth expected him to agree to the projected match without hesitation. The young man seemed desirable enough. Perhaps he was as eligible a husband for the girl as he, her father, could have picked. But how know? The responsibility rested with him; and he felt singularly disinclined to take risks. Was he getting old? All life consisted in taking risks.

At dinner Abe met his three children around the board; and with them McCrae; for Ruth, yielding to necessity, had offered to give him his meals. Even at table Abe was preoccupied. An occasional scrap of the conversation he caught caused him surprise; Jim, McCrae, and Frances had much to laugh about. Marion smiled in an absent way.

In the midst of haying Abe left the farm on Saturday at noon, three weeks after young Harrison's first visit to the place. The other settlers were waiting for a rain which would make the grass grow. Abe knew better; he even left the windrows on the ground over Sunday.

In town, he had a half-hour's consultation with his brother-in-law, and together they went to Somerville in the latter's car, to gather information about the young lawyer. Between them, they talked every angle of the matter over; and when Abe reached home late in the day, he had made up his mind to speak to his daughter.

After supper, he switched the light on in the den and lingered in the dining-room. Marion, too, stayed behind, as if anticipating what was to follow. Ruth and Frances were in the kitchen where Marion rarely helped now. Abe caught the girl's eye and nodded towards his little room. As they entered, he closed the door behind his back.

"Sit down," he said in a kindly voice, pointing to a chair at the end of the library table; and on his heavy, broad forehead appeared his settled frown. He wished to say what was in his mind in such a way as to spare her. But no matter how he might put it, it was bound to hold a note of reproach. In the sharp light of an unshaded bulb black shadows came into his face. "I wish you had let me know about this sooner."

"Everything happened within a few hours," Marion said. "We met at a young people's club, and I wrote mother the next day."

Abe could hardly ask why she had not written to him. "Everything?"

"Before I knew it, I was engaged to be married."

"At seventeen years? There are laws; and those who made them were guided by the wisdom of the ages."

"They put the age below which a girl may not marry at sixteen."

"With the consent of the parents."

"That consent . . ."

"I cannot give within a year."

Pallor spread over the face of the girl; the look in her eyes became tragic. But her voice was tinged by a challenge. "In a year I won't need any one's consent."

Abe placed a hand on the table between them as if he were reaching for hers. "You won't be without it."

"Father," the girl cried, rising in the ecstasy of her passion. "You don't understand. We cannot wait. We cannot live without each other. A year. . . . If you understood, you would not keep us apart. I felt so sure that all would be well as soon as I came home. . . ."

"All will be well," Abe said almost impatiently. "But you must wait. That is all there is to say." And, with a shrug of his shoulders, he left the room while the girl sank back on her chair. . . .

At night, when the children had gone to bed, anxious to

escape the charged atmosphere of the dining-room, Abe and Ruth confronted each other. It was she who spoke first.

"Just what is your objection to John, Abe?"

He stopped in his walk. "I have no objection to him. I have made inquiries. But the girl is too young to think of marriage."

"Marion *is* rather young. But hardly too young to be happy."

"Let her be happy in the way of her years."

"It is too late to consider that."

"That is not my fault."

"You mean it was I who sent her to high school?"

"Exactly."

"It proves that I was right. Whom could she meet in a place like this? Henry Topp? The time would have come when she would have wanted a home of her own. She would have had to take what she could get."

"She would have had the maturity to make her choice."

"When there would have been no choice to make."

"She fell a victim to the first man bold enough to make love to her."

"Do you think a girl like Marion could live in a town for three years without more than one man trying to make love to her?"

"And to that you were willing to expose your child?"

"You are old-fashioned, Abe."

"That means I am sensible."

"Marion has seen others. Young people have their meetings these days. She has chosen well."

Abe took several turns through the room. "She is in her puberty," he said at last. "Just ready to develop her inner life. Satisfy sexual instincts at that stage, and higher things cease."

Ruth looked up. "Abe, I hear your brother-in-law through you."

"My brother-in-law has seen much of life. I am not ashamed to admit that I learn from him." Abe sat down. "Ruth! You speak as if you wished to hurt my pride. I have no pride left. I am anxious to do what seems right to me according to my lights. I will be frank. This comes at a time when it disturbs me greatly. I wish we could see eye to eye. Is it so much that I ask? I want her to wait a year, that is all."

And for the moment, Ruth being under the influence of Abe's plea, it did not seem much. Ten years later it would seem a trifle. Yet she could hardly give in quite gracefully. "Since she needs your consent," she said, "she will have to wait, I suppose."

And there, for the time being, the matter rested.

NEXT day, Mr. Harrison arrived in the early afternoon and had a long interview with Abe from which he emerged frowning. Yet a formal engagement was recognized to exist between the lovers. Henceforth he came every Sunday and often, on weekdays, at night. Marion, Frances, he, and Jim played ball on the lawn east of the house; and Marion and he had long walks in the windbreaks where regular footpaths were becoming established among the trees. In the evenings, Ruth went with them, allowing the young people to pair off by themselves. At ten or eleven, the patient lover returned to Somerville in his car.

Time went by; and the district was shaken by things hardly noticed at Abe's farm. The crops had suffered from drought; partly because the spring work had been poorly done. Everybody except Abe had strained his credit in securing help at peak prices in order to put flax in the ground. But in midsummer the price of that flax had broken at last, with the yield averaging less than five bushels an acre.

"Well," Jim said to Abe, "this time you were right."

From week to week farmers watched the market, hoping it would recover. But, once broken, the price tumbled steadily till, late in the fall, it reached pre-war levels. All farm products fell in value in 1920, but none to the same ruinous extent; and therefore no land depreciated to the same extent as flax land.

It was staggering. John Elliot who, a year ago, had declined an offer of twenty thousand dollars was now anxious to sell but could find no buyer. He was told that he could not expect to get more than a thousand dollars a quarter. His annual interest charges would, under changed conditions, have paid for a farm.

Henry Topp, who had not succeeded in renewing his contract to drive the school van—Baker had taken his place—was in a similar plight; and Hilmer and the Ukrainians were hiring out by the month.

Again all eyes were focused on Abe Spalding. It was a repetition of his spectacular achievement of 1912, though in a negative sense. His crop was nothing to boast of; but it was raised at insignificant cost.

During the fall, a renewal of neighbourly relations came about between Nicoll and Abe. Nicoll's son Dick came home from overseas, with Slim Topp. According to the Soldier Settlement Act of 1919, they were entitled to financial assistance by the Federal Government: a loan of three thousand dollars for building, stock, and equipment. Dick, who had brought a wife from England, was still in the city but had filed a claim on the quarter west of his father's. Nicoll, seeing Abe pass one day, came out to the road.

"I've been thinking, Abe," he said as if there had never been any break in their friendship. "Dick's coming home. Do you figure on putting another man on your place?"

Abe was looking straight ahead; his heart was beating faster. He had missed the friendly contact with his neighbour. "Do you mean Dick . . .?"

"No. I'd like to buy the house you have on your place."

"Oh? Yes, I might sell it."

"How much do you want?"

Abe mused, then, in an impulse of generosity, "Two hundred dollars if you haul it yourself."

"I'll haul it," Nicoll replied, "as soon as there's snow."

Abe nodded and clicked his tongue. Few words to pass between them! But they were precious to him. Yet, this was a first step towards the dismemberment of his farm.

Snow fell in November. One morning Nicoll came with ten horses, four trucks, a load of timbers, and a number of men to draw away the house.

Abe was feeding his horses when he saw them passing; and for half an hour he went on with his work. Already he had laid down the fence in front of the lot; Nicoll would notice that he had made things easy for him. After breakfast he did more; he went over to help. Among the men Abe noticed McCrae, Hilmer, and Shilloe. Abe's help was welcome, for he had moved a house before. As though it went without saying that, where he appeared, he would take the lead, everybody watched him, ready to assist, though it was Nicoll who spoke when explicit orders were needed.

This aid given to Nicoll set Abe thinking of another man whom, for no reason whatever, he had included in his stubborn avoidance of contacts: old man Blaine. The next time he passed his cottage, he stopped and went in. On the opposite quarter the frame of a new, unfinished structure was standing like a skeleton against the sky: Slim Topp's new barn. Neither he nor Dave Topp could live in peace with Henry any longer; and so the partnership had been dissolved. That gave Abe his opening as he knocked at Blaine's kitchen door. "Getting married?" he asked with a nod across the road.

"So they say; so they say," the old man replied in a childish treble. "He came back without a scratch."

Abe went through the kitchen into the living-room beyond. Two rocking-chairs, a table, and a few bookshelves were covered with dust, testifying to the old man's diminishing eyesight.

As Blain followed him, Abe realized with a shock how much his old friend had aged. While he had been at work, something outside him had sustained him; when he had retired, he had been left without that support. He looked shrunk; his limbs were like thin rods housed in his clothes. His hoary beard, white as snow, seemed the only part of his body undiminished in size. His step was uncertain. As Abe sat down, the old man stood in the door and grinned at him.

"How old are you now?" Abe asked, speaking as to a child.

"Eighty," replied the senile voice proudly. "Eighty years and sixty-three days. And sound as a dollar."

Abe looked out of the window. "I see you had a garden." He inferred the fact from such dry vines as were standing up through the snow.

"Yes. I grew all the plants in the house. I've got a great recipe." He looked about to make sure they were alone. "No ladies around, eh?" And he tittered. "I wrote to my brother in Ontario for a pound of sheep manure. The real thing. Of that I made a decoction—boiled it for three hours. That's a sweet smell! With that I watered the plants. Made them grow like a miracle. You must try that one day." He was standing unsteadily, supporting himself now with one hand now with the other against the frame.

"All right," Abe said, too painfully impressed to wish for a longer stay. "I must move on. I was going to town."

But Blaine, anxious to detain his caller, began to talk precipitately. "They say they are going to use the school as a community hall and have dances there. Slim Topp has learned to play the saxophone; and McCrae, over there, hits it off on the trombone." And he imitated the notes of these instruments, using his hands like a trumpet.

"You keeping all right?" Abe asked, not having the heart to leave.

"Fine," Blaine boasted. "I take a walk every day. I still have the bicycle. But I'd rather walk now, all the way to Horanski's. His missus bakes my bread for me; and he brings me candy from town. I have a sweet tooth, Abe. How are the little ones?"

"The little ones? Oh, Marion's going to be married next year. Jim and Frances are attending high school in town."

The old man looked sobered; but comprehension was beyond his powers. The near past had disappeared; he was living in years far removed from the present. "There was another one, wasn't there? A boy, Charlie? . . . Or was he not yours?"

"He was mine," Abe said. "He is dead. Good-bye, Blaine."

The decay of the human faculties impressed him as part of the human tragedy inherent in the fundamental conditions of man's life on earth. That was a thing ever present now. What, as compared with this fact—that, having lived, we must die— did such inessentials matter as economic success or the fleeting happiness of the moment?

When, at Somerville, he turned into Main Street, identical with the highway in town, he caught sight of young Harrison on the sidewalk to his right and stopped to speak to him. A few commonplace remarks were exchanged. Then Abe asked, "Have you told your father?"

"My father? Yes, I have told him."

"Does he agree?"

"He disadvises. He does not object."

"What's his reason?"

"He thinks a professional man married is a professional man arrested in his career."

After a brief silence Abe nodded and drove on. On his way home, he was steeped in thought.

He knew nothing of what was going on in the district. Yet, as he passed Hilmer's Corner, he was conscious of a pair of malicious eyes in a wrinkled face following his progress from a square little window in the shack. Hilmer who had returned with the freeze-up was busy at the stable behind the house. Within, old Mrs. Grappentin was muttering to herself. "The great lord is going to build his fortunes still higher! A lawyer to be his son-in-law! He has grown too great for the likes of us! Too great indeed!"

For, as a consequence of the respect for any sort of education common to the peasant classes of Europe, this fact, known to every one, that a professional man was going to marry into the family, had almost succeeded in changing her attitude to Abe as a person.

Opposite Hilmer's, there was John Elliot's vastly greater establishment, well-kept, apart from a pile of opened tins near the house, a four-roomed cottage painted brown.

Abe noticed these things; but before they became a thought, he had reverted to that girl in his house who, during the last few months, had so greatly changed. Throughout the weeks she was listless now, her face pale, her features drawn; only on Sundays did she revive. Abe was aware of the fact that between her and her mother there was often a pleasant and lively exchange of words; but when he entered, a silence fell. With a pang Abe realized that, in the eyes of the girl, he lived as a sort of doom personified, as a law from the verdict of which there is no appeal. That misconception put him on the defensive; he justified himself to himself. But as a matter of fact he felt far from certain that what he did was the right thing to do.

A great task was ahead of him : the task of making clear to himself what his life had been worth to him; and this necessity filled him with a passionate longing for peace and moral support within his own house. No matter what he had said in the past, his isolation in the district weighed heavily on him. Since that August day when Harrison had interviewed him, he had seemed isolated even in his house.

All these things were coming to a head now, as a consequence of many things : of his renewed though slight contact with Nicoll; of the way in which Blaine's sight had affected him; even of his instinctive revolt against the opinion of Judge Harrison. Abe had had an unavowed suspicion that the judge's hostile attitude, never admitted by his son, had been against Marion as the daughter of a mere farmer. That was not the case. His objection was based on the opinion that marriage meant the end of ambition. But even ambition might be enhanced by the right marriage. Abe was suddenly inclined to think that Marion was the proper wife for the man. Why not let her have her desire?

Had he indeed lost his grip that such thoughts should come? How about the farm? He no longer raised crops to compare with that of 1912. Yet, a few days ago he had heard John Elliot say in town, "Thank the Lord it was a poor crop. The greater the yield, the greater the loss!" That, at any rate, was not his, Abe's case. He was earning enough to carry him from year to year.

But he wanted peace and goodwill in his house; and thus, a week or so before Christmas, he proposed to Ruth that they invite the Vanbruiks and young Harrison for their Christmas dinner. Ruth agreed at once. A year ago, the Spaldings had been the guests of the Vanbruiks; this was an opportunity to reciprocate.

From that moment on Abe nursed a secret plan. Every night when his family was assembled in the dining-room, he sat at the end of the table, apparently absorbed in a book or a paper, in reality watching Marion. Had she risen from that arm-chair in the corner of the room, and had she come to him to put an arm about him and to say, "I know you are against me only because you think you see more clearly into the future than I do, not because you wish to inflict pain upon me," he would, for the moment, have been entirely happy.

XXII * THE CHRISTMAS DINNER

ABE slept little during the night before Christmas. Dimly and distantly he was aware, long before he rose, that the threatened break in the fine winter weather preceding the festival had come at last.

Dimly and distantly. . . . There had been a time when they would all have been aware of it in a very direct way; when the old house would have shaken and quivered under the impact of the blows which the wind levelled at its walls; when, even in bed, they would have shrunk into the smallest possible space in order to retain the warmth of their bodies. That had been before the wind-breaks had attained the height and density with which they protected them; before the great quadrangle of the yard had been closed by the double row of buildings in the north; and, above all, before that great house of his had been erected in which one had to listen closely in order to hear the tumult of the blizzard which raced and raged over the open prairie.

It was four o'clock. As a rule Abe rose at that hour; to-day he lingered in bed. It was not cold in the room, nor anywhere in the house. But he indulged in a feeling of infinite comfort; this was what he had striven for; this brought home his achievement.

But a disquieting thought arose. This was the day on which he was to carry out his secret plan. Young Harrison's presence was essential to its success; what if the blizzard prevented his coming?

Abe switched on the reading light at the head of his bed and swung his feet to the floor. He went to the window to look out; but it was too dark to see. Hurriedly he dressed. When he had done so, he went down into the basement to shake the furnace into life. He called no one; nor did he light the kitchen fire.

Instead, he went out through the front door; and as he stood on the stoop, he shivered, drawing his sheepskin more closely about him. To realize the fury of the storm, one had to be in it.

Sheltered as the yard was, it was bitterly cold out there. In the huge enclosure the air swayed in canting sheets, now horizontal, now tilted, rising and falling as if the flawed blast of the wind were reaching down now and then into the basin of comparative calm; or as if it found a sudden entrance along the ground, through the wind-break, throwing the snow aloft in a fine, dusty, prickling spray.

He made his way to the barn; and, having entered, he felt impressed with the perfect shelter which even his brute beasts enjoyed. Not a stable on the windswept prairie offered such protection; on the inside the door was covered with a fur of hoar-frost.

He was greeted by a vast stir of feet and a multiple nicker. Groping for the switch, he flashed a light on. He shook himself to expel the icy air; and slowly, deliberately, he fed his horses.

He went from place to place, looking after cows, pigs, and fowl. It was the same thing everywhere; the shelter was perfect. At last he milked—by hand as he had always done.

It was six when he re-entered the sleeping house. He sat down in the rarely-used living-room. On any other day he would have fallen asleep; but the furious blizzard of the prairie forces the hearer to listen. This wind, with its onsets and lulls and its sudden cannonading attacks, infuses into the blood a rhythm which defies sleep. Will anything withstand it? Or is it going to level the work of man, turning a slow and gradual destruction into a cataclysm momentary and catastrophic?

Repeatedly Abe went out again. Slowly a grey light crept into things, and the short, crepuscular day began. Abe lighted the fire in the kitchen. It was all settled: to-night, at supper, he would make the announcement; the date would be set. Provided the groom arrived!

At half-past eight Abe went to the stairway and called: a great shout which woke every one in the house; then he shouldered into his sheepskin to issue forth into the yard for the dozenth time.

There was light to see by. Above, the hollow of the yard was covered as with a lid: a moving, scurrying lid consisting of infinitely small particles, some of which, dropping into the calm of the space enclosed by wind-break and buildings, were arrested in their wild flight, caught in the stagnant, swaying air where they filtered to the ground, to be swept up again and whirled aloft in fluttering sheets which rocked according to the whim of eddying counter-currents within the shelter belts. Again Abe went all over his yard. . . .

Let the girl have her wish!

Lights flashed on in the house. Abe waited; but at last, expecting breakfast to be ready, he entered through the shed at the rear.

In the kitchen all but Jim were busy, their faces flushed, tongues babbling, for they had found the presents which, the night before, had been scattered over the dining table. Abe was greeted with a shout of "Merry Christmas!" and answered like the beloved head of a family, giver of all good gifts to them. His eye sought a face and found it.

In entering he had admitted a whiff of icy air; and for a moment he stood in an evanescent cloud arising from the condensation of the moisture in the room. Huge and tall he towered in the door, dusted over from head to foot with a fine, glittering snow. What a contrast to the girl in her beige-coloured dress of georgette silk over which she had donned a large starched overall apron of pale-blue cambric!

She had shed that air of suffering and languor which she had worn for months except on Sundays; never before had she shed it so completely. Yet a slight change came over her at sight of her father.

They had breakfast. And after breakfast Abe went out again, restless and disturbed. It was partly the effect of the weather.

Even though the poplars stood bare and leafless, the wind bent and twisted them, straining at every twig and bough, whipping their swaying tops. Everything that could move moved under the impact of that aerial turmoil; everything that could rattle rattled; and since trees and timbers were frozen to the core, the sum total of the sounds produced was that of a dry, feverish chatter which set the nerves on edge as though things had a sort of insane voice of their own. The twigs which broke in the girdle of trees snapped with the splintering crackle of rifle fire. When, in a down-sweep of the captured air, the hard, fine granules of the snow, which had no trace of their crystalline structure left, hit the ground or the roofs of the lower buildings, they did so with a swishing sound. And to all that was added the music of the air itself which, like a floating shroud, kept swinging and swaying.

Abe's powerful physique enjoyed the flooding turbulence as others may enjoy a dip through rolling breakers of brine.

Again he went to the house. "It's doubtful," he said in the kitchen.

Ruth and the girls looked at him; and so did Jim who was helping.

On Marion's face lay a peculiar smile. "Would you go yourself?"

"I don't believe a horse would face that wind."

Marion shrugged her shoulders. "I don't know about uncle and auntie; but John will come!" This was said with unalterable conviction.

The noon hour came. The girl knew no doubt. Abe went upstairs to change into his Sunday clothes.

In the old coonskin coat which had belonged to his father before him, he went to the gate of his yard. He knew it was impossible to see far on the prairie; he had always liked the feeling of isolation produced by a blizzard, as if the farm were shut off from all the entanglements of contact with a turbulent world: that world which demanded a surrender of individual freedom and independence and with which he need have nothing more to do. Knowing that in house and granaries provisions were stored which would secure the continuance of life for weeks, he felt the very fierceness and aggressiveness of this winter orgy as enhancing rather than diminishing the sense of safety: no matter what might happen in the outer world, this farm was a world in itself which would endure while he lasted, defying the forces of nature.

The great farm gate, open as always in winter, creaked on its hinges. Outside, the flying snow swooped to the ground like a sloping roof, hiding even the ditch. Everything was sketched in white and grey. No, they could not come. They could never hold their direction.

The drift-laden wind leapt the shelter of the yard as a hunting animal might leap stone or shrub in its way; the very ground seemed to be slipping forward. Since the trees formed a trap for whatever snow fell below the carrying blast, the fence was half buried.

Without thought of what he was doing, Abe turned west, close to the fence. Twenty rods from the gate the wind-break bent to the north. Beyond, the field of vision was closed by flying, whirling, streaky walls of drift. Abe went on to that corner, stopping in the sharp-rested wave of closely packed snow which traversed the road like a boldly flung promontory, losing itself in the ditch which was completely filled. The world seemed to end beyond the wind-break. The snow came in waves and flaws; but these spectral waves did not advance in straight lines; and so there were no vistas between them such as occur between vertical veils of mist. Sometimes those sheet-like waves were thrown down by a canting of the wind; then they looked like enormous, airy beings which stretched aloft before they blotted themselves on their faces in a unison of supplication. At other times, a sheet resolved itself, under the impact of an adventitious blow, into a rounded thing bounding along like a galloping animal multiplied a thousand-fold in size : and before it had crossed the road, it, too, was flung down by a chute of the gale or blown aloft, disintegrated into its elements.

Glowing with inner warmth, Abe turned. He was at peace with himself; the question which had disturbed him was settled. This inner peace was enhanced into positive happiness by the reaction to the turmoil about.

He reached the gate and went on, from a mere aversion to enter yard or house. He came to the eastern corner of the wind-break. No, that prairie, ordinarily so open, did not exist to the eye. Nothing was left but the farm behind his back, nothing of all the world.

Convinced, and sorry in the conviction, that no callers could come, he was on the point of turning once more when he was caught up in a whirl of a different kind.

From out of the swaying drifts to the east two horses emerged whose jingling bells became audible with startling suddeness as they entered the shelter belt; their nostrils raised and wide, with icicles hanging from nose and lips, they plunged through the snow. Abe had just time to leap aside. But they, no less startled than he, reared and upset the cutter, throwing its inmates into the snow. They were on the point of bolting in a panic when Abe leapt forward and caught their bridles.

From behind came the sound of muffled laughter. Three figures, hardly recognizable in their wraps, struggled to their feet. Two of them, one tall and strong, the other short and spare, showed no trace of their faces which were hidden by woollen scarfs; the last, of medium height, had its eyes bare in a slit between fur cap and wrappings.

Abe felt almost disappointed at their arrival; but he remembered his duty as host. "I didn't think you would venture out," he said.

"We'd never have started," said Mary, laughing and shaking the snow from her coat, her voice sounding as though she were singing against the wind. "But Mr. Harrison came at nine; and he swore he would be responsible for our safe arrival."

"I got you here, did I not?" young Harrison laughed.

"You might have been lost!"

"We *were* lost half a dozen times. But Charlie and I never

stirred from our seats. We left it to Mr. Harrison to find his way back to the road."

Abe was leading the horses by their bridles; the guests followed.

"Better go to the house," he said as he stopped at the barn.

"You go," young Harrison said to the Vanbruiks, untying the scarf from around his head. "I'll help Mr. Spalding."

Abe took the sleigh into the driveway of the barn and watered the horses at the inside trough. "You'll have to stay overnight."

"We'll see," said John,

At the house, all lights had been turned on, for even at mid-day it remained murky. In the kitchen the last preparations for dinner were going forward. Like Ruth, the girls, and Mary Van-bruik, Jim had donned an overall apron. Somehow, this seemed to impart even to the aprons of the women the character of a disguise.

When Abe and John entered, the latter joined those in the kitchen; and the gaiety reached a climax when, in addition to donning an apron, he twisted a towel into a turban and, reach-ing for a ladle, walked about like a chef supervising the work. His disguise was all the more comically effective as the apron served to set off his blue shirt with the excessively wide trousers which he affected.

Abe and the doctor sat down in the living-room.

During the next half-hour—whenever the swing-door from the kitchen admitted someone to the dining-room—a burst of voices and laughter ran through the house. Once Mary came to the door and spoke to her brother. "I should have been sorry to miss this. It is lovely out here in this weather."

Abe followed her with his eyes as she returned to the kitchen. In spite of her age she looked like a girl.

Shortly after, the ladies passed through the room to run out into the hall and upstairs. Even Ruth seemed rejuvenated. They removed their aprons, touched up their hair, and "powdered their noses," as the doctor expressed it. When they returned, they stood for a moment in the living-room, laughing and jest-ing. John, still in his cook's disguise, appeared in the door and announced solemnly, bowing and swinging his ladle, that "madame was served."

This brought a new burst of laughter; and Dr. Vanbruik, "rising to the occasion"—he always used set phrases when he was jesting—offered his arm to Ruth. Abe did the same with his sister; and, the girls following, they took their seats. John con-trived to divest himself with magic speed of apron and turban.

Ruth had taken out her best dinner set and the sterling flatware which Abe had given her on completion of the house. The tablecloth was of cut-work embroidery; and the whole arrangement of the room betrayed the endeavour, not unsuccessful, to produce an impression of festive splendour. Abe, expecting his guests to stay for the night, the first time such a thing had happened, was conscious of a feeling of satisfaction. Ruth deserved credit.

The doctor exerted his conversational powers, though even to-day he could not entirely remove the impression that he was descending into a lower arena when mingling with his fellow beings; but he succeeded in making himself agreeable to his nieces and Ruth; which meant that he indulged in an old-fashioned, cumbersome sort of banter.

"Uncle!" Marion exclaimed on such an occasion, with a flash of her even teeth. "You are trying to fluster me."

"To judge from your blush, I succeeded," he said, looking at her through his gold-rimmed glasses.

"I may have blushed——"

"You are still blushing. Never mind. Even a plain girl grows pretty when the colour mounts to her hair. And you——"

"Now you are going to say what you don't mean."

"You contradict to give emphasis to my words. Admit it."

"Not at all!"

"Of course," he went on, "that is as it should be. Who does not like to be praised? And you, I was going to say, are far from plain. I appeal to Mr. Harrison's judgment."

John looked at her, laughing. Her blushes deepened.

"Perhaps," the doctor still pursued the subject, with a bow to the young man, "that appeal is hardly fair."

"John," Marion cried, "I forbid you to answer."

Which brought a laugh around the board. Ruth felt perhaps even more flattered than the girl herself.

Dinner over, Jim went to the hall and climbed into a suit of overalls to feed the strange horses.

"I'll go along." said John Harrison.

"All right, Bud."

"And I!" Frances joined in.

But Ruth objected. "You and I, my dear, are going to do the dishes."

"Let her go," Mary said. "I'll help you."

So the girls, too, put on coats and wraps. Jim ran to the kitchen to fetch his sheepskin from the narrow closet. Rapid whispers sprang up in the hall; the girls intended to race him to the stable. But Jim divined their intention, and in spite of their hurry he reached the corner of the house at the very moment when they descended the steps of the stoop. They were nearer the gate in the fence of the house-yard; but, presuming on this advantage, they failed to put forth their best effort; and Jim defeated them by vaulting the fence. Yet none of them gave up. On such a day it seemed the only fit way of locomotion to run as fast as one could; it sent a glow of health into the cheeks and gave all eyes the polish of jewels. Marion's looked like veined agate, harmonizing with her complexion of ivory and red, in striking contrast to her sister's which was pure white and apple-blossom pink.

Being the only one properly dressed, Jim did the work in his noisy, slapdash way, shouting raucously and elbowing the horses aside.

Marion and John had gone to the west door which led into the run-way and the pasture beyond. This door was exposed to the full impact of the wind, there being a gap in the trees behind. Ineffectively Marion pulled at its handle; but when John grasped one of the diagonal timbers which braced it, it gave abruptly, admitting blasts of bitter cold air awhirl with snow-dust which swept along the floor of the building, stirring up chaff and dust. Jim shouted at them.

"Hi there; What do you think you are doing?"

"Never mind," Marion said, laughing. "That's a good boy."

Jim, coming over, removed his mitt and took her chin in his hand, bending her head back till her eyes met his.

She laughed and shook the imprisoned head; but as she did so, bright tears were scattered from the corners of her eyes.

"What's that?" Jim asked in a whisper.

"I could laugh and weep at the same time. You don't understand, Jim."

"I don't?" he asked. "I have eyes in my head."

With a startled look Marion freed herself.

Frances had gone through the wings of the barn, picking her way between the rumps of the horses in their stalls. From childhood on she had liked the smell of the barn and shown a morbid interest in animals kept on the farm; her father had often sharply sent her away.

Marion's glance became pointed, as if she were warning her brother not to betray her to the girl. She turned; and, her eye alighting on John, her face melted in a smile.

Jim bent down for the gallon measure which he had used and which he now threw under the hinged cover of the feed box.

When he returned, John, Marion, and Frances were standing by the cutter in which the guests had come, in the transverse driveway. They were shaking out the robes.

"That's that," said Jim. "Go back to the house?"

"You go, Jim," Marion answered. "Take Frances. John and I are going to have a walk. I love to be out in weather like this."

"I'll go with you," said Frances.

"No, you won't." With the authority of an elder sister.

"I guess I can go if I want to."

"We can't keep you from having a walk. But ours we are going to have by ourselves."

Jim took a little note-book from an inner pocket and scribbled a line or two. Then he tore the page out and crushed it in his palm. Above them, the loft boomed with the wind like a resonance board. As he returned the note-book to his pocket, he "tagged" Frances.

"Come on, sis," he cried. "You're it!" And with a leap he reached the door to the yard.

Frances ill-humouredly ran after him, overtaking him before he had had time to push the door back.

For a minute they stood, tagging and retagging each other as fast as they could; Frances, with hard slaps of her gauntleted hand; Jim barely touching her arm with quick reaches of two extended fingers. "You're it!"—"No, you!"—"You!"—"You!"

Jim, working with one free hand and his heels, had pushed the door open bit by bit; and just as Frances was on the point of bursting into tears, he had widened the crack sufficiently to slip out, still continuing the game. Catching Marions eye, he winked and tossed her the crumpled ball of paper in his hand. Tagging Frances a last time—"You're it!"—he twisted himself from under her hand and escaped across the yard. At the fence he waited; and when Frances felt sure she could reach him, he retreated skilfully to the stoop of the house. Again he waited, letting her approach before he disappeared into the hall.

John and Marion had been watching them through the crack of the barn door. There could be no doubt; Jim was luring Frances away with his antics! They looked at each other. Then they closed the door, leaving a crack less than an inch wide to look through with a single eye. Dusk was settling over the storm-ridden prairie.

That done, Marion turned to the nearest light and unfolded the paper which Jim had tossed her. Her look became troubled. "Third tree, second row north of runway. That is the place where the suitcase is hidden. Jim knows."

"So long as he does not talk!" John said, bursting into activity. "Quick. Watch the door."

And he ran to the stall where the horses stood. Backing them out, he led them to the sleigh; but he had difficulty in making the off horse step over the pole. Marion left her post to help him. She was less awkward with horses than he.

Both were feverishly excited. They worked together now, though Marion stepped back to the door every few seconds, to peer out. Jim, knowing their secret, must be playing into their hands. They wrapped up in robes and scarfs which John pulled from under the seat, together with overshoes and caps. For a second they looked at each other in their disguise. They kissed and, running to the west door, united their efforts in pushing it far enough back for the sleigh to pass through. Then Marion returned once more to the yard door, to wave a futile hand at the house where all was quiet. A second later, they pushed it shut. They were leaving an unmistakable trail, for the floor of the driveway was at once covered with snow. It could not be helped. Outside, the wind would obliterate their tracks.

"The weather's all in our favour," said John as he climbed in.

"It's glorious!" Marion cried back.

They drove into the gap of the wind-break, and Marion pointed to a tree on their right. John, alighting, withdrew a suitcase from under the snow. . . .

At the house, Jim, in sudden alarm, spoke to his mother; and Ruth appearing in the door of the livingroom, signalled to Abe to follow her into the kitchen.

"Abe," she said breathlessly, "John and Marion——"

"Where?" Abe exclaimed, divining the plot; at a bound he was at the closet and reached for his sheepskin.

"At the barn," Ruth answered.

Abe rushed through the back-door.

John Harrison had not yet returned to the sleigh when Abe laid a hand on Marion's shoulder. "This will not do," he said gently.

Marion felt as though she were going to faint.

"Come to the house," Abe went on, speaking now to John as well as to her. "We shall set the date. I withdraw my objection."

"Daddy!" Marion cried.

"Come in," he repeated. "As far as I am concerned you can be married on New Year's Day. But the wedding must be from the house."

Marion's arms closed about her father's neck.

ABE looked aged and tired. Throughout the district people watched him. It did not seem as if the marriage of his daughter had made him happy; again he took to driving about, often returning only after dark.

On one such occasion, he passed the old school-house at night when the building was brilliantly lighted, probably with the lamp which he had given years ago. The sound of music issued through its walls.

Abe stopped on the culvert and looked back. Through the windows in the north wall he saw human shapes moving in the figures of a dance. The music was more distinct on this side.

He alighted and walked over to the building. The music ceased, and the dancers stopped. Standing close to one of the windows, he saw someone pouring from a bottle into glasses held by half a dozen young men and women. He retraced his steps to the cutter. When he reached his gate, the small lights on the gate-posts which had been out of order for some time were incandescent: Jim would never stay on the farm!

Abe's life had taken on an almost furtive cast when, in municipality and district, movements arose to draw him back into politics.

In the municipality, a leader was needed to co-ordinate those activities which had been suspended during the war. Nobody had forgotten the single-minded economy with which Abe had administered the business; many municipalities had gone into the hands of receivers; Somerville had never been in a sounder financial condition than at the time when Rogers took Abe's place for the remainder of the latter's term as reeve. Rogers had declined re-election; a new man had taken office; and already there was dissatisfaction. The roads were deteriorating; grades built at great expense were sinking back into a primeval swamp; the ditches were choked; farmers were suffering from the sudden deflation after the war; and, as in the way of farmers all over the world, they blamed the Government for their plight which was often the effect of their own improvidence; taxes were rising; incomes decreasing; public money was spent to no purpose; relief was given only in such districts as were directly represented on the council. It was the old story of democratic institutions exploited for the benefit of individuals.

Rogers, meeting Abe at Somerville, pleaded with him. He claimed to be voicing the wish of a large majority in urging Abe to accept nomination next fall. Abe did as he had done before : he listened; but, having listened, he shook his head and drove on. Rogers changed his tactics and came back to the attack. He asked Abe about the methods he used in haying; for Abe had the reputation of being the "uncrowned champion stacker" of the west. Abe did not know that Rogers's sole purpose was to bring him into contact with public opinion once more; for the scheme which Rogers proposed sounded reasonable enough in itself. He offered to loan Abe two of his men if Abe, in return, would come to direct operations on his place for an equal number of days. The offer was flattering, for it assumed that Abe's help was worth the help of two men in return. Rogers claimed that his haying was done at a cost out of proportion to the value of the roughage secured. Abe promised.

Locally, in Spalding District, it was Nicoll, of course, who voiced what he called the wishes of many. When asked who they were, he named Stanley, Horanski, Hilmer, Shilloe, Elliot, and others. The complaints centred around the use to which the old school was put. Nicoll spoke of unbearable scandals. In spite of nation-wide prohibition liquor flowed freely at these dances which had become weekly, even twice-weekly affairs. Worse things were mentioned. Seeing that these meetings were sponsored by the returned men, a number of farmers, including Nicoll, had allowed their daughters to go. Some, like the Ukrainians, having once allowed it, found themselves unable to stop it. Girls from other districts came in : undesirable elements from town and city. To his amazement Abe was told that three or four children had been born out of wedlock; more were expected; the dances had degenerated into drunken orgies. The names mentioned as those of the guilty were McCrae and Henry and Slim Topp. McCrae, according to Nicoll, though a married man, could not be trusted with any woman.

Abe had nothing to say for those implicated, least of all for McCrae; but he needed the man; he was the only one on whom he could count when he wanted help; the others were making progress on their own farms; not many were working at a profit; but land once broken must be cultivated. John Elliot, for instance, had to work from dawn to dark in order to make at least part of his interest payments, helping to make the country prosperous while he remained poor himself.

"What could I do about it?" Abe asked.

"It's the school board," Nicoll said. "They rent the building to this gang. The school should be sold. But Wheeldon refuses to propose anything of the sort; he depends on the votes of these men. He wants to run the district. We need a man who will stand up for the good of the whole. We need you, Abe."

Abe laughed mirthlessly. "You put consolidation over on me; now you want me to run it for you."

"I know, Abe. But something has to be done. Wherever there are children going to school, they are getting out of hand."

"That's it, is it? Are you finding it out?"

Nicoll looked gloomy. "Even the little ones."

"Of course."

"Are we simply old-fashioned, Abe?"

"That may be; the fact remains that you are losing control."

"We are between the devil and the deep sea," Nicoll said.

But Abe replied in a tone of finality: "You have made your bed, you must lie in it."

Yet Nicoll did not give up. He, too, was becoming an influence in the community; his corner now consisted of three farms; his third son Stan was taking up land. But his two youngest sons had taken the infection of the age and refused to work at home except for wages. Besides, Dick, now the oldest one, had given at least part of his allegiance to the gang. Nicoll felt old age approaching: the district had gone wild: nobody wanted to farm any longer; they wanted to make money instead.

Nicoll tried Elliot. "I know," Elliot said, "you must count me out. I have my hands full. Get Spalding. My children are small. If things go on the way they're going when they grow up, I'll know what to do."

"I wish you'd tell me what that is," Nicoll said.

Elliot looked at him, pushed his sombrero back, and wiped his brow. Then, with a savage fling of his long arms, "Take the shotgun out and go after the gang."

In the surrounding towns, Somerville, Morley, Ferney, Torquay, Arkwright, Spalding District was beginning to bear a "hard name." Whenever McCrae and his cronies appeared— and wherever a dance was held, they furnished the music— social events, staid and wooden as they had been in the past, degenerated into drunkenness and immorality. Their professed intention was to show the older people post-war life.

Just before the thaw-up of 1921, the oldest Stanley girl, somewhat "simple"—rumour said praying and fasting had made her so—disappeared from the district. The reason assigned by the one-armed man, that an aunt in the city wished to have one of her nieces with her, satisfied nobody; Nawosad had heard

Stanley forbidding his yard to McCrae. Three Ukrainian girls were reported to have "gone wrong." Indignation waxed furious. But since, with the disintegration of the district, the meetings at Nicoll's Corner had ceased, there was no way for public opinion to crystallize and to express itself. Hartley was peddling groceries and buying chickens in competition with Schweigel. Shilloe, Nawosad, Hilmer had withdrawn during the war; as former Austrians and Russo-Germans they were under a cloud, perhaps more in their own imagination than in the minds of responsible settlers; though Henry Topp had done a great deal to make them feel that way, and Wheeldon not much less. The only public opinion which was organized was that of the gang.

Since, however, Nicoll did not despair of ultimately winning Abe back to his abandoned leadership, he was glad, in spring, of an opportunity to render Abe a great service.

The two great floods through which the district had lived were those of 1910 and 1919. People derived a comforting thought from the interval that had elapsed between them. But Nicoll and a few others, more clear-sighted, were well aware that the flood of 1919 had been caused only by the neglected state of the ditches. They saw with concern that, in spite of all their complaints, nothing had been done in 1920. When the flood of 1921 arrived, disastrous in its sequel, they were ready with their "I told you so." The flood was less in volume than normal; but its effect was worse than that of either of the great floods.

If Abe had been cooperating with his district, Nicoll and others said, the disaster would have been avoided. He would, in 1920, have organized a volunteer crew to do what had to be done. True, nobody needed to stir a finger unless paid by the municipality; and that was the answer Nicoll had received from every one he had approached; though Nicoll knew what should be done, he lacked that compelling element which forced others to fall in line, be it against their will and inclination. Abe would have furnished ten or sixteen horses; and the rest would have followed.

The flood came late; it covered the fields to a depth of only a few inches; Abe's yard remained dry. But very little of the water ran out. The ditches filled; and in them as well as the fields the flood stood stagnant. Slowly it disappeared; the weather having turned hot, most of it simply evaporated, leaving an alkaline slime behind. This slime ultimately dried into a whitish, hygroscopic incrustation which liquefied nightly by imbibing the dew, thus preventing the ground from drying.

It was a general condition : a new Egyptian plague afflicting the district and a large part of the province. There was a panic. The drought of the previous year, combined with the decline in the value of farm products, had prepared the minds of the people to expect the worst. The old superstition—or was it observation?—that disastrous years run in threes was revived. Farmers cast about in their minds for ways and means of weathering evil times. One single product commanded a price above the normal : hay.

In Spalding District and east and west of it the greater part of the land was wild prairie. Nobody had ever worried about hay; since less than half the land was cultivated, every settler had more wild land to cut from than he owned. So far, nobody had even known that there were ways of securing the exclusive right of cutting grass on a given area.

But this spring the flood had hardly disappeared when people came from south of the Line, from twenty, thirty miles away, and inquired, often in a secretive and circuitous manner, which were the best meadows; and, having received ungrudging information, they disappeared and were, for the time being, not seen again. Nicoll, happening to drop in at the municipal office at Somerville, was asked by the secretary why the settlers of Spalding District allowed the best hay lands to pass into the hands of outsiders. He learned that these outsiders had secured haying permits from province and Crown which gave them the exclusive right to cut on such areas as were designated in their permits. For these they had paid certain fees. Incidentally, Nicoll received one item of news which he promptly communicated to Abe.

This was that Wheeldon had taken out a permit for the section west of Abe's land. Abe frowned. Within the district, that section was, by prescription, considered almost as part of his farm.

Money was scarce; Nicoll himself was in a bad plight. Abe saw it all at a glance and promptly went to Somerville.

On the way, he thought the situation over with the utmost care. If this was going to be a wet year, and though there might be little rain, the soil was bound to be wet for at least part of the summer—meadowlands might be inaccessible to horses and such heavy machinery as was used in haying. There was one section, however, even more than a section, south of his farm, which had a gravelly subsoil, forming part of the slight ridge on which his own land lay; it was higher than the rest of the district. In dry years, therefore, the grass was thin and short. Every trip into that meadow involved such loss of time for him as was required to travel four miles, to Nicoll's Corner and back again, for there was no other bridge to cross the ditch. In an exceptionally wet season, however, it would prove his salvation.

At Somerville he found that the section in question was available. He wrote a cheque and secured a permit from the Crown.

When he met Nicoll, he said, "I'll let you have what you need on shares."

"All right," Nicoll said. He still felt hurt by the way in which Abe restricted their intercourse to business; but there had been years when they had never exchanged a word.

Seeding time came and went, and no work was done in the district. Gumbo clay cannot be ploughed till the clods are dry enough to crumble; but wherever one stepped on the soil, one slipped; the crust was an alkaline smear. Even Abe did nothing till the second half of May had arrived. In Nicoll's fallow water stood in the furrows; the ridges looked like brown sugar melting in the flood. It was the same with all the fields along the road to town; the road itself, though graded up to a height of two or three feet above the prairie, was deeply rutted; and the ruts remained full of water. In front of Hilmer's, the grade had been washed out in 1919; and there remained a bad hole. Baker drove his van with four horses, at six and a half dollars a day. The ditches held the water like irrigation ditches—a curse instead of a blessing. People talked of suing province or municipality for their losses.

Meanwhile, a perhaps trifling occurrence disturbed Abe at Easter which came on 27th March/that year; the roads, though still frozen, were almost bare of snow. On Thursday before the festival Abe was taking a cream-can to town; and, thinking of his children, he arranged to get there about four o'clock.

As soon as he issued from his gate, he began, according to his habit, to scan the horizon; and he was at once aware of something moving on the road from town. At once also, like the prairie dweller he had become, he followed that moving point with his eyes.

Suddenly he noticed that the car—for nothing but a car could have moved so fast—had come to a stop, half-way between town and Hilmer's Corner. No settler had ever squatted down there; not even good grass grew in that alkaline marsh.

Then his attention was claimed by an unexpected snow-drift remaining in the trail. His horses were high-strung and restive and plunged in passing through. One of the traces broke;

and in order to affect a temporary repair, Abe had to descend to the road.

When he resumed his seat, he swept the horizon again, searching for the spot he had seen; but a point at rest is not so easily found as a point in motion. His horses fell into a trot at the very moment when the point began to move once more. There was no doubt any longer about its being a car. North of Hilmer's, it dipped steeply down into the hole, slowed, and rose again. Then it became more distinct; and the two vehicles would have met at Nicoll's Corner had not Abe held his hackneys back: they were not entirely broken to cars. The car was slowing down and came to a stop on the culvert south of the corner. Some person who was with the driver alighted on the far side and stood a moment, talking or waiting. Then the car moved on.

Abe had just reached Nicoll's wind-break when, to his amazement, he recognized in the person who had alighted his own daughter Frances. Waves of anger and passion ran through him. Was the school-house thrusting itself across his path? For the car had turned east; it was McCrae's.

Abe turned at Nicoll's gate and waited. When the girl reached him, she had just subdued the worst of a furious blush. "Hello," she said briefly and climbed to her father's side, the fact that he had waited becoming a summons. The cream-can being in her way, she had an excuse for turning her back to her father.

A hundred impulses urged Abe to angry speech; but he touched his horses with the whip in silence. When they had entered the yard, Abe drove to the small gate and tied the lead horse. Frances made at once for the house. "Wait for me in the living-room!" Abe said grimly. When he followed her, he saw Ruth coming down from upstairs.

"How did you come to be in that man's car?" he asked.

Frances, plump, dimpled, with large blue eyes in a flushed face, winced at the sound of his voice. But she raised her glance to meet his with an almost hostile stare. "School was dismissed at three. He happened to pass and offered the ride. Why shouldn't I take it?"

"Why did the car stop so long on the road?"

"Stop? Where?"

"On the road. North of town."

"Oh, that! Engine trouble. How should I know?"

Abe stood and lowered down on the girl. Behind him, Ruth filled the door, silent, straight-lipped. All sorts of things passed through his mind: he did not know the girl very well; he doubted whether Ruth knew her. McCrae had a most unsavoury reputation; though he employed him, he objected to contact between him and members of his household. Yet he thought of a remark of his brother-in-law's: "A suspicion cast on a girl's character does not remain without its effect on the girl."

"Listen here," he said with an effort to speak evenly. "No matter what happens, you don't accept favours from that man. If I ever see you with him again, that's the end of your school days. You understand?"

"I understand you," Frances said, callous, sullen, defiant.

Abe scowled; but after a moment's hesitation he turned, passing Ruth in the door, left the house, and drove to town.

Again and again when Nicoll had told him of the goings-on in the school, he had said to himself that he would not interfere; the thing was none of his business; he was living in isolation; *his* daughter, the only one left, would never attend any dance organized by the gang.

But he lived in the district after all; these people of the gang were his neighbours. No one can live in isolation unless his neighbours allow him to do so; and not only him but his to boot.

Would the day come when he would be forced to interfere?

XXIV * THE LURE OF THE TOWN

On 30th April, a Saturday, Abe happened to overhear part of a conversation between Jim and Ruth.

He was in the shed behind the house, putting on his hip-boots; and the door to the kitchen stood ajar. Abe was on the point of closing it when he heard the first words and refrained.

"Why," Ruth was saying, "has your recommendation been refused?"

This referred to the final high-school examinations on which Jim was to write in June. At the time, no candidate could write on any examination without the teacher's recommendation. In the final year, this recommendation referred only to the character of the candidate; but neither Ruth nor Abe knew that. In the lower grades the certificate of the school was accepted for certain subjects; and the recommendation referred partly to the work done in the class.

"I don't know," Jim replied evasively.

"How did you make out in the Easter tests?"

"None too well."

"Jim," his mother pleaded, "I want you so to do well at school."

"I know, mother. But it's all such nonsense. And without that recommendation I can't write."

"You are over twenty, Jim. I'll apply to the department again. They have given credit for work on the farm before."

"Not for the final year."

"How do you know? Then it means another year."

"Mother," the boy exclaimed, "what's the use? I want to be a mechanic. I don't need any standing for that. I simply can't get along at school. Duncan and Ferris offer me a hundred a month. I'd take it for a while. But I'll tell you. There's a chap by name of Cope who's going to open a high-class garage at Somerville. He offers me a partnership if I can come in with two thousand dollars. I could borrow the money."

"I'll *give* it to you the moment you finish high school."

"What's the use!" Jim cried in desperation.

"I shall never give my consent to your leaving school before you are through. I insisted on that in Marion's case. Make up your mind that I shall insist on it with you."

At this moment she noticed that the door was open and closed it.

Abe had heard enough and watched. The conversation had the result that Jim went back to school on Monday.

All about, boys were leaving the land. Their education was bringing them in contact with what appeared to them to be a world wider than that of the farm. Abe hardly knew whether he would hold Jim if he could. There was good stuff in the boy; he was old enough to know what he wanted.

Yet the thought was weariness. What was to become of the farm? What had all the work been for if Jim refused to take it up where his father must leave it? He might just as well have "mined" the soil and taken from it what it would give. Instead, he had built house and barns and acquired two square miles of land, to be divided among his descendants!

On Tuesday, 17th May, Abe took the seeder out on the fallow; even now he had to leave many places untouched because they were too wet. There was no work for more than a single man.

He was on the long narrow strip east of the pasture, when, about eleven o'clock, he saw Jim coming home, afoot. But not before twelve did he leave the field. Impersonally he wondered what might have happened. At half-past twelve, the usual hour, he entered the house.

Jim, visibly nervous, was sitting in the kitchen, a strange figure of dejection for a boy six feet tall. Ruth's eyes were red.

Abe went to the wash-basin, stripped off his smock, pushed his shirt-sleeves up, and prepared with great deliberation for his ablutions. While he slowly cleaned hands, arms, face, and head, Ruth was going about between kitchen and dining-room. The fact that Abe accepted his son's presence without comment had something profoundly disquieting.

Having finished, he turned to the dining-room. "Well, let's have dinner first!" He meant his tone to be humorous; but the word "first" had the effect that neither Ruth nor Jim made more than a pretence at eating. Abe ate slowly and with relish, a still more disconcerting fact. But at last he pushed his chair back.

"Well," he said, "what's your story?"

"I didn't get my recommendation."

"That I know. But why did you leave school to-day when your mother wished you to continue?"

The mother sat motionless; Jim was playing with a fork.

Abe waited. At last, again in that disquieting, half humorous tone, "Out with it now! What is you story?"

Jim collected himself. "Well, they'd been hinting at school——"

"Who's they?"

"The teachers."

"Been hinting at what?"

"That I'd better stay at home."

"My own opinion. But what business is it of theirs? I am paying toward that school and the salaries."

"They say I am holding the whole class back."

"How?"

Jim, not understanding his father, was on the point of becoming defiant. He shrugged his shoulders.

"What I want to know is why you left school to-day. Why not yesterday or to-morrow? What has happened to-day?"

"The board met last night."

"What's the board got to do with it?"

Jim braced himself. "They told me the board had resolved——"

"Out with it! . . . I'll tell you. They've expelled you. Right?"

"It amounts to that," Jim said with a shrug. Only shrugs could express his full meaning.

"What for?"

"Oh, I don't know."

Unreasonable anger surged in Abe, not against the boy but against the school system which they had set up to defy him. "You don't know? I'll have to go to town then, to find out. I have no objection to your leaving school. I don't want a boy of mine to press the school bench, advertising the fact that he has no brains. But they can't expel him without reasons. Unless their reasons are mighty good, back you go."

The boy looked doubtfully at his father, realizing at last that he was an ally. "Their reasons are good enough," he said, ready at last to explain. "I've goaded them into doing what they have done. I want to go to work. I didn't want to leave the way Marion tried to."

"Leave? If you quit school, you'll help on the farm, I suppose."

"No, father. I don't like the dust and the dirt. I'm a mechanic."

"You like the grease and the dirt better than the dust and the dirt, do you?"

Jim disregarded his father's sarcasm. "You said you don't want me to advertise the fact that I have no brains. It isn't a question of brains. All decent boys leave school. Only the sheiks stick it out."

"What's a sheik?"

Jim laughed. "A boy that runs after girls and thinks more of the way his necktie is tied than of what he wants to do in the world."

"Go on," Abe said.

"If I'd applied myself, I could have done as well as the next one. I don't want to learn silly verses by heart and French phrases. I don't want to be a writer chap. I want to do a man's work. Work in which brains count. Not turn furrows."

"They've taught you to despise what your father's doing, eh?"

"That's what they say," Jim defended himself. "He's got no brains, they say; he'll never make anything but a farmer."

"They say that, do they?" Abe's tone required no answer. "And so you want to leave father and mother?"

Ruth redoubled her sobbing.

"I've had a job waiting for me for two years. Since I left Somerville." Jim spoke as an equal now, confiding what was in his heart. "I've given this school game a try-out. It hasn't advanced me an inch. And now I want to quit." With a laugh, he added, "I've given the teachers a run for their money anyway."

"And they've expelled you," Abe said evenly. "Nothing to boast of. What did you do, by the way?"

But Jim was serious again. "Unless they had expelled me, mother would never have let me quit."

"And you don't want the farm?" Abe rose as if to leave the room. But he turned in the door. "All we can do on earth is to make our living, directly or in a roundabout way. I don't mean to hold you. But I've built this house and these barns to keep my children on the farm. If you go, my work is for nothing. I have no pleasure in it myself any longer. If you stay, half the farm is yours. To-day if you want it. Think it over. Then let me know." With that he went out.

About four o'clock Abe heard the hum of Jim's car in the yard. When he reached the southern edge of the field, he waited.

"You've come to say good-bye?" he asked when Jim arrived.

"Yes, I am going to town." Jim hesitated. "I want to say one more thing, father. If I cared for a farm, I'd take up a homestead myself, to build a place of my own."

Abe looked at Jim. That was the way he had felt himself. . . .

A week later, rain having stopped the work again. Abe went to Somerville, made inquiries about a certain Mr. Cope, saw him, and entered into an agreement with him whereby he, Abe, became a sleeping partner in the new firm of Spalding, Spalding, and Cope. He invested five thousand dollars in the venture.

XXV ✴ DISTRESS

ALTHOUGH Abe co-operated in the matter of his son's establishment, he became very taciturn when Jim had left.

This reacted on his relations to the rest of the district where, during the summer of 1921, as a consequence of the economic situation, he might have re-established his former prestige; for many of those even who were hostile to him began to realize that a leader was needed. The peculiarity of the situation consisted in this that, while prices of farm products continued to decline, such commodities as the farmer had to buy were reaching their peak. What with the failure of the farmers to complete their seeding operations, things worked up to a climax which only Abe could remedy. But matters of actual fact were not the only ones to enter as factors into the situation. The war had unsettled men's minds. There was a tremendous new urge towards immediacy of results; there was general dissatisfaction. Irrespective of their economic ability, people craved things which they had never craved before. Democracy was interpreted as the right of everybody to everything that the stimulated inventive power of mankind in the mass could furnish in the way of conveniences and luxuries. Amusements became a necessity of daily life. A tendency to spend recklessly and to use credit on a scale hitherto unknown was linked with a pronounced weakening of the moral fibre. In the homes of the Hartleys, McCraes, Wheeldons, Topps, gramophones and similar knick-knacks made their appearance; young men wore flashy clothes, paying or owing from forty to a hundred dollars for a suit. Girls wore silk stockings, silk underwear, silk dresses; and nothing destroys modesty and sexual morality in a girl more quickly than the consciousness that suddenly she wears attractive *dessous.* This orgy of spending had been enormously stimulated by the easy money of the flax boom; and the rate of expenditure was hardly retarded by the subsequent disaster of the slump. A standard of expenditure once arrived at is not so easily abandoned as established.

So far, the district had been a grain district. Only Abe had, to any extent, raised cattle. In that disastrous spring land could not be worked; credit was at once cut off. Instead of being able to go to the bank and borrow, the settlers were molested by collectors trying to squeeze water out of a stone; their mail consisted of dunning letters. Against the holdings of not a few legal judgments were secured, among them McCrae. As Abe was seeding, people came humbly and asked, "How are the chances for a job?" He looked at them and replied laconically, "Not a chance on earth, now."

And haying permits could not be had on credit. To make this situation doubly ironic, hay was the only thing of which there was an abundance and which, nevertheless, stubbornly held to its price.

This seemed puzzzling; but as, with the advancing season, the truly dramatic condition unfolded itself, it found its natural explanation. The abundance of grass proceeded from the very circumstance which prevented its being harvested. And this was general, brought about by an excess of rain. In the rolling parts of the country, the rains had neither delayed seeding nor prevented the growth of the grain. But on the flat prairie the ground never dried out; and so it could not absorb the rains which began with the early summer. What grain had been seeded was drowned. But through the natural selection which had been going on for centuries and millennia, the prairie grasses had adjusted themselves to excessive moisture; they grew knee-high, hip-high in places. In the rolling parts of the country only such areas as, by reason of their low, sloughy character, had never been tilled were left to the native growth; and consequently, what applied to the hay of the plain applied to the hay of the hills as well: hay land remained inaccessible to horses and heavy machinery; where the soil was not covered with water, it was so soft that a harvest of the grass was out of the question. In places, stacks of last year's hay rotted in the meadows because they could not be taken out. In Spalding District meadows were bottomless; the roads, with ruts filled and ditches overflowing, were mires of mud; in going to town, farmers used four horses and wagons.

The rains continued through the whole of June. Two, three sunny days were at once followed by devastating thunderstorms which spared no corner. The traditional haying season went by with nothing done.

To make matters worse, this combination of a surplus of the growing grass with a scarcity of the marketable product began to cut with a double edge. Few settlers had hay left from the previous year. When their stock began to suffer—they could not even turn the beasts out without danger of seeing them engulfed—those who had money or credit shipped in hay from across the border or from Ontario. Farmers were bidding against each other and against city buyers; the price of hay rose and rose. End of May it had been twelve dollars a ton; by the end of June when, before the war, wild hay had been three dollars, it sold at twenty. Timothy and clover went as high as thirty-two.

One dry day in June Abe went into his field to look at the ruin of his wheat. He saw Wheeldon and Nawosad on the section west of his farm, cutting by hand. Hip-boots on their legs, they stood in water; when they swung their scythes, jets of spray flew over their heads. There was no way of getting the fodder they needed except by such antiquated methods. They gathered their cuttings in bundles secured by ropes and carried them on their backs to a point north of the Hudson's Bay section where a hayrack stood, hitched with eight horses. That hayrack stood aslant, on the point of toppling over. When, late in the day, the men tried to draw their load away, they broke a wheel and went home on horseback. Even that green feed turned black with decay.

When Wheeldon had secured the west section as it was commonly called he had disregarded Abe's prescriptive claim. Some had rejoiced at his boldness in doing so; others said now, "It served Wheeldon right." That section, in dry years, yielded the best and most abundant fodder; it was low, with a subsoil of impermeable clay. In any other year, Wheeldon might simply have looked elsewhere for hay; but every single spot which was not irreclaimable swamp had been pre-empted by a permit. Permit holders objected to any encroachment on their rights. Wheeldon did cut a strip north of his farm where in a dry year there would have been only a scab of turf. Horanski promptly presented him with a claim for damages amounting to fifty dollars. Threatened with legal proceedings, Wheeldon paid by a note without securing the hay. Not only the settlers of the district watched jealously over their rights; people living at a distance paid local men for looking after their interests, such as Anderson, the hardware dealer, or Elliot or Baker.

Just how dramatic the situation had become was brought home to Abe when, around the middle of July, a dairy man from near the city, having looked the land over, offered him five hundred dollars for a sub-permit valid for one quarter-section. Abe declined. Incidentally he bought on a falling market steers and heifers wherever he could. He held the purse-strings; and though he occasionally paid more than was asked, many looked at his deals with the green eye of jealousy.

Wheeldon could not cut; Horanski might have cut but could not reach his meadow; Abe alone might have taken hundreds of tons of green feed off his land; to reach it, he had the dam formed by the soil taken from the ditch; but he held off; he could not have cured the grass.

The district was awed. Even Wheeldon's treachery turned to Spalding's profit. There was no hurry about cutting; the grass did not mature; like any other crop it needed dry weather to ripen. Dry weather would come. The longer it was delayed, the more pronounced would Spalding's advantage be over the rest of the district. Wealth untold would be his. "A marvellous man!" most settlers said. Others asked, "How does he do it?" And a small minority exclaimed, "What the devil——"

Towards the middle of July a dry spell came, lasting five days. For three days Abe waited anxiously. On the fourth he took a trench plough and eight horses and made the trip around Nicoll's Corner and over the dam to his meadow. Working with a four-horse team and changing horses every two hours, he cross-ditched the section from north to south. It was not a neat job; but that did not matter. For two days he worked with dogged determination, ploughing and reploughing a fourteen-foot furrow till he reached the gravel underneath.

He had barely finished when a three-day rain of unheard-of violence started, with sheet-lightning and rolling thunder all around. This rain produced a situation with which it seemed impossible to cope.

South of Nicoll's farm, beyond the ditch, a lake was produced resembling the spring flood, a mile and a half long from north to south, and half a mile wide, covering the Topp holdings. It was ten inches deep, with soft mud underneath. The water massed itself on the west side of the road to town which acted as a dam, most of the flood coming from the drainage shed by Abe's meadow; and slowly the lake backed towards that meadow. The Topp buildings stood in water, their cellars drowned; but neither Slim nor Henry minded it so long as the flood backed into Abe's hay land. Spalding was, after all, not going to get away with his devil's luck or whatever it was, be it only his confounded shrewdness or initiative; all his ditching and cross-ditching was not going to help him.

They could not know that Abe's heart was anywhere but in his work. In 1912 he had exulted in his victory; that he had worried at the time was forgotten; he saw only the contrast of the past with the present. Now he fought because farm and weather ruled him with a logic of their own.

And then the amazing thing happened. During the night of the third day the grade which held the water broke. Beginning as a mere trickle, the runnel soon became a washout; the water disappeared from the Topp holdings and flooded Horanski's and Elliot's instead. Abe's hay land lay high and dry while the current played havoc with the road to town.

It was unnatural; it could not be. Was he possessed of superior powers? Or had he gone by night and opened the road? Mrs. Grappentin said you could weaken a dam by thinking of it. The devil would do the rest.

Nobody remembered that Abe, in 1899, had simply shown ordinary sagacity in the choice of his location. So long as the ditches had functioned, that sagacity had not been conspicuous; circumstances had restored conditions as they had been before the advent of these ditches. But nobody gave Abe credit for his foresight except Nicoll. Everything, at all times, people said, was in Spalding's favour. To him that hath shall be given. Had Wheeldon not forestalled him, he would have had the west section; and though Nicoll laughed at such an idea, even Stanley, Wheeldon, and Elliot had an uncanny feeling that to his horses it would not have been inaccessible. "Perhaps not,"

Nicoll said. "He would have found a way to drain it in time."

Abe gave no thought to such matters. A more oppressing thing held him in its grip: he had worked and slaved: what for? His great house was useless: the three people left in it would have had ample room in the patchwork shack. Soon he and Ruth would be alone, lost in that structure which, from behind the rustling wind-breaks, looked out over that prairie which it had been built to dominate.

And then dry, settled weather came at last. The crop failure was general; the compensation, peculiar to Abe. Wild hay, for immediate delivery, stood at twenty-five dollars a ton.

Abe went to town. Opposite Blaine's cottage there was a gap in the road twenty feet long and four feet deep. The fields beyond looked like the sleek, smooth bottom of a gigantic mud-hole.

Abe called Rogers over the telephone; and the latter promised to bring his two men at once; they were to board at Nicoll's.

Nicoll would come with two boys; in addition, Abe hired McCrae to help in the field; and he made it known that everybody who had a team would find work in hauling the hay to the track in town.

XXVI * HAYING

THE weather held. Elsewhere, the wheat harvest began; in Spalding District there was no wheat. Abe had started the cutting of the hay at the southern edge of his meadow. For a few days, another, a Mennonite crew had been working south of it, on the spur of high land that lost itself west of Scheigel's. For two weeks the work had gone on, and Abe had moved north. For the week of 17th August a last strip remained. Rogers's two young Englishmen were delighted at the chance of learning his methods.

On the afternoon of that first Monday of the second half of August the whole life of the landscape seemed to come to a focus in that meadow, now mamillated with stacks of hay. Nowhere else was any work possible. The haystacks stood uniform over the field, thirty feet wide at the base, tapering to the top, a hundred feet long, their longitudinal axis running from north-west to south-east, in the direction of the prevailing winds. Only the northernmost edge of the field, twenty rods wide, was still bare, the cut hay lying in wind-rows or, farther west, in such swaths as were being gathered up even then by the rakes. These rakes were being operated by Nicoll's two youngest boys, Bill and Norman, fourteen and fifteen years old.

The life of the meadow centred at a point directly south of the gap in Abe's wind-break where a new stack was growing up. Two enormous "bucks" drawn by two four-horse teams each, swept the wind-rows up and drew the hay to the stack which, so far, looked perilously tall and slender like a spire. At the unfinished end a huge scaffolding of heavy timbers slanted to the top, forming an angle of thirty degrees with the level prairie.

There, between the last two planks of the scaffold, reaching into the air like horns or jumping board, Abe worked with his fork, putting a semblance of order into the chaotic masses of freshly-cured hay. His movements were slow and deliberate. A glance showed that he was no longer young; a stranger might have placed his age even higher than it was. The methodical sweeps of his arms were performed with that economy of motion and effort which comes with long experience and which counts the cost, in energy as well as time, of every lifting of the fork. Thus, standing up to his knees and often his hips in loose hay, he worked forkful after forkful upwards, the base of the stack taking care of itself.

His glance did not roam far over the field. Yet there was present to his mental vision the whole area in which the work went on. East of the stack stood two wagons with low boxes, their tongues trailing on the ground. The bucks described ever-widening circles; and the horse-drawn rakes, never resting, swept wind-row after wind-row into place farther west. The work, proceeding in an apparently leisurely way, was surprisingly fast in its results, chiefly because it was so thoroughly organized, though also because the capacity of these bucks was immense: whenever one of them swept up to the stack, and they came in steady succession, two tons of hay were lifted to the top.

To such as had known Abe in years gone by he looked weary and grey. He wore a khaki-coloured suit of overalls. In his face, the ruddy colour of his skin was overlain by a layer of dust and chaff. At this northern end of the meadow, the grass contained an admixture of skunk-tail the seed of which was annually spread by the flood; and the barbed awns of this grassy weed were sticking in his hair and eyebrows, giving him the hoary appearance of some rustic harvest god.

In the short intervals of rest he stood leaning on his fork

and allowed his small, blue eyes to sweep the horizon, hardly moving his head. The weather was incredibly golden; the light, bronzed.

Once every ten or fifteen minutes Abe's full, though silent, attention was claimed by one or other of the bucks which, having scooped up a wind-row of hay, swept into position, south-east of the stack, in line with its axis. There it stopped for a few seconds to give the horses a breathing space before their last, desperate effort in forcing their load over the inclined planks to the top of the scaffold. They came on, at first slowly, merely bending their weights into their collars; then, urged by the drivers, faster and faster; till, when the buck struck the upward slanting planks, they strained every muscle, clamping their feet like grappling-hooks into the yielding soil, while behind them the long chains to which the eveners were fastened rose with the buck which their pull lifted up; and those eveners, finally, quivered high above their rumps, one on each side of the stack. Simultaneously, their drivers became vocal : Nicoll and the Englishmen calling their horses by their names and shouting, "Get up, there! Now! Get up! Get up!" McCrae cursing and swearing while he swung loose lines down on straining rumps and arching backs.

The buck was hanging in the air, perched on the last projecting planks of the scaffold, holding its load on wide, pointed, wooden prongs set in the huge cross timbers which were the exact length of the width of the stack; and the horses, in order not to let it slide back, dug their forefeet into the ground while, with their heads, they reached for such stray wisps of hay as littered the ground.

Abe, meanwhile, had climbed to the top of the stack and, thence, stepped across to a plank below the horns of the scaffold. Having passed under the buck, he tilted the evenly poised machine with a single reach of his powerful arms; and an avalanche of hay poured down the sloping unfinished end of the stack. Then he bent to let the buck pass over his head as the horses backed away and allowed it to slip to the ground. Next they swung around in a huge half circle; the buck was hooked on to the lower timbers of the scaffold; and the latter was pulled back a foot or so. The hooks were reversed, and the buck swung free, these prongs which, on the previous trip, had stood upright now sweeping the ground. Abe stepped back to the stack and worked quietly on, finishing off the top to a thatch.

As he worked, his consciousness, apart from definite thoughts, was made up of three distinct and separate complexes which yet remained intertwined and blurred in their demarcations.

One of them was composed of such elements of his immediate surroundings as obtruded on his senses: the hayfield with its crew; the ditch bordering the field to the north, brimful of water; the trail beyond; his farmstead within its wind-break, with the roofs of barns and house out-topping the autumnally dark-green trees and a vista through the gap of the gate to the yard; the illimitable horizon to the west; the district with its roads and its two bridges, one of them of fatal memory, to the east; and the hamlet of Morley. But his consciousness of this landscape also comprised many things unseen: the towns of Somerville and St. Cecile beyond the horizon, joined by the highway to the city sixty miles away. More than that: as it extended in space to things imperceptible to the eye, so it extended in time beyond the present; it comprised the two-roomed and later three-and four-roomed shack in which he had lived for fourteen years till it had been replaced by that palatial structure with its green roof: a possession of no value now, a mere ostentation.

The second complex concerned itself with the economic situation that had arisen during the last few years. Abe had failed to take advantage of the flax boom; and, therefore, he had escaped the disaster of the slump. For two years he had done no fall-ploughing; and his seeming neglect had turned to his profit. This hay crop represented unheard-of wealth. He had bought steers and heifers by the dozen and the score, to convert the poorer parts of this crop into gold; he would once more live up to the obligation of his wealth and give the district work; he would, in the bank and in sound investments, replace all that the house and the new barn had taken seven years ago, and more. . . .

The third complex was that concerned with his own personal life and its extension into the life of a family. Over there, in that house, Ruth was alone. Frances, seventeen years old and just promoted into the final high-school grade, had been sent to town in the little buggy which he had bought for his children to drive to school in; for none of the men could be spared. How Ruth spent her days when she was alone Abe had often wondered. But to his household belonged other children: even Charlie who haunted a room in that house as a mere memory now, slowly paling; and Marion who had moved into the city where her husband had bought a partnership in a great law firm; and Jim who preferred the grease and the dirt to the dust and the dirt and was part owner of a prosperous garage at Somerville, selling high-priced cars. Incomprehensibly, there was also Frances, a source of disquietude even to Ruth. Like so many others she had grown out of hand. She did not rebel or disobey; but she lived a life of her own, admitting no one into her confidence. And further, there were the Vanbruiks in town: Abe's sister Mary, ageing, brave in her loneliness, disappointed of children; and the enigmatic doctor, owner of the most flourishing business outside of the city, yet professing that he could not afford to buy any but the cheapest car : a doctor who had abandoned his practice and to whom many turned when they were in distress.

All these things were present to Abe. His mind hovered over his life as the marsh-hawk hovers over the prairie lifted to the sky.

It was between three and four o'clock when the first of the three complexes was invaded by a new element.

The landscape of the prairie is so vast that a stranger might think a new detail must be of considerable magnitude or striking colour or outline to attract attention. But it is also so simple and unrelieved that he who knows it detects the most insignificant change, especially when it arises along the well-known lines of the roads.

As Abe proceeded in his work, slowly and deliberately, yet without a break, he became aware that once more something was moving on the road from town, five miles away in a direct line. Every now and then he raised his eyes and looked. A stranger would not have found what attracted Abe's attention without having it pointed out to him.

In years long gone by, Abe would have refused to allow such a trifle to intrude on his thought; it would have seemed a fit occupation for such as Hartley or Mrs. Grappentin. It was his disinclination to spy upon his possible neighbours, more perhaps than his disinclination to be spied upon, which had induced him to plant his wind-break all around his yard; south of the Somerville Line, wind-breaks were drawn only north and west of the buildings; for south and east winds were rarely violent and never cold. Abe had excluded all views; even on himself his place had made the impression of a walled castle. Nicoll, Stanley, and Shilloe had followed his plan. The district bore the imprint of his mind.

Along the road from town a black spot was crawling north. Abe had learned to interpret such things with an unfailing accuracy : it was a buggy coming from town.

Now Abe had been in the field all day and knew that no buggy had gone to town but his. Strangers visiting the district, salesmen and collectors, did not travel in horse-drawn vehicles. This was a small buggy drawn by a single horse: Frances was coming home.

Nothing strange about that. Ruth had been in need of supplies from the store and had wished to send Mary a message. The girl, having attended to her errands, was coming home. Nothing strange about that.

Yet, as the buggy crept north—the pony was ageing—Abe felt disquieted. When it had crossed the ditch at Hilmer's Corner, horse and vehicle became articulated against the sky, distorted by the mirage. The horse looked like a long, cylindrical body with mere hair-lines for its legs, as a child would draw it with a few strokes of the pencil. Behind it, the box floated on a silver surface, its wheels eclipsed by the eddies set up by the horse in the wavy air.

The only strange thing about it was that, in the morning, Frances had worn a light dress; and whoever sat on the near side of the buggy now wore dark clothes. Once seen and noted, this seemed sufficient to disquiet Abe. Who was with the girl?

Abe was still watching the buggy as it approached the washout in the grade when his attention was claimed by a buck which swung into line with the skids of the scaffold. Yet even while, with automatic precision, he dumped the load, he kept an eye on the vehicle as the horse hesitated on the brink and gingerly descended into the gap, completely eclipsed by the mirage. By the time the horses were circling away, the vehicle had reached the bridge at Nicoll's Corner. Before Abe began to work the newly-dumped load upwards, he stood for a moment leaning on the handle of his fork, up to his hips in hay.

The buggy turned at the corner, and the mystery resolved itself. Frances was not alone; but the person with her was a woman. At least there was nothing in her companion for gossip to take hold of; for Abe knew that everybody in the district, down to the men and boys in the field, had watched the vehicle as closely as he himself.

A few minutes later, the woman with Frances revealed her identity by a characteristic motion in readjusting herself on her seat, it was Mary. Quietly Abe went on creating order out of chaos.

Steadily the slow-trotting horse approached beyond the ditch; again a buck claimed Abe's attention. As he dumped it, he glanced about. Another half-day would finish their work.

When the buck departed, Abe could no longer see the buggy; it had disappeared behind the stack. He went on with his work; but when he had finished, he took a few plunging steps upward, steadying himself with his fork, till he could look over the top of the now considerably lengthened stack, straight into his yard, through the gap in the wind-break. The buggy had turned in and was heading for the little gate in the fence of the house-yard. With the back of his hand Abe wiped the sweat off his brow.

Never before had Mary come in a vehicle not her own, except on that Christmas Day when Marion had tried to elope. But this was summer; the doctor kept a small car which Mary drove. How did she intend to go home? Did she mean to stay overnight? It must have been something of importance which had brought her out. Abe waited till she and Frances had alighted, tying the horse to the gate-post in which there was a ring. Then, on the way to the house, they disappeared behind the wind-break. Abe returned to his work. Had he been on his own side of the full-flowing ditch, he would have gone to the house to inquire; as it was, his gate, twenty rods away, was four miles distant.

For the rest of the afternoon a certain disquietude did not leave him, not even when, about six o'clock, he saw Mary returning to town, alone, in the buggy. He was restless. More and more frequently he looked about to see whether the next buck was not yet coming, as though to accelerate the work. Not that the speed would have made any difference, for the work would go on till dark in any case. It was just a feeling of impatience with a day which seemed unwilling to end.

Behind the wind-break, the house stood undisturbed, its dark-red walls showing here and there between the thinning masses of foliage. At times the pleasant picture darkened to his eye till it seemed silent and sinister, holding a secret. Till Mary had departed, the little horse had stood between its shafts, knock-kneed, its head hanging low.

At last the dark rose like a wave rolling up from the east. The mown grass and the stubble became beaded with dew, its scent intensified. Dusk comes fast on the level prairie, and with a tremendously accentuated contrast against the bright light of day. Horizons are hazy; the sun, perhaps still above the rim of the world, loses its power of orienting such light as remains. It turns into a vermilion disk. Dampness wells up with a chill. . . And still the work went on.

But at last, all sorts of uncanny changes having taken place, work had to stop. Abe spoke to Nicoll; and Nicoll sent a call through the thickening twilight, a signal for the boys to gather at the stack where Abe did the last capping-off. Then he, too, slipped to the ground, while his helpers unhooked the horses from the draw-chains of the bucks.

The ground being saturated with moisture, the lower air, heated by contact with the soil, had drunk itself full of vapour during the day. But radiation is swift on flat, unrelieved ground; and, with the gathering dusk, the moisture held by the air began to condense into a thick white mist. Already horses and men were wading about in this mist which, so far, lay knee-high. This gave a peculiar detached air to the scene: the day was done; the time to rest at hand; and a great, overwhelming lassitude came over the workers.

One of the two wagons east of the stack, Abe's, held two clothes-baskets filled with the dishes in which the noonday meal had been brought; besides, earthenware jugs which had held water, repair parts for mowers and rakes, a few spare forks, and a tin box used as a stove to make coffee on, with such of the hay for fuel as was rejected because it held too much skunk-tail. The other wagon, Nicoll's, was filled with fresh hay. Abe threw his fork into the former and spead a canvas sheet over its contents.

McCrae and Nicoll were hitching two horses each to the wagons; the Englishmen were stringing the others together into two lines, one long, consisting of Abe's ten Clydes; the other short, of two horses, which were Nicoll's. These they tied behind the wagons.

The mist was rising. At this moment the horses that had been working beyond the gully came galloping in like a herd of wild beasts, with cocked ears flicking forward and backward: horses are easily frightened in a mist at night. With them came McCrae's pony. Two of the draught horses that came thundering in bore their riders, the Nicoll boys.

For a minute the scene was one of utter confusion; for all horses pranced and stirred as if expecting an attack; some reared, others whinnied. Nicoll spoke a word of reproach to the boys, in subdued accents; but their voices and laughter sounded unnaturally loud. The mist was still rising, forming in ever-higher layers. Then the horses that had arrived last disappeared as they had come. McCrae had captured his mount. The others galloped away to the east, along the dam; and the laughter and the shouts of the boys echoed over the plain.

Abe climbed into the front of his wagon and took the lines. It was now so dark that he could no longer see his companions. He stood and listened, inferring the progress made from sounds.

"Ready?" he asked at last.

A grunt answered him, as if those who had no driving to do

were too exhausted for articulate speech. The caravan started, the horses following the wagons like trains of satellites. Without raising himself from the floor of Abe's wagon where he was reclining, McCrae lighted a cigarette; and the flicker of the match showed Abe standing in front. The horses moved their ears; the mist enveloped them all.

They went on for half an hour. Apart from the creaking of the wheels there was silence till the hollow thud of the horses' hoofs proclaimed that they had turned on to the bridge. Abe stopped with a "Whoa there!"

McCrae jumped to the ground. His leap scared the pony which had been tied to the stepping board, and it wheeled, straining at the line. When McCrae had untied it, it backed away till it stood in front of Abe's horses so that, when Abe clicked his tongue, they fidgeted but did not move. McCrae had rolled another cigarette and, hooking the pony's bridle over a shoulder, proceeded to light it.

As the match flared up, its flame illuminated the raw, cynical face of the man and the wide, quivering nostrils of his frightened mount. All about, it threw a momentary sphere of visibility into the enveloping mist; and the pony, head raised, its eyes full of fright, was trying to break away. McCrae, once more in the dark, vaulted on to the bare back of the animal and galloped away through the night. By the gentle way in which Abe said, "Get up!" he seemed to express his disapproval of the man's methods in dealing with animals.

As he went on, Nicoll's wagon drew up behind him; and "Good night" sounded on every hand. Abe had turned west.

When he reached his barn and unhooked his horses, throwing the traces over their backs, he touched their rumps one by one, a signal that they might go and drink at the outside trough. The yard was unlighted. Abe had expressed his opinion that it was a waste to turn lights on when only he was working in the yard at night. Darkness felt grateful.

The last hour of the day's work had come: the hour he liked best. As he entered the horse barn, switching on a single light, he was greeted by a nicker from those of the animals which had come in from the pasture at dark. The horses that had drunk at the trough filed in and went to their stalls; and, as Abe moved about, carrying them their rations, they turned their heads and touched his arm with exploring noses. Having finished, he stood for a moment in the open door.

The things of the day had fallen away before the utter peace of the night. Abe's disquietude was a mere memory now. The tiny droplets of the mist held, dissolved in them, a trace of the wood smoke from the chimney of the kitchen which imparted to them a scent as of spring.

Yet a remnant of curiousity remained; and before he went to the new barn to admit the cows crowding about its western door, he crossed over to the house through the driving gate north of the barn. The back doors of shed and kitchen stood open; and the light from the kitchen fell through the shed on the ground. Toned down by the mist, it, too, held a note of peace and drowsiness. Abe looked at his watch: a little after ten. The house was plunged in utter silence. Nothing stirred; curiosity vanished. In a strange impulse Abe reached for the coal-oil lantern. He did not light it till he was in the cow barn.

Having admitted the cows, some twenty of them, for steers and heifers were left in the pasture, he distributed hay and shorts—crushed wheat with most of the flour removed—fetched a milking stool, washed his hands, and squatted down by the side of one of the two cows which were to be milked; the rest had their calves at foot.

For many years Abe had not milked by lantern light. That he did so now, carried him back through the years to a time when he had been filled with ambition; when yard and barns as they were had existed only in dreams. He had been happy then; all his wishes had been of a realizable kind; he had lived in a future which he desired; that future had come disappointingly. Youth and the ardent urge; age and poignant regret: where was the life in between? Peace and happiness? He sought them in the past. In the present were only exhaustion and weariness: weariness even unto death. . . . Yet this was the last turning point in Abe's life.

He took the milk to the separator in the milk room; and after a while, breathing deeply in the fresh, misty air, he took the skimmed milk to the pig pen where he stirred barley chop into it before he poured it into the troughs, the animals squealing as they shouldered each other aside.

It was past eleven when, carrying the cream pail, he entered the house. Ruth was sitting in the dining-room, half asleep no doubt as was her custom when Abe was late. As he bent over the wash-basin, she came and busied herself at the white-panelled range.

It had never been Abe's way to speak readily. All things come to him who waits. What did it matter? Having finished, he turned, his limbs feeling heavy as lead. His question, when it was uttered at last, came as though advanced against some resistance. "Frances in bed?"

"Yes," Ruth said without turning from the stove where the eggs were sizzling. "It's quite late."

"I know." That was all.

Abe entered the dining-room and dropped into his chair. When Ruth placed his supper before him, he ate slowly, enjoying the additional drowsiness induced by the food. He was half conscious of the fact that Ruth had not mentioned Mary's call. He looked at her where she sat sewing; but he lowered his eyes again to his plate. He felt drugged with sleep. When he pushed his chair back and rose, stretching, he had almost forgotten about Mary. Sleep! "Well," he said, omitting the rest which was obvious.

But Ruth, putting her sewing away, said casually, "Mary was here."

"So I saw." He felt disinclined to go into that now.

"She had a telephone message from Rogers," Ruth went on. "He has started cutting and wants you for stacking."

"Was that what she came for?"

"Yes. He'll call for you and his men to-morrow after dinner."

"All right."

"Whom are you going to get for the chores?"

"McCrae, I suppose."

Ruth winced. Abe hesitated at the door, frowning. But no. Not now. Let it go. Still, he asked, "Why did Mary not come in the car?"

"Charles was in the city. She'll send the buggy back with a boy."

"That's all right." A moment longer he lingered. There was something strange. Mary might have sent the message through Frances. But he gave in to his desire for sleep. He yawned. "Good night."

"Good night."

XXVII * RUTH

Ruth did not sleep that night. She cried into her pillow. In the dark, what had happened came back with cruel vividness; every word that had been spoken during Mary's visit.

Entering the house, Mary had nodded, saying nothing by way of greeting but "Ruth!" Frances had slunk in, a picture of dejection.

"You better sit down, Ruth," Mary had said in the living-room.

"Why? What is wrong?"

"Sit down before I tell you."

Frightened, Ruth had obeyed.

Mary, too, had sat down. "I am bringing Frances home as you see. She can't be trusted out of sight. The girl is with child."

"No!"

"No use saying no, Ruth. She has confessed."

There had been a silence, Ruth staring at Frances with tears in her eyes. The girl, head bent, had stood pale but defiant. No admission was needed. Once attention had been called to it, her condition was evident.

"You might at least have told me," Ruth said bitterly to her child. "It would have saved half the disgrace."

"It's plainly to be seen," Mary had sternly gone on. "But I'll admit I did not suspect her till this afternoon. I was in the garden. Across the fence was Ethel Reilly with another girl. "Look at that Spalding kid!" one said to the other. "Surely, she's got herself into trouble?" I couldn't see Frances. But it struck me at once with the force of conviction. Only in the morning I had been thinking that she had grown astonishingly stout since school had closed. But you are stout yourself; and it hadn't been striking so far."

"I wasn't stout when I was her age," Ruth had said.

"Perhaps not. But she's been at home for two months, and you have noticed nothing yourself. I have blamed and blamed myself ever since. When she came in, I charged her with the fact. She denied it. I made her undress; and she broke down and admitted it all . . . No use crying, Ruth, now the thing's done. I came because I knew Abe wasn't at home. The problem is how to keep it from his knowledge."

"How *can* it be kept from his knowledge?"

"That you will have to think out. I wonder whether you realize what this would mean to him. He would kill the man."

"Who *is* the man?"

"Let Frances tell you. I don't mean to go into the details of the sordid story. But the man is married and has a family of his own. That ghost of an excuse Frances has. But it is all the worse for Abe."

"Why?"

"Ruth, I know what this must mean to you. I don't want to be harsh. But I must speak. I wish to God I had said long ago what I have to say. You have not always been the right wife for Abe. When you saw what it meant to carve a farm out of raw prairie, you gave up and threw the whole burden on him. You thought your children should have a freer and easier life. You taught them to look for fulfilment of their wishes away from home. They have learned the lesson."

"If you want to speak ill of my children——"

"I am not speaking ill of them. If you had given them the right kind of home, this would not have happened. Marion would not have married against Abe's wishes. Jim would have stayed at home. Frances would be a decent girl. What has Abe left? He works like a slave to preserve that semblance of a home which he thinks he still has. He is over fifty. He has always worked too hard. And this is what you hold in reserve for him. Go if you want to. Tell him what you have done, yes, you! Tell him that this girl and a scoundrel have brought shame on his greying head. Do! And see what will come of it."

Ruth had listened, half in despair half in revolt. Some of the things Mary had said were true; others were not. What did it matter? If Abe could be spared, he must be spared, with that she agreed.

"He will kill the man!" Mary had repeated.

"If he is a married man, he deserves it."

"But what about Abe? He will hang."

Ruth had started to her feet with a cry.

Mary had gone on speaking passionately. All that had stood between the two women had come from her lips, things just and unjust. To Ruth they had seemed irrelevant. Mary had concluded by saying, "He will do justice regardless of consequences."

Yes, so Ruth had thought at that moment of emotional upheaval. Abe stood at the centre of it all. She understood him better than his sister. He must be protected. The whole load of the crisis settled down on her shoulders. "Have you a plan?" she had asked.

"That," Mary had said, rising and going to the window, "I will tell you when Frances has told you what she has told me. Better take her upstairs and keep her there, out of Abe's sight."

Ruth, with the uneasy memory in her mind of what Abe had said at the mere thought of just what had happened, had done as Mary bade; and in this room where she spent the night Frances had told the tale of that ride from town in McCrae's car. Ruth had shuddered; but the thought of Abe had saved her from breaking down. As, during the night, she lay there, she was torn between two desires: that of saving Abe and that of handing "that man" over to him. A ruthless power had twisted her purpose into its opposite. An easier and higher life than she had led !

Abe was the child's father; he was the man to punish the offender; and yet he must be spared. Much of what Mary had said Ruth was willing to admit. It had come to the point where Abe, with all his faults, meant manhood to her, power, tenacity, perseverance in the face of adversity; yes, and forbearance. The very things which she had resented in him she had come to admire. He must be spared. And a crooked little by-thought had crept in : by sparing him, she could protect the girl from his wrath. For already Ruth was building a defence around her child; in defending her she was defending herself. McCrae alone was to blame; he must be punished, or she would lose her faith in life !

Abe must be kept in ignorance : that, the two women had agreed upon. A plan had suggested itself to Mary, starting from the coincidence of Mr. Rogers's telephone call; so she had made a definite arrangement for her brother to be fetched in the afternoon of the following day. Abe being out of the·way, she would run Ruth and Frances to the city where Marion's approaching confinement would furnish a pretext for this visit of her sister. Frances would remain in the city till all was over; she need never even see her own child; that remained to be arranged for.

There seemed to be no flaw in this plan, provided Ruth was willing to let McCrae go unpunished. That Ruth might for a moment weigh her desire for his punishment against the necessity of keeping the thing from Abe had never occurred to Mary. But Ruth plotted and planned till she seemed to see a way of achieving both ends. McCrae must be punished; he was the guilty one; Frances was his innocent victim. His punishment would restore to Ruth a measure of confidence in herself.

She had reached no definite conclusion yet when Abe stirred to rise for the day. He stretched and yawned in his room, stretched and yawned.

Frances was innocent. Ruth had told Mary so. "Force was used."

"Why is force not used against other girls?"

"We don't need to discuss that," Ruth had said. . . .

She must get up to prepare breakfast and pack the noonday lunch. She waited till Abe had gone to the barn. Then, having washed, she slipped down to the kitchen. . . .

At ten o'clock a boy from town brought the buggy, leading a saddle-horse behind. He came to the house and brought Ruth a note.

"I have arranged everything. Rogers will call for Abe at three. I shall come for you to-morrow morning at seven.— Mary."

"There is no answer," Ruth had said to the messenger. . . .

McCrae looked at Abe with a supercilious glance when he asked him that morning whether he would look after his stock for a few days.

"Sure. Going away?"

"Yes. I am going to help Mr. Rogers stack his hay."

McCrae even inquired, "Leaving the missus and daughter at home?"

Abe nodded.

The mist had crawled south; the day was as brilliant as ever; the work would be finished by noon.

Abe could not remember the time when he had worked in such utter peace. Last night resignation had come to him. In no other way could he find happiness: a life in the present, looking neither backward nor forward. The air was crisp; the warmth of the rising sun felt grateful.

When, at two o'clock, his haying finished, he returned to the house, Frances had lain down with a headache.

Abe planned retrenchments: cross-fence his farm a mile north; seed the Hudson's Bay section to grass; keep stock there; rebuild life on a smaller scale; do things in a leisurely way; enjoy the doing of them; taste every season, every hour, every task to the full! Had he done so years ago, he would have saved much of life.

Shortly after three Rogers drove into the yard. Abe admired the man. Perfect in poise and control, endowed with the ease of speech, he took pleasure out of life; he never overreached himself; he spoke to his daughters as though flirting with them. The crow's feet about his eyes came from much laughter. Abe felt as if he were going on a holiday.

Ruth watched from behind the curtains of a window. They went through the barns, the pig pen, the fowl house. When they returned to the car, they were laughing. . . .

Till Abe came back, all action was transferred to Ruth. She was gliding down a smooth river which plunged over a ledge of rock to a whirlpool beneath. She had seen Niagara in her youth.

For a moment, when the car swung out through the gate, she felt overwhelmed with the desire to call Abe back. She went to an arm-chair and sank down. Exhaustion hung over her like a threat. Glimpses of thought were endowed with a life of their own: of the dead child; of Jim who had not yet come home; of

Marion who preferred to go to a hospital and did not call her mother to her side. And now this!

She rose. No use thinking; action was needed. She busied herself.

She must see a lawyer. The law was supposed to be just; if it was, it would protect her. Yet, *had* it protected her? This thing was done against all law! Then the law must set it right again!

A lawyer? Which lawyer? Her son-in-law? No. Her other children, too, must be protected from even the knowledge of this thing.

She would have to get rid of Mary. Mary must not know of her plan. She would argue that it was imperative to let the man go unpunished. That, Ruth could not concede. Never had she thought it possible that she should hate a man as she hated him who had brought this wreckage into her life. Again she began to plan, to weigh every circumstance. Yes, if she could hand the man over into the grip of the law, he would be removed from Abe; even for Abe her plan was best.

At night, she grimly watched the object of her hatred jauntily going about the yard and glancing up at the windows of the house, looking for an opportunity of seeing the girl, no doubt.

Then, right after dark, feeling the unescapable need for rest, she made preparations for going to bed.

Frances had kept out of her way all day, coming down only for her meals. She avoided all discussion.

After another sleepless night, Ruth rose on Wednesday excited and confused. As she pulled at the laces of her corsets, she burst into tears. She must find a lawyer. . . . But the difficulty about Mary remained unsolved.

She went to waken Frances and returned to her room. Ruth, too, was overwhelmed with the feeling of the uselessness of this great house. She looked at the costly fittings of her room: bedstead, dresser, chest of drawers, rug. . . .

Before she went downstairs, she returned to the girl's room. She found her laying out her best clothes; she had rouged and powdered her face. "Frances!" she cried in an undefinable voice.

"Nonsense, mother!" Then, in a changed tone, "Mother, come here!" And, in a whisper, "I'm afraid, mother. Does it hurt much?"

"Too late to think of that" Ruth replied and turned away.

The two were sitting at the breakfast table when the purr

of a car in the yard announced Mary's arrival. They rose to get their hats.

It was another cloudless day, with the sun emerging hotly out of the eastern haze. The run to the city took three hours—a stifling run for the first thirty miles; for Mary kept the curtains of the car closed against prying eyes till they had left St. Cecile behind. Ruth sat with Mary in the front; Frances in the tonneau, dressed as for a conquest. On the way, Mary explained the arrangements she had made. Frances would go to a private hospital where such cases were taken care of. When they approached the city, the sun stood high in the sky, burning down through a hot, blue, charged air which made beads of perspiration stand on every brow.

In the city, thanks to Mary's foresight, everything concerning Frances was attended to by noon. When the two women were alone, Mary asked, "I suppose you want to look in on Marion?"

Here was the looked-for pretext. "When do you wish to leave?"

"I'll run you out. I'll have lunch with Charles's sister. I can fetch you after that. It will be time if we leave at four."

"Set me down at the Corner of Grande Pré," Ruth said; for she knew that to be the principal business street. "I want to go to a store and I'll take a street car. We'll meet in front of the Parliament Buildings."

Mary nodded and turned left at the next corner. When Ruth had alighted, she watched the car out of sight. She had no desire to call on Marion; other things were on her mind; she must do what she had never done before : she must act for herself.

She walked down the chief business artery of the city, looking uncouth and out of place. She kept scanning the signs in doors and windows, paying no attention to the passers-by who stared at her funny little mauve hat, many years old. She was melting with the heat but did not feel her discomfort.

She went a mile before she saw a sign such as she was looking for. It was across the street, in an upper window, "Craig, McPherson, McPherson, Barristers and Attorneys-at-Law." She crossed the maze of the driveway, crowded with street cars, automobiles, and delivery wagons; and within a few minutes she found herself in a huge building where a man whom she asked beckoned her into a crowded elevator. She had to hold on to herself not to betray how unfamiliar it all was to her. When the cage shot up, she gave a half-stifled scream. Yet she kept her head by sheer effort. The elevator coming to a stop, the attendant touched her arm, naming a number and pointing a direction.

In a large deserted office a young lady approached her between the desks. With arrogant politeness she asked Ruth for her errand.

"I wish to see Mr. McPherson."

"Junior or senior, madam?"

"Senior," Ruth answered at random.

The young lady disappeared, not without smiling to herself at Ruth's hat. A few minutes later an elderly man came to the partition dividing the office, small, cool, distant, bored.

"I am Mr. McPherson, madam. What can I do for you?"

"Could I see you privately for a moment?"

The elderly man hesitated before he swung a small gate in the railing open. Ruth followed him into a private office. At a motion of the lawyer's she sat down on the edge of a chair.

"Mr. McPherson," she said, "I want to consult you about a case. What can a person do when a man has taken advantage of a girl?" She wondered at her own fluency.

Mr. McPherson smiled. "We don't handle such cases, madam. You want to see Mr. Inkster of Inglewood, Inkster, and McIntosh. He will give you competent advice."

Ruth rose. "Mr. Inkster?"

"I'll see whether he is in." He reached for the receiver of a telephone and made an inquiry. "One block east. You will find him there."

At the offices of Inglewood, Inkster, and McIntosh, Ruth had to wait half an hour before she was admitted. When she entered the private room, she found a middle-aged man of powerful build who held his half-bald head to one side where his chin jerked over his shoulder. His face was expressive of utter disillusionment. He did not rise or look up from his papers as he asked her to be seated and to state her case.

She repeated the question which she had asked Mr. McPherson.

"I can't tell without knowing the details. It is for you to know whether you want to disclose them or not."

Ruth told the story as she knew it; and now and then the lawyer jotted down a note on a pad of paper. He seemed to pay the closest attention, but whether to her story or to his papers was hard to say. He asked a few questions, so brutal that she winced. She quailed before his indifference; but she answered to the best of her knowledge.

Then, "You say the girl was innocent before this happened?"

"I do."

The man shot her a shrewd glance. "Does she use rouge?"

Ruth bridled. "I don't see——"

Mr. Inkster smiled at his papers. "You wouldn't, madam. My question is answered." He leaned back, relaxing, spreading out. "May I ask what your purpose is in proceeding against the man?"

"Surely he should be punished for ruining the life of a child?"

Again he smiled. "If your story is strictly true, madam; if you can persuade a jury to accept it, you may have a case. I won't say offhandedly on what charge: rape or seduction of a girl under eighteen. I do not mean to cast any doubt on your veracity, madam. But there are two sides to every case. A conviction is never certain. Every trial is full of surprises. May I call your attention to another thing? If the girl was not strictly innocent, the trial is bound to bring the fact to light. I do not say that she was not; understand me, madam. I am merely putting the case for your consideration. You may not be fully informed. Parents rarely are. In that case, a trial can bring only additional sorrow. But even if she was strictly innocent when this thing happened, you might, if you knew how such trials are necessarily conducted, not wish to expose your daughter to the sort of cross-examination which she will have to undergo. The opposing lawyer will ply her with questions about the minutest and most unsavoury details of the act. . . ."

Ruth gasped. "Will he be able to get a lawyer?"

Mr. Inkster's broad body swung forward, his head jerking over his shoulder. "Even the guilty are entitled to the protection of the law, madam. I'll be quite frank. If what has happened to your daughter had happened to mine, I should not proceed. Suppose her essentially innocent. I assure you, a girl that has stood in the witness-box in a trial for rape or seduction can never again be called innocent in any sense but that of the law. She knows human nature in its worst aspects more thoroughly than any one except a criminal lawyer. From what she learns in the trial she can never recover. Her imagination is sullied for life. That is the way this thing looks to me; and I should know."

Ruth was speechless. The lawyer's eyes remained on his papers.

At last she recovered sufficiently to ask, "What is your advice?"

"That depends on your reason for proceeding against the man. As for the thing itself, it is done; nothing can undo it."

"I want him punished."

Mr. Inkster raised a weary hand. "The full rigour of the law! If I were without a conscience, madam, I should confirm you in that wish."

"Cannot the girl be left out of the proceedings?"

"She cannot."

Ruth rebelled. "If that is justice——"

The lawyer spoke tentatively. "Are there other considerations, madam? Financial ones?"

"No. Except inasmuch as they might embarrass the man."

"In that case you might do almost anything with him, provided you get him to admit the fact before witnesses."

"That would be very hard to do."

"May I suggest a proceeding?"

"If you please."

"Suppose you sign an information in blank. I shall have it filled in with due care. I shall get a warrant for the man's arrest and send a detective down. You procure another witness and hide the two in your house. Invite the man in under some pretext and talk matters over so as to make him involve himself. Get his admission, as if you were willing to compromise. The detective will place him under arrest and take him to the city. He will engage counsel and ask to be admitted to bail. Bail will be granted; but the sum fixed will depend on the girl's previous innocence. He may know more than you. The sum imposed will tell us. That he will claim knowledge of the girl's bad character goes without saying. Every man accused of such things does. It will depend on the degree to which he can substantiate his claim. If the trial judge disbelieves him, bail may be as high as a thousand dollars; but if makes his defence plausible, it may be as low as two hundred. We force him to show his cards; you will have time to consider whether you want to proceed or not. A trial offers small chance of success when a man can show cause why his bail should be low. If bail is high, it remains to be considered whether you wish to expose the girl to a trial or not. If the problem is money, that is the time to settle out of court."

Ruth became hopeful once more. "We can get an arrest, then?"

"You can get an arrest on any kind of a charge."

"That is something," Ruth muttered.

"You agree to the plan?"

"I believe I do."

"If you will take a seat in the waiting-room, I will have the papers prepared when my secretary returns from her luncheon.

We need your signature. In an hour you will be able to go home. Sixty miles, you said? The detective will be down by five to-morrow. Will that do?"

"Yes. The man comes at six to do the chores at my place."

At four o'clock, Ruth met Mary on Broadway. For the moment she felt as if her action had invested her with a consciously heroic attitude towards life.

XXVIII ✳ THE CONFLICT

Ruth had succeeded in evading Mary's questions and declined her offer to stay with her at the farm. But as soon as her sister-in-law had left, she surrendered to fears and doubts. She suspected the world to be vastly more complex than it appeared to be. New and unforeseen possibilities constantly arose before her imagination. The man was a returned soldier; did that give him privileges before the law? He had friends in the district; would they defend and help him?

There was the difficulty of procuring a witness. Whom could she ask? How was she to induce McCrae to come into the house? What, when she had him there, was she going to say? If she could not adequately punish, she craved the satisfaction of striking at least a telling blow.

But her hatred was complicated by such a longing for Abe and his support as she had never felt before. Love? What was love! She wished for a quiet, harmonious life by his side—a life of mutual forbearance if not understanding. But with this secret in her heart, how could she ever look Abe in the face again?

She had taken on herself a responsibility in which she needed the support of him in whom she discovered herself to believe more unconditionally than in God. When she had rebelled against him in the past, she had done so not the least because she had felt that she could never fulfil his expectation of her. She was not what he had thought her to be; thence had sprung a devastating jealousy of an ideal in his heart.

Repeatedly Ruth sat down, in dining- or living-room, and later at the foot of her bed, to abandon herself to a paroxysm of sobbing.

Again the unchained emotional possibilities dormant in her took their direction against McCrae; him she hated so that she could have annihilated the world to annihilate him. What he had done, made her past life one utter, dismal failure. The intensity of her hatred appalled her. He *must* be punished though it meant ruin to herself.

Whom could she ask to act as witness? Whom but Nicoll!

Night came, and practical things demanded to be done. She must see Nicoll. With the need for action her agitation subsided. She waited till it was quite dark before she went to the road to break into a needless run; but when the unwonted exertion affected her heart, she forced herself to go at a more leisurely gait.

She passed Dick Nicoll's new place which looked deserted; but the windows of the school were ablaze with light; there, the young people were assembled for a dance. A dance!

When she reached the gate of the farm at the corner, a light was moving near the stables. She stopped and called.

The light approached. "Mrs. Spalding?" Nicoll asked, surprised.

"Mr. Nicoll, I have come to ask you to do me a favour."

"Anything I can do——"

"Will you come to the house to-morrow, between four and five, and listen to a conversation. I need a witness."

Nicoll looked at her uncomprehendingly.

"I am in great need of help."

"Of course, I'll come. But what is it?"

"You will hear. You must arrange to get there without being seen. Abe is away. It's McCrae who mustn't see you."

"I'll go through the field. It is muddy, but——"

"Thanks," Ruth said. She had spoken evenly throughout; but as she turned away, her knees shook. . . .

Another night without sleep: a vague, chaotic night, full of tossings and lapses, accelerated heartbeats and bottomless voids.

And a morning, seemingly endless, yet regretted when it was gone.

As the afternoon wore on, a dull, feverish excitement invaded her, with no articulate thought, only feelings undefined and full of menace.

It was hardly four o'clock when a sound in the yard proclaimed the fact that a car had arrived. Ruth ran to the window in Abe's den. A medium-sized stranger was coming to the house.

"Mrs. Spalding?" he asked at the door, with a liveliness of speech in contrast to the mournful expression of his face. "Stuart, P.P., from headquarters, request Mr. Inkster."

"Come in," Ruth said faintly.

The man laughed mirthlessly. "The cah, madam. We'd bettah not leave the cah in the yahd. I have a drivah along."

"I'll show you." And, running, she led the way to the new barn.

"All-l-l right," said the stranger, looking in. "Be at the house in a minute."

Ruth felt no longer exhausted; but she hardly knew what she was doing. In the kitchen, she caught herself in the act of putting on an apron as if to wash the dishes which had accumulated since Tuesday.

The detective reappeared. "Your man isn't heah yet?"

"My man? . . . Oh, McCrae. No, I don't expect him till six o'clock."

"A witness?"

"Will be here any moment."

"Does the man suspect?"

"I don't think so."

"That's the dining-room? No, leave the blinds drawn. A den? All-l-l right. We'll be in theah. You get your man into this room heah . . ."

There was a knock at the back door. It was Nicoll; returning, she introduced the men to each other.

"P.P.," the stranger said in explanation.

"McCrae is going to be arrested," Ruth said to make it all clear. Nicoll betrayed no surprise. Perhaps he understood.

Ruth did wash the dishes, leaving the men to themselves. Nicoll was on the point of lighting a cigarette when the detective stopped him. . . .

McCrae appeared a few minutes to six, on horseback. Ruth was upstairs watching from Jim's window. She ran down to tell the detective.

"Don't be in a hurry," the stranger advised. "Call him in casually."

She returned to her post at the upper window. McCrae was behind the barn, calling to horses and cows, "Come on—come on—come on!"

Half an hour went by; the horses came; and McCrae fed them.

Impatient for action, Ruth went down again. Again the stranger warned her against hurry. "He mustn't suspect a trap."

If only it were over. A plan was forming in her mind. Yet she wished she could postpone it all. Once more she returned upstairs.

McCrae was in the cow barn. Again half an hour went by.

For the third time he appeared, carrying two pails of skimmed milk. A dull shock went through Ruth at his sight. How she hated him! How she hated every jaunty motion of his! She went down; and the detective nodded to her, all but closing the door of the den; she went to the shed.

Five minutes later, she saw the man returning from the pig pen, holding his head high, his cap aslant on his skull. Ruth's excitement reached such a pitch that she feared she would fall and scream.

Now! As by a miracle her mind became clear. McCrae was on the point of turning the corner of the barn when she ran out, her bulk shaking. "Mr. McCrae!" She marvelled at the friendliness which she succeeded in putting into her voice. She was listening to its sound.

He stopped in his tracks.

"Would you mind coming in for a moment? I want you to do me a favour."

"Sure," he replied in cynical surprise. "Not at all."

Ruth was conscious of the fact that she could not readjust her features from the ghastly smile she had put on. Yet she said coolly, "Come right in," as she led the way through shed and kitchen. "Sit down." She moved a chair in the dining-room. "Are the fields drying?"

"They're drying, yes. Unless we get more rain."

"Well," Ruth said evenly, "nobody wants more rain."

"Guess not." McCrae looked about the room. "You all alone?"

"Yes. My daughter is away."

"That so?"

Ruth, taking the bull by the horns, turned full on him, one arm on the table. "Mr. McCrae, why did you take advantage of Frances?"

His eyes narrowed; but he held his smile. "I? Take advantage of Frances?"

"Yes."

"Who says I did?"

"She does."

"Frances, eh?"

"I got Abe out of the way to talk matters over. I was afraid he might go to extremes."

"He doesn't know?"

"He doesn't suspect."

The young man sat very still. His smile vanished as if he were dropping a mask. "Mrs. Spalding, I love Frances."

Ruth winced. But as she went on, she might have been

discussing a trifle of no importance. "Then why did you take advantage of her?"

"I don't know," he replied with a despondent shrug of his shoulders. "Something in me does these things. I can't help myself."

"You don't know why. But you don't deny the fact?"

"I don't deny."

Ruth's resolution gave way. Her bosom heaving, she burst into tears.

The young man felt shaken. Resting one elbow on the table and ruffling his hair, he looked up. "Where is Frances?"

"I won't tell you."

"Mrs. Spalding, we must talk this over."

"What is there to talk about?"

"You take this too hard. What difference does it make? Not many girls marry to-day without having had to do with a man."

Through her tears Ruth looked straight at him. "Is that so?"

"Believe me, you are old-fashioned. These things mean nothing."

"Does a child mean nothing?"

He leaned back, bewildered. "There's a child? Surely not yet?"

"Not yet, of course," Ruth said dryly.

Again he ruffled his hair. "I'll have to take care of the child."

"In your own family?"

"No!" he said precipitately. "Grace mustn't know."

"How can you keep it a secret?"

"I'll pay for the child's keep."

"And the other expenses?" Ruth sat as if driving a bargain, uncertain whether she had gone far enough.

"I'll pay for everything. As sure as I live."

"Where is the money to come from?"

"I'll find it. I'll borrow. I have friends."

"Then," Ruth lifted herself to her feet, unable to go on, "you will have to ask them first to go bail for you."

The detective stepped forth, baring the badge on his vest.

"I suppose that will do?" Ruth asked.

"That will do nicely, madam. Thank you." He stepped to McCrae's side and fastened a handcuff around his right wrist.

McCrae, standing rigid, made no resistance. "Mrs. Spalding," he said, "I'll get a divorce from Grace and marry Frances."

"Marry Frances!" Then, scornfully, "I thought you loved your wife so much that you did not even want her to know."

"You'll be sorry for this!" he threatened in sudden anger.

Nicoll stirred in the den. McCrae, becoming aware of this further presence, turned to the man by his side. "Can I see my wife?"

"Right-o! Take you theah myself," the constable answered politely.

Half an hour later, certain papers having been signed by Ruth and Nicoll, these two were left alone for a moment.

"I'm sorry," Nicoll said, clasping his grey beard pensively with one hand. "That's all I can say, Mrs. Spalding."

Ruth nodded, in tears. "You'll act as though you knew nothing?"

"Of course," Nicoll replied and took his leave. . . .

That night, Ruth slept from sheer exhaustion: a dull, dead sleep annulling reality. Next morning, not a memory seemed left of what she had gone through. She lay between sleeping and waking, listening for sounds to tell her that Abe was stirring. When the ghost of a memory returned, she sat up; and inconsequently the fact that she was stout and unwieldy interfered with the realization of other things. She cried. She was all alone, helpless and alone. That was what twenty-one years had brought her to. Twenty-one years ago she had been full of hope, joy, pride. Only now did she understand Abe. But if he had remained faithful to her it was because other things had occupied him to the exclusion of guilty thoughts: not because he had desired only her. The struggle which that insight had cost her had made her hard; but she did not blame him. She rose and went to the dresser to put her clothes on before the mirror, looking at herself with that distaste which, in the past, she had often thought she saw in Abe's face.

Then she went down. The huge, empty house oppressed her. She took her breakfast in the kitchen, standing, feeling desolate.

Then she left the house to do the chores which, but for her, would remain undone. By doing them, she was asking Abe's forgiveness. The bitterness of a past decade was gone. Would Abe ever seek her because he needed her as she needed him? That would redeem her life. . . .

She was glad to find the work hard as she carried oats and hay. . . .

The morning wore on. Another hot day. The season of storms was past: this was the last of the summer before the fall. From all about, as Ruth went to and fro, the deafening trilling of the crickets invaded the oasis of the yard. The sky was filled with the haze which, disappearing, left the atmosphere dry with summer dust. For the first time Ruth, too, felt the immensity of the prairie like a menace : as if she must get away from its threat. Yet she dreaded the house.

As the morning merged into noon, her excitement gained on her again. Her pulse was fast; she could hear the thud of her heart. At last she went in and mechanically tidied the rooms. Then she went upstairs and lay down on her bed. The house, the farm, all life were disorganized.

What did it mean? The law! The common justification of punishment is its deterrent effect. With that justification something was wrong : punishment arose from another cause : from the feeling which invaded her when she thought of McCrae: he deserved death because she must revenge herself; his death would give her satisfaction. Oh, how she needed Abe! How absolutely she would trust him!

"You take this too hard. . . . These things mean nothing." That was not Abe's view. Yet, what had happened, had happened. It could not be changed. Suddenly she regretted what she had done. Her hatred had exhausted itself by being indulged in. She felt uncertain again. . . .

The day went by. Ruth did not even think of rising for her dinner. She had to get these things clear in her mind.

They were clear as night fell; and a measure of firmness returned. The whole trend of her resolutions had been reversed. She would go to town in the morning and, over the telephone, withdraw the charge. Others were involved; let them act; she must save what was left to her : the chance of a peaceful old age with Abe. Mary had been right; she, Ruth, had made a mistake. If she withdrew in time, the man would be careful what he said. Abe might still be kept in ignorance.

On Saturday morning, having done the chores, she dressed for the trip and hitched the aged pony to what had been the children's buggy.

By ten, the weather still being unchanged, she arrived at Morley. Her conveyance she left at the livery stable.

Thence she went to the telephone office to put in a long-distance call for Mr. Inkster. She waited till the connection was made, surprised to find nothing disturbed in the routine of things.

She was going to undo what she had done. She felt that she was going to act on a lower plane : listening to the voice of expediency. Like Abe she had been urged on by the fundamental revolt against injustice : by the age-old desire to replace the blind flow of events and the yielding to impulse by something conformable to human reason; by the need to make a moral order prevail where chaos had ruled. This man had transgressed the law that is born within us; she had tried to vindicate that law by invoking another, made by men, never doubting that in the result the two were identical. She had done exactly what Abe would have done. In doing what she was going to do, she was frustrating the very course which he would have taken. She was plunged back into uncertainty.

A bell rang in the toll booth. "Mr. Inkster is on the wire."

Blindly she stumbled into the booth, her hands trembling. "That Mr. Inkster? Mrs. Spalding speaking."

"Oh, yes. The preliminary hearing is over. McCrae is out on bail."

"He is out?" Ruth asked in amazement.

"He handled his case very skilfully. He had witnesses on hand to confirm his assertions."

Ruth trembled from head to foot. She knew that the operator was listening in. How could she put her question without letting her into the secret? "What was the sum?" she stammered.

"Two hundred dollars."

A cry broke from the woman in the booth.

"In my opinion," the lawyer went on, callous to implications conveyed by his words, "a trial, therefore, will offer no chance."

Ruth felt a sudden revulsion which impelled her in the very direction which she meant to reverse. She could not accept the verdict implied. She would have been willing to withdraw a charge which offered a chance of success. To do so under defeat was bitter. "What happened?"

"He made it appear highly probable that the girl——"

"It went without saying that he would try to do that."

"That he would try. Not that he would succeed."

"Succeed? With whom?"

"With the magistrate and—myself."

"You don't mean to say——"

"It went like most cases. His witness was willing to go under oath."

"Who was it?"

"I forget the name—an engineer with one of the railways."

Ruth was unconscious of the fact that she was holding the receiver in her hand. She did not grasp the words she heard. Then she realized that the man would never be silent when he triumphed. He would boast of the fact. "What do you advise?" she asked at last.

"Settle out of court. If it's a question of money, now is the time."

"But it is not."

"You gave me to understand——"

"I wanted him punished. I wanted justice done. I wanted——"

"Mrs. Spalding, all this leads to nothing. Will you kindly instruct me whether to get in touch with defendant's counsel?"

"No." Then, seeing no way out, she did under compulsion what she had come to do of her own free will. "I withdraw the charge."

"Very well," said the voice at the other end of the wire. "I shall send the papers for your signature by to-morrow's mail."

Mechanically Ruth replaced the receiver and left the booth. The operator called after her. She had forgotten to pay the fee.

She was in a turmoil. She did not believe in the guilt of the girl. How could a daughter of hers be guilty? The path of the law was closed; but the desire to see the man punished revived in all its strength.

Where was she to go? Not to Mary's house. There she would go when her mind was made up. To protect Abe was no longer an issue with Ruth. She knew she was vastly more at one with him than his sister. Through her own feelings she had had another revelation of Abe. Abe must come at once. Human law left her without support. The letter killeth. . . .

She went to the end of Main Street where the road led north. She turned and went on into the open prairie. In front of the trees which screened the village in the north, she would be invisible from Hilmer's and Elliot's houses. She crossed the ditch and went east to the grove of poplars invading the prairie. There she sat down on the ground.

A long while she cried, her feeling of helplessness and impotence poignant. Her whole being was once more a single urge and impulse: to crush that man! For a decade she had lived only in her children and through them. And this man had arisen. . . .

Then the chaos of her feelings resolved itself again into that call for Abe. She staggered to her feet. There was only one course left.

Mary and the doctor were at home. For the first time in Ruth's experience, there was disagreement between man and wife.

"You know?" Ruth asked as she sat down.

"About the arrest?" Mary asked with acerbity. "It's the talk of the countryside. The papers report it."

"You will find it was a useless step, Ruth," said the doctor.

"The man must be punished."

"It is not a case for the law."

"He is out on bail."

The doctor nodded. "So the papers say. I should withdraw the charge."

"And let the man go unpunished?"

"It is my belief that no flagrant wrong goes unpunished."

"If you had listened to me," Mary said, "you would not have started this. The more you bestir yourself, the sooner Abe will know."

"The sooner Abe knows," said the doctor, "the better."

Ruth looked at him. Was he an ally?

"Frances," he went on, "is Abe's child as well as Ruth's. You want to keep him in ignorance. It cannot be done; if it could, it would be wrong. When he hears of it, we shall all be to blame in his eyes."

"He will do something rash!" Mary exclaimed.

"No matter what he will do. Nobody has the right to do it for him."

"You said," Ruth interposed, "this is not a case for the law. For whom is it a case?"

"For me and others. For all who know of it. This thing is vastly more ramified than you think; and not only McCrae is involved. I have talked to a number of people who do not know that Frances is among the victims. For two years there has been talk. Half the district has run wild. There's the oldest Hartley boy; there is Henry Topp; and Slim. It is a whole gang. The district has been without its leader. It has been run in opposition to its natural leader. That is an acknowledged fact. McCrae and others, it is said, cannot be trusted with woman or girl for the space of minutes. I have urged certain parents to take action; we wished to place the guilt. In this case, at last, we know. One man, at least, will be an outlaw henceforth. His neighbours will close their doors against him. No merchant in town will sell him supplies. On the road, people will refuse him the time of the day. Unless he can live on his farm as in the wilderness, he will have to leave."

"And do elsewhere as he has done here," Ruth said.

"That risk we must take. We shall find out where he goes and shall warn his neighbours. Wherever he goes, this will follow him."

Mary moved. "That is all very well. But how about Abe? If he is to be told, it would have been better to tell him in the first place."

"Exactly," the doctor said. "Who proposed to keep it from him?"

"I did not propose to bring an action behind his back."

"I wanted to see the man punished," Ruth cried in despair.

"And to punish him you were willing to expose your husband to danger!"

"My husband's place is by my side!"

Mary raised her hands in angry protest.

The doctor cleared his throat. "Mary, I do not like to act against your wish. But I agree with Ruth. If her action, ill-advised as it was, has cleared the air for the recognition that Abe must be told, then I am glad it was taken. Abe will hear of it in any case: the question is merely from whom."

"Not from me."

"Very well. There is Ruth. She is the only person in the world who has both the right and the duty to tell him. Abe will not act on impulse. I know what I should do; I think I know what he will do. But no matter what is to be done, it is for him to do it. To deprive him of the possibility to act for himself is to deprive him of his birthright. Besides, as you say, it cannot be done."

"Then," Mary said, "I wash my hands of the whole affair."

"Just a moment, Mary. I do not wish to go against your wishes; but I cannot act against my own judgment. Let me put a case. Suppose we had children; suppose I knew that a child of ours had run up against such a thing; and suppose I kept it from you, and you found out."

Mary stared at her husband. It had been the most cruel disappointment of her life when, twenty-five years ago, he had told her that she must never have children. Since that day the fact had not been touched on between them except in a painful silence. By mentioning it now, he placed the whole case on a different plane. She had thought him only mildly interested. This argument undeceived her. *She* had made the mistake which strangers often made about him: she had under-estimated his emotional involvement, intense to a degree of passion. He was voicing a protest against the violation of a fundamental right: the right of every human being to determine his own course of action. She thought she knew Abe; she thought she knew exactly what he would do. She felt sorry for him; more than she could express. But if her husband thought that Abe, no matter what might be the consequence, would have wanted to know; if he thought Abe would consider himself deprived of his very freedom unless he were told, then, indeed, there was no way but to tell him. "I hope you are right," she said. "What do you propose?"

The doctor smiled at her from where he sat, his right foot drawn up on his left knee. "I advise to withdraw the charge."

"The charge has been withdrawn."

"Good. Then I shall without delay run down in the car and fetch Abe home. What do you say, Ruth?"

"I think so," Ruth said with an immense relief in her voice.

XXIX * ABE

W HEN Abe, in the field, was told that his brother-in-law was waiting for him at the gate of Rogers's yard, the mood of the last day spent in his own meadow still persisted. He had resigned himself; he would rebuild life on a smaller scale. There was peace ahead: rest after a feverish life. Ruth, too, would be willing to give and to take. . . .

He crossed the field and yard and went to the highway. "Anything wrong?" he asked when he saw the doctor behind the wheel of his car.

"Ruth wants you, Abe."

"All right. I'll be back in a minute. I must wash."

A quarter of an hour later they were gliding north along the highway, in silence.

"Abe," said the doctor after a while, "I want to tell you something."

Abe looked up, still half withdrawn.

"I want to tell you why I gave up my practice."

Again there was a silence before the doctor went on:

"One night, twenty-four years ago, I was called out of bed by a message summoning me to the house of a farmer whom I knew slightly. I was called in as a consultant; a doctor from St. Cecile was in charge. When I arrived, after a drive of fifteen miles, I found a competent nurse in the house. Everything was ready for an emergency operation. I met my colleague in the parlour; and he told me about the course of the illness without giving me his own diagnosis. It was he who had called me in, not the patient's wife. At the bedside, I made my own diagnosis with the greatest care. When I returned to my colleague, I found we were in complete agreement. An immediate operation seemed to offer the only chance of life. But there was one trouble. The condition of the respiratory organs contra-indicated an ether anaesthesia. It was a serious case. If our diagnosis was correct—and we did not doubt it—delay spelt danger. On the other hand, so long as there was a ghost of a chance of recovery without the operation, it was our duty to wait and to get an anaesthetic other than ether. The chances of the patient's living through an ether, anaesthesia were one in ten. No other anaesthetic was available; we were many hours from the nearest source of supply; it was before the day of the car; and it was winter. My colleague had been prepared to proceed even before I arrived. That I came in time was a tremendous relief to him. We weighed every possibility; we decided not to wait and reported accordingly to the patient's wife, not disguising the fact that the operation might be fatal. She placed her husband in our hands. As soon as the incision was made, the man died under the anaesthetic. My colleague, bent over the body while the nurse and I tried artificial respiration, looked up at me, ghastly white. A glance showed me that our diagnosis had been mistaken. If we had waited, the man would have lived."

Abe sat and pondered, resenting the fact that this tale should be intruded on his mood. "Why," he asked, "do you tell me that now?"

"Abe," said the doctor, "I never trusted myself again. My colleague had a more robust conscience. He is in practice to-day. I sold out."

"That I understand. But why tell me to-day?"

"Nobody knows except that colleague, Mary, and you. I tell you because it might be well for you to know before you go home. It has ruined my career and darkened my life. I was a young man then and have been an old man since. A human life was given into my hands, and I took it. Of that fact I cannot dispose. Not even to-day does it avail me that I acted according to the best of my knowledge; not that probably any other consultant would have made the same mistake. We never see all the facts of a case. The greatest in my profession might have erred. Few, perhaps, leave this life without having to look back on similar errors. But all that is beside the point. We act and blunder. We can never tell. Perhaps this knowledge may help to sustain you."

Abe sat silent, huge, disturbed. "Sustain me in what?"

The doctor shrugged a shoulder and raised a hand from the wheel.

Again there was silence. The prairie to both sides of the highway was as flat as in Spalding District; but it was densely settled; and every farmstead was sheltered by wind-breaks and drained by shallow ditches. To the east, the bush fringe of the river closed the horizon.

In the north, the grain elevators of Somerville rose up; and in twenty minutes they turned west in the centre of the town.

"Any one sick?" Abe asked as the car sped into the open country again which here looked less cared for, even the road being rougher.

"It isn't that."

Abe half turned to his companion. "Well, tell me, what is it?"

"Ruth wants you. Be patient."

They were nearing Morley when Abe's groping thought hit on the school-house in his district. That district was claiming him. He would have to obey the call. . . .

The car passed Morley School. "Ruth is with Mary," the doctor said. "We shall pick her up."

At the house Ruth came down the steps as the car came to a stop. Abe noticed every detail: the faded mauve hat, too small and too glossy, the dress of black, flowered voile, too tight over the hips. In times past he would have been touched by distaste at her sight; to-day he saw that this woman, human like himself, was stirred to her depth; and he noticed her immense relief at his return. He nodded to Mary who stood on the stoop and, in answer, raised her brows.

At the stable, Ruth and the doctor remained in their seats while Abe fetched the horse. It was four o'clock. While they waited, the whistle of the afternoon train which was late shrilled over the prairie from the east. When the buggy was ready, Ruth alighted; and the doctor, with a brief nod, backed his car away.

Abe turned into Main Street. To their left, the train was slowing down for the stop at the station, two hundred yards ahead. The ordinarily deserted platform burst into momentary life. Bags were thrown from the mail car; cream cans clattered from the van. A few passengers alighted as the buggy passed in the rear of the buildings.

Abe happened to look at Ruth. Her face held the same expression of a veiled reticence which he had seen in the doctor and Mary.

Then several things happened at once.

From the group of people who had alighted and were now passing out, one figure detached itself at a run. Abe was on the point of pulling the pony to a stop; but Ruth reached for the whip in its socket and brought it down on the horse's back. People stopped, laughing.

The little horse broke into a trot and, at a second blow from the whip, into a gallop.

The man who had started to run was still following them,

shouting. Abe, whose attention was claimed by the horse, did not understand all he said, but he caught a few words about "getting even with the whole Spalding outfit." He had not recognized the man.

Then came Ruth's voice. "Don't stop. I must talk to you first."

The whip coming down a third time, the horse took the turn to the north at a gallop, with the buggy running precariously on two wheels.

For several minutes Abe did not speak. When he did, his voice held a note of weary patience. "Was that McCrae at the station?"

"Yes."

"You mustn't get so upset about things. . . . Is Frances alone?"

Ruth's heart pounded. "Take me home first. Then I shall tell you."

Abe nodded; a deep, trench-like frown settled on his brow.

They came to the second mile-crossing with the bridge over the so-called first ditch. Beyond, to the right, John Elliot was crossing his yard, swinging his long arms, his bullet head bent to one side. As he heard the rumble of the buggy on the culvert, he stopped and turned. Seeing Abe, he broke into a sort of gallop to intercept him.

To the left, an old woman, working on a flower bed close to the road, in front of Hilmer's shack, rested from her labours, leaning on the handle of her hoe, her wide, ragged skirt hanging unevenly about her broomstick legs. She stared at the two, the man in the buggy, straight and stern, and the other by his side, one hand on a wheel.

"I've been wanting to see you, Spalding," Elliot said. "Things can't go on the way they're going down there at the school. Drinking and dancing all night and every night. And worse things. It's got to be stopped. We have to have someone else on the board. We're all agreed that you are the man. But I've promised, if you refuse, I'll run myself."

Abe nodded. Then, to the other's amazement, he said slowly, "I suppose I'll have to go on that board."

"All right. I am with you. And so is every decent settler."

As Abe moved on, Mrs. Grappentin shouted after him; but as she spoke in German, he did not understand. "Ah now!" she called. "Is the great lord stepping down from his shining height? Now he's got a whore in the family like other common folk?" And she broke into a cackling laugh, waving her hand after the buggy in the greeting of fellowship. Grappentin, her sponging husband who had come back since his stepson was working for wages again, stepped into the open door and joined in her villainous laugh, spitting tobacco juice into a bed of blooming asters.

A shudder ran down Abe's spine at the sound; and Ruth paled. The voice, unintelligible though it was, sounded like the voice of the prairie which lay swooning under the afternoon sun.

They passed Dave Topp's place, a one-roomed shed resembling a granary. He lived very quietly now and played his violin of an evening in front of his door. Next, Henry Topp's yard, unchanged in all these years. Of the three brothers, only Slim succeeded in making his place look like a farm; but people said that, at the rate at which he spent money, he would never "make his place a go," to say nothing of paying his debt to the Government. His new white house presented a striking contrast to Horanski's establishment across the road with its low, dark buildings in keeping with the soil. Yet Horanski was said to be making money.

Old man Blaine's cottage followed next, to the right and just south of the school which had become the abode of iniquity. A curtain moved in the window; and behind the pane trembled a leonine head. Man passes, they say; his work remains. Does it? It seemed vain in the face of the composure of this prairie. This was the district: farmsteads to east, west, south, and north: and that district was calling for Abe. Dare he decline to take hold?

Nicoll's wind-break across the corner was mature now, too; and when the buggy turned the corner, Abe almost felt compassionate eyes peering after him. At the gate, he caught a glimpse of a stout, towering female in the shade, no doubt muttering in her pathetic way, "There goes the fallen hero! The shame and pity of it!" In days long past Abe had laughed at her dramatic ways.

And on, past Dick Nicoll's, for another two miles, to his own place which, for a while, would stand as a monument to man's endeavour. South of the ditch, the meadow stretched away, mamillated with haystacks.

Alighting at the little gate near the house, Abe said with sombre sobriety, "Go in. I'll turn the pony out. I won't need him again."

A lump rose in Ruth's throat. His was a commonplace remark, meaning only that, for the day, Abe's driving was done. Yet, in the light of Mary's forebodings, it had a sinister sound. "Abe, I'll go with you."

He looked at her. Then, "Come along if you want to."

And so, as in years long gone by, Ruth stood in the door of the barn as Abe stripped the harness off the pony's back and turned him out.

Then, side by side, they went to the house and sat down in the dining-room. Abe was visibly, painstakingly collecting his thoughts.

"Tell me in detail just what you have done," he said at last.

Ruth told her story without the slightest attempt to shield man or girl: for her, something more than Frances was at stake.

Abe listened patiently, letting her go back and forth over the story and asking her to repeat certain statements—as that regarding the significance of the amount at which bail had been fixed. At last he nodded. "You did right. You did right even in getting me out of the way. I might not have had the patience to go through with it." And, after a while, "It is a case where the law fails us."

"Then the law is evil," Ruth cried.

"No. It is merely imperfect." And again he sat and pondered, Ruth torturing a handkerchief in her hands. "You have done," he repeated, "what I should have done. I am glad it isn't to do over again."

"I felt that the man must be punished," Ruth said as if still in self-defence.

"I could not have done what you did in getting the admission from the man," Abe said, rising. "It clears the case. And now I want to be alone for a while. Don't follow me; and don't worry."

He went out and across the yard, through the old barn, into the pasture where he stared unseeingly at horses and cows. Every now and then a tremor ran through his body.

In the hall of the house stood a gun-rack; and he thought of it. He might load one of these guns, go down to the man's shack, call him out, and shoot him down like a dog. His hand seemed to close about the weapon where stock and barrel join, a finger on the trigger. . . .

But what would be gained by it? Abe's body relaxed. The district, the municipality, the province, the country would be supplied with a thrill, to be forgotten the next day or the day after; and then the matter would pass into the void of oblivion, to be revived perhaps now and then in tales around the stove.

What else? The district was calling. There, too, he had started a machinery which he could not stop and which imposed its law upon him. But suddenly he felt that, if he followed its call, that district would rally about him: the Ukrainians, Hilmer, the Jew, and Baker; Dave Topp, Stanley, Elliot, Nicoll—a clear majority over the gang—the moment he gave them a chance to align themselves by his side. The gang had been running the district because he, Abe, had stood aloof.

Resignation? The thing he had dreamt of for a week had been no resignation at all: he had nursed his anger and shut himself off. He had meant to do what, in his weariness, seemed fulfilment of his desires. True resignation meant accepting one's destiny; to him, it meant accepting the burden of leadership; and the moment he saw that, he felt at one with the district, with his brother-in-law who had told him his story, with Ruth in her sorrow, and, strangely, with himself; for here was something to do once more: the gang would vanish into thin air. His own life had been wrong, or all this would not have happened. He had lived to himself and had had to learn that it could not be done. . . .

There were further searchings, painfully probing; but all led to the same result. "Yes," he muttered to himself, "I'll go on. . . . To the end. . . . Whatever it may be."

And when, in the dusk, he returned to the house where he knew Ruth was waiting in distress and anxiety, his mind was made up.

He sat down in the dining-room; and in a sudden impulse Ruth came to his side and half bent over him. "Abe," she said, "for my sake, let him go."

He placed his hand on hers which rested on the table; and for the first time in many years, he felt her touch on his shoulder. "I can hardly do that," he said with an effort. "He is not alone in his doings. And this is my district, founded by me and bearing my name. Shall his example stand for all time to come? What would it mean? That a man can do as he pleases, living the life of the beast within him. If Frances was in any way to blame, that is her concern. But McCrae is not a giddy boy. If he were, I'd make him marry the girl and keep him straight. But look at the case. He is married. He has children of his own. He is a ratepayer, entitled to office if he can muster followers enough to elect him as Wheeldon did. He enjoys all the rights and privileges of others. Has he none of their duties? I had withdrawn from the district; I did wrong; and this has risen up against me. I see my duty again. It is out of cases of self-help that the law has arisen; whatever I do will have its effect on the law; or at least on its interpretation within this district. No, I shall have to act. I shall have to drive him out."

Ruth was tense, tears streaming down her cheeks.

"I have wronged the district," he went on. "And, Ruth, I have wronged you."

She sobbed convulsively; her hand gripped his shoulder.

"And I have wronged my children as well," he added painfully.

"Abe——" But she could not speak.

"You thought I should kill him," he went on more composedly. "It would not serve the case. On that score you may be at rest. The district as well as I will have to live this down; it will have to vindicate me and itself by casting him out. I shall have to take office again, and not only here but in the municipality as well."

At ten o'clock, that night, Abe was at Nicoll's Corner, looking across at the meeting place of the gang; and then, through the utter darkness of a moonless night, he approached the building. As he came in line with the open door, he could see through the whole of the classroom to the far end where the three musicians sat: Slim, Henry, and a stranger. Abe stopped for a second and then went on till he was mounting the concrete steps and entering the vestibule. He passed the cloakroom to his left and the partition of the office to his right. Up to the moment when he actually entered the dance-floor where half a dozen couples were turning, he was in deep shade, for the gasoline lamp which lighted the dancers was suspended close to the ceiling.

His appearance there, in the entrance, caused an instant hush. The music broke off, and the dancing ceased. Two couples near the door disappeared at once behind his back. All others stood and stared.

Among the musicians, Henry Topp had risen. Through the door of the office, Abe was dimly aware of a group of girls sitting on chairs. McCrae was not present. Abe turned slowly, surveying the scene. The deep, trench-like frown on his brow made him look formidable.

"Who has the key to this building?" he asked.

Strangely, Slim Topp held it out to him.

He took it and went on, "This building is closed." He looked like an irresistible force of nature; and his composure seemed uncanny.

For a second no one stirred. Then Henry Topp tried to spring. "Hold on!" he yelled. But Slim who was almost as tall as Abe held him back.

"Here, let me go!" Henry roared.

And a girl, a stranger to the district, dressed in an excessively short and provokingly open sleeveless dress—she was more than a little tipsy—asked with a hiccup, "What does that guy want?"

Abe fixed a look on her under which she was silenced.

"Go home," he said, standing perfectly still.

"I'll be jiggered," Henry Topp said from behind Abe's back; and, though his brother held him, he executed a dance step and, pantomimically, aimed a blow at Abe's head. A tall, gawky youth burst into a guffaw which ceased abruptly in the general silence; he reddened.

Abe, still standing perfectly still, was patiently waiting. Yet, to these people, his seeming mildness gave his words a compelling power; more than one of them shivered at his sight.

"Oh, come on!" Slim Topp said at last with an embarrassed grin.

Everybody was half convinced that Abe was insane.

There was a movement towards the door. The girls from the office slipped into the cloakroom. A moment later there was a stampede.

Only Henry Topp still wriggled in his brother's grasp. "Hold on, there!" he shouted.

"Shut up!" Slim hissed in his ear. "What's the use? Let's go!"

"Oh, all right then!" And arm in arm the two brothers followed the others, swaggering. Slim carried his saxophone; Henry his violin. In the cloakroom, there was a scramble. A moment later the school-house was empty except for Abe who locked the windows and turned the lamp off.

Outside, there was whispering and excited talk. Then Slim blew a rally on the saxophone, from the road. A burst of laughter answered him, sounding weirdly through the night. Then a shout and a summons to meet at Slim's house; and an answer from two or three, "No, I'm going home." And, within five or ten minutes, silence utter and complete.

Abe went out, locked the door, and turned away. . . .

The news of his action spread through the district that very night; and there were not a few who breathed the traditional sigh of relief.

THE AUTHOR

FREDERICK PHILIP GROVE was born in 1871 in southern Sweden. In Toronto in 1892 he learned of the death of his father and the collapse of the family fortunes. For twenty years he roamed the continent, working as a farmhand in the West. In 1912 he became a school teacher in Manitoba and continued in that profession until 1924, when deafness obliged him to resign. Meanwhile he had married very happily, but a great grief was added to the trials of financial stringency and uncertain health when his young daughter died in 1927. Two years later, he and his wife left the West; they settled in Simcoe, Ontario, and it was there that Grove died in 1948.

He is the author of eight published novels, an autobiography, three volumes of essays and sketches, and many short stories. In 1934 the Royal Society of Canada awarded him the Lorne Pierce Gold Medal for Literature, and in 1945 he received an honorary degree from the University of Manitoba. His best work—with the exception of his autobiography, *In Search of Myself* (1946), which won him a Governor-General's prize, and an early autobiographical novel entitled *A Search for America* —has the Canadian West as its setting and inspiration. In addition to the present volume, it includes *Over Prairie Trails*, *The Turn of the Year*, *Settlers of the Marsh*, *Our Daily Bread*, *The Yoke of Life*, and *The Master of the Mill*.

Map of
Spalding
District

(*within the
broken line*)

and adjacent
territories
in 1921

7	8
	Spalding Farm
6	5
31	32
30	29

Baker

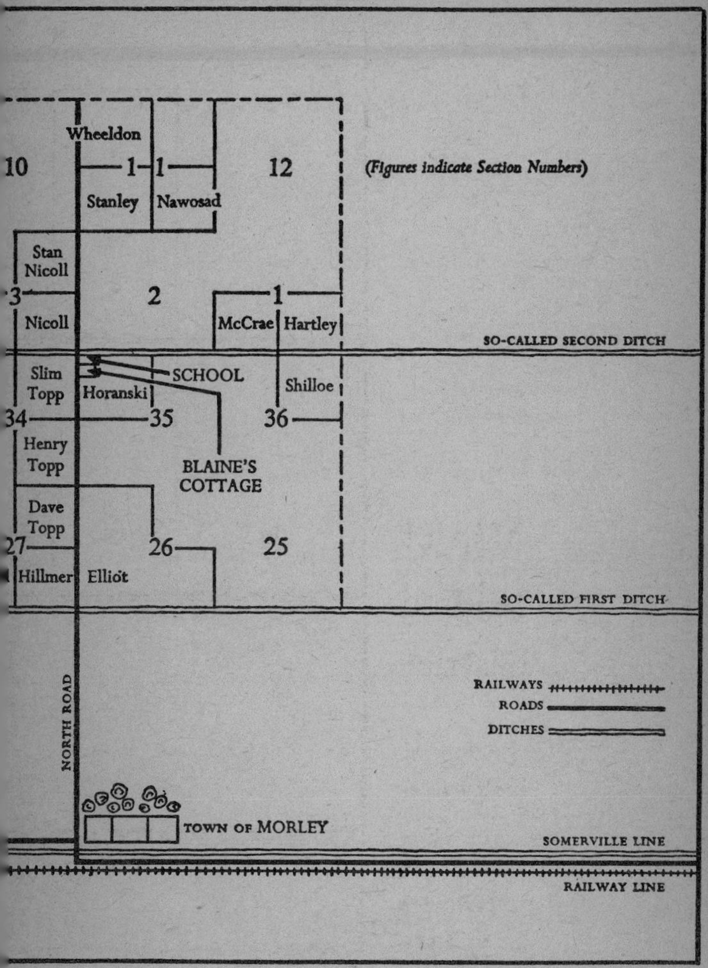

Wheeldon
10
1
1
12
(Figures indicate Section Numbers)
Stanley
Nawosad
Stan
Nicoll
3
2
1
Nicoll
McCrae
Hartley
SO-CALLED SECOND DITCH
Slim
Topp
SCHOOL
Horanski
Shilloe
34
35
36
Henry
Topp
BLAINE'S
COTTAGE
Dave
Topp
27
26
25
Hillmer
Elliot
SO-CALLED FIRST DITCH
NORTH ROAD
RAILWAYS
ROADS
DITCHES
TOWN OF MORLEY
SOMERVILLE LINE
RAILWAY LINE

THE NEW CANADIAN LIBRARY LIST